THE FAIR FOLK

ALSO BY

SU BRISTOW

Sealskin

Su Bristow

THE FAIR FOLK

Europa
editions

Europa Editions
27 Union Square West, Suite 302
New York NY 10003
www.europaeditions.com
info@europaeditions.com

First publication 2024 by Europa Editions

Library of Congress Cataloging in Publication Data is available
ISBN 979-8-88966-012-5

Bristow, Su
The Fair Folk

Cover design and illustration by Ginevra Rapisardi

Prepress by Grafica Punto Print—Rome

Printed in Canada

CONTENTS

In th'olde days of the Kyng Arthour,
Of which that Britons speken greet honour,
Al was this land fulfild of fayerye.
The elf-queene, with hir joly compaignye,
Daunced ful ofte in many a grene mede.
This was the olde opinion, as I rede;
I speke of manye hundred yeres ago.
But now kan no man se none elves mo . . .

From *The Wyf of Bathe, The Canterbury Tales*
—Geoffrey Chaucer, 1392

Newnham College, Cambridge
April 1969

Dear Professor Edgerley,

Enclosed is the next instalment of my story. I'm sorry it's taking so long, but coursework has to come first, and I feel the need to be careful where and when I work on this. The Faculty Library is good, I've found, and so is the University Library. So far, I think, it's been fine, and I have no sense that They have any suspicions about what we are doing. Touch wood!

Thank you for taking the time and trouble to help me in this way. I know you say it's of great value to your work, and I'm glad of that, of course. But making myself remember and record everything that happened—even things I'd forgotten about until now—is helping me too. There are things I took for granted as a child that I wonder about now, and some things make more sense in hindsight. Most of all, though, this "unburdening," as you called it, is something I desperately needed. It's such a relief to share what I know, and to be able to talk about Them with you. So thank you for that too.

You asked me last time where I thought my story began. The best answer I can give is "Once upon a time," and certainly long before I was born on a small farm in the Surrey hills. And of course I can't tell you where it ends.

You told me that you have never met anyone else like me, but I'd be very sad to think that there are no others, and that perhaps the time is coming when They will be gone from the world.

I hope, despite everything, that somehow, somewhere, it's still going on.

Looking forward to hearing your thoughts,

Felicity Turner

Part One:
Three Times the Charm

There was once a farmer who took his goods to market, and did well. He started home late in the day, so that it was already dark by the time his cart entered the woods. The horse was ambling along, when some way off between the trees he saw lights, and heard the sound of merrymaking.

"Now, who can that be?" he wondered. Getting down from the cart, he set off through the woods; but as he got close, lights, music and people all vanished, leaving him alone in the dark. Shaking his head in bewilderment, he was about to turn back when the lights appeared again, some way off.

He took great care this time, moving as quietly as he could, but still, just as he got near enough to see that there were a great many strange folk seated around a bonfire, once again they disappeared. And now, in the dark and far from the road, he did not know which way to turn. But as he stood there, tired and befuddled, what do you think?

There was the bonfire, and there were the folk drinking and laughing, just a little way off among the trees. And this time, when he stumbled into their circle, they did not vanish away but led him to an empty seat, offered him food and drink, and welcomed him to their company. And so he feasted with them far into the night, until at length he was overcome by sleep, and they covered him with a fine embroidered cloth and left him to his slumbers.

Well, it was long past daybreak when he awoke. Gone was the bonfire, gone the merry folk. He was lying in a pile of leaves, stiff and sore. He had a deal of trouble finding his way back to the road and, when he reached it at last, the horse and cart were nowhere to be found. That old horse had a lot more sense than her master, and she had made her own way home.

Traditional tale, British Isles

Chapter 1

Well Farm, Surrey, 1959

"Best get on." My father put down his mug, scraped back his chair. Crouched on the landing, I watched with my mind's eye as he swiped his hand across his mouth, dried it on his overalls. "There's another gap in the hedge down on Low Field."

"I need you to run me into town this morning. I told you."

"Holes don't mend themselves." He went out, leaving the kitchen door ajar. There was a heavy silence, then "Out! Out with you!" and the sudden clatter and squawk of escaping chickens. While my mother was occupied, I made it to the front door, wrestled with the latch and got out onto the front step, pulled it shut and was away before she could stop me. Once I reached the trees, I'd be safe.

I'd only got my school plimsolls, and by the time I'd crossed the yard and passed the barns, they were already wet and muddy. The cats came, picking their way between the puddles, but I had nothing for them today. Malkin followed me right to the edge of the woods, but she wouldn't come any further. She curled her tail around her feet and sat up tall, watching. They all said the same; her unblinking eyes, my mother's scolding, my father's hand. *Don't go there. It's not for you.*

When I can't see the buildings any longer, I stop. Let the woods enfold me, the quiet that's never really quiet, full of the huge slow life of trees, the quick busy life of insects. And if I'm lucky, other things too. This is the boundary.

In the hollow where the woodpeckers nested last year, I leave my watch, tucked in so it won't get wet. My birthday present—"So you won't have any excuse for being late now, will you?"—and it has a stupid cartoon picture of Cinderella on the face. They don't like cold iron; all the stories say so. And I don't like it either.

Today I'm going to the clearing again, where I found the hazelnuts last time. A perfect circle in a place swept clear of leaves, each one right way up. Squirrels never did that. I had to hunt around to find the hazel tree, with its roots in black water hidden under layers of rotten leaves and dead branches, and I got scratched and smeared with green mould before I found one, whole and nearly ripe, and put it right in the centre so they'd know, so they'd understand.

When I get there, I close my eyes and wish as hard as I can, but when I open them there's nothing, nothing but leaves and the sound of birds. No sign of hazelnuts; all gone. Surely that means something?

"I've brought you apricots," I say, and my voice sounds small and shaky. Stupid. Stupid kid. Why would they be interested in you? But I clear a space and make a circle, with a little pile in the middle. The dried apricots look too bright, as though the sun is shining on them. Already, ants are coming; but maybe something else will come too.

I lie down on the dry leaves, looking up through those still growing, hanging on for the first big wind of autumn. Today it's misty, nothing moving up there; the top branches disappearing into greyness. "Not a breath of wind," Mum says, and the wind is a huge animal, somewhere far beyond the horizon, that wakes and roars across the land; but today it's sleeping. Waiting.

Already the damp is seeping into my t-shirt, and the ants are beginning to explore me. Maybe spiders, too. There's a root under my back, but I've trained myself to sink into the ground and be part of it all. I'm a tree root, an ant path. I'm leaf litter. I take a deep breath and close my eyes.

Time goes by, and it doesn't matter. When I grow up I'm going to be a naturalist, and you have to know how to stay still for hours, maybe all day, so the forest doesn't know you're there any more. And you have to use not just your eyes. What things look like, that's only a little bit of what they are, and it's maybe not even true, because caterpillars try to look like leaves, and insects try to look like sticks, and leopards look like sunlight falling through trees.

So why are foxes red? I'm wondering about that, feeling the scratch and tickle of tiny feet finding their way through the hairs on my arms, up under my t-shirt, when there's a sudden sharp pain in my side. My eyes fly open, and there's something right close to my face, too close to see properly, and next second it's gone, so I can't be sure I saw what I thought I saw—

An eye. A blue eye, looking straight into mine!

I've jumped up before I realise, shaking ants out of my clothes, trying to see everywhere at once, even though there's nothing to see. Just the trees and the mist, and my circle of apricots, just the same, only the heap in the middle is gone, and there's something else, something brown like the leaves, that blinks at me.

A toad. It begins to crawl, not in a hurry, but wanting to be somewhere dark and wet. Out of the circle, towards the stream. Apricots have nothing to offer a toad, and the toad has nothing to say to me. Except, somebody put it there, and that means it's a message.

I lift my t-shirt and look down at my side. On the pale skin there are two red marks, and the curved imprint of fingernails. I put my own finger and thumb over the marks, and they fit almost perfectly.

Somebody pinched me, hard.

I lost my nerve, then. I ran, slipping and skidding in the black mud under the leaves, splashing through the puddles in the yard. There might have been laughter; I couldn't be sure at the time, though now I've no doubt at all. I climbed up the hay bales in the barn, and curled there in the prickly scent of summer. The marks were still there; there'd be bruises later. And I had my answer. I knew for certain.

They were out there. And I had found them.

Chapter 2

Of course, I know better now. All that time when I was playing cat and mouse, leaving little treats and traps, thinking I had to lure them out of hiding and make them trust me. Who was the cat, and who was the mouse?

There came a day when I got home from school to find my mother clearing out the larder. Damp had got in, turning sugar into solid rock and flour into sour-smelling paste, and the kitchen table was covered with jars and cans. She looked at me over her shoulder, reaching down something from the highest shelf.

"Go and get changed and you can give me a hand." Then she looked again. "What have you done to your glasses?"

I took them off, and the jagged lines across my right eye went away. "Dropped them."

"Let me see." She got down off the steps and came over, dusting off her hands. As she took the glasses, her hand touched mine, just a little. And then she took both my hands in hers, turned them over, looked at the grazes and beads of blood.

"How did this happen?"

"I fell over." But the stupid tears welled up, and I couldn't pull my hands away.

"Fliss. Have you been fighting again?" She wouldn't let go. "Answer me!"

"They started it!" The words burst out of me now. "They waited on the path home, and they took my bag and tore my library book, and the librarian said if it happens again I might lose my ticket." All the way home I had kept the sobs at bay—there was always someone watching—but now I wailed aloud.

The sound appalled both of us. My mother shook my hands, quite hard, and then let go, stepped back.

"Oh, Fliss. When will you learn? Just don't give them cause. Ignore them and they'll soon get bored. If you weren't so—"

She seemed to run out of words, then. If I weren't so—what? But as soon as she let go of me I ran for the stairs. She called, once, and then gave it up.

Behind the locked bathroom door, I washed gravel out of my hands and knees and stuck on plasters as best I could. The landing floor creaked as I crossed it, but there was no sound from below. I got out of my school uniform, put on trousers and a long-sleeved top. As an afterthought, I stuffed the blanket off my bed into my backpack. It gets cold in the woods at night.

I'd miss tea, but there were some supplies in my den, if the mice hadn't got to them. It would only be eating up the out-of-date cans from the back of the cupboard, anyway. I hoped she wouldn't notice that things had gone missing, but it didn't really matter; they wouldn't come looking for me, I was sure.

It wasn't that hard to climb out of the bedroom window, slide down the back porch roof and land in the yard, but the kitchen window looked that way, and my hands were still stinging, so I just went quietly down the stairs. But the front door always stuck, even in summer, and we only opened it for company. I had to pull with both hands, and then it came open suddenly and a swirl of dust and hot air blew in. I heard Mum call out "Fliss?" but I pulled it shut behind me and ran.

Since the day I first knew for sure, I'd done everything the same way, in case it was part of the magic. In through the hole in the fence along Low Field, where the oak tree has swallowed up the barbed wire, and wriggle through under the hedge, where foxes and badgers have made a secret tunnel. Leave my watch in the hollow tree, and step off the path into the deeper woods.

With eyes closed, I took nine steps, and turned around three times.

In the woods, you leave behind the heat and the glare. You leave behind the sweet smell of cows and the hum of insects. It's somewhere else, even if you don't manage to step into Somewhere Else. And when you open your eyes, you're never quite sure.

I went to my den by a roundabout way, because they don't like straight lines, and when I got close I didn't go in right away. The feathers were there just as I'd left them, woven into the bushes as though the wind brought them: black crow and the barred brown of a tawny owl, and a white gull feather. You never saw gulls here, this deep in the woods, but the white stood out well against the undergrowth.

The dry grass and sticks were undisturbed, too, and I pulled them back into place behind me. Boys sometimes passed through, even though it was our farm and there was no public right of way. They used the "Trespassers will be prosecuted" sign for target practice, and they took all the eggs from the blackbird nest by the gate that year.

Inside, you couldn't see out much, but you would start to listen in a different way, as though you were reading a map made from sounds. I curled up in my blanket against the tree trunk, and ate some of the biscuits I left there in the old cake tin that Mum used to keep buttons in. She never sewed on buttons any more. The biscuits had gone soft, but they were ginger nuts so they still tasted good, and I had an apple as well.

I could hear a few birds calling, and the little rustle of voles in the grass, and the deep, slow sigh of the trees overhead. If I put my ear to the ground I would hear when the deer came out, though it was hard to tell where they were. The scent of me was masked by layers of leaves and branches, and sometimes they came really close. Once, a fox nosed his way right into my den. He stopped when he saw me, and we just looked at each other, and then he turned and went on his way. I closed my eyes and let myself drift out into the wood, like an owl that flies soundlessly, ghosting through and never touching.

When I wake up it's almost dark, the time when badgers and foxes come out. I'm not sure what woke me. There's no sound nearby, no rain pattering on the leaves overhead, and the wind has died down. But there's a listening feeling, as though the whole wood is waiting for something. And then—

Right on the edge of hearing, and gone almost before my ears can make sense of it; a brief thread of music. And there it is again, coming in snatches, broken pieces that can't quite make a tune. It can't be men, out lamping for deer or rabbits; they try to be quiet though you can hear them a mile off. And it's not like any wireless music I've ever heard. A pipe or a whistle, rising and falling like lark song. No one round here makes music like that.

As quietly as I can, I untangle myself from the blanket and crawl towards the entrance. The dry leaves I put there to warn me if anyone comes near are my enemies now, but I try to move like a badger, stopping and starting, deliberately scrunching about. Badgers have nothing to fear, except men and their dogs.

Every time I pause, I wait to hear the music again. And when I'm finally out of the den, I stay crouching low, turning my head like a fox catching the scent, until I'm sure. That way.

It's no good trying to be quiet, but I can't help it. One step at a time, testing before I put my foot down. There's light as well as music now; flickering firelight between the trees, and the little pulsing lights of glow-worms. Someone talking, though I can't make out the words, and then a burst of laughter.

Could it be people camping, here in our woods? But I know already, by the prickling of my skin and the singing in my ears, that this is something else. And when, finally, I get close enough to see, through the yellow sparks from the fire and the green dance of the glow-worms, those faces! Some young and beautiful, like heroes from a book of legends, and others . . .

Even now, remembering, it's so hard to put into words. They are seated in a circle around the fire, except for one, standing back and half in shadow, playing that little piping tune. There is a feast, the wonderful stomach-wrenching savour of roast meat, and piles of perfect fruit, grapes and peaches and other things I can't name. They are drinking from sparkling goblets, laughing and talking. I have time to see that their clothes gleam with jewels, catching the firelight as they move.

Then one who sits on the far side of the fire, so that I can clearly see the fantastic shadows made by that nutcracker face as he turns to his neighbour, that one raises his eyes in the act of lifting a grape to his mouth, and for one eternal second, our eyes meet.

The next instant, up goes the fire in a great whoosh of sparks and flame, and up goes a great screeching and laughing so loud that I cower down with my hands over my ears.

And when I look again, there is nothing.

No fire, no feast, no faces. Only the after-images burned into my eyes, and the quiet sounds of the night; no alarm calls from birds roused from their roosts, no deer crashing away through the undergrowth. I am cold, and wet, and alone.

For a long time, I don't move. The darkness presses down on me, and even my ears don't know how to listen any more. I bring my hands to my face, smell leaf-mould and dank mud, and crouch there, hearing only my own heart jumping in my chest like a trapped animal. Slowly, slowly, hearing and seeing come back to me. It's never completely dark outdoors, and now I can see the shapes of the trees around me. At long last, I get up, and walk forward a few steps into the clearing where they had been.

The ground is cold. I crouch again, put my hands down flat, and there is no ash. No fire, no feast, no sign that anyone had ever been there. But inside, my whole body is full of singing. If only for an instant, I had seen them, face to face. I raise my head and speak into the dark.

"Thank you."

There is no response, but I don't really expect it. I stand up again, meaning to go back to my den, and then realise I have no idea which way to go. Where had I come from? In the dark, off the path, there is nothing familiar. And that joyful singing inside me gets stronger, as I realise how they have led me on, just as all the old stories say. Only this isn't an old story in a book; this is happening now, to me.

And as I think that, I hear the music again.

Chapter 3

"Knock three times, and you shall enter." That's what it says in all the old stories. Three times is the charm. So now, standing there in the dark, I take my courage in both hands. Not lost, but on a path I can't see. Well, then.

I close my eyes, take a moment to listen for that elusive thread of music, and then turn around, slowly, full circle. And again, until I am sure the sound is clearest from *that* direction. Then once more, because there must never be two without three. I open my eyes, take a deep breath, and set off again.

They lead me on a merry dance, through brambles and across a stream, by ways that feel completely unfamiliar. I know these woods better than anyone, but I am no longer in any place I recognise, and that in itself is a sign that I am on the right track. Many times, the music fades, and I have to stop and wait, trusting that it will return. And at last I begin to see the lights again too, flickering between the trees. I am almost there.

And yet, knowing how the stories go, I stop again, just short of the circle of firelight. I am scratched and bruised, wet and tired, and I want to prolong the moment before the inevitable. But then, standing there on the threshold, neither in nor out, I find a courage that amazes me. The bullies in the playground would not have recognised this Felicity—not that I give them a thought, as I step forward, right into the circle, and say, loud and clear,

"Here I am."

There is one moment of stillness; time enough to notice her

as she turns her face towards me. The queen, crowned with mayflowers (May blossom? In August?). Her long dark hair floats around a narrow face and laughing eyes, and she opens her mouth as though to speak, and then—

Uproar! Once again, a great screeching and a rush of flames, so that I step back despite myself. It seems to go on for longer this time, and I feel—or imagine I feel—people jostling me as they pass. There is laughter, and someone pulls my hair. Without meaning to, I crouch down again, and put my hands over my ears until the tumult has died down.

When at last everything is quiet, I venture once more into the place where the circle had been. This time, I don't expect to find anything; but there to one side is a gleam of white in the near-darkness. Lying on the moss, impossible and perfect: the mayflower crown.

I kneel down on the cold, damp ground, and put out my hand, half expecting it to vanish at my touch. But it is real; the flowers are fresh, newly picked, the scent strong as I bring it to my face. Mayflowers, in August.

The scent drifts around me as I put it on. Is that the wrong thing to do? Nothing ventured, nothing gained; and I've come this far, after all. Her hair had been smooth and dark, and it wouldn't sit well on my springy curls, but even so. She'd left it for me, and that must mean something.

The third journey is the hardest of all. They lead me into a bog, and then the music vanishes and I stand there amid the marsh lights, fighting terror as the cold mud creeps up almost to my knees. Later, there is a grove of ancient, twisted oak trees, all hung with swags of lichen, that reach out for me as I stumble among the rocks. I twist an ankle, and sit down and cry, until the sense of eyes watching in the dark gets too much to bear. What might there be, in this wood that was no part of the everyday world? I think of wolves, and bears, and maybe worse things, and fear drives me onward.

It feels like hours, long enough for the moon to set and the sky to grow paler, before I see firelight again. The trees are further apart here, and there is nowhere to hide, but this time I don't even pause. They are sitting in an open area, almost like a lawn, and the sound of singing comes to me as I step out from behind the last tree and limp forward into the firelight.

Their faces are all turned towards me as I approach, but the singing never pauses, and the music goes on until I come to the circle itself, and pass in between two seated ones, and around to where she stands, waiting, with an empty place at her side.

I stand there before the queen. She's not much taller than me, and our eyes are almost level as she steps forward and takes my hands. There's a thrill like the prickle of pins and needles as we touch, and I look down, almost expecting my hands to transform into paws or claws; but there they are, brown and scratched, resting in her own slim, perfect ones. It's only for a second and then she lets go, but the prickling continues as she says,

"Welcome, little firefly." She reaches out to touch the mayflower crown, all askew on my tangled hair. Then she gestures to the seat beside her, and there's a grand flourish from the piper, and a chorus of voices raised in welcome.

Before me there stands a little man, bowing low, presenting me with a crystal goblet and a plate of food. But I've no attention to spare for that, as he straightens up and meets my gaze. How to describe that face? I've tried to draw it a hundred times, and it's always a caricature; a cartoon goblin with a long and twisted nose, huge misshapen ears, and bushy eyebrows almost meeting in the middle. But those eyes! Young and sparkling with mischief, and a smile full of small, perfect teeth. He makes me a low bow, and then suddenly cartwheels sideways and out of the circle, and while I'm looking to see where he went, I'm grabbed from behind and almost spill the drink I'm holding.

"Hob. Let her be." The queen is watching, smiling, and now she gestures to the moss-covered log beside her. I take a step forward, but she holds up her hand.

"A moment, Felicity. Shall you attend our revels looking like a vagabond?"

While I'm wondering how she knows my name (my real name, not Fliss or Fizz or any of the names they call me at school), I'm surrounded by glow-worms. They whirl around me, faster and closer, until I close my eyes against the streaks of light. And when I open them—

You move differently, when you're clothed in green silk that floats around you, shimmering with silver thread. Your feet dance when they are shod with little silver slippers. I'm no longer cold, or weary, or scratched and bleeding, as I sit beside her. But I am hungry, and I eat everything they bring to me. "Don't eat the food," the old stories say, "or you'll be in their power forever." But if that's true, then I'm already lost. Sitting there, surrounded by marvels, I'm at my journey's end, and I never want to leave.

For a long time, I only watch, and listen. They offer me one delicacy after another, and I try them all, and when the feast is done there is more music, fiddle and drum and pipes, and dancing beside the fire. When a young man, tall and lordly like a knight in a storybook, stands before me and offers his hand, I rise without hesitation and join the dance, and it's almost like flying, so fast and fearless, and no one stumbles or bumps into anyone else. I have time to see that none of them is much taller than I am, and that some are very far from beautiful, but in that first encounter I am beyond observing and judging, beyond anything but being there, in that magical present that I hope will never end.

But there comes a time when I am seated again beside the queen, watching the revellers in the firelight, and I feel her eyes upon me. The question is out almost before I've thought it:

"Your Majesty, how can I repay you?"

There is a wild cackle from Hob and some of the others nearby; some clap their hands, while he rolls on the ground and kicks his feet in the air. "Your Majesty! Your Majesty!" he says, gets up and makes a low bow that turns into a somersault.

The queen smiles. "You shall, in time. For now, your own sweet presence is payment enough."

"Your Majesty!" says Hob again. "Will you join the dance with me?" And he's off again, capering through the dancers who never miss a step.

I grow a little bolder. "So what should I call you, O Queen?"

"The night is getting old," she says, as though I haven't spoken. I'll learn this, in the times to come: if the question is not the right one, she simply ignores it. And now the music is softer, slower; a gentle lullaby to which the last dancers tread a slow and stately measure. Another young man with a face like Apollo in my book of Greek myths comes over and places a cloak around my shoulders. It's light and soft as thistledown, and as soon as it envelops me I feel wonderfully sleepy. The queen looks down as I curl up beside her, and her hand just touches my hair. I yearn, then, for her to sweep me up, to hug me close the way my parents never do, but she only smiles, as if from a long way away, and says, "Sweet dreams, little firefly."

It's a sleep full of dreams, both sweet and strange, and sometimes there are goblin faces that leer at me in the dying firelight, but somehow I have never felt safer. This is where I belong, and here I shall stay, for ever and ever.

Well. Poor little Felicity! It still makes me smile, thinking of that night; that marvellous night, and the morning that followed. Waking stiff and sore and gritty-eyed, not wrapped in a cloak of thistledown but half-covered in last year's dry, scratchy leaves. Waking hours after first light, hot and thirsty, with no crystal goblet to hand filled with nectar. My scrapes and bruises were gone, though. And tangled in my hair were the long-withered flowers of May.

Chapter 4

It took me a long time to find my way to a familiar path. To be sure, I was back in the ordinary, everyday world, but they had left me in a place ringed by bogland and brambles. By the time I emerged into Low Field, I had a new set of scratches and bruises, and the dank smell of marsh-water hung about me. And as I started to cross the barnyard, my father was there.

He grabbed my arm and towed me across the yard towards the house. He never spoke a word to me as he dragged me to the kitchen door and pushed me in. Only then, just before he shouted for my mother, did he look me in the face.

"You stay out of them woods. You hear me?" And he was off down the garden again, leaving me to my mother's scolding. "Fliss, look at the state of you! Those shoes are ruined! I don't know what gets into you, really I don't. And your hair! One of these days, my girl, I'll take the scissors to it, and serve you right. What's this?" She pulled at the tangles, and then suddenly went still.

"Out! Out of my kitchen! You know better than to bring may into the house." She shooed me out into the garden like a marauding cat and backed away, wide-eyed. "You stay right there while I fetch the hairbrush, and you don't set foot in this house until you've got rid of every last flower."

Left blessedly alone for a few moments, I sat down on the back step. She was angry, yes, but there was something else; I'd never seen her look at me like that before. I hadn't brought flowers into the house since I was very young, but I did remember once making a bouquet from the hedgerow on the way home from somewhere, and presenting it to my mother. She was in the garden, pegging out washing, and she looked down at me, took the limp bunch from my hand and threw it aside. The chickens came running to shred the flowers, campion and stitchwort, meadowsweet and may.

"Never bring mayflowers indoors. Don't you know it's bad luck?" she said. And that was it. Not anger, or not only that. She was afraid.

She had words enough for both of them, and questions too, but they dried up soon enough. I suppose, looking back, my shining eyes and lack of response must have unnerved them; I had something that was beyond their reach.

I felt now that I could bear anything. The bullies at school, my cousins looking down on me; even—if it came to that—being banned from the library. I had something far more precious and wonderful, and now that I had eaten and drunk and danced with Them, I knew that next time, the way would not be so hard. I had found my own people at last, and they had crowned me with may.

CHAPTER 5

Of course, it was not so simple. Coming and going was at their behest, always. Two days later, when I slipped out to my den with neither food nor drink—why would I need everyday food, after all?—I fell asleep to the calling of owls, and woke to the whisper of rain all about me the next morning. I went home cold and wet and hungry, wondering if I'd ever see them again. That happened many times. The button tin became the place to store my library book of the moment, because after all, I could not simply sit and wait.

"You'll have to pay for a new one," Mrs. Hutchings the librarian had said when I took back the torn book, though I know she mended the cover with sticky tape and the book stayed on the shelves. So I forfeited my pocket money for the rest of the summer. An easy price to pay, for an excuse not to go to the holiday activities in the school playground, and not run the gauntlet of the school bullies afterwards. I went to the woods every time I could get away, and after that first time my father let me be. I thought he had given up. Where else, after all, would a child go? He must have done it himself in his time, though of course I never thought of that.

I'm not sure how long it was until the next time, though I remember very clearly what came before. Even now, I don't want to look directly at that memory. You'd think a child growing up on a farm would be used to the everyday brutality of it. In those days, you could slaughter your own beasts and carry out the butchery in your own kitchen, though regulations were coming in that made it harder. Neighbours would come to help, and everyone had a job to do. I hated the whole business, the stink and the blood that got everywhere, the boys with their hot eyes leaving fag-ends outside the back door, the younger children that I was supposed to look after while their mothers were up to their elbows in guts.

But it wasn't the bull calves and the ram lambs I minded so much; that was just farming. I had no link with them, really. But I did have a link—a kind of kinship, in fact—with the barn cats, scruffy and half-wild as they were. You couldn't pet the working dogs; they answered only to my father and would never come to hand when I called. But the cats did. Little grey Malkin the grandmother cat was my friend, and that meant that when I went into the barn and made the special low crooning call, they would come running. To a child starved of touch, their soft fur and shining eyes answered a hunger that was direct and simple. To lay my head gently on the flank of Mitten the tortoiseshell or Big Ginger, and awaken that deep throbbing purr, was a joy that never failed.

I was there in the barn that evening, after all the neighbours had gone at last. I'd kept back some of the offal for the nursing mothers; there were two that summer, and six kittens who tumbled about in the straw, suckling from whichever mother was nearest. Until now they'd mostly stayed hidden, deep among the hay bales, but after the feast they were all sleeping, round-bellied, in the scattered straw. And I fell asleep too, briefly, curled up among the cats.

It was the urgent calling of the mothers that woke me, in time to see my father slipping out of the barn door with a sack hanging heavy in one hand. Not the first time, of course, but usually he'd leave it until I was at school. Just one more necessary job on a farm, and the less fuss the better. This was something else, though. This felt like punishment.

What could I do? The cats were clawing at the door, mewing

desperately. Oh yes, I knew they'd get over it, I knew they'd call for a few days and then give up, and next year there'd be more kittens. But this time, it felt like my fault.

"I'm sorry! I'm sorry!" I sobbed. Malkin came and butted me with her hard little head. How many kittens had she borne and lost? Most of the barn cats were her children and grandchildren; usually he left one, at least. But they were all gone.

Much later, long after milking, when the owls were calling and the poor cats, exhausted, had fallen asleep, I crawled out of my hiding-place in the straw, and went off down to Low Field. My face felt stiff from crying, and my head ached. I didn't even look back at the house, though it was getting cold now and a light rain was falling. My mother had called, once or twice, when tea was ready, but after that they'd left me alone. They didn't have time to go looking for me, and they knew I'd turn up eventually, like any country child in those days.

By the time I got down to the hole in the fence, it was almost dark. I never used a torch in the woods, and I knew my way to the den almost without using my eyes. This time, though, it was different. Across the hole there was barbed wire, new and tight, too low to crawl under and too close to the old strands to get between. I tore my t-shirt and scratched my arm quite badly, before giving up and sitting down with my back to the oak tree.

I don't suppose my father meant it that way, but to my eight-year-old self the two things were linked. He'd taken the kittens and closed off my way into the wood. What else did I have, apart from books? It seemed to me that all they wanted was to make me smaller, closing me into a box like a cow in the crush. They'd take the books, too, if they could. You have no choice, as a child; you're born into a family and there you must stay until you're old enough to run.

Or maybe not, after all. It was full dark by the time I got up and made my way slowly down the fence to the bottom, where the ditch got deep and the nettles grew high. He'd stretched the new wire all the way along, but he'd stopped short of the corner. There was black, stagnant water there, and brambles too, but I was past caring.

Once I'd struggled through the stinking black water in the ditch, and pulled myself up the bank by the tree-roots, the wire on the other side was no barrier. It was old and loose, and probably not touched since my grandfather's time, or even before. There had been a hedge-bank once, the layered stems of blackthorn growing thick as small trees now, and with plenty of gaps where someone small and determined could slip through. And beyond that, the woods began; first a stand of coppiced hazels, where they used to cut poles for hurdles and fences, and then the old woods, oak and holly and alder by the stream.

I'd come the wrong way. It was all wrong, and I had no way to make it right. Without even noticing where I was going, I just walked, and kept walking. Some part of me knew that I should have come to another boundary by now, and rejoiced, but I couldn't stop. I never wanted to stop, and the only thing that finally brought me to a halt was the realisation that the water I was splashing through was getting deeper, and I could see light through the trees.

There are willows here with their feet in the water, and then there is nothing but the quiet surface of a pond, reflecting the rising moon and a few wisps of cloud. The rain has stopped, and the surface is utterly smooth, except where my own ripples have disturbed it. On the far side, the ground rises up bare of trees to a hill crowned with something dark against the sky. A pile of rocks, or maybe a building? Either way, I know there is nothing like that anywhere nearby.

I am shivering, and the water trembles around me. What to do? There is no way across that I can see, and something about that sombre hillside and its burden makes me want to hide, not wade out into the silent water. Slowly, trying not to make a sound, I feel my way backwards onto something like solid ground. The ripples spread out, breaking up the moonlight into silver slivers, and then stop. Only when I am completely hidden by trees do I take a breath.

"Please, show me the way," I say aloud. My voice sounds very small and shaky in that huge silence, and there is no answer. I have no idea which way I came, or what to do next. Although I very much do not want to be near whatever lies across the water, the thought of turning my back on it gives me goosebumps.

And then, as I hesitate, the water begins to move again. Little waves are lapping against the tree trunks, breaking on the muddy ground beyond. I look down, and the water is rising around my sodden shoes, creeping up onto the drier ground. Something is moving, out there in the dark. Something big.

There is no decision; I simply run. Or rather, scramble, splash and fall, get up and run again, as fast as I can, away from whatever is coming. Panic takes me, lends wings to my stumbling feet and sends fire through my veins. I've no idea how far I run, but I don't stop until, pushing my way between close-growing saplings, I fall out suddenly onto clear ground.

There is grass under my hands and knees. Grass, and smooth stones, set into the earth. For a while I see no more than that. When at last I can breathe again, and the thumping of my heart is no longer the only thing I can hear, I sit up and look around.

I am on a path. On either side, trees and undergrowth crowd in. Branches almost meet overhead, but on the path itself, nothing grows except short, fine grass. One way, downhill, leads into the darkness of the woods. Uphill, the trees thin out, and there is moonlight.

Don't we always choose to move towards the light if we can? I get up and walk that way without thinking about it. It isn't far. The path leads on across a bare hillside, bordered now by stones instead of trees, and just beyond where the ground dips a little, there is a crossroads.

I stop. No signposts, no clues. Which way should I go? Back into the shadowy woods, or down towards where—I guess—the pond waits with its dark secrets. Somewhere, probably on the road that runs straight ahead, that hilltop is looming. I shudder. Left, then, on the open ground but away from where I've been. What else can I do?

Behind me, someone speaks.

"Go that way, and you won't come back."

Perhaps I would have run again, if my legs had not been shaking with cold and exhaustion. But what would I be running to? Slowly, I turn around. There is nothing to be seen but the path emerging from the trees, and those irregular rocks that border it.

"Who's there?"

Nothing moves, and there is no reply. After a few moments, I am no longer sure I've heard anything at all. But as I start to turn back towards the higher ground, the voice comes again.

"Onward is not for you, Felicity Turner. Elfrida waits for you."

"Elfrida—is she the Queen? Where is she?" I take a step or two back along the path. But again, there is no reply, only a thin wind that whispers in the long grass. Shivering, I move into the lee of the nearest stone, crouch down and wrap my arms around my knees. I am cold and wet, and tired of being frightened.

"Please help me. I don't know what to do."

A part of the next stone along splits away, rises up and becomes a small man, about my own height. He stands looking down at me.

"Turn again, Felicity. Choose the woods and the water. She waits for you there." He holds out a hand to me, and as I stand up the world spins around us, and we seem to be turning and turning, he and I, dancing to music that comes out of the ground all about us.

"You danced with me! The other night—didn't you?" But,

as I speak, the music stops and I come to rest again, at arm's length from my partner. I can see the shine of the moonlight in his eyes.

No questions. I am learning. I point down towards the trees and say, "I'll go that way then." And he steps back, out of my way. After a few paces I look back, saying "Thank you!" but there is nobody there.

My courage almost fails me as I pass once more into the shadow of the trees. What if it's a trick? But I am so tired now, and I want to trust. So I go on, past the place where I'd broken through onto the path, always downhill. Branches meet overhead, shutting out the moonlight, but on the path itself there are no fallen leaves or twigs. There isn't much light either, but after a while I realise that the path gleams with a faint light of its own.

And it isn't very far, in the end. Other paths lead off into the forest, but I keep going, on the level now, until the path ends at a wall of rock and earth. A little stream trickles down through the moss, forming a pool fringed by flat stones. And beside the pool, set in the side of the hill, there is a door.

CHAPTER 6

I go straight up to the door, and knock. It is solid oak, joined with wooden pegs and carved all over with curling lines, and I don't expect my little knock to be heard at all. But the door swings open at once. There on the threshold stands a tall young man, who sweeps off his cap when he sees me, makes a low bow, and says,

"Welcome, Felicity!"

I cross the threshold. He takes my hand, and once again there is that dizzy, whirling sensation, and the sound of birds singing. I had been looking up at him, but now my eyes are almost on a level with his, and I am clothed in midnight blue velvet, sewn with tiny pearls that gleam in the light of hundreds of candles.

It's hard to know what to attend to first: the beautiful room that opens out before me, hung with tapestries and full—or so it seems at first—of marvellous people; the feast laid out on long tables; the queen, seated on a high dais at the far end; or my own self, moving slow and stately in my finery. It takes me a few minutes to work it out, and then I want very much to find a mirror, to see what I have become. No longer eight years old, no longer little Fliss, but a graceful young woman with hips and breasts and—I squint sidelong—hair now long and flowing, but still a fiery red.

We have arrived at the dais, and there is the queen, rising to greet me. She claps her hands together.

"You've attired her in the night sky, Lord Ember! It suits

her very well. Felicity, come sit by me. You've come by long and weary ways, and now you shall rest." She waves at the chair next to hers—had it been empty before?—and, as I come around the table, there is Hob, drawing out the chair for me to sit. Certainly, an empty plate and a goblet full of something pale and sparkling are waiting for me.

Once again, I am too hungry and thirsty to pay much attention to anything else, at first. I simply eat, and drink, with my eyes and ears and all of my senses. They are laughing and talking around me, but the words are strange, and I listen without really hearing.

"And so they set snares, limed the branches and all. Do they think we are birds now?"

"Ha! We sprang their gin traps, every one; set poppets in their snares. Took down the crows from Jack Wheeler's barn—dead a fortnight since, the last of them—and hung them in a row along the branch. Dan Miller's boy will get another beating for it, I'll wager."

On the floor by the hearth, Hob and another goblin roll each other over, shrieking with laughter. Then one of the speakers says,

"Maybe he'll come to us after all, think you?" and they stop, in the act of pummelling each other, staring at the one who'd spoken.

"Dick Miller? Not he," says another, picking a bone from between his teeth and throwing it at Hob. It becomes a tiny arrow, but before it reaches its target it grows wings and veers away, to dart back and peck at his ear and then zoom away into the darkness beyond the fire.

"Why so? Did we not make him welcome?"

The one who threw the bone leans back. He grimaces, and his face changes for an instant, becomes a mask like a snarling fox, and is back again almost too fast to see. "Him? He's found another kind of welcome with a come-hither wench from the town. He won't be back."

I try to make sense of this. The Dick Miller I know is a hulking youth who went off to secondary school three years ago, leaving a vacancy in the playground that was soon filled by another bully. I can't imagine him here, wearing silks and velvet and joining the dance. Nor do I want to, of course; I want them to be my secret and mine alone. But I must have misunderstood, after all.

"So no one new since—when?"

"Till now, mayhap." And my skin tingles again, almost painfully. But then Elfrida claps her hands.

"Felicity, what's your pleasure?"

I'm not sure what she means, but suddenly all their faces are turned towards me, and the talking ceases. There is only the crackle and hiss of the fire. Somewhere in the shadows, the piper plays a little run of notes that ends mid-phrase, like a question.

"Please, what was that thing in the water?" I hadn't meant to say that at all, but I do really want to know.

There is a sort of hiss or gasp from the company, and Hob scuttles under the table, to peer out at me from behind a table leg. His eyes get bigger and bigger until he looks like the dog in the fairy tale whose eyes were as big as dinner plates.

"Do not go that way again. It will know you next time," Elfrida says.

"I won't, I promise! But someone helped me. I didn't know which way to go, and he told me you were waiting."

She only looks at me, and the firelight flickers in her eyes. Behind me, someone says,

"Thomas walks the border. He'll go one day."

"Peace!" says Elfrida. And to me, "You were fortunate, Felicity. Stay within the woods, and we will always find you if you have need. Or if you are with us, then you are safe."

"But—" and I falter, not wanting to offend her. "But sometimes I can't find you. Please, tell me what to do."

She laughs, then, and others laugh with her. As though some danger has passed, they begin to move and talk again. Hob comes out from under the table, seizes a bone and begins to worry it like a dog. I wait for an answer, but although I seem to have said the right thing, none comes.

I am afraid to speak now, but my need to know is greater than my fear. Moving a little closer to Elfrida, I wait until there is a burst of shouting and laughter from further down the table, and then say quietly,

"My pleasure is to stay here with you, and never go back."

I hold my breath. What if I've asked for too much? What if the spell breaks and they all disappear, leaving me stranded once again? But she only looks at me steadily—and our eyes are on a level now—and says,

"One day, maybe. But not yet."

"What do I have to do?" The question bursts out of me, borne on the tide of grief and rage and despair that rises when I think of home.

"You will know when the time comes." And then she turns away, claps her hands again and calls aloud:

"The moon is high! Let us go hunting!"

The piper plays a two-note call, like the one the foxhunters use. When they are abroad, my mother and I have to run to shut up the hens; if the fox comes our way, the hounds will stream through the barnyard tearing at anything in their path. My hands are seized on both sides, and my feet seem to leave the ground as we pour out of the door into the cold night air.

I have just time to notice that not everyone is on the move; in the shadows beyond the fire, a girl sits singing to something on her lap—a dog? a baby?—and seems to take no notice of the tumult around her. And then we really are flying, swooping and diving over the tops of the trees. They don't have wings, I know that. It's like flying in a dream, except that I am terrified they might let go and, alone, I'll go crashing down through the branches. Yet at the same time I am filled with wild elation, screaming for pure joy amid the whooping and catcalling all around me. I want to look for landmarks, to see where we re-enter the familiar woods, but all of that goes out of my head. Better than riding a horse, better than any roller-coaster ride; those are just sad attempts to experience this. This is the real thing.

Chapter 7

We're coming down to the ground now. Fields and hedges are rushing up towards us, and my terror returns at the thought of landing, but when it comes it's slow and gentle, like stepping from water onto soft grass. And it is grass we stand on, under the twisted oak tree at Wycherley Cross.

I look around. There is the lane leading down into the village. The other way, uphill, winds its way between hedges to within half a mile of our farm. The school bus will come by that road to pick me up when term starts again in a week or two. I turn away from that thought. And yet; what if they let me stay? What if I never go back? Although I want that more than anything, something in me curls up small and closes its eyes.

"Be still. They are coming." I can't see who has spoken, but the whole company falls silent, and a moment later they have melted into the shadows. For a few seconds I think they've left me, and then someone takes my hand. I too become a shimmer of leaves in moonlight, a breath of wind through the hedge. Only Elfrida stands alone under the tree.

From around the corner comes the sound of voices, talking over each other. Two or three men, making their slow and stumbling way home from the pub. When they round the corner, surely they will see her. Why doesn't she hide herself?

"Damn!" One of the speakers rounds the bend and then stops suddenly, so that the others run into him. There is some pushing and shoving as he sways but stands his ground.

"Left my lighter in the pub," he says, patting at his pockets, first jacket and then trousers. Then he starts again.

"Want a light? Here," says one of the others, digging in his own pocket.

The first man starts to turn around. "That thieving bastard'll have it off me."

"Hoy!" The third man has grabbed him by the arm. "Pub's shut now. Come on, let's go home." They stand there, pulling in opposite directions, while the second—Jimmy Blackett from Ward's Farm—holds out his lighter. This seems likely to go on all night, but at last Jimmy says, "Fuck's sake!" Putting the lighter away, he plods on up the lane.

The other two stay where they are for a few seconds more, and then the third man gives the other a shove that sends him into the hedge, and turns away. As the moonlight falls on his face, I recognise him too; Dave Brooks, big brother of Joe Brooks who is in my class at school. He had been at our farm this afternoon, though it seems a lifetime ago now. The boys on the back step saw me sneaking off to the barn, and they laughed and jeered; but he had winked at me.

He is trudging on up the hill towards the turning now, head down and hands in his pockets, so he almost runs into Jimmy standing stock still in the middle of the road. He raises his head to look where Jimmy is looking.

"Bloody hell!" he says.

Elfrida stands there, glowing against the dark trunk of the twisted oak. I can't see her face, but she seems to be holding out her hands to the two men. Their faces are plain enough, though. Mouths open, eyes stretched wide in—what? Wonder, certainly, and fear too. And something else I can't put a name to; something that fills me with dread.

Dave is pulling at Jimmy's arm. "Come away. Let's go! Jimmy!"

Jimmy takes a step forward. "Not seen you round here before," he says. And another step.

When Elfrida answers, I can hear the smile in her voice. "But I have seen you, Jimmy Blackett."

He takes another step. "Have you, now? Liked what you saw, did you?"

"Jesus, Jimmy, come back here!" Dave stands rooted, and there is terror in his voice now. From beyond the bend in the road comes the voice of the third man, singing as he begins to plod back down the road. Dave starts, and looks back with yearning.

He tries once more. "Jimmy. What about your Emma?" But it comes out in a whisper, and gets no response at all from Jimmy, who takes another couple of steps, and lifts his hands towards Elfrida.

"Oh yes," says Elfrida. "You, and your father before you, and your father's father. Liars and drunkards, all of you."

He keeps moving, as though the sense of her words has not reached him. He looms over her, standing there so slight and straight under the tree. But just as he reaches out to touch her, she begins to change. I still can't see her face, but she seems to grow taller and darker, and her arms grow longer, sending out twigs and branches that begin to encircle him. The wide, soft grin on his face vanishes, and he lets out a wail of pure terror.

At the same time, Dave makes his decision, or his legs make it for him. He bolts, only to run straight into his friend, coming back up the hill saying too loudly,

"Found it in my sodding pocket! Whoa!" And then they are both rolling over in the road. Jimmy is screaming now, and he is not alone. The rest of the hunters break cover, howling and whooping. They rise into the air, changing as they go. Black and ragged against the night sky, they look now like creatures from my nightmares; bat-winged, long-beaked, sharp-clawed. They fall on the two prone men like a flock of crows on a carcass, and the noises they make are more animal than human.

I think—well, I don't know what I think. Will they stop

short of killing? There is squealing, like the pigs when they are cornered for the slaughter. I put my hands over my ears, and as I do so, see that I have become my own self again, small and mud-streaked, all alone by the blackthorn hedge. For a moment Jimmy's eyes meet mine, though I can't tell whether he knows me, or whether he is seeing only his own horror as the brambles grow up around him, faster than anything could possibly grow, holding him upright even as his eyes roll upward and his head falls back.

Is he dead? Are they all dead? I am sobbing now, open-mouthed. Distant and unreal, the thought comes to me that maybe I should fetch help, or at least try to get away. I don't move. And now the nightmare horde begins to break up; here and there, I see shapes emerging that I recognise. They draw back from the two men on the ground, and I see with relief that they are moving. Hissing like snakes, the brambles uncoil themselves from around Jimmy, and he falls, limp as a rag doll. Elfrida steps back, and the whole troupe now stands with her.

"Go home, Jimmy Blackett. Get you hence, David Brooks and Peter Green. Stray not from the path, or we will find you."

From either side, my hands are taken once more, and then the wind is rushing past, cold on my tear-streaked face. I hold on for dear life, not caring now where we're going or what sights we might see, until we come once more to that door in the hillside, and pass through. The fire is still burning, and by it sits the girl, crooning a lullaby to the creature in her arms.

The troupe bursts in, laughing and chattering like a flight of rooks, and she stands up, letting the creature slide to the floor. It sits there, rocking a little, and I see that it is neither dog nor baby, but something very strange, something betwixt and between. It looks up at me, and holds up its arms, and grins like a jack o'lantern, showing three crooked teeth.

"How now," she says, and touches the side of my face. "Here's a sight to behold."

"Felicity!" Lord Ember stands beside me, holding out his hand. And for a moment I feel an odd reluctance, although I stand out in that splendid company like a starling among the peacocks. Is it my true self they showed to me, or is it all make-believe? But I give him my hand even as I think it, and a moment later stand tall and elegant again, with flowers in my hair instead of twigs and leaves, and a wide sweep of skirts that fall to my feet. Where the creature is sitting, looking up at me. It gathers a fistful of my skirt in one chubby hand, and pulls at it, and begins to whine.

"Alys! Take your poppet and let Felicity be." Ember twitches my skirt out of its grasp and sweeps me away as the music starts up again. I look back, once, as the dance whirls me past the hearth. It's still sitting there, too close to the unguarded flames, and Alys is nowhere to be seen.

By the time the dance is over, it seems that the hunt is over and done with too, and no one is giving it a second thought. I have so many questions! How can I frame them, without actually asking?

Nearby, Hob and his friends are changing chicken bones into swords, mock-fighting like the boys in the playground at school. But the swords are real; they ring against each other, and when Hob lunges at his friend I see the blade go right into him. I gasp aloud as Hob yells in triumph. His friend looks down, clutches at his stomach and sinks to his knees. He opens his mouth as though trying to speak.

There is silence, maybe for a second or two, while Hob and the others watch. And then out of his mouth pours a black cloud, swirling and buzzing. It splits into three groups, and they fly straight at Hob and his friends.

Bees! Thousands and thousands of them, impossibly many, pouring out while the goblins screech and caper, trying to beat them off. Others are watching now, laughing and applauding. Slowly, I take my hands from my face and look around. And then Elfrida points, says something I can't hear, and—pop!—all the bees become bright stars, drifting slowly downward like the end of a firework display. They lie glowing on the floor for a few moments, and then go out.

Hob and his friends jump up, and one of them begins juggling with apples. There is no blood, no stings, not even any bruises that I can see. Is it all play-acting, then?

"Be not afraid, Felicity." Elfrida is at my side. "No one shall come to harm here."

I've thought carefully about what to say next; how to find out what I need to know without seeming to ask.

"Dave Brooks was at our farm today. He's quite nice to us kids."

Elfrida raises her eyebrows. "David, son of John, son of Aldo Ricci, though he thinks that William Brooks is his father."

That throws me off track, and it takes me some time to work it out. "Can you do that with my family, too? How far can you go back?"

Immediately, I kick myself for asking. But surprisingly, she answers.

"Further back than I can count, Felicity Turner. There have been Turners at Well Farm as long as I have dwelt in these woods. But you'll be the last, it seems."

Now I'm really thrown. I forget all about poor Dave Brooks and his friends.

"Why? What do you mean?"

"Do you want to be a farmer, Felicity?"

I stare at her. Without thinking, I put my hands to my dress, and run them slowly down the smooth velvet. She sees the movement, and smiles.

"No need for such thoughts now. It's time for you to go home."

"No! I don't want to go! Please, please let me stay with you. What do I have to do?"

"The time will come." She raises her hand. "Fairies, away!"

Around the table, everyone gets to their feet. They bow and curtsey to me, and Hob blows me a kiss that turns into a shining dragonfly. *Fairies*, I think. And I hold that word in my heart, as once more we go rushing through the air, too fast to see much beyond the dawn-streaked sky, and then a tumble of flying leaves. And I'm standing alone, just inside the boundary of the woods, by the oak tree where I leave my watch. The new barbed wire has been unstapled and rolled back to either side, and the hole is easily big enough for me to get through.

And I did, in the end. What choice did I have? But she did say the time would come. I held on to that, as I made my way along the side of the field and into the barnyard. It wasn't even milking time yet, and no one was about as I eased open the back door, unlaced my muddy shoes and crept upstairs to my bedroom. Someone—it could only be my mother—had left an apple and a chocolate bar by my bed. Of course, she meant to be kind, but it felt like just the opposite. *I have feasted with the fairies*, I thought. *You can give me nothing that I want*. Although, at that moment, all I wanted was the soft cocoon of my own bed, and the sleep that rushed up to pull me in.

CHAPTER 8

The autumn term began. That meant I had less time to spend in the woods, and as the nights grew longer and colder, it wasn't so easy to stay there. Darkness held no fear for me, but the cold was hard to bear. I searched for the door in the hillside, though I knew it was beyond the familiar pathways, but I never found it. There were signs, though. A daisy chain hanging on a branch above the entrance to my den; a spray of fresh green beech leaves on the path where no beeches grew; and once, when I'd fallen asleep in my den huddled in my blanket, a honey-cake still warm from the baking, placed just by my hand.

Although it seemed that there was nothing they wanted from me, I kept on trying to find gifts for them. But there were no treasures that I could offer, nothing that could come close to the splendour that was theirs whenever they chose. It made me look at my own home with fresh eyes.

When you live on a farm, things don't stay bright and new and clean for very long. There was the front parlour, which we never used except on special occasions, where the best china lived in a glass-fronted cabinet and the curtains were closed against the sun; but even there, spiders made dusty webs in the high corners, and the folded tablecloths in the dresser smelled of mould and damp. It was a chilly and unwelcoming place where you had to be on your best behaviour.

The kitchen was the heart of the house, always warm because of the range that was never allowed to go out. Clothes dried there, food was cooked there, cats and dogs were always underfoot. Orphan lambs and new chicks could be kept alive in the warming oven. I did my homework there, at the far end of the long table, while at the other end my mother rolled out pastry and the radio chattered and sang to itself. But everything in it was well-used and worn down, from the battered tabletop to the range with its baked-on layers of old spillages, to the tiles underfoot that might once, long ago, have been red and shiny.

And my parents were part of that. Well-used, worn down, though of course I didn't see it that way then. I just thought that was how they were. But Elfrida's words, like a stone thrown into a pond, had started ripples that broke up the picture and made strange, unsettling new patterns.

"Do you want to be a farmer, Felicity?"

I shied away from the thought of it. From any thought of the future, out there waiting to use me up and wear me down. They had seen generations come and go, and they never changed. When I had mentioned Dave Brooks, Elfrida had named his father and grandfather, and she had said something similar to Jimmy Miller, "Liars and drunkards, all of them." How far did they go back? It made me feel strange and small to think of it; those people in the photo albums, foxed and faded, working in our fields and driving their produce to the market. And others, before there were photos. In the churchyard there were plenty of Millers and Turners, Coopers and Brooks, and I went to school with children who bore those names still.

"You'll be the last, it seems." Parts of what she'd said kept coming back to me. Why would I be the last? Was it because I would choose not to be a farmer—and if not, what?—or because maybe, just maybe, I'd be allowed to stay with them and never come back? Those were not the only possibilities, of course, but back then, they were the only ones I could let myself think about. I was bursting with questions, but I knew now that when I did see them again, it was likely to leave me with more questions than answers. All I could do was wait, and hope.

Chapter 9

Two days before they were coming to stay for the week-end, my mother started cleaning. When I got home from school, she wasn't sitting in her chair with her magazine. She was in the kitchen baking cakes, and the whole house smelled of food and floor polish. She'd washed the tiles in the hall so you could see all the colours, where it was usually just mud, but she couldn't get rid of the scrapes along the walls, or the spiders up in the corners where even the long brush wouldn't reach.

I went to take one of the cakes off the rack where they were cooling, and she slapped my hand away.

"Those are for the weekend! Don't touch!" She had flour on her face and in her hair, and a sort of wild look in her eyes.

"What's for tea, then? I'm really hungry."

"Oh, I haven't got time to bother with cooking now. There's a tin of spaghetti in the larder, you can heat that up. Sort yourself out, and then you can make yourself useful."

"I've got to work on my bird project, it's due in tomorrow." I crossed my fingers in my pocket when I said that. Really we had another week, but I wasn't going to say so. "Please can I have just one cake?"

"You leave those alone! And if you're not going to help, get out of the way and let me get on with it!"

I didn't know why they had Aunty Marjorie and the rest to stay at all. They got in a bad mood all week, and then we had to sit in the parlour and they talked for hours, or Mum and

Aunty Marjorie did, and I wasn't allowed to go out or anything, or if I did I had to take the cousins with me. I had to share my bed with Angie, top and tail, and she kicked and wriggled all night. So I went and got the tin of spaghetti, and opened it just enough to get a spoon in, and then I took it upstairs and grabbed a cake on the way as well. They'd be stale by Saturday, anyway, and we'd all have to pretend to like them.

It was cold upstairs, but Mum had taken away the electric heater to warm up the spare bedroom for Aunty Marjorie and Uncle Bob, so I got under the covers. I ate the cake first, still warm and smelling of vanilla, and then I spooned the spaghetti out of the tin and got the rest of the sauce out with my finger. The edges of the lid were very sharp; if I were imprisoned in a dungeon I could use it to dig through the wall, a little bit at a time, and drop the dirt out of the window so the guards wouldn't notice. And I'd mark the days with scratches under the bed where no one could see. Then I'd know how long I'd been there and whether it was winter or spring outside.

When it was all gone, I got one of the blankets Mum had hung over the banisters to air, and stowed it in my backpack. They always smelled musty, and there were brown mould spots on them, but I knew wool was the best thing because it stays warm even if it's wet. The men who climbed Everest wore layers of wool, and the new synthetic materials weren't a patch on the old stuff, or that's what Dad always said. Mum would notice there was a blanket missing, but I'd be gone by then. There was enough food to last a few days in the den now, and with an extra blanket as well, I could manage even when it got very cold. Next time, I was planning to stay out all night again.

They arrived mid-morning on Saturday. I went to the hay barn with my book, but Dad came and found me, even though I was up in my nest near the ceiling. I didn't think he knew about the ginger kittens though. They were a late litter, too small to run about, so maybe they'd be safe. Maybe he'd leave them alone this time. I had to go in and put on the dress that Aunty Marjorie sent me, though it was too big; Angie had outgrown it and it wouldn't be warm enough in the winter.

"That looks like a sack on you," Mum said, and she made me stand while she plaited my hair and put ribbons on the ends.

"Let me wear something else then."

"Oh, hold still, for goodness" sake! As if I hadn't got anything better to do!"

"It hurts! You're pulling it too tight. Oww!"

"If you just stay put, it'll be done all the faster. There; that'll have to do. Now don't fiddle with the bows or it'll all come undone. Put that apron on and shell some peas for me."

I liked shelling peas. The best pods made a nice snap and the peas all came jumping out into the colander. People said, "As like as peas in a pod," but they weren't really the same at all. They got smaller towards the end. Each pod was a family, with the parents at one end and then all the children in order of size. Some families had seven or eight children, like the Tanners in the village, and sometimes there were just two or three good peas and the rest were little and squashy. I only put good ones into the colander.

"Aren't you finished yet? Don't go off into a daydream, there's work to be done." She was cooking a roast dinner even though it wasn't Sunday, and she was all hot and red in the face.

"Give that here, I'll finish it. We'll be here till next week waiting for you." I was saving the best ones till last, but she took the colander away and said, "Go and lay the table, they'll be here soon. Seven places, remember. There's only six of the good knives and forks, so you children will have to use the ordinary ones. And get the glasses out of the cabinet, but be careful!"

Dad had put the extra leaf on the dining table in the parlour, and there was only just room to get around it, with the chairs and everything. He'd brought the electric fire in as well, but he'd have to turn it off when they came, or whoever sat near it would get their legs burnt. It would have to be me and Angie and Tommy along one side, or we wouldn't all fit in, and Mum would make me sit in the middle where the table legs were, so I wouldn't be able to sit properly and I'd get told off, as usual.

I was putting the cutlery out, lining them all up carefully with the spoons across the top, when I heard their car coming into the yard. The geese started screeching at them, and I watched behind the net curtain. Angie was afraid, and she wouldn't get out of the car. So was Tommy, but he pretended not to be. Uncle Bob pulled the back door open and said, "Come on, scaredy cat!"

Angie got out and went a little way, and then one of the geese came around the side of the car, and she screamed and ran to Uncle Bob. He had to pick her up, though she's ten and much too big for that, and her shoes made a smear of dirt on his coat. Camel, that's what the colour was called, though it looked like beige to me. Beige with streaks of goose poo.

I ducked down behind the table, and listened while Mum fussed around them, taking their coats off and everything. She opened the door and looked in, but she couldn't see me, so she closed it again and shouted up the stairs.

"Felicity! Come down and say hello!"

"Nose in a book again, I expect." That was Uncle Bob, too loud in the hallway with everyone clattering about. "Angie, go and find your cousin."

I waited until they'd all gone into the sitting room, except for Mum and Aunty Marjorie making tea in the kitchen, and then I came out into the hall. Really, I wanted to get out of the front door and away, but my best shoes would get all muddy and they'd find me in the end anyway, so I went upstairs and listened outside my bedroom door. I couldn't hear any noise. What was she doing in there?

You can't open the bedroom door without making it creak, so I just pushed it open really quickly. Angie was sitting on my bed, and she jumped. She had my diary in her hands.

"Leave that alone! That's private!" I should have hidden it in my den like last time, but I'd been drawing pictures of the barn owls. She was looking at the writing, but I couldn't see what it was.

"You're really strange. You know that, don't you?" she said in her superior, I'm-two-years-older-and-I-live-in-town-and-I-know-everything voice.

"Give it to me!"

She tried to hold it out of my reach, but I pushed her over and climbed on her so she couldn't get away. She screamed, but she kept her arm up, and with her other hand she grabbed one of my plaits and pulled it, hard.

"Give it back!" I could have scratched her face, but I didn't quite dare. Then Tommy came in. He said "Oi! Play nice, children" like Aunty Marjorie, and he took my diary out of Angie's hand.

"What's this, then?" He opened the front and started to read in a pretend little-girl voice. "January the first, 1960. My name is Felicity Turner, but people usually call me Fliss. My eyes are blue and my hair is red and frizzy. I've got sticky-out teeth and knobbly knees and freckles, and nobody likes me." He stopped then, and I thought he was going to laugh, but he just stood there for a minute as though he'd forgotten what he was doing, and then he said, "Come on, you two, they want us downstairs," and he put the diary down on the bedside table.

I got off Angie, then, and grabbed it before she could get it back. She smoothed down her dress and said, "Your hair's a mess, you look really stupid," and went out. After a moment, Tommy went too, and then I hid the diary in one of the jigsaws on the shelf. It was the most boring one, like a map of Britain with all the industries marked on it, that Aunty Marjorie gave me for Christmas because it was educational, and no one ever wanted to do it, so they wouldn't look there.

One of my ribbons had come undone and bits of hair were sticking out everywhere, but there was nothing I could do about it. I went down as slowly as I could, imagining myself tall and beautiful in the blue velvet dress, with a net of tiny seed-pearls shimmering in my hair, but I could already hear Aunty Marjorie talking in her loud voice, like she did for Grandma who was a bit deaf. Only Grandma wasn't here, so it must be to make sure we all listened properly. Because mostly people didn't, especially Uncle Bob. Sometimes he pretended to be asleep and snoring. Tommy tried that once, but he got a slap for it, which wasn't really fair.

"And it's got its own little cabinet with doors that close, so it just looks like a cupboard when you're not watching it. Walnut veneer. I've put a nice plant on the top, one of those African violets. Mrs. Searle down the road says the rays from the television set will kill it, but Bob says that can't be right. If it killed pot plants, it wouldn't do the rest of us much good."

Uncle Bob grunted. "If you believed half of what that woman says, you'd never go out of the house. Silly cow."

"Bob! Not in front of the children! Well, anyway, I think it's a good test. If the plant dies we'll know, won't we? And I make the children sit at least six feet away, just in case."

"You can't make out the picture most of the time, anyway." That was Tommy. "It's all fuzzy with lines across it, and if you move the aerial it goes like a snowstorm."

"Tommy! Your father paid good money for that television set, and no one else in our street has got one yet, except for Mrs. Anstey on the corner. Not that she speaks to anybody, she's too stuck-up, but I saw it being delivered last week."

"Lot of nonsense if you ask me." My Dad's voice always sounded sort of rusty, as though if you didn't speak much it stopped working properly, like the hinges of the little door into the hay barn. "We've managed fine without it so far."

"Well, there are some very good educational programmes for the children," she said. She liked the word "educational"; she said it a lot. "And we watch the six o'clock news too. It's good to keep abreast of current affairs."

The door was open a little bit, and I could see Tommy with his legs wound round the legs of his chair, but when Aunty Marjorie said "abreast" he made a sort of snorting noise, and Angie giggled.

"Stop that, you two, or you'll feel the back of my hand!" Uncle Bob wasn't snoring now. "Honestly, they don't miss a trick."

I pushed the door and went in, and they all looked up. Mum said "Oh, Fliss! It's not five minutes since I did your hair and look at the state of it already. I give up, I really do."

I wished she would, but she never really meant it. I said, "My plait got caught on the door-handle," because that did happen once, and I crossed my fingers and looked out of the window so as not to see Angie.

Aunty Marjorie said "I don't know how you manage. Thank goodness Angie's got naturally curly hair." Which is a lie, because she made Angie have it in curlers before they went out anywhere. Grown-ups told us off for making things up, but they did it all the time.

"Shut the door, for goodness sake! You're letting in the draught," said Mum. "Come here and let me sort you out."

"So, Felicity, how are you getting on at school?" It was Uncle Bob's turn to talk too loudly now. "Still top of the class?"

"Yes," I said, and then "Ow!" because Mum stuck a hairpin into my head.

"Don't boast, Fliss. It's not becoming."

"It's true! They've put me in a special group of my own for spelling, because the ones the others are doing are too easy."

"Is that so? Well, you try spelling this for me." Uncle Bob paused, and then he said a very long word. He said it slowly, as though he had to feel his way through it. I looked it up afterwards, and it was

"FLOCCINAUCINIHILIPILIFICATION."

It meant "the estimation of something as valueless", and it took up a whole line in my diary. I'll never forget it for the rest of my life, but then I just looked at him, and they all laughed.

"Ah!" said Uncle Bob as though he'd done something really clever. "So, you don't know everything yet."

I thought: *But I know things you can't imagine.* And it was easier, somehow, than it used to be.

Mum said, "Well, long words won't get dinner under way," and she got up and went into the kitchen. Aunty Marjorie went too, and then it was dead quiet, because no one could think of anything to say.

I'd noticed that, although Dad and Uncle Bob said things like, "You can't get a word in edgeways!" when Mum and Aunty Marjorie were talking, they didn't really want to talk much themselves when they did get the chance. If they had a newspaper, they'd go behind it and rustle a bit. And if they hadn't got a newspaper, they just sat there.

Mum and Grandma and the aunties did the same when they'd finished making food and washing up and all that. All grown-ups did. They'd sit down with this big sigh, as though it was the best thing they'd done all day, the thing they'd been really looking forward to. So then they'd ask you, "How are you getting on at school?" though they didn't really want to know. And the next question after that was, "So, what do you want to do when you grow up?"

I don't think they really wanted to know that either. Because I think what they really wanted, whether they were a farmer like Dad or worked in an office like Uncle Bob, or were housewives like Mum and Aunty Marjorie, was to sit down and do nothing at all. In fact, what they really wanted was to

TURN INTO STONE.

So if I told the truth when they asked me what I wanted to do when I grew up, which they were always telling me I should do instead of making things up; if I said what I really thought in my secret inside self (which I never did, because they just got angry or laughed at me), it would have been this:

"I don't want to grow up. Ever."

Chapter 10

But even if you did want to turn into stone, you couldn't do it in the middle of the morning before lunch was ready. So after a long time, Dad said to Uncle Bob, "Coming to look at the cows?"

"Might as well. You coming, young Tommy?"

I crossed my fingers and wished, hard, but the magic only worked when I was out there, with Them. There could never be any magic inside the house.

"No thanks," said Tommy.

"All right," said Dad. "You youngsters go off and play, and don't get into mischief." He and Uncle Bob got out of their chairs, with a lot of creaking, and went off to put on overalls and wellies. As soon as they shut the door, Tommy said,

"Let's go in the woods! I've got this new air rifle for my birthday. You can have a go if you like, Fliss."

"He's not allowed to use it in our garden at home," said Angie. "He shot a squirrel, and then he nearly shot the cat from next door."

"It was digging up the flowerbed! Dad's always saying, 'I'm going to shoot that ruddy cat one of these days,' so I did."

"Don't swear, or I'll tell Mum," said Angie. "Anyway, you're not allowed to point it at anything except your target, Dad said."

"What's the point of having an airgun if you can't shoot things? Anyway, that only counts at home in our garden. It's different in the woods. And squirrels are vermin, Dad says."

"You can't take that into our woods," I said. And I remembered what Elfrida told me: *No bird nor beast shall come to harm in our domain, but we shall hear of it. All are under our protection.*

"Says who?"

Says the Queen of the Fairies, that's who. Aloud, I said,

"Tommy, if you hurt any of our animals, you'll be in trouble."

He laughed. "I'm not going to shoot at cows or sheep, dumbo!" He went off down the passage to the back door, where all the coats and boots are kept. Angie hung back in case there were spiders, while Tommy and I banged the boots together. Sure enough, a big black spider fell out of one and ran along by the wall. Angie started screaming, and Tommy aimed the gun and shot it, just like that.

I screamed too, then. A big flake of plaster fell off the wall. The spider was still alive, but it was dragging itself along, and two of its legs were smashed. Tommy bent down to get a closer look, and he made that yelping noise boys make when they're excited, sort of laughing and shouting at the same time.

We heard Mum calling out,

"What's going on out there?" And Tommy said,

"Quick, run!" and shoved me in the back, but then Mum and Aunty Marjorie came out into the passage, and anyway I'd only got one boot on.

"For crying out loud!" Mum said, and she picked up a boot and killed the spider as though it was the same as rolling out pastry or peeling potatoes. Angie screamed again, but I was glad. If the spider could have been screaming, it would, and now everything went quiet although people were still talking and making a fuss.

"If I've told you once, I've told you a thousand times," said Aunty Marjorie. "You do not shoot that thing indoors!"

"It was frightening Angie," said Tommy. "I was protecting her."

"You wait till your father hears about this! Look at the mess you've made of that wall!" Actually, bits of plaster fell off in the passage all the time, and the walls were all scuffed and scarred where people had kicked them or bashed things against them on their way in or out. But that was just the sort of thing grownups said.

"Don't worry about that, Marge. Ray will sort it out," Mum said. And that's another thing they said. Dad never sorted things out unless he had to, like when the cows got out through the hedge by the lane. He used to mend things, but not any more.

"We're just going to see the animals," said Tommy, and he ran out before Aunty Marjorie could take the gun away from him. She was fussing over Angie, anyway, making sure her boots were safe before she put them on, and she didn't notice.

"Go on, get out from under our feet," said Mum. "Fliss, can you pick some parsley from the garden for me? And mind you're back before lunchtime." She went back into the kitchen.

I looked out into the yard, but I couldn't see Tommy anywhere.

"He's gone," I said to Angie. "D'you want to come to the barn and see the kittens?" It was raining a bit, and she didn't like getting wet. Mum said it was because they were townies, and a bit of good honest rain never did anyone any harm, but she never said that when they were actually there.

"All right," said Angie. She looked at the squashed spider, and sort of shivered all over. "I hate my stupid brother and his stupid gun," she said.

"Me too. Come on, let's hide in the barn."

We ran to the garden wall, and then I made her crouch down. "We're scouts in enemy territory, and if they see us they'll take us prisoner," I told her. She just looked at me as if I was mad, but she crouched down anyway.

"When the coast is clear, we'll run across to the corner of the milking parlour. That gives us cover, and then it's just over the barnyard to the barn. Are you ready?" I peered over the wall. "All clear. Now run!"

I splashed straight through the puddles to the milking parlour; you can't worry about mud when you're hiding from the enemy. But then I had to wait for Angie, and she took ages, picking her way between the puddles, holding up the hem of her dress.

"It's all pooey!" she said when she got there. "I've got poo on my best dress."

"It's only cow dung, it won't hurt you. Come on; we won't be out of danger until we reach the barn." She made a face, but she followed me round the milking parlour wall. The barnyard was always wet and muddy, because that was where the cows waited when they came in for milking. You couldn't really run, it was too deep and slippery in places, so I held her hand and said,

"Just walk where I walk. Follow in my footsteps, like King Wenceslas and his page," and so we got across safely.

The barn door was shut so the cows couldn't go in and eat the hay. It was hard to lift the latch on your own, but I made Angie lean against the door, and then I could push it up more easily. Apart from the woods, the barn was my best place. It smelled nice from all the hay, and it was a little bit warm, especially when it was full of bales. You could make yourself a kind of den, like an igloo only made of hay, up at the back where it wouldn't be disturbed until springtime.

"Promise you won't tell if I show you my den?" Angie nodded, so we climbed up there. I remembered I had some books in the den, but I thought she wouldn't laugh at me now I'd helped her escape and shown her my secret place. Fingers crossed.

The den was a bit small for two people, so we sat on the bales just outside it. Angie didn't even look at my books properly, so that was all right. She wriggled.

"It's all prickly," she said in a whiny voice. "And there might be creepy-crawlies in it."

"Do you want to see the kittens?" I knew that it was pointless trying to make people not mind about things like creepy-crawlies. All you could do was to try to take their minds off it, which was what Mum said when we went to the dentist. So we climbed across to where the kittens were, and it was just as prickly there, but Angie forgot all about that. There were three kittens, all ginger, but one had white feet, and their eyes were only just open. Their mother was one of Malkin's daughters, and she didn't mind me, but she hissed when she saw Angie.

"Let me go first, she's used to me," I said. I stroked her a bit, and then I picked up one of the kittens and gave it to Angie, and the mother cat watched but she stayed calm.

Angie cuddled it like a baby. It squirmed a bit and started to mew.

"You've got to be gentle. Here, let me hold it."

"I know how to do it!" Angie held on to the kitten. "I'm going to ask if we can have one of them."

"You can't! You promised you wouldn't say anything!"

"No I didn't, I had my fingers crossed, so there. Anyway, why can't we? You've got lots of cats, and we've only got a stupid budgie."

"That's not fair! I wouldn't have shown you if I'd known you would tell. I'm not showing you anything else, ever." Why couldn't I just tell her what would happen to the kittens if my dad knew about them? It was shame that stopped me; not just about the kittens, but everything to do with the farm. Everything about it that Angie despised, and I felt I had to defend.

"Keep your hair on," said Angie in her superior voice. "There will be two left for you. You're just selfish."

I stared at her, and all the words I was trying not to say got stuck in my throat, and then I couldn't hold them back any longer, and they came out in one great big sob.

"Cry-baby, cry-baby!" she said, and she held up the kitten

over the edge of the hay bales, so it mewed loudly. The mother cat stopped nursing the others, and hissed again.

"Put it back! Please, Angie!" And after a moment, she did, and it scrambled back in between the other two. We didn't look at each other. I didn't want to say the words, but I had to make her understand.

"If Dad knows about them, he'll drown them. Please don't say anything. You did promise."

I held my breath, looking away. And then she said, "Well, anyway, we're getting something better than a kitten. We're going to have a baby!"

Then I did look at her. How could a baby be better than a kitten? But at least it would mean they would be safe, for now. Angie had gone pink in the face.

"You're supposed to say congratulations. And how lovely, and when's it due, and all that. That's why they wanted us out of the house, so Mum could tell your mum all about it."

"Oh." I really couldn't think of anything else to say.

"You're hopeless! And your mum will pretend to be pleased but she'll be really upset, because she can't have any more babies."

"Oh," I said again. The idea of more babies was a new and startling one. It had always been just me. Mum and Dad weren't very interested in me, so why would they want more children?

"Don't you know anything? That's why this farm will have to be sold. If they had a boy, he would carry it on, but there's only you. It's a matter of time, Dad says. He thinks Uncle Ray should give it up now, the way things are going with farming, but Uncle Ray won't listen."

I know lots of things, I thought inside my head. *I know about centipedes and millipedes, and where to find a butterfly chrysalis in wintertime. But I don't know about the ground I stand on.* Our family has always farmed this land. There have been Turners here for hundreds of years; their names are on the gravestones in the churchyard. How could that come to an end because of me? But Elfrida's words came back to me: *You'll be the last, it seems.*

That was too big and too strange for me to deal with, so I came back to the other thing.

"Mum doesn't want another baby."

Angie looked sideways at me. "You don't know, do you?"

"What don't I know?" I could see she was torn between having a secret that I didn't share, and wanting to tell me. So I looked away and stroked the mother cat, who was quietly purring now while she fed her kittens, as though I didn't care either way.

After a few moments, she went on. "I heard them talking about it when they thought I was upstairs. Mum said, 'We'll have to tell Ray and Jane, now we've told the children. And Dad said, 'Can't we just leave it for a bit?' And she said 'No, we can't! They're bound to find out soon enough. Poor June will be devastated.' Then he said, 'Well, we can't go tiptoeing round them forever. It's three years now since they lost the last one. And it's not as though we did it on purpose to spite them. No one's more surprised than me, I can tell you!"

"Then Mum laughed in a funny sort of way, and said, 'But you are really pleased, aren't you?' and he said, 'Course I am, love,' and then I ran upstairs because they were coming out into the hall. So that's how I know," Angie finished, looking expectantly at me.

But I didn't understand what she was telling me. "What do you mean, 'lost the last one'? We haven't had any babies, except me, of course. I'd know about it if we had!"

Angie went pink again. She didn't say anything for a minute, and then she spoke very slowly and carefully, as though she thought I didn't understand English or something. "You do know where babies come from, don't you?"

"Of course I do!" I was outraged; I was the one who lived on a farm, after all.

"Well, sometimes when a lady is expecting a baby, something goes wrong and it comes out too soon."

I thought about this. "You mean like when the sheep have been serviced and there's one or two that drop their lambs before they're ready?" I had helped with lambing, of course. Everyone did; and my small hands could do the work that grown-ups couldn't manage.

"People aren't like sheep, dummy! But yes, sort of like that."

"What's that got to do with us having babies?"

Angie rolled her eyes. "Well, that's what happened to your mum. Three times before you were born, and then two more times. That's what my mum said, and then the doctor told her she mustn't try any more."

I couldn't look at her. How could she know such things about my family, when I didn't? And it was too big, too private to talk about, even to think about, with Angie there, watching me.

"Let's play sliding down the haystacks!" I said, too loudly, and I jumped up and threw myself into the next row of bales. I couldn't keep still, couldn't stay near her.

"Not likely! We'll be all over straw and get really told off. You've got loads in your hair now."

"It's not straw, it's hay," I said, but I didn't have the heart to score points off her. I wanted to go to the woods, crawl into my den and pull the blankets over my head. Only then would it be safe to take out the new knowledge she'd given me, and feel my way into it. But they were staying all day, and night-time too, and not going home until after lunch tomorrow. How could I bear it?

"You've got to pick some parsley," said Angie from her perch up on the high bales. "Or your mum will be cross and dinner will be ruined." She said the last bit in Aunty Marjorie's voice. It was a sort of peace-offering, and we were both grateful.

Chapter 11

Family dinners were always strange; everyone on their best behaviour and saying things they'd never think of normally. We hardly ever had meals together on ordinary days. I'd have tea when I got home from school, and my parents would have theirs later, after the outdoor work was done. I got my own breakfast on school mornings, and sometimes hardly saw my mother and father for days. But now here we were, all in one room, and the new secret knowledge like an invisible extra guest. I imagined those babies, three of them and maybe more. How old would they be now? There wouldn't be enough room for all of us round the table. Brothers and sisters, kicking each other and fighting over who got the pork crackling.

Brothers. Boys who would have airguns and shoot squirrels, who would help on the farm when they were old enough, so Dad wouldn't have to hire help. Who would carry it on in their turn, perhaps. But instead, there was only me. *You'll be the last, it seems.*

"Lovely bit of pork." Uncle Bob leaned back in his chair. "You can't beat home-grown, eh? Sorry I couldn't get away to help this year; you know how it is with the annual leave allowance."

"We managed. The Miller boys came over—not that they're a lot of use—and John Brooks's boy, and a few others."

"That Dave Brooks seems a steady sort of lad. You thought of asking him on a regular basis?"

Dad grunted. "He used to be up for any work going, but he's changed his tune lately."

Uncle Bob looked knowing. "None of them want to go into farming these days, not any more. Got their eyes on the bright lights. Clean hands and a regular wage, that's all they're interested in."

"Tidn't that." Dad was annoyed, I could see, and that made him more talkative than usual. "Him and his mates, they spent their earnings down at the pub in Wycherley after the butchering. Went home by the twisted oak, and it seems they had a little encounter with the spirit there."

He had everyone's attention now.

"What spirit?" Tommy demanded, and Aunty Marjorie said,

"Elbows off the table, young man. Some spirit out of a bottle, I'd imagine."

"What, like a genie?" All the grown-ups laughed. Angie smirked at her brother's embarrassment, and he kicked her quite hard.

"Children, honestly! Who'd have them?" Too late, Uncle Bob realised what he had said. There was a small, charged silence.

"But what is the spirit really?" That was Angie; she hated not knowing things. And for once, she didn't get told off for interrupting.

"Well." Dad cleared his throat. "There's supposed to be some kind of a spirit imprisoned in the oak tree at the crossroads. That's why it's twisted, see, on account of the spirit trying to get out. And Dave Brooks and his mates reckoned they saw it."

"What did it look like?"

"Depends who you ask. Peter Green, now, he said it were like a mob of black birds, only bigger than any birds could be, all coming at them screeching and tearing with their beaks and claws. But Dave Brooks said he saw a beautiful lady all dressed in white. And young Jimmy Miller, well, he won't say nothing at all."

This was the longest speech I had ever heard my father make. We all stared at him in astonishment. And yet, I had the feeling there was more he could have said; something he had held back. He would not look at me.

Uncle Bob laughed. "That'll teach them to keep their money in their pockets! Though there is something about that tree, especially at the full moon, or so they say . . ." He looked sidelong at us children. "Do you remember, Ray, when big John Miller tried to burn it down? Folks said he'd let the spirit out and there'd be no end of trouble, but he wasn't having it. Poured petrol all round and then set a match to it. We was supposed to be in bed, but we sneaked out to watch. Us and most of the boys in the neighbourhood."

Dad grunted again, busy with his dinner. He had had his say. Uncle Bob carried on, and his voice got richer, less townified, as he told his tale. Aunty Marjorie looked as though she'd swallowed a beetle, but she didn't interrupt. She wanted to hear the story too.

"What happened?" Tommy was there in his imagination, waiting for the whoosh of flame, the crackle of fireworks.

Uncle Bob put down his knife and fork. "A huge black shape come out the tree. It leaned down over big John, and what d'you think happened next?"

"Bob!" said Aunty Marjorie. "You'll be giving them nightmares. Talk sense, now."

"What did happen? Tell us!" That was Angie and Tommy together. I kept my mouth shut, feeling my father watching me.

Uncle Bob went "Whoooh!" the way ghosts are supposed to, and Angie screamed.

"Nothing happened, that's what," said Dad. "The tree lost a few leaves, and big John lost his eyebrows, and that's about the size of it. Any farm boy could have told him you can't burn down an oak tree. And we all got a leathering next day for being out of bed and playing with matches."

I'd been holding my breath, and now I let it out slowly, trying not to be noticed. Tommy slumped in disappointment, and Aunty Marjorie said,

"Sit up straight, for goodness sake. What a lot of nonsense! Any excuse to avoid an honest day's work."

Dad said, "The other two, maybe. Dave Brooks ent like that, though. Shame to lose him." And I felt again, though I did not dare to look up, that his eyes were on me.

"We'll manage, Ray." Mum had hardly spoken over dinner, and she hadn't even told me off about the state of my hair and the wisps of hay stuck to my cardigan. Sometimes it felt as though there was a sort of mist around her, so I couldn't see her properly, or she was too far away. *All those babies.* For some reason, I thought of Alys, singing to her strange, ugly creature. Her *poppet*: that was what Lord Ember had called it.

Dad didn't reply, and after a few moments Mum said,

"Would anyone like some more before I clear away?"

"No thanks, June. That was a smashing dinner." Uncle Bob leaned back in his chair again, and patted his stomach. "Got to leave some room for pudding, eh, kids?"

"Let me give you a hand." Aunty Marjorie started to get to her feet, but Uncle Bob said,

"No, no, you stay where you are. Let the girls do their bit." Usually she would have insisted on helping, and ordered Angie and me around as well, but now she just sat down, and there was another odd silence. Angie jumped up straight away, and began to stack plates with a lot of noise, but I didn't move. I was worrying over the twisted oak. Had the men told my father they'd seen me? What might he do?

"Fliss!" His voice made me jump. "Don't let your cousin do all the work."

I scrambled up, and we had a sort of race to see who could

collect more plates. Angie won, of course, because she'd started first, and we carried them out to the kitchen together. As soon as we were out in the hall, she shot me a triumphant look and said, "See?"

But I didn't see. Not at all.

Chapter 12

The weekend seemed endless. I yearned to see Elfrida, to understand more about the hunt and the things she'd said to me, and maybe to find out—in a roundabout way, of course—about my parents, and the lost babies, and the farm. Everything seemed to lead back into everything else, and I didn't understand why. And the thought that the future of the farm might depend on me was just too big to deal with. But more than anything else, of course, I just wanted to be in that magic place, feeling blue velvet under my fingertips, tasting marvellous things, immersed in wonders and far from everyday life.

Instead, I had to answer politely when the grown-ups spoke to me, and "play nicely" with Angie and Tommy. That meant not getting dirty, and that meant not really going outside at all, except for my usual jobs of collecting the eggs or picking herbs for my mother. By Sunday afternoon, we were all fed up with jigsaws and board games and sitting still. They were going home after tea, and even the grown-ups seemed relieved, talking more than usual and not expecting us to entertain them. The questions about school had all been asked, so our job was to be seen and not heard.

"Fliss! Aunty Marjorie asked you a question!" I came back with a start, to find everyone looking at me.

"Miles away," said Uncle Bob. "The house could catch fire and she'd never notice. Too busy thinking deep thoughts, eh?"

"Felicity," said Aunty Marjorie loudly, "I was just wondering whether you'd like to come and stay with us in town for a bit; give your parents a break."

I shook my head. "No, thank you."

"Fliss, don't be so rude! It's very kind of you to offer, Marge. It would save her the bus ride, and she could keep Angie company." I knew, in some complicated way, that my mother did not want me to go, but that something had been decided between the adults and she had gone along with it. And as usual, I would have no choice, unless I could think of some excuse that they would understand.

"I can't go! We've got a project at school about rivers, and we've got to measure a curve and look at the wildlife and that."

"No you haven't," said Tommy instantly, "That's only for the top class." He turned to his father. "Remember when I did it? And you said I could go with you when you went fishing and bring Tony and Peter with me, so you could keep an eye on us."

"So I did," said Uncle Bob, though he didn't sound very pleased to be reminded.

"Yes, but we've got to do a sort of easier version," I said desperately. "We had tadpoles last term in my class, and now we've got to see what else lives there. I've already found a good place, and I've been counting dragonflies. There are three species in our bourn, and damselflies too."

"Ugh!" said Angie. "We never had to do that last year, thank goodness."

"Well, maybe you could just go for half term then." I was right; my mother was on my side. But half term? That was even worse. A whole week away?

I said, "I can't go away for a whole week!" at the same time as Angie said, "She's not coming with us to the seaside, is she?"

"Angie! Manners!" said Aunty Marjorie. "Well, that's decided then. Bob's taken some annual leave," she said, looking at Mum and Dad, "And we're going to a guest house in Bognor. It'll be cheaper out of season, and we could do with a break."

To me, she added, "Your mum and dad can't get away because of the animals, but you're coming with us this time. Won't that be fun?"

I stared at her. My plans for the half-term break involved camping in my den and spending as much time with Them as possible. To lose those precious few days was beyond unfair, it was unthinkable. And my father's words came to mind: *You stay away from them woods, you hear me?* I looked at him, but again, he would not meet my eyes.

What could I do? One story after another went through my head and out again. Perhaps I could be ill; a short illness that would mean I had to stay at home, but not stay in bed for too long. A tummy bug, maybe? And although it felt dangerous even to think it, I couldn't stop myself. *I could ask Them. Maybe They would help me.* This gave me a glimmer of hope, and I held on to that for the rest of the meal.

When they'd gone, I had to help Mum with the washing up, and then the guest beds had to be stripped ready for doing the washing on Monday. By the time I could get away and change out of my Sunday clothes, it was already getting dark. Out in the woods, although a lot of the leaves were down now, it was even darker. Heavy weather, my father called it, when the hens stopped laying and the cows stood around looking sulky. I went to my den, where the music had first come to me, but before I went in I closed my eyes and said aloud,

"Please, I need your help."

Nothing happened, of course. But I didn't expect it to be that easy. Inside the den, I wrapped myself in the blankets I'd left there, and curled up on the ground. It was too gloomy for reading, but I had plenty to think about, and I was prepared to wait for as long as it took.

Noises! Noises in the dark. I came awake all at once, listening hard. Rustling and scuffling, quite nearby. Whatever it was made no attempt at stealth. For a while I lay still, but in the end boredom got the better of me, and I began to stretch out my legs. And then all of a sudden something landed right on top of me. I screamed, flailing desperately at the enclosing blankets, and whatever it was leaped around me, crashing about in the small space of the den. It seemed to take forever to fight my way out of my cocoon, feel about for my rucksack and switch on my torch.

There, grotesque in the beam of torchlight, was Hob.

"You were affrighted," he said, and went off into a parody of my reaction, screeching and rolling about, kicking his legs in the air.

"You're as bad as the boys at school!" That wasn't what I'd meant to say, and I was afraid I'd offended him, but he only cackled gleefully.

"No school for Hob! Over the hills and far away, that's where he'll be." He sat upright and hugged his knees. "And all among the daisies-O."

"Where are the others?"

"Here and there and anywhere. Will you come, Felicity Turner?"

"Of course I will."

I held out my hand to him, but instead he turned and crawled out of the den. By the time I'd scrambled after him, leaving torch and rucksack and everything else behind, all was quiet. Alone in the dark, I braced myself for another shock. Would he jump at me again? Or take my hand and sweep me up into the air? Or—and I crossed my fingers and wished, *not that*—would I have to make my way through bogs and briars?

Nothing happened. And slowly, I realised that it was not just dark around me. I could see nothing at all, not even my own hands, though when I rubbed my eyes I could feel them well enough. It was as though I myself was still there—wherever *there* was—but the rest of the world had gone away. And I did not dare to move, in case there might be no ground under my feet. I stood there, and nothing changed.

I imagined them out there, watching me. Waiting. For what? *Three times is the charm.* I took a deep breath, and spoke into the nothingness.

"Please help me. I don't know the way."

There was only darkness and silence. Terror rose up in me, and I clenched my fists, trying not to cry out. Sparks were swimming in front of my eyes now. I screwed them shut and counted slowly to three, hoping against hope. But when I looked again the sparks were still there, swarming more and more thickly all around me, and then, all at once, I knew it was all going to be all right. Even before my eyes understood how to see again, I could feel brocaded silk under my fingertips, and the scent of roses was all around me, and the sound of laughter and singing came to my ears.

"Felicity. You asked for our help."

Elfrida stands there, smiling. And all the love and longing inside me seems to rise up into my throat, so that I cannot speak at all. Besides, now that I am There, with Them, none of it seems to matter any more.

"Walk with me," she says. At first I am aware of others around us, and then it is just she and I, moving along a path that is wide enough for two to walk abreast without touching. It is night-time now, but lanterns hang from the trees and nestle in the moss among their roots, sending huge fantastic shadows into the forest as we pass by.

And somehow, side by side, it is easier. I talk, and she listens, and words pour out of me in a crazy jumble, as though now that I have found my tongue, everything has to be said all at once. The twisted oak, and Jimmy Miller who saw me there, and what it might mean. My mother and father, and the farm, and the baby that is coming and the ones that never came, and my whole family wanting to keep me away, I was almost sure of it, although they couldn't know why. Could they? And now I am to be taken away for a whole week, off to the seaside where it would be cold and boring and far from Them, and what am I to do?

In the end, I run out of words. We walk in silence for a little while, and then she says,

"I have never seen the sea."

I stop and stare at her, shocked out of my own concerns.

"Oh! Well, it's really big, like that lake, only you can't see the end of it. And there's sand, and donkey rides, and a fairground. Only all that will be closed now, and it'll just be cold." I run out of words again, feeling small, and stupid, and selfish.

I try again. "But you can go anywhere you like. Can't you?"

She says nothing. And then, while I am still trying to think how to make it all right again, she speaks very quietly, as if to herself.

"Such a beautiful boy, he was. Hair of just your colour, and the light in his eyes! You'd never guess it now, to look at him."

This time, I know better than to ask. After a few moments, she goes on.

"He's afraid. He doesn't remember, and he fears what he has lost, what he could have had. Such a short time, and then the way grows over and there is nothing to mark where it once was. He never comes to the woods now, even so. He is afraid, and he fears for you, too."

Now it is my turn to be afraid. "You're talking about my father. Aren't you?"

"Father, grandfather, what does it matter? They all leave us behind, in the end."

"I won't! I'll never, never do that! I promise."

She turns to look at me then, and puts a finger to her lips. "Have a care, Felicity. In this place, promises are binding."

"Good! I mean it." I stop, and speak aloud into the listening shadows. "I won't forget. I don't want to go back, ever. They don't want me there, not really. They wanted a boy so he could work with my dad and be a farmer when he grew up. They wouldn't care if I never came back." The look on my mother's face comes back to me, but I put it aside.

Elfrida moves closer to me. She reaches out a hand, and I lift my own hand to take it, but instead she touches my eyelids with her fingertip. I have closed my eyes, and can't tell when the touch ends. It is warm like a candle flame, and makes a red glow the way a torch does when you shine it through your hand. I don't move, waiting for whatever comes next.

"Look yonder, Felicity." At first I can see nothing but dancing lights, but I blink hard and rub my eyes, and gradually sight returns. We are standing at the edge of the woods, in that high place where the open moorland begins. Far away, outlined against a sky that holds the promise of morning, there are mountains. Snow-capped, jagged, impossible. I turn to look at her.

"Those weren't there before!"

She smiles. "And maybe they won't be there again, next time. There are no maps or charts when you go Onward."

"Onward?"

She makes a wide sweep of her arm. "Beyond the crossroads. East of the sun and west of the moon. The paths change. Go too far and you might never find your way back; or if you did, the place where you started would no longer be as you left it. Thomas stopped you just in time."

I look at the line of stones, throwing long shadows towards us in the dawn light. "I'd like to say 'Thank you' to him. Is he here?"

"He went Onward at the dark of the moon. We shall not see him again."

She sounds sad; once again, she has distracted me from my own troubles by giving me more mysteries to ponder. It seems to be a dangerous business, asking questions.

"But as long as we stay in the woods, we're safe." I make it a statement rather than a question, hoping to get back onto familiar ground.

Elfrida laughs aloud. "Safe? The woods are our domain,

and we keep watch, but we cannot hold back everything that comes from beyond. From your side, yes. We can lead them astray when they come with lamps to catch deer, and charm them or terrify them or send them into a deep sleep. But what lies Onward is stranger than you can imagine."

I think, *I can imagine some very strange things,* and then decide that perhaps it would be better not to. I shiver, though not from cold.

She is watching me. "Tell me, Felicity. Why do they not come as they used to?"

I don't understand what she is asking me. "Who doesn't come?"

She has turned to face the trees, and now she throws out her arm again, including them all. "Families came, to pollard the willows and gather osiers for baskets. Charcoal burners came and stayed for weeks beside their kilns. That bank of hazels was coppiced for poles to make hurdles and fences; those elms were felled and sawn up where they lay, for benches and coffins. There were always children, gathering the long fingers of the ash for firewood, the sloes after a hard frost, the wool caught in fences. The gypsies passed through, and some came to talk with us, and sometimes we answered. Where do they go now?"

Now I am completely lost. "There are gypsies down by the recreation ground in the village sometimes. We're not allowed to talk to them if they come to school, but they never stay long. They have nits, my mother says."

But Elfrida is not interested in what my mother says. "The coppices have grown into thickets, and no one gathers the fallen timber, not since your grandfather's day. Have they stopped building houses and mending fences? Do they not need to cook and warm themselves?"

Too many questions. They all add up to one big question, but to me, at nine years old, the world simply is as it is, and I cannot begin to see what she is asking me. Timidly, I offer,

"They've got an electric cooker at Angie's house, and they might be getting central heating." I have no idea what this is, but I heard the grown-ups discussing it during the endless weekend. The questions distress me, and I want some answers of my own. "Isn't it better when people don't come to the woods? I like it best when it's just me. And you, of course."

She turns and smiles at me. And although she has made me a full-grown woman and clothed me in silk brocade, I feel like what I truly am; a child in the presence of someone immensely old, who has seen things and knows things that are far beyond my understanding. I am ashamed. How did I dare to think that I might ask for favours, or have my wishes granted? I drop my gaze so that she will not see the tears in my eyes.

"Felicity." Her voice is kind, and a little sad. "There are very few who find their way to us, and only when we choose. Even when the woods were thronged with folk going about their business, it was only once in a great while that a child might look beyond the everyday world. Most are too afraid, or too attached to the life they know, to stay beyond for long. You are rare and special, never doubt it."

I am looking at her now, drinking in her words, and the tears are falling freely. "Rare and special," she called me. In all my life, no one has ever said anything like that to me before. In that moment, I would give her anything she asked.

As if she has heard my thought, she says,

"And we will help you if we can. The time will come when we may ask a favour of you in return. But not yet. For now, you must return to your family. But rest assured," and she holds up a hand as I start to protest, "For you, the way is open. And I have already granted you a gift."

I open my mouth to ask, and close it again. The sun is up now, and on those distant dog-toothed mountains, the snow shines dazzling white. In between, mist fills all the hollows and valleys, and the hilltops rise out of it like islands in a pearly sea.

The Onward road is only visible for a little way, and it seems no longer threatening, but full of promise. And yet, I turn away without regret and let Elfrida set me on the homeward path.

She has promised help, and for the time being, that is enough.

Chapter 13

They gave me chickenpox.

Of course, I couldn't be sure of that, and half my class at school had it too, but I was quarantined at home and there was no question of going to the seaside, let alone anywhere else. My cousins went, and stayed for two weeks in the end, and Uncle Bob came home and went back to work. My mother fretted about him looking after himself, but they couldn't invite him over while I was infectious. Aunty Marjorie must be protected "at all costs," they said, and so I had not one but two blissful weeks, with nothing to do but read and stay out of everyone's way.

And Elfrida kept her word. After the first few days I wasn't actively unwell, just itchy, and tired of being indoors. My mother had seemed reluctant to let me go away with my cousins, but she certainly wasn't overjoyed at having me "underfoot," as she put it, for two whole weeks. So I went off into the woods, and whenever I called, They answered.

When I was with Them, the spots and the itching vanished away. Sometimes I was my child-self, and I learned to enjoy the rough-and-tumble games They played, though I'd always feared them in the playground at school. With Them, it was different. There were no bruises or scraped knees, no vicious taunting or bullying. To be sure, They loved vying with each other to come up with the most outrageous and fantastical insults, but in the end, it was all make-believe. There was a companionship there of a kind I had never known, and never even known that I needed.

When They went "hunting," though, it was a different story. Big groups of people were usually safe, at least in daylight. After dark, or in the autumn mists that came up along the bourn, anyone was fair game. Men stumbling home from the pub, especially if they cut through the woods, would sometimes have a story to tell to their disbelieving families when they got home late, muddy and dishevelled, or even woke up far from the path the following day. Courting couples made for great sport. But in all that blessed time, though there were gangs of boys out setting snares for rabbits or shooting at squirrels, there were no other children alone. Elfrida was right; I was the only one.

I never wanted it to end, but although I often stayed far into the night, or crept out before milking time, she always made me go home to sleep. "Time runs differently here," she said. "Many years might pass in a single night. How would you like to return and find your parents grown old and feeble, or even vanished away, and strangers sitting at your table?"

I would have answered that I never wanted to go back at all, but I had learned that it did no good to say so. I would fall into my own bed and sleep for hours, and if I slept half the day away, it was only to be expected when you were not well. At the time I simply took it for granted that my parents let me come and go as I pleased, and never asked what I got up to. Now, I imagine that they knew it would do no good to ask. Like my companions, I had become very good at not answering questions.

That time seemed to stretch on forever, although in the real world it was just a few weeks. Gradually, the classroom filled up again, some of us a little paler and thinner than we had been. I was a little taller, too. But that was not the only change. I don't remember saying or doing anything different, but the bullies left me alone. Sometimes, the popular girls even asked me to join in their games, and no longer found ways to punish me if I turned them down. I wondered whether Elfrida had worked some magic on me. Perhaps, when she touched my eyelids, it wasn't just about seeing things in Their world. I couldn't ask, and so I simply accepted the new way of things, and was glad to be left in peace.

For Christmas dinner that year, we went for the first time to Uncle Bob and Aunty Marjorie in their new house on the edge of town. The fabled central heating had been installed, and Angie told me that her mother "couldn't bear the thought of spending Christmas in that freezing, draughty farmhouse." Aunty Marjorie was stately in late pregnancy, though she said her ankles were giving her gip; she stroked her stomach a lot, looking, as my father said in a rare outburst on the way home, "Like the cat that got the cream."

We had all had to inspect the newly decorated nursery and give our opinions on whether "it" was a girl or a boy. I had no strong feelings on the subject, but I saw that my mother was even more silent than usual. She had knitted a little cardigan—"Yellow, to suit either way"—and presented it with a kind of shy desperation that made me want to shout at somebody. The new knowledge made everything look subtly different, and we were all glad to be able to go home after the Queen's speech, "because animals don't look after themselves."

That winter was a hard one, and snow lay for weeks in the lee of walls. Along the edges of the bourn, twigs and roots were encased in ice, though the water midstream flowed too fast to freeze. Usually, when I was with Them, it was springtime or even high summer, but there was one whole long day when I walked into deep, deep winter, and the kind of weather that is rare and precious in the everyday world: dry, brilliant, and freezing hard. The snow squeaked underfoot, and the bourn itself froze over. We skated and slid on the ice, played in the snow, and made marvellous sculptures, deer and owl and bear, and at our command they came to life and flew or ran, glittering and gorgeous.

Elfrida said that winters used to be colder, once upon a time, and I asked my father later if he remembered this. But he only gave me a sharp look and said, "Not in my day."

Towards the end of February, when snowdrops and crocuses were out, Aunty Marjorie's baby was born. She had it in the maternity home in town, and so I did not meet my little cousin Christine for almost two weeks, when they had brought her home and got settled in. My own tenth birthday had come and gone, with a card and a birthday cake at home, and a pair of new shoes that I needed anyway. But I didn't care. In the hollow hill, we had feasted, and They had told fantastical tales and showered me with extravagant gifts that vanished away before morning. So when Angie showed off the little bootees and matinee jackets and tiny dresses that Christine was to wear, I admired them dutifully. I was even given the baby to hold, just for a minute or two, and she lay heavy and slack across my lap, dribbling over my arm. Kittens were definitely better.

Chapter 14

When the summer holidays came, my cousins went away to the seaside again, but this time there was no question of my going with them. If my father did try to suggest it, he didn't get far. "We're getting a bigger car," Angie told me, "and Christine has to have her own room because she wakes up and cries in the night. Mum says it's a full-time job, having a baby." But they came to stay at the end of the summer holidays, because Angie was going to the secondary school and I wouldn't see her in the playground any more, and they thought we should spend some time together.

Baby Christine could sit up now, and even I had to admit that she was getting a little more interesting. When she smiled at you, she did it with her whole body, and you couldn't help smiling back. We spread a blanket on the grass under the apple tree, and played with her while Aunty Marjorie took an afternoon nap indoors. Perhaps They watched us from afar. I don't know, although when the baby slept in her pram, it stirred a half-memory in me, of lying in my own pram watching the dance of light and shadow through the branches above, and seeing laughing faces among the leaves. I liked to think of Them watching over me, keeping me safe.

That evening when I slipped away to the woods while Angie helped her mother put Christine to bed, Hob pounced on me even before I got to the den. It wouldn't be dark for hours yet, but he grabbed me and spun me around and around until I fell down, laughing, and the ground rocked crazily under me.

When I finally sit up again, They are there. Hob climbs an oak tree, hand over hand like a monkey, and throws down small unripe acorns that turn into little singing birds and fly around us, making a net of sound and colour in the air.

Lord Ember helps me to my feet, and I am tall and beautiful and clothed in green and silver.

"Felicity," he says, and bows. "We would ask our favour tonight."

"Oh!" I say. "I can't stay long. My cousins are here, and I have to share with Angie. She'll notice if I'm not in bed."

"No matter," he says. "When you open the door to us, we will give them a deep sleep and dreams full of wonder."

"Open the door? What do you mean?"

"We'll come after moonrise. You will awaken, but no one else. Come down to the kitchen, open the door to the garden, and invite us to come in. That is all we ask of you."

"But why? What will you do?"

He turns away, and I don't think I'm going to get an answer, but just as he reaches the edge of the charmed circle, he says,

"We have a fancy to revisit the hearth of the Turners." Then he passes through the net, and it glows more brightly so that I cannot see what lies beyond. They are all going, waving farewell to me, and I'm turning around again, trying to keep them in sight, but they've all slipped away, and the net itself is fading, fragmenting into bright tatters that waft away like cinders on the evening breeze.

And I am my own self again.

It all happened in no more than a few minutes. What had I agreed to? I remembered thinking that there could never be any magic inside the house. It seemed, after all, that there could, and I wasn't sure how I felt about that. What if I pretended to be asleep, and didn't let them in? Would they come anyway, or would they stop me coming to them? It didn't matter, in the end; my choice had been made long ago.

It was hard to sleep that night. Angie and I lay top to toe in my single bed. She sighed, and wriggled, and said that my feet smelled. We had both grown over the summer, and there was not enough room to curl up as I liked to do. But at last we both fell asleep, and even when Christine cried for her night feed, neither of us woke for long.

I'm not sure what did rouse me, in the end. I only know that I was suddenly and completely awake, wide-eyed in the dark. Around the edges of the curtains, moonlight beamed, and although Angie had insisted that I close the window "because of bugs," I could hear the business of the night going on outside: wind shifting the trees, a late owl using the moonlight for hunting, the creak of the garden gate. The latch was broken and it was closed with a loop of baler twine, but on windy nights it moved to and fro. The owl sounded again, right outside my window, and all at once I remembered. They were here.

Cautiously, I eased myself out of bed. I had to pull a fold of my nightdress out from under Angie's legs, but she only shifted a little and muttered something I couldn't understand. Under her eyelids, her eyes were moving, and I knew that meant she was dreaming. What dreams had they sent her? If I woke her I could ask, but I was afraid. If she woke up the plan would be spoiled, but what if I shook her and shook her and still she slept? In a kind of horror, I stepped away from the bed, felt for the door handle behind me, and slipped out onto the landing.

Even though I knew that no one would wake, I was careful to avoid the stairs that creaked. The hall tiles were cold under my bare feet, but nothing would make me go back for my slippers now. Once in the kitchen, it was a little warmer, and moonlight streamed in through the uncurtained window. I made it across to the Rayburn, and hung on to the rail as though it were a lifeline.

The kettle sat to one side, black-crusted on the sides but gleaming silver underneath, waiting for dawn and the first cup of tea before milking. Under my hands was the kitchen towel, warm and dry and smelling of old biscuits, stained from a thousand uses. There was a streak of flour on the table from the day's baking, and under the table lay a few potato peelings that had escaped the brush of my mother's hand. On the dresser were her reading glasses, a hand-me-down school blouse of Angie's that needed a new button, and the wireless that murmured constantly to itself while my mother worked. It was silent now.

Outside, the owl called. I jumped, and shuddered all over. It was time.

I crossed the kitchen, running my hand along the edge of the table as I went. By the back door there was a dip, where generations of feet had stopped on their way in or out, and I had to use both hands to turn the door handle. The door scraped a little as I pulled it inward, and then I was in the back porch. I'd thought the dogs might be asleep too, but they were watching me from their basket, prick-eared and alert. Good sheepdogs don't bark much, but the younger one, Jess, whined a little and thumped her tail on the floor. Cap, the elder, just watched me, with his chin on his paws.

There was a window beside the back door, but the glass was dull, mud-crusted, and anyway I did not want to look through, to see what I might see. Too late for that. The door was never locked; all I had to do was lean on the handle and push, and it swung wide, coming to rest against the stone that was used to prop it open in the daytime.

They were there, right inside the garden, waiting for me. For a long moment, we just looked at each other. I had never seen them outside the woods, and I had never thought about how many there might be. Here in my garden, there were no more than fifteen or so. They stood among my mother's lettuces and onions, trampling where I had sown rows of carrots a few days ago.

I recognised Elfrida, and Alys with her poppet in her arms, but the rest seemed somehow diminished, small and misshapen.

Where were the lordly ones? Maybe their magic would not reach so far, or maybe they simply did not choose to put on their finery tonight. I searched for faces I might recognise, but the moon was behind them, throwing them into shadow.

Elfrida took a step forward.

"Felicity Turner," she said. "You must ask us to cross your threshold."

These are my people, I thought. *If they would let me, I would be one of them.* And yet, I thought of my sleeping family, and a great dry sob heaved its way out of me. Then I stood aside and said,

"Come in."

Chapter 15

The next moment, the stillness and silence vanished. They erupted into motion, pouring past me and over me like a living wave, shrieking. Much faster than any human could move, they were gone while I was turning away from the empty garden, but I could hear thumping and shouting from all over the house. I had never thought about what might happen next. The two dogs were on their feet, stiff-legged and growling, pacing about on the path. They were not allowed inside the house, and without orders, they had no idea what to do, how to be. I could not help them. I almost wanted to run for the woods and burrow into my den, my refuge. But I turned, and went into the kitchen.

The wave had become a hurricane. The larder door swung open, and inside it were two goblins. One wore my mother's glasses and the other the tea cosy, and they were opening jars of jam, tasting and smearing and throwing it at each other. They saw me and howled with joy, and the next moment my nightdress was splattered with blackberry jam. The blackberries were just starting to ripen, and I had spent all of one afternoon picking the best of the crop. I scraped one from my front and put it in my mouth, felt another catch in my hair. I backed out of there quickly, treading on something soft and sticky.

In the kitchen, someone was crouched on the dresser, playing with the wireless dial. A crackle of sound came out of it, and he screeched and hurled it across the room, where it crashed against the cast-iron front of the Rayburn and split open like a ripe plum. A bag of flour hit me in the back and burst on the floor, white turning purple as it soaked up the blackberry juice. We had had blackberry and apple pie for pudding, and eaten every last piece; even the baby had had a taste. *At least they won't get that*, I thought.

What were they doing upstairs? Where was Elfrida? I ran from room to room, finding a trail of havoc. Hob was in the parlour, springing from chair to chair and hurling cushions about; he seized me and tried to whirl me around in a mad dance, but I tore myself away and went upstairs, holding on to the banister as two or three more came tumbling past. They were everywhere, even up in the attic, but I could not find Elfrida, nor anyone that I recognised except for Hob.

In their beds, my family slept, while devastation went on around them. I tried to shake my father awake. He would rouse at the sound of a fox digging under the wire of the henhouse, right across the yard, but now he would not stir. At the dressing table sat a creature wearing one of my mother's two hats. She only wore them for special occasions, and they lived in round boxes on top of the wardrobe, but now the boxes were strewn about the floor. It—was it a he or a she?—smeared my mother's lipstick in a great red gash across its face, and leered at me in the mirror. Elsewhere, the crashing and running footsteps went on, and then I heard something that stopped my heart.

From the little box room next to the spare bedroom where Uncle Bob and Aunty Marjorie were staying, there came the wail of a baby.

Christine was awake.

I ran across the landing and through the open door. She was sitting up in her cot, wide-eyed, watching as two or three creatures threw her toys around the room. There was quite a collection of stuffed animals; far too many for one small person. They had been carefully placed by Angie in the cot when Christine was put to bed, but now they were hurtling through the air too fast for my eyes to follow. I went towards Christine, though I had no idea of how to soothe her, but then a plush rabbit struck her full in the chest and she fell over. I braced myself for a bloodcurdling howl—surely that would wake Aunty Marjorie, even from an enchanted sleep?—but instead, she sat up again.

And she laughed.

A knitted cat with string whiskers fell into her cot, and she seized it and tried to throw it. Her whole body was shaking with laughter, and the toy fell at her feet. As she reached for it, one of Them jumped right into the cot and snatched up the cat. He brandished it in her face, going "Miaow, miaow," and then made it rub up against her. And again, I had a vivid sudden memory of looking up at the leaves of the apple tree in the garden, framed by the hood of my pram, laughing at the strange faces that peered in at me over the top. Had They been watching me, even then?

Something pulled at the hem of my nightdress, and I came back with a start. There was the poppet grinning up at me, drooling. Alys was nowhere to be seen, and Christine was fine for now, and I had to find Elfrida. Surely, she would still be her own self? I could not bear the thought of Elfrida grown hideous, inhuman, screeching and rampaging with the rest. I twitched my nightie out of that damp little hand, and ran from the room.

In the end, I curled up in my father's armchair in the parlour. No one else ever sat there, and it smelled of tobacco, of wool and the liniment he used on the cattle; comforting, everyday things. I must have fallen asleep. When I opened my eyes, Elfrida was standing by the chair, quite close, looking down at me. There was no one else, and the house was completely silent.

"There have been changes afoot," she said.

I neither knew nor cared what she might mean. I stared at her, and tears welled from my eyes.

She reached out one finger, touched my wet cheek, and put her finger in her mouth.

"Ah, Felicity," she said. "Be of good cheer. All is restored. Well, almost all."

"Have they gone?" My voice sounded very small and shaky.

"When the blackbirds fledge. Look for us then," she said. Suddenly I was alone in my father's chair, in the parlour that was only for company, at the coldest time that comes just after sunrise. And there I stayed, curled tight inside my thin nightdress, until I heard my father come downstairs for the morning milking. He went along the hall and into the kitchen, and stopped, and my heart stopped too. And then, after a long moment, I heard the rush of water from the kitchen tap, and the scrape of the kettle on the range.

As quietly as I could, I got up, stretched my cramped arms and legs, and went to the door. The handle was stiff, and the door creaked. I opened it just enough to slip through, hoping to creep up to the bathroom, but it scraped across the flagstones and then my father was there, in the kitchen doorway, looking down at me.

"You're up early," he said. He had a mug of tea in one hand, and a piece of toast in the other. "Want some toast?"

I stared at him, and he made a small, impatient noise and went back into the kitchen. And now I did not know what to think. Had they somehow made him blind to what they had done? Curiosity warred with dread; but after a moment, curiosity won. I followed him into the kitchen.

My first thought was for my bare feet on the glass-strewn floor. But there was no glass, no smears of jam, no sign of anything amiss. Except for the wireless, which stood now on the kitchen table, with one dial hanging off and a crack down the side. My father saw me looking.

"Did you open the window, Fliss?"

I saw that the window above the sink stood ajar. "No," I said, truthfully enough.

"Hmph. Looks like a cat got in," he said. "Bit of a mess in

the larder. See if you can clear it up before your mother comes down." He rinsed out his mug, swallowed the last bite of toast and went to the door. Then he hesitated.

"Come and give a hand with the milking if you like," he said. He went out, not looking at me, and I heard him greeting the dogs in the porch.

Then I was alone in the kitchen. The teapot stood at the side of the range, and the tea cosy lay nearby, just as usual. Everything was in its place, and the floor was completely clean; even the stray potato peelings had vanished. Near the larder door there was a faint purplish stain that might have been blackberry jam, but you would only notice it if you knew where to look. And on the dresser, neatly folded, lay the school blouse, which had been Angie's and was now mine, with all its buttons and a neat darn where one cuff had been torn.

I was beginning to understand. In the larder, I saw what my father meant. The remains of yesterday's joint of beef looked as though mice had been at it, and the bowl of cream had been uncovered and half-eaten. But that was all. I counted the jars of jam, and there were two missing. Why hadn't they mended the wireless? And even as I thought it, the answer came to me: *Too modern. They didn't know what to make of it.* I stood there on the cold stone floor, and took a huge breath in, and held it as long as I could, then let it out in one big whoosh.

It was all going to be all right.

Suddenly, I wanted to go with my father to the milking parlour, to sit on a stool and watch while he stripped out the difficult milkers by hand in the old way, leaning against their sides as their breath steamed and the milk zinged into the tin pail, and the cats crowded around, waiting for their share. I pulled on my coat over my nightdress and stamped my feet into my boots; too big without socks on, but I wasn't going far. I clomped out into the dew-fresh morning, noticing a few broken stems among the young lettuces and onions, but nothing too terrible.

And then, down at the end where a newly raked bed awaited the young pea plants from the greenhouse, right across the levelled earth and standing out darkly in the early sunlight, I saw the footprints. Little naked feet, all the toe-prints clear and deep, running here and there. Standing on one leg, I took off my left boot, and fitted my own foot over the nearest print. Smaller than mine. Should I brush them away? After a long moment, I pulled my boot on again, and went on down the path.

The latch on the garden gate had been mended.

CHAPTER 16

When the blackbirds fledge," she had said. "Look for us then." But I went all the same, after the guests had gone and I'd helped my mother with the washing. Everything was back in place, as far as I could tell, and no one seemed to have noticed anything amiss. What had they dreamed about? If they remembered anything, they weren't saying. The grown-ups were fussing over baby Christine, who was teething this morning, and cried solidly until they left.

The house seemed blessedly quiet after that; and so did the woods, when I went to my den late in the afternoon. At the end of August, even the birds don't sing much, and there's a kind of breathless feeling, as though the trees know that change is coming. There was no sign of Them, but I didn't really expect that. For the first time, in fact, I was glad to be able to curl up with my book and my own thoughts, and go home at the end of the day.

In any case, I thought I knew what Elfrida had meant. Blackbirds can be nesting at any time from May until late August, and of course there had been many nests that year. But there was one I'd been watching, in the hedge bank by the sunken lane that ran through the woods near the village. Boys from my class had taken the eggs in July, and when the blackbirds laid again, They had promised to look after them. With great glee, Hob had acted out for me how They had hidden in the bushes nearby. When the boys came by, they heard strange noises. Just grunts and squeaks at first, and then howling like wolves from both sides of the path. But it was the deep-voiced laughter that finally proved too much for them, and they fled, empty-handed.

So the eggs were saved, and I'd seen the baby birds with my own eyes. They couldn't be more than a few days away from fledging now, and school was starting again next week too. I wouldn't be there to see them fly, but after that, I thought, the way would be open to me once more.

On the last day of the summer holidays, they flew, early in the morning before I got there. But there was a lot to do that day. My mother and I went into town on the bus, to get the last few things I needed for school, and we even had lunch in a café as a special treat. It was the end of the week before I went back to the woods. We'd been settling into a new classroom, with a new teacher, and I was too tired after school, or so I told myself. But it was a golden morning, that Saturday, and the blackberries were fully ripe now. I took a bowl, left my watch behind, and set out.

The best blackberries grew along the edges of High Top, where nothing grazed but two rough ponies which belonged to a neighbour. We used to make hay there, and the tedder had been left to rust quietly in the corner of the field, woven through with tall grass, home to fieldmice and late-nesting wrens. The ponies stood nose to tail in the shade, flicking their tails against the clouds of flies; they watched me for a while, and then lost interest.

I loved picking blackberries. When my cousins were here, they'd eat a few, then get bored and start throwing them at each other. It was far better to be alone, with the deep hum of insects and the hush of the trees. As I worked my way along the hedgerow towards the top of the field, getting scratched and insect-bitten and purple-stained, my thoughts got bigger and slower and time seemed almost to stop. It was a good crop this year; more than enough to replace the broken jars of jam.

Although even that had been managed, somehow. When my mother had looked in the larder to see the damage the "cat" had done, she noticed the missing jars, but all she said was,

"Oh, Marjorie must have taken some jam after all," in a strange vague voice, as though she was thinking about something else.

The bowl was almost full, and the shade of the oaks at the top had lengthened. In the tall elms on the crest of the hill, the rooks were talking to each other as they settled to roost. I chose one perfect blackberry to eat, and closed my eyes while the juice filled my mouth and sunshine warmed my eyelids. *I am a tree*, I thought. *A young sapling, moving out from the shade so I can grow tall and strong. If there were no ponies to graze here, no one to farm the land, the forest would take it back.*

My eyes sprang open at a sudden squeal from the ponies, and then the thunder of hooves as they surged up the hill towards me. They would do that sometimes, maddened by flies or simply bored with standing about, although that was not the reason this time. On the hill, the rooks went up with a great clatter and racket, but I stood my ground, waved my arms and shouted "Whoa!" as loudly as I could, just as we did when we were herding cattle along the lanes. One of the ponies wheeled away, but the other galloped right past me, so close that I felt the wind of it, and then someone sprang off its back and landed a few feet away.

"Good even to you, Felicity Turner," said Hob, and snatched a handful of blackberries from the bowl at my feet.

"You could hurt yourself, doing that," I said, hearing my mother's voice even as I spoke the words.

Hob laughed. "Not I!" he said. "Nor sticks nor stones, nor strike of lightning nor sting of bee shall harm me. Nor you, while I am nigh."

"How do you stay on?" I asked, really wanting to know. I had never had proper riding lessons, but Mr. Jones had let me take a turn around the yard once, after his children had been out on the ponies. Even with a saddle and bridle and stirrups, it had felt very unstable, and when he made the pony trot I had begged to be let down. The Jones boys had laughed, and I avoided them from then on.

"I am a burr. She won't unseat me, try she never so hard," he said. He held out some berries to the horse, and though she rolled her eyes and put back her ears, she came to him and lipped them off his outstretched palm. I saw that her mane had been woven into twists, almost like plaits. Something to hold on to, or perhaps just a bit of mischief; and I remembered that my mother called them "elf-locks" when she found them in my hair, and threatened to fetch the scissors.

"Poor Goldie," I said. "They'll have trouble combing those out next time they want to ride her."

"Then I shall weave some more." He gave her a final pat, and she moved away to join her mate. "Now, Felicity, will you come?"

Standing there in the field, casting a long shadow down the hill, he looked almost like an outpost of the forest himself; not a sapling, but a gnarled and ancient stump left over from more expansive days. His clothes were the colour of leaves and lichen, and his skin was brown as bark and almost as deeply lined; he had only to close those bright blue eyes. And there was something odd, something different. For a moment I could not put my finger on it, and then it came to me. When I had first encountered Hob, a year or more ago, we had been about the same height. Now, I was an inch or two taller.

But there was no time to wonder about that. He seized my hand, and the next minute the world was spinning around me. Trees, hedges and sky tilted crazily. I stumbled and fell, but instead of landing on grass, I seemed to be whirled upwards like a leaf in a sudden gust of wind, and the firm grasp of Hob's hand was the only certain thing in all the world.

And it is leaves that I fall into, a drift of last year's dry and crumbling beech litter. We are in the woods, among the stately beech trees on the higher ground, and as I pick myself up I can see Them a little way off, no longer a ragamuffin band of troublemakers but a royal company, taking their ease in the magnificent hall made by the trees.

There is Elfrida, turning to laugh over her shoulder at something one of the lords is saying, and there again is Hob, turning somersaults in the leaf-drifts between them, like a child trying to get the attention of its elders. And yet, I know now that I cannot trust the evidence of my senses. Hob can be bird or beast, but his human form never seems to change. The rest, though; can they take any form they choose? And if so, what are they really like?

I'm eager to talk to Elfrida, though I know better than to expect clear answers about what happened. And, after all, I'm so glad to be here that I can't keep the smile off my face. Now everything can go back to the way it was, and I won't have to try to make sense of anything. I start towards her, making a detour to avoid Alys, who is sitting on a tree trunk cradling her poppet, singing to it in a strange, tuneless voice. Alys makes me uneasy. She is another one who never seems to change, but neither does she truly join in with the others. She is just there, shadowy, on the edge of things. She looks up at me as I pass, sidewise through the curtain of her long, matted hair, and draws the creature closer to her chest.

Hob and his friends come barging between us, hurling leaves at each other. One leaps on another's back, and they career around the clearing, leaping over logs and tree roots, until they tumble down among the leaves. I avoid them too, as best I can. There is a light wind now, and sunlight spangles the leaf litter, dancing over the heads of the company. Will they make me one of them this time? I stand at the edge of the group, awkward, a child among adults, waiting to be noticed.

And then Elfrida is at my side. Just for a moment, her hand touches my head.

"My Felicity," she says. "Welcome. The blackbirds have long flown."

"I know," I say. "We had to go to town to get things for school. Term's just started." My voice sounds small, and my words childish; what could school possibly mean to Them? And the next moment, as if he had heard my thought, Lord Ember says, "What need does a maid have of schooling? We can teach you far more wondrous things."

I look up at him. If only they would! And yet, since they came to the house, something has changed. I don't want to look at it too closely, but that fierce longing is not quite so strong.

"All children have to go to school. It's the law. Next year it'll be secondary school, or the grammar school in town if I pass my 11-plus." I've hardly ever talked about the ordinary world when I'm with Them, except for that one time when I asked for Their help. My words are a challenge: this is what will happen unless you let me stay. I clench my fists, waiting for a response, but it's as though I've said nothing at all, or nothing that made sense to Them.

"Shall we go hunting tonight, think you?" He has turned away, talking to one of the others. "Peer in at the windows and keep them from their sleep? There are fine new horses over at Burnt House Farm; I've a mind to ride them before the next full moon."

Elfrida is watching me. "Do you want to go to school, Felicity?"

"I don't know! It's just what you do, what everyone does."

"You spin no wool and weave no cloth; you make no cheese and salt no meat. Only sweet pickles and conserves; and in your cupboards there are boxes and metal containers of a kind that I have never seen. So many changes. Does it make a better world?"

"I don't know," I say again. "What was it like before?"

"I watched your parents as they lay sleeping," she says. "And it did not seem to me that these changes have brought them joy."

This time I don't bother to answer. She is following her own train of thought. But it's true; joy is not a word I associate with my parents. Or any adults, really. Joy belongs to children, and to Them.

"Thank you for mending my blouse," I say. "And clearing up all the mess. They didn't even really notice anything had happened."

"Ah, but they dreamed!" she says. "Those dreams will trouble them for many a day. And you too, I think, though your eyes were open."

"I remembered something," I say. "When I was a baby, in the pram under the apple tree, you were watching me. Or was that a dream?"

"We have watched you always," she says. And I glow inside at the thought. My parents may have yearned for a different child, but I have always been special to Them. I stand a little taller, looking up at her. Today she is wearing a silver snood woven with pearls on her dark hair, and the pearls gleam as the sunlight catches them.

"When I first saw you—properly, I mean—I thought you were Queen Mab. But there must be other groups, in other places. Is there a queen of all the—of all of you?" I've never called them *fairies* except in my own thoughts, and the stories say they don't like to be named that way. But she's not interested in the question. She's looking over my head at the others, at Lovet the piper, who has begun to play a lively dance tune. He stops after a few notes, and says,

"The harvest is in and they'll be merrymaking tonight! The weather is changing." It's true; in the west, there are mackerel clouds gathering, gilded by the setting sun. Our own wheat and barley were cut a few days ago, and the bales must be stacked high in the barn by tomorrow night. But I've missed his next words, thinking of that.

"—And there'll be good sport to be had as they wend their way homeward!"

"Come, Felicity." Lord Ember holds out a hand to me, but for the first time, I hesitate.

"I'd better not come tonight. It's school tomorrow. But I'll come with you soon, I promise."

It feels strange and dangerous to refuse. What if They never ask me again? But we've got a history lesson tomorrow with the new teacher, and I don't want to be half-asleep at school. Besides, a tiny bit of me is looking forward to it. Who will I sit next to? And what will the top class be like?

"As you will." He gives Elfrida a strange look, but she doesn't seem concerned.

"On your way, then. The light is fading." Once again, she touches my head, so softly I can barely feel it. "Look for us at the new moon, Felicity." And she turns away, already moving to the next thing. I almost change my mind then, but the moment is past, and they are drifting between the trees, leaving me behind. Hob and his friends have gone already, and Alys passes me by, holding her poppet at her shoulder. I can see one little hand grasping her hair, and then she pulls it free, and just for a moment I see its face, looking over her shoulder as she walks away.

It is my cousin Christine.

Part Two: Changeling

A couple of Strathspey lads who dealt in whiskey that never paid duty, which they used to purchase in Glenlivat, and sell at Badenoch and Fort William, were one night laying in stock at Glenlivat when they heard the child in the cradle give a piercing cry, just as if it had been shot. The mother, of course, blessed it, and the Strathspey lads took no further notice, and soon after set out with their goods.

They had not gone far when they found a fine healthy child lying all alone on the roadside, which they soon recognized as that of their friend. They saw at once how the thing was. The fairies had taken away the real child and left a stock, but, owing to the pious ejaculation of the mother, they had been forced to drop it.

As the urgency of their business did not permit them to return, they took the child with them, and kept it till the next time they had occasion to visit Glenlivat. On their arrival they said nothing about the child, which they kept concealed. In the course of conversation, the mother took occasion to remark that the disease which had attacked the child the last time they were there had never left it, and she had not little hopes of its recovery. As if to confirm her statement, it continued uttering most piteous cries.

To end the matter at once, the lads produced the real child healthy and hearty, and told how they had found it. An exchange was at once effected, and they forthwith proceeded to dispose of their new charge. For this purpose they got an old creel to put him in and some straw to light under it. Seeing the serious turn matters were likely to take, he resolved not to await the trial, but flew up the smoke-hole, and when at the top he cried out that things would have gone very differently with them had it not been for the arrival of their guests.

Thomas Keightley, *The Fairy Mythology, Illustrative of the Romance and Superstition of Various Countries, A new edition, revised and greatly enlarged* (London: H. G. Bohn, 1850), p. 393.

Chapter 17

Did I call out? Or was it only in my head? In any case, they were already gone, and I was standing in the half-dark, with only the muttering of the rooks overhead for company. Already, I was doubting what I'd seen.

It was a seeming. It must have been. If They could make me look grown-up and beautiful, they could do it to anybody, surely? Though I'd never seen the poppet change before. Of course, Alys would have seen Christine, she would have been in the nursery, maybe even when I was there. That had to be it; she had seen the baby with her fine blonde curls and her lovely laughing face, and she wanted to make her poppet look like a real baby. Who could blame her for that?

And yet . . . It was one thing to change how a thing seemed. But could you change its nature? Dressing me in fine silks didn't make me a princess; I knew that well enough. It was just a piece of joyful make-believe, like so much of what They did. But in all the time I'd spent with Them, that creature had never looked at me the way it had just now. Its gaze was always squinty, sidelong. It grinned, or it grizzled, and its eyes were dull. Christine's gaze was clear and direct, and you could tell that she was thinking something, even if you didn't know what it might be.

What was I to do? "Look for us at the new moon," Elfrida had said. It had been full when they came to the house, so it would be another week or so before there was a new moon. Somehow, I had to find a way to see Christine, to make sure. What if They really had taken her? My stomach clenched at the thought, and I reached out to touch the nearest tree. Three times, for luck, or to ward off misfortune. It was almost dark now, and I had to start for home, stumbling my way down from the hill to where the fields began.

On High Top, the ponies were grazing at the far end, and rabbits scuttered into the hedge as I climbed the gate. I couldn't see my bowl at first; the ponies had eaten most of the blackberries, and pushed it into the nettles that grew rank around the water trough. It was full dark by the time I got home, nettle-stung and empty-handed.

It was true that I'd been looking forward to school, but after all, the history lesson about the Tudors passed me by. I tried to concentrate, but then I'd come back with a start when Miss Stevens asked somebody a question, and realise I'd been there again, seeing my cousin Christine's face as it vanished into the twilight. What if it really was her?

I had to find some way of seeing my cousins. Angie was now at the secondary school on the edge of town, so I wouldn't be able to talk to her in the playground any more—not that she would talk to me if her friends were around in any case. I had to find some excuse to go to their house, to see for myself. Only then could I decide what to do next.

By the end of the school day, I had concocted a sort of plan. I ran upstairs to change as soon as I got home, and then called down to mum in the kitchen.

"I'm going over to Angie's on my bike. She's got my protractor and I need it for school tomorrow. Won't be long!"

Mum came into the hall, drying her hands on her apron. "Can't you borrow one?" she said. "I could do with your help sorting the apples."

"I'll come straight back."

"Why on earth has she got your protractor, anyway? Are

you sure? I'll give Marjorie a ring," and she went to pick up the telephone in the hall.

"Umm, we did some maths homework when they were here, and she put it in her pencil case by mistake," I said. "Aunty Marjorie won't know where it is. I'll be back before tea." I ran for the door before she could ask any more questions.

My cousins lived on the far side of the village, in a new housing development that had been fields a few years ago. Each house had its own garage with a connecting door, as though the car were a part of the family like a big dog or maybe a horse, and a little bit of lawn and flowerbed at the front with no garden walls. You went up a step to ring the bell, and there was patterned glass in the door so you could see when someone was coming. To me, the house felt insubstantial, as light as a leaf that might blow away on the wind.

Aunty Marjorie opened the door. "Fliss!" she said, and she didn't sound pleased to see me. "Whatever are you doing here?" She looked over my shoulder at my bike, lying askew on the grass. "Lean that against the garage door, would you—and take your shoes off when you come in." She went back along the hall, not waiting for an answer. "Angie!" she called upstairs, and I could hear the sound of a wireless playing the kind of music my mother never listened to.

I scrambled to undo my shoelaces, hoping to get a look at Christine before Angie came down. She might be in the front room in her playpen, or maybe in the kitchen having tea. But as I was taking off my shoes, Aunty Marjorie came back with the baby in her arms. She was patting her back and rocking her to and fro as she walked.

"Angie!" she called again. "Turn that thing off!" The music suddenly got much louder, and Angie was standing at the top of the stairs. She hadn't changed out of her school uniform, but the tie was half undone and her skirt was rolled up to way above her knees. She had been backcombing her hair, so that it stuck out in clumps.

"For goodness sake, whatever do you look like?" From the back, the baby looked like Christine, but I couldn't be sure without seeing her face. *And maybe not even then,* I thought, and crossed my fingers.

Angie said, "What're you doing here?" just like her mother, and they both looked at me, waiting for an answer. Then Christine let out a thin wailing noise, and Aunty Marjorie jiggled her up and down again. "Hush, now. Are those toothy pegs bothering you? Let's find a rusk in the kitchen, shall we?" I stared, hoping for a clue, but the baby's face was hidden against her shoulder. That fine gold hair, though; that was right. Maybe I'd been worrying for nothing.

"What d'you want, squirt?" I looked up to see that Angie had been joined by a friend. They stood at the top of the stairs, almost identical, and I noticed they'd put on eyeshadow too. *It's just a different kind of uniform,* I thought. They looked like little girls pretending to be older ones. The irony of that made me smile, knowing what I knew.

"What are you laughing at?" Angie came down a step or two, and I smelled cigarette smoke.

"I'm not laughing. Aunty Marjorie will kill you if she finds out you've been smoking."

They both started flapping their hands around. "Who says we've been smoking?"

Inspiration came to me. "I won't tell. But I said you'd got my protractor, so can you say that if they want to know why I'm here?" Before they could ask why, I went along the hall and into the kitchen.

"Here, drink this. You must be thirsty after that ride." Aunty Marjorie handed me a glass of orange squash, then turned back to the stove to stir something in a saucepan. Afternoon sunshine streamed in through the glass doors—French windows, they were called—that took up most of the back wall. The cupboards were all the same, and they had a name too: units, as though they were part of a maths puzzle. Christine was in her high chair now, chewing on a rusk. She looked at me and squealed, banging her hands on her tray.

"Hello, Christine!" I said, making my voice bright and high, the way the grown-ups did when they talked to babies. "What have you got there?" And I went towards her.

I don't quite know how to describe what happened next. She *flickered,* the way films do at the cinema when the projectionist gets the speed wrong. There was my little cousin, pink-cheeked and laughing, holding up her sticky hands to show me. And somehow, at the same time, there was that other thing, its eyes gleaming with a kind of dull cunning. It opened its mouth wide, spilling out a wad of half-chewed rusk, and stuck out its tongue.

I stopped dead. I might even have taken a step back. The next moment I was retching, so suddenly that there was no time to run to the bathroom, and orange juice spilled out through my nose and mouth and splattered on the shiny kitchen floor.

"Good gracious, Fliss! Whatever's the matter?" Aunty Marjorie was at my side, thrusting a bowl under my nose. "Here, hold this. I'll get some kitchen roll."

"Sorry, sorry," I gasped. My nose and eyes were streaming. I couldn't bear to risk another glance at the baby, who was now banging a spoon on her tray. My stomach heaved again, but there was really nothing to come up; I hadn't stopped to eat before I set off. Aunty Marjorie fussed around me with pieces of thick paper torn off a roll, and shouted up to Angie to find an old top to lend me. "Get that off now, Fliss, and I'll put it straight in the machine. No, don't go near Christine, we don't want her catching anything. She's already off-colour with her teeth."

Now I did look at Christine, and again, she *flickered.* The thing was rocking to and fro, making a sort of gasping noise, gaping at me. After a moment or two, I realised that it was laughing.

"She's just started doing that, I don't know why. What's the matter, poppet?" said Aunty Marjorie, and once more, I retched. Angie opened the kitchen door, said "Ugh!" and backed out again. I felt for a chair, but Aunty Marjorie said "Don't touch anything! Go to the cloakroom and sort yourself out."

The cloakroom was at the end of the hall, though there weren't any cloaks in it, just a toilet and a handbasin, with a toilet roll hidden under the wide crocheted skirt of a doll with empty blue eyes. In the mirror, my face looked green, and the freckles stood out across my nose. At that moment I looked exactly how I felt: young, and small, and terrified. What on earth was I going to do?

"Oi, squirt!" said Angie from outside the door. "Here's a t-shirt. No, don't come near me," as I started to open the door. "I'm not catching it off you. You stay downstairs. And I haven't got your stupid protractor anyway."

"I know," I started to say, but she was already halfway up the stairs. The shirt was one of Tommy's and way too big for me, but I picked it up anyway. What choice did I have?

"Did you wash your hands?" asked Aunty Marjorie the minute I went back into the kitchen. "Now sit over there and stay away from the baby. Bob'll have to run you home when he gets in."

"I'm feeling better now," I said. As long as I didn't look at Christine again.

"Don't be silly, Fliss. You can't cycle home in that state. Whatever will your mother think?"

"I'm all right. Sorry. I'll go now," and I ran for the front door. Aunty Marjorie followed me, but really she was glad to have me out of the house. And so was I. I pedalled home as fast as I could, ignoring the boys from my class who were hanging about outside the sweet shop, and went straight upstairs to change for the third time that afternoon.

Chapter 18

Mum was picking peas in the vegetable garden, but she had left some ham sandwiches for me on the kitchen table. I sat in the familiar kitchen, close to the Rayburn for its comforting warmth, even though it was a golden afternoon. Aunty Marjorie's kitchen hardly felt like a kitchen at all; everything was hidden away inside the units and drawers, the surfaces were all shiny and clean, and it had no *depth*, somehow. I couldn't think of a better word. Here, you could read the history of this kitchen in every stain and scratch on the table, the dips in the flagstones where people had stood at the stove and the sink, even the paler places on the wall where the old copper warming pans used to hang. My father had sent them off to auction just last year, but their shadows were with us still.

It stirred inside me, all that history. It was part of me. I wondered, suddenly, about the changes Elfrida had mentioned. What did she remember?

But that brought me back to the place I was avoiding, the place I never wanted to go to again. She must have known what Alys had done. They had invited me to stay with them that evening; they knew I would see Christine there, in Alys's arms.

And they didn't care.

I felt sick again, and the ham sandwich turned to slime in my mouth. In my mind's eye I saw Christine under the hollow hill, sometimes petted and sometimes ignored, playing too close to the fire. I saw the poppet, the *changeling*, sitting in her high chair in that clean kitchen like a cuckoo in a reed warbler's nest, grinning as Aunty Marjorie fussed and worried, opening its mouth to be fed, giving nothing back. Would it grow as time went on? Would it learn to walk, to speak, to be human? And what would become of Christine?

It was wrong. It was all wrong. And it was my fault, even though I had never meant any of this. Once, at school, we were supposed to be working quietly in class. The girl next to me had whispered something, and I had whispered back, "No talking, remember?" The teacher had seen me, and I had to stay in at playtime and write a hundred lines. It wasn't fair. The shame and the sense of injustice burned in me still. But this was far worse, more than a hundred times worse, and it couldn't be put right however many lines I wrote. What was I to do?

I thought about Them, my beautiful friends. I loved the magic and the glamour, and their gleeful enjoyment of the tricks they played. Sometimes, though, it wasn't so different from the bullying that went on at school, and sometimes it was downright cruel.

On that awful night when they had rampaged through the house—when I had stood aside and let them in—I had been truly terrified at what they might do. But never, not in my worst nightmares, had I imagined what had actually happened. Of course, I knew there were stories about changelings, and grown-ups too, kidnapped by the fairies against their will, but I never thought my friends would do such a thing.

Were they really my friends, after all?

That thought was much too big for me. I came back, once again, to my little cousin. I had wanted more than anything to be one of Them, but she couldn't choose for herself. That made it wrong; that much I was sure of. But how could I put it right?

I could go back to Aunty Marjorie's house, take the changeling and go to the woods. What then? Even if I could take the baby without anyone noticing, and carry it all that way (and the thought of touching that creature made me shudder), what if They didn't come? Or what if they did, but they wouldn't give

Christine back? Either way, I would lose them. I would never be able to see them again. It was no good.

I would have to wait until the new moon, and then talk to Elfrida. Surely, somehow, I could make her see how wrong this was. Surely she could make Alys take back her poppet, and return Christine to her mother. The new moon was nearly a week away, but it seemed to me that the only choice was to wait, and hope that they took good care of Christine until then.

That week passed very, very slowly. The lovely autumn weather continued, and I should have been out every day after school while the evenings were long and warm, but I couldn't bring myself to go to my den, or anywhere near the woods at all. Instead, I helped my mother pick beans and marrows, collected windfall apples for chutney, and stayed close to home. But no matter how busy I was, I could not shut out the sight of that Thing, sitting in Christine's high chair, grinning.

"All is restored. Well, almost all." That was what Elfrida had said to me when They came to the house. I'd thought she meant the broken radio and the smashed jam jars, but like so many of her words, they could have more than one meaning. The more I thought about it, the more it seemed to me that she must have known. Maybe it had even been planned? They would know all the comings and goings on the farm if they cared to. But that was a step too far for me to take. Elfrida was my friend. My only friend, really; why would I need any others, when I had her?

I couldn't bear to think that she might do such a thing to me. And yet, of course, I knew already that their sense of right and wrong was not at all the same as mine. They were Outside, in more ways than one. Maybe they thought that taking my cousin would make no difference to me? My own thoughts went around and around until I was sick of them, and I surprised my mother by asking for more jobs to do.

Harvest was always a busy time, and on those farms that still followed the old ways, neighbours helped each other out to get the crops safely stored before the weather changed. Usually I avoided going to other farms, because it was a chance to be alone and peaceful at home, but this year I went whenever I could. I was still too small to wield a pitchfork, but I could fetch and carry, open gates and lay tables, and there was no time to think.

The first time I ran into Jimmy Miller, he looked askance at me and I avoided him for the rest of the day, but as time went on he seemed to have put aside his memory of that night at the twisted oak, though folk were never tired of teasing him about it. He did not go about with Dave Brooks and Peter Green any more. Ordinary life flowed on and swallowed up anything that couldn't be explained, anything too wonderful or too colourful or just too big. My father—not that he ever talked about such things—would have said that it had to be so. I knew otherwise; I *yearned* for it to be otherwise. Still, I was glad that Jimmy Miller and his one-time friends did not see it that way.

So, one way or another, the time passed, until it was the night before the new moon and I had run out of distractions. It was a Friday; no school tomorrow, no excuse not to go to my den after tea, with a book and a blanket, and wait for whatever came next.

I took my time along the way, picking blackberries as I went, inspecting the ripening hazelnuts in the old coppice along the edge of the woods. When I got there, I found the entrance to the den clogged with leaves, and new growth had made the space smaller inside. Maybe I had grown too. I resolved to bring a pair of secateurs next time. For now, I went instead to a place by the bourn, and settled there.

Chapter 19

Sunlight played on the surface of the water, sparkling where it rushed over pebbles in the shallows, catching the dancing gnats as it slanted through the trees. Fallen leaves had built up against the larger stones, yellow birch and brown oak packed like the pages of a book. Over in the shady depths where tree roots overhung and the stream slowed down, I could see minnows facing into the current, visible only when they moved. I closed my eyes to listen to the water, a quiet constant sound made up of a thousand different notes, almost but not quite music. Lovet would make it into a tune, I thought. I began to hear it emerging from the background net of sound, the notes of the pipe hesitant at first, feeling its way, and then growing louder and more confident, taking the water music and the birdsong and the sound of the wind, and telling them somehow more truly.

I open my eyes, and They are there. Immediately, Hob and his friends are in the water, splashing and shrieking, drowning out the music. I scramble away as they shower me with drops, but before they hit me they become bubbles, each one carrying a tiny rainbow. Where they touch my skin and clothes, they vanish, leaving bright scales of colour until I am covered in red and gold and copper, like autumn leaves but gleaming, metallic. I raise my arms, and sunlight dazzles off them.

"Today you are a dragon, Felicity!" Elfrida stands before me. Somehow, I had thought that they would share my mood. I had imagined that they might be subdued, or even guilty, but everything is as usual. Alys is not among them. Is that significant?

"My mother says I should never wear red," I say, touching my hair.

"Your mother has forgotten her colours," says Elfrida. "Come and see."

She leads me to the water's edge, and suddenly the stream is as clear and bright as a mirror, even though Hob and his friends are splashing and shouting just a few feet away. I see the two of us side by side, not quite touching, nearly the same height. Her hair is smooth and dark, but she too is clothed in autumn leaves, and we could almost be sisters. As we move, the leaves ripple and shift like the scales on a snake, though the colours are like no snake I've ever seen. They flash and glitter in the sunlight, and she's right. In this guise, I'm not the quiet, watchful Felicity, who never draws attention to herself; but I'm still me. My mother wouldn't recognise me, though. I look *dangerous.* I'm a dragon.

Then the ripples return and the picture breaks into dancing fragments, as Hob sends another wave of water towards us. This time, Elfrida stops it in mid-air, building a shimmering wall of water between us and the stream, and then she turns back towards the trees.

"This is a good place," she says. "Shall we feast here tonight, do you think?"

She doesn't really expect an answer, and it's just as well. I may look like a dragon, but my heart is thumping hard and I feel sick. Very soon, I have to say the words that will bar me from all this forever, and I can't bear it. I clench my fists and look down at the ground, willing away tears.

Elfrida is watching me. "You are troubled, Felicity," she says.

Mutely, I nod. Then, not looking up, I say, "I don't know what to do."

"Come," she says. There is a path leading away under the trees, where in the ordinary world—the real world?—is nothing but brambles and dense undergrowth. I follow her. What else can I do?

The path winds uphill, and great rocks begin to appear between the trees. They are smaller now, birch and rowan and hawthorn, twisting into strange shapes among the rocks. We emerge onto a hillside by a small stream, and I recognise the moorland, the boundary land, though not the place itself. The boulders by the stream are sun-warmed, and Elfrida settles there.

"Sit by me," she says, but I stay on my feet, a little way away. Somehow, it seems important. I smooth my dragon scales. Perhaps they will lend me the fire of a dragon, too.

"Alys is not with you this evening," I say. No questions.

Elfrida is looking afar, at the distant hills she calls Onward, where things get even stranger. There are no mountains today.

"That one goes her own way," she says, absently.

I take a deep breath. "When you came to my house, she did something."

I wait. I can't seem to get enough air into my lungs.

"Did she so?" she says at last.

"She took something," I say. "And she left something of hers."

"A fair exchange, meseems." Elfrida is watching me, not quite smiling, and I have the feeling she knows exactly what I'm talking about. She might even be enjoying this; and as I think that, I feel the clench of anger in my belly.

"It's not right!" The words tumble out of me now. "She's taken my cousin, and she has to give her back!"

Nothing changes. Elfrida continues to watch me, and the afternoon sun dances on my scales, and bees murmur in the heather. It's as though I haven't spoken at all. No, that's not it. My words don't matter. They change nothing.

"Please!" My hands curl into fists. "You have to make her give Christine back! Please."

Still, she says nothing, only stretches her legs in front of her, making the scales ripple. Are we going to stay like this forever? I take a step forward, though I have no idea what to do next, and then suddenly she speaks.

"Tell me, then," she says, watching as a ladybird lands on her forearm, walking unafraid towards her wrist. "Does your aunt miss her child? Are her arms empty and her heart full of grief? Does she weep and mourn for her lost darling?"

I shake my head. "She doesn't know," I say, slowly. "Nobody knows except me. But—but I think they know something's wrong."

Again, my words blow away like spider silk on the wind. But then suddenly she looks up, directly at me, and I've never seen her look so fierce.

"Alys wept," she says, speaking low, almost hissing. "Alys begged and screamed. She ran to the woods and they came after her. Oh, not he; not the one who planted the seed. He sent his men to tear the babe from her arms, and they laughed at her. They took it away, to be a gift for his lady who had miscarried her own, and left Alys bereft and alone. Was that right, do you think?"

Now it's my turn for silence. I don't understand what she's telling me, not really; or not enough. The ladybird has reached her fingers, and she lifts her hand high.

"Fly away home, little clock-a-clay," she says. "Your house is on fire and your children have flown." And as if it hears her, it opens its wings and lifts away.

"What happened to the baby?" I ask at last. Somehow, it's the only part of the story I can bear to talk about.

She lifts one shoulder. "It lived, for a time," she says. "But it did not thrive."

I take a deep, deep breath, and then let it all out at once, trying to ease the tightness around my heart. It doesn't help. Then, out of all the terrible things she just told me, a small part falls into place.

"Alys was human," I say, slowly. "She came to you and you took her in."

Elfrida huffs out a little laugh. I have surprised her. Of all the things I might have said, she wasn't expecting that. "Of course, human," she says. "What else?"

There's something important here, something I desperately need to understand, but I can't think about that just now. I must not be thrown off course.

"So she came to the woods, and they took her baby away, and then you looked after her," I say, as though working it out for myself. "But where did her poppet come from?"

"I forget," she says, as though it doesn't matter at all.

"But it isn't human," I say. "I don't know what it is, but it's not—"

"It was, once," she says.

None of it makes sense, or no sense I want to hear. And abruptly I can't keep still; I turn away, pacing the length of the hilltop to where it falls away in a jumble of rocks and bracken. My scales shimmer as I move, but I'm not a dragon. I'm not beautiful, not magic; I'm just Felicity, ten years old and in far too deep. *You're supposed to help me!* I think at Elfrida, and then realise that she never made me any promises. I made assumptions, and she let me. *Fairies grant wishes, don't they?*

At last, I turn back, to where she waits in the sunlight, because there is nothing else I can do, and I have to play this through to the end.

"What happened to the poppet?" I ask, and I don't really care any more whether she answers or not.

"Nothing happened," she says. "Things change."

"But if that—*thing*—used to be human, something definitely happened to it." I face her squarely.

"Nothing happened," she says again. "Only time."

I'm afraid, now. "But that's not how it works. Babies get bigger. They learn to walk and talk and everything. They start off looking ugly, and then they get prettier, and then they are proper children. That's what should happen."

"And then they grow up, and they get old, and die," she finishes the story for me. "And their children die, and their children's children. That is what happens in your world, over and over again." She looks straight at me, and I see them in her eyes, all those generations passing while she stays forever the same. But something is bothering me; something that doesn't quite make sense, and I have to think carefully about what to say next.

"So you and the others don't change, or grow old, or die," I say slowly. "But if the poppet,"—I didn't know what else to call it—"was an ordinary baby once, then it *has* changed. A lot." A thought occurs to me, and I speak it without thinking. "Or does Alys just make it look like that? But why would she want to?"

Elfrida smiles. "Why, indeed?" she says. "Alys never makes anything look other than what it is. Not even herself, poor foolish girl. She dwells in a land of plenty, but all she can think about is the one thing she lacks."

I can't let myself be distracted. "How old is the poppet?" I demand suddenly. Sometimes she does answer my questions, even if I can't make sense of the answers. It's worth a try.

She looks thoughtful. "It crawls, but has no words. Nine months or so, maybe? And such a bonny child, when first it came to us."

Now I can only stare at her. "How long ago was that?"

She shrugs, looking down at her feet, where ants are milling about, their nest disturbed. "A time, and a time."

Horror is growing in me. I hardly dare speak my thought aloud, and yet I must. I've come this far, and I must go all the way, wherever the path takes me.

"So Christine will change like that," I say, carefully, trying not to sound as though I care one way or the other. "She won't grow up, she'll just stay the same size, and never learn to walk, or anything."

"Such a winsome little face," she says absently. "Alys is well pleased."

"And what will happen to the poppet, now it's back in the human world? Will it start to grow, after all?" I'm looking out at those distant hills as I speak, as though I were simply thinking aloud. The truth is, I can't bear to look at her, to see that to her, it simply does not matter.

She doesn't answer, only stirs the ants about with one foot. I suppose it's a kind of answer, really. It's all I'm going to get.

"It looks like Christine now," I say abruptly, speaking my thoughts aloud. "That's why they don't mind yet. They think it's just teething, or something. But if it can only look like itself, that must be a spell you've put on it. So what happens when it wears off?"

Elfrida sighs. "It is a glamour, just as your appearance is a glamour now. When you cross over to us, you too will be able to cast your own glamours. You too will live, and live, and change only very slowly. But a babe cannot cast glamours of its own, or not for long. We have ensorcelled it to please its mother, but of course it will wear off, in your world. In time."

I hadn't expected an answer at all, let alone one that told me much more than I had asked. It doesn't get me any closer to a solution, though. I look out towards those distant hills, glowing in the afternoon light of a sun that will never set, or at least not while Elfrida and I are here. In the real world—if that's the right word for it—it will be growing dark already. I'll miss teatime; not that my parents will mind, or even notice.

At last, I turn to face her. "It's not fair," I say, and hear the childish whine in my voice. "Life's not fair," my mother would say, with a kind of satisfaction, almost glee, as though she had scored points in some game I didn't even know we were playing. And Elfrida says nothing, only looks at me steadily.

So. They won't put things right just because I want them to. Alys matters more to them than my Aunty Marjorie, and why not? But I know with all of my being that it matters to me, more than anything else. Dimly, I sense a future, in this world or theirs, seeing the changeling not grow up, seeing Christine change until she, too, became a grotesque goblin, and Alys would tire of her and look for a new poppet to play with. To live with that, and know that I had let it happen, would change me too.

"What can I give you if you'll return Christine to her family?" The words are out, and I can't take them back. In the next few minutes, I'll be banished forever. With both hands, I lift the folds of my dress, turning to make the scales flash and glitter, as though I could somehow hold on to that marvel. Soon, the glamour will be gone.

She doesn't look at me, but she is suddenly still. At last, I have said something that matters. And yet when she speaks, she says only,

"But you have nothing that Alys desires."

Now, we are coming to it; now, here is something I do understand.

"What do *you* want from me, Elfrida? Help me get Christine back, and I will give it to you, if I can." It's the first time I've ever called her by her name, face to face, and in that moment, just for that moment, it feels as though we are equals. I have never felt that before, with anyone. She rises, and takes both my hands.

"My brave Felicity," she says. She lifts her hands, so that our arms are upraised and our sleeves fall back, and all the scales catch fire in the sun's light, turning to gold. Then she lets go and our hands drop to our sides, but the golden glory does not dim. We seem to scatter light around us; it dances off the rocks as we walk together along the path. When we get to the end, gazing out side by side over the folds and slopes of moorland to those faraway hills, I feel that if I could stop time now, I would ask for nothing more. I am full up and brimming over. I don't know what she wants from me, but for now, I am at peace.

"So," she says at last, and her voice is quiet and sad. "There is something I would ask of you, Felicity Turner, but the time is not yet come. Your cousin will be restored to her family. Will you be ready to pay the price?"

My mouth is dry now, and my voice trembles as I say, "And you'll take the changeling back to Alys?" That's not what I really want to ask, of course, but I can't bring myself to put the bigger question—and besides, I don't think she's going to tell me. I'm going to have to agree to pay the price, without knowing what it is. That's how it is, in stories.

She sighs. "That creature has no place now in any world. But I will return it if you wish."

For the first time, it comes home to me. The changeling—*that creature*—used to be human. It used to be a beautiful baby, loved and cherished. Then the fairies came and stole it from its mother, to be a plaything for Alys until it was no longer beautiful, and she grew tired of it. And what had they left in its place? My heart aches for those lost children, carried away from their own lives before they had a chance to choose for themselves. How many had there been? And I know, beyond all doubt now, that I've made the right choice, whatever the price may be. It's too late for the poppet, but it's not too late for Christine.

Chapter 20

I take a deep breath. "I'm ready," I say quietly, still looking Onward, where I cannot go. After a moment, she takes my hand.

"Let us return to the feast," she says. And we walk together down the path, into the shade of the trees, where we cast our own light as we pass. The sound of pipes floats up to us, and then there is a light drumbeat, so that our steps are already moving in time as we enter the clearing side by side. Lights glow among the trees, throwing grotesque shadows on the faces of the company as they turn to face us. Some beautiful, some very far from human, but all as familiar and as beloved to me as my own self. Although, on this night, I hardly know myself any more.

Then the rhythm of the drum quickens, the music lifts into a wild skirling reel, and someone—Lord Ember?—takes both my hands and whirls me into the dance. I am passed from hand to hand, and somehow my steps never falter, and the lights that spark from my scales take flight and dart around and between the dancers, weaving a net that holds us all, now and in this moment forever.

But of course, it can't be forever. Maybe for them, but not for me. The dance comes to an end, and we move to where the feast is laid out, waiting. It's harvest time in the world, but the food they eat takes no account of the seasons. There are fruits I've never seen before, and maybe they don't exist at all outside this magic place, where the only limit is your own imagination.

I could have had that. But then I think again of Christine, far from her mother, and my resolve is firm. I'll enjoy tonight while I can, and take the memory back with me.

Elfrida is dancing, a slow and graceful measure, moving between three of the lordly ones. The music stops, and she drops a deep curtsey to her partner, scattering golden gleams. He takes her hand and raises her up, and as they come towards us, he glances at me in sudden surprise, and then back down at Elfrida, eyebrows raised. She smiles. The look she sends me is shocking, just before she sees that I am watching her; the fierce, intent look of a cat about to pounce. What have I promised her?

I discover something then, for the first time; a lesson I'll have to learn over and over again. Once you've decided to leave something behind, you can't have one last wonderful time there. It's like spending a last few minutes with your friend on the railway station before their train arrives. Really, they've already gone; you're just marking time until you can move on to the next thing. Abruptly, I decide that it's time to go home.

Then someone barges into me and I'm knocked sideways, almost off my feet. My hands are grabbed and I'm dancing—capering, really—with Hob and his friends, whirling around and bumping into the other dancers. At first I have to reach down to keep hold of their hands, but I'm changing as we dance, shrinking down almost to their level, and before the music stops I'm my own self again, ten-year-old Felicity in my old trousers with twigs in my hair. In a strange kind of way, it's almost a relief.

It must be time to go, but Hob is pulling at me, urging me back to the feasting.

"I have to go home now," I say, and he clutches my arm with a kind of desperation.

"Coming and going and going and coming," he chants. "When will you stay, Felicity? If you keep getting bigger, you won't fit through! And what will the robin do then, poor thing?

Winter's coming, and the north wind blows." He makes a sad face, hugging himself and chattering his teeth.

"No it doesn't, not yet. I'll come back soon." One more time, perhaps, to take Christine away. I can't bring myself to say that out loud, but he knows or guesses something. He looks at me sidelong, a desolate look like the dogs when my father leaves the house without them. Should I tell him? Where's the harm?

"Hob," I say, and then stop. I try again. "Hob, if I can't come back for any reason, I won't forget you. Not ever. I promise."

It's too much for him. He turns a somersault and comes up ten feet away, shouting "Promises are piecrusts! Crumbs for the little birds and fishes!" And he's off again, as though the only thing to do with difficult things is to outrun them. But that won't work for me.

I turn my back on them all, and start along the path away from the bourn; the path that leads past my den and towards the farm. I've never left Them of my own accord, and I don't even know if I can, but I haven't gone more than a dozen steps before Elfrida is there, standing in front of me.

"Well, then," she says.

I look up at her, so tall and powerful and lovely. She can make everything right if she chooses. I wait.

"If it's to be done," she says, "It must be now." She holds out her hand to me. And after a moment, I take it.

At once, the world rushes away. That's how it feels, as though we two are standing still while everything shifts around us. Then it stops, and we are looking at the door in the hillside. Birds are singing, and primroses bloom in the grass around the spring, where there should be fallen leaves at this time of year. No matter. Elfrida pulls the door open, and we go in.

Inside, it could be any time of day or season. There is candlelight, and flickering firelight, and shadows in the corners. On the hearth sits a tortoiseshell cat, one of Malkin's grandchildren who was born in our barn. She stretches out one leg as we approach, and begins to wash. Well, cats can come and go as they please.

I can't see Alys at first, but I can hear her, singing in her strange, cracked voice:

"Rings on her fingers and bells on her toes,
She shall have music wherever she goes."

She is sitting on the floor behind the long table, dancing Christine up and down. I never saw the changeling in anything but dirty rags, but Christine is dressed in an elaborate long white dress, sewn with tiny bells that jingle as she moves, and her golden curls gleam in the firelight. The relief I feel is shocking; I go weak at the knees and almost sob. They both look up at us and, as Christine sees me, she holds out her arms and smiles her unearthly smile. She knows me!

I am moving forward before I realise, but Alys draws Christine to her breast and rocks her, singing close to her ear. I stop, but the child is squirming now, trying to turn around. Alys holds her more tightly, and she begins to whimper.

For a long moment, nothing changes. I glance up at Elfrida, expecting her to say something, to take Christine away, but she just stands there, watching. And then I realise; she's brought me here not as a witness, but because the task is mine. I must be the one who takes away Alys's child, again.

Once more the outrage rises in me: It's not fair! Not fair on me, and certainly not fair on poor Alys, who probably never had any luck in her short life as a human. But I have no choice, now.

"Alys," I say, hearing the tremble in my voice, "Can I hold her for a moment?"

She shakes her head, shrinking away from me. Christine is crying now, pushing at her.

"Alys, you're hurting her!" That doesn't help; she only hunches over the child, rocking back and forth. Her lips are moving, but I can't hear what she's saying over Christine's rising wails. Again, I look to Elfrida, but she doesn't move. *I'm only ten*, I think. *I don't know what to do.*

What would a grown-up do? Aunty Marjorie would rush to take the baby, and that would be that. But Alys thinks Christine is her own child, and who has a better right to hold her than her own mother?

"Alys," I try again. "She's a beautiful baby, isn't she? Such pretty hair, and those lovely blue eyes!" That's what I've heard people saying, in the village, when Aunty Marjorie goes to the shops. Alys has stopped squeezing her now. She lifts one hand to run her fingers through Christine's curls.

"She's got a special brush at home," I say, "with soft bristles so it doesn't hurt. Sometimes she has ribbons in her hair, but she usually pulls them out pretty soon, and then you have to be careful she doesn't put them in her mouth."

Alys won't look at me, but I can tell she's listening.

"When she cries like that," I go on, "Aunty Marjorie usually gives her a rusk or a piece of carrot to chew on. It could be her teeth. Or sometimes if you read her a story, she stops crying so she can listen. I don't think she really understands, though."

Does Alys understand? There are no books here, I realise, though I never thought about it before. They tell stories, but they don't read.

"Do you know her name, Alys?" I'm not expecting an answer, but she gathers Christine close again and speaks at last. Her voice is low and hoarse, almost a growl. "Eleonora."

"Oh." My mouth is very dry. "Was that your baby's name?"

From behind me, startling us both, Elfrida says, "Her baby's name was Annie, though they gave her another name later. Didn't they, Alys?"

Alys is rocking again, to and fro, to and fro. "Florabel," she says. "Anna Maria. Melisande. Miranda."

I crouch down now, making myself small. "It's Christine," I say quietly. "Her name is Christine." And at the sound of her name, the baby turns again to look at me. Her face is red from crying, and there is snot like a snail trail down one cheek. Aunty Marjorie would have wiped it off straight away. For a moment, I see how it would be, if Christine stayed with Alys. The slow changes, year on year, until she became a creature no one would want to look at, let alone touch.

"Her name is Christine," I say again, more loudly. "Christine Turner. Her parents are Bob and Marjorie Turner. She has a big brother called Tommy and a sister called Angie. And I'm her cousin. She knows me. Don't you, Christine?"

She stares at me, quite still, in that way that babies do.

"Christine," I repeat, and she leans towards me, her face intent. Each time I say her name, Alys jumps a little as though something had startled her. "Your mummy is worried about you, Christine. It's time to go home now. Shall we go and see your mummy?"

She holds out her arms again, and then, without warning, she throws herself forward. Alys sits there, not moving to save her, not doing anything. I'm just in time to catch her, awkwardly, before she hits her head on the floor. I pull her up and into my arms, and she nestles in my lap, quite still, though my arms are shaking so hard I can barely hold her.

"Alys," I say, when my voice is almost steady. She doesn't react at all. "They shouldn't have taken your baby. Your Annie. That was wrong. But you can't take Christine to make it right. She needs her mummy. I'm going to take her back to her mummy now."

Alys looks down at her empty hands. She is utterly still, and there is something about that stillness that terrifies me. It's like the time I met an adder on the common, and neither of us knew whether to attack or flee. That time, a dog came bounding along the path, and the snake slithered off. This time, I'm on my own. Christine pulls at my hair, so hard it makes me wince.

Carefully, without letting go of her, I start to move, to get to my feet. I have to put her down, then lift her into my arms, warm and solid. She doesn't smell the way she usually does, of Aunty Marjorie's scented washing powder and sour milk. It's a woodland smell, like tree sap and wild mushrooms, and I wonder what else has changed.

When I'm safely standing, I look down at Alys. She hasn't moved.

"I'm sorry, Alys," I say. My voice sounds small and foolish, but it's the only one I have. "Christine has to go back to her mother. Elfrida will bring you back your poppet." I am backing away as I speak, one careful step at a time. I daren't look round to see where Elfrida is, or where I'm going, but I just want to get as far away as possible.

Alys suddenly looks up, straight at me, and then she lifts her empty arms and lets out a howl like an animal in mortal pain, and all the hairs on my arms stand up. Christine starts to cry again, and I turn to run, to get away, and there at last is Elfrida, standing by the door, waiting.

Chapter 21

I haven't got a free hand to give her. I'm stumbling with the weight of Christine in my arms, and the awful sounds that Alys is making behind me feel like brambles, pulling and tearing at me, holding me back. It seems to take forever to get to the door, as though the distance is stretching further, or I'm getting smaller. Christine is howling and twisting, and I'm sobbing too now, my hair in my eyes, and she's slipping out of my grip. I can't hold on, and I'll either have to drop her or sink to the floor. We both fall, and I hit my head against a chair, but I manage to shield Christine, and I don't let go. She has a hank of my hair clasped in her fist, and it really hurts, but I twist my head to look up, and there is Elfrida, only a few feet away, and beyond her the spring sunshine sparkling through green leaves.

"Help me," I say. "Please!"

Now, at last, she stoops down. I'm expecting her to take Christine from me, but somehow she gathers us both up, as though I were very small and Christine just a doll in my arms. Nobody has held me like that for a long, long time. Elfrida is as tall and strong as a tree, and now it's all up to her. I don't have to do anything any more. I lean my head against her chest, feeling her heartbeat inside my own head, as she steps across the threshold and out into the afternoon sunshine.

Then we are gliding through the woods, not flying exactly but moving swift and sure between the trees, along the stream for a bit, and on again, too fast for me to see where we're going.

Christine sits very upright, bright-eyed and laughing for joy, and I never want this journey to end.

It doesn't take long, after all. We come to a stop and I open my eyes—when did I close them?—and we are standing in the field behind the row of new houses where Uncle Bob and Aunty Marjorie live. Platts Close, it's called, after the field that used to be there. There are bullocks grazing, and if I were on my own they would come up and try to lick me, but they take no notice of us at all. Maybe we're invisible. That would be good; I feel the gaze of all those big blank windows in the bedrooms upstairs. Angie's room has her old teddy bear sitting on the windowsill, but I can't see into the kitchen because of the new fence Uncle Bob put up. Mr. Green next door just has barbed wire at the end of the garden, though, and he's tipped a lot of garden rubbish over it into the field.

"You must do the rest," says Elfrida, and her voice vibrates in her chest like a drumbeat. In one stride, she reaches the fence, and leans over it to set me down. I want to cling to her, but my own arms are full, and then I'm on my feet at the bottom of the garden, looking up as Elfrida towers above me.

"Aren't you coming? Can't I let you in?" I ask.

"It is not your home," she says, as though that was an answer.

"But they'll see me! What shall I say? I don't know what to do!"

"They will not see you, not for a time. Be quick and silent, and do not look directly at them. I shall wait here." She stands up straight and folds her arms, and disappears. Or no, not exactly; I can see her in a vague sort of way, like in the old mirror in our hall that's lost a lot of its backing, but I can see the sky and the clouds at the same time, somehow. Is that how I look? To myself I seem as solid as ever, but I'll have to trust her. I have no choice.

I take a step, and then stop. There is one more thing.

"Elfrida," I say. "Can you tell me its name? Please?"

There is a long silence. I think she isn't going to answer, but just as I start to move again, she says, "Its mother called it Annie."

"Thank you," I say.

I hitch Christine up to get a better grip, and turn towards the house. The French windows are open, but the first thing I see is the pram, parked in the shade. What if the poppet is there? Then all I'll have to do is lift it out and put Christine in, and I won't have to go into the house at all. As fast as I can, I make my way over there, but as soon as I can see inside, my hope dies. The pram is empty.

For a moment, I think about putting Christine into the pram and just running away. That part would be easy; it's the thought of touching that goblin thing, the changeling, that makes my skin crawl.

And as I stand there, I hear Aunty Marjorie's voice in the kitchen, and then the awful thin wailing noise it makes. It's in there, and that's where I must go.

When I get to the French doors, the noise gets louder. Grizzling, my mother calls it. It's a good word. Aunty Marjorie is at the stove, but just as I step inside, she turns around sharply. I freeze, thinking she's seen me, but her head is turned away, towards the playpen on the far side of the kitchen.

"For goodness's sake, just stop!" she hisses, in a voice I hardly recognise. Her fists are clenched. "I don't know what you want. Please, please, just five minutes. I can't do this." She covers her face with her hands, and the awful grizzling gets louder. Then she makes a sound of her own, something like a growl or a scream, and I've never heard any grown-up make a noise like that, let alone my Aunty Marjorie, always so superior and composed.

From the sitting room, I can hear the sound of the television. Angie and Tommy must be in there, watching some programme I know nothing about. They all talk about television programmes at school, and I have nothing to say. There is music, and then suddenly it gets much louder, and Aunty Marjorie looks up like a dog scenting a rabbit.

"Turn that down!" she yells. If anything, it gets louder. Her face is red and twisted with fury; she grabs a wooden spoon and rushes out into the hall. "Turn that bloody racket off this minute!" she shouts, and then there are yells of protest from the sitting room, and now's my chance. It's now or never.

The changeling looks up as we come around the kitchen table. Its mouth is stretched wide in a horrible goblin grin, and there's no *flickering* now, no chance you could ever mistake it for a normal baby. It rocks to and fro, snickering and wheezing. There are toys strewn about in the playpen, smeared with food of some sort, or maybe worse. It smells foul, and I think I'm going to be sick again; just the thought of touching it makes me gag. I've only got a few minutes. No time to think.

Turning my face away from the ghastly thing, I say to Christine, "I'm going to put you in the playpen now. It's not very nice, but your mummy will be back soon, and then everything will be all right." Will it? I've never heard Aunty Marjorie swear before, never seen her look so dangerous. But I can't help it. This is what has to happen, now.

Christine clings to me as I lower her into the playpen, and then she spies one of her dolls, and reaches for it. Just for a moment, she and the changeling touch, and then I get my hands under its armpits and heave it out and over the side. It seems to get heavier, and it hooks one foot over the top rail, dragging the playpen out of shape. Its fingernails dig into my arms, and it begins to scream, a high keening noise that tears at my ears.

"Annie," I say, keeping my face turned away so I don't have to see what I'm holding. "Annie, you have to go back to Alys now. Christine needs her mummy. I know you need yours too, but I'm doing the best I can. You can't stay here. I'm sorry."

I've unhooked its foot and I'm stumbling towards the French

windows, and it's scratching me and butting with its head, leaving trails of snot and dribble on my jumper. Through the noise in my ears I can hear that the music has stopped, and then a door slams and the sound of angry voices from the sitting room is cut off. At the French windows I turn to look back. Aunty Marjorie is standing in the doorway, looking straight at me.

That's how it feels at first, but after that first frozen moment, I realise that what Elfrida says is true: she's looking at me, but she's not seeing me. She stands there, a little puzzled frown on her face, holding the wooden spoon. The creature in my arms is yelling even more loudly, and writhing so hard that I can't move; all I can do is to hold on with all my strength. Surely she can hear something? Then Christine in the playpen gives a little crow of joy. She picks up a red wooden brick and throws it out of the playpen. It skitters across the shiny floor, crashes into the leg of the table, and she gurgles with laughter.

Aunty Marjorie's gaze snaps away. She's staring at Christine, mouth open, and then she drops the spoon and puts both hands up to her face. The changeling is yelling, but somehow it feels as though everything has gone quiet. We all watch as Christine picks up another brick. This time, it hits the bar of the playpen and falls down in front of her. For a moment, she is startled, and then her whole body rocks with glee.

Aunty Marjorie lets her hands fall, and I can't bear to see her face. I've never seen a grown-up cry like that, not even bothering to wipe her nose, her eyes shining with hope. She starts towards the playpen, and Christine holds up her arms.

It's time to go. I hoist the changeling up again, and turn to trudge across the garden. "Shh, Annie, shh, it's all right," I'm saying, and I realise now why grown-ups say things like that when of course, it's not all right and it never can be, not for her. It's not the words, it's the feeling; the intention. It's what you want to be true, even if it can't possibly be.

By the time we get to the bottom of the garden, she's sagging in my arms, her feet almost trailing in the long grass. I can't see Elfrida, so when I get there I sit down, holding her between my knees. I know she can crawl, so I keep a good hold, and for the first time I look straight at her. Her ugly little wizened face is turned away from me, so I'm looking at one ear, much too big for her head. Her hair is pale brown and baby-fine, but her skin is weathered like an old person's. Like Hob's, I realise suddenly. But Hob is a goblin; he's supposed to look grotesque. On a baby, it's all wrong.

"Annie," I say. She won't meet my eyes, and she's still grizzling, but more quietly now, like a wasp buzzing against a windowpane. I know she's listening. I'm not sure if she knows her own name after all this time, but it seems to calm her, somehow.

I try again. "Annie, Elfrida is going to take you back. You can't stay here. Christine is with her mummy, where she needs to be. And maybe Alys will take better care of you now."

I gaze at her, trying to see the lovely baby she must have been, and she pushes at my knees, trying to get away. It's no good.

"Elfrida!" I raise my voice, sure now that no one in the house will see or hear me.

"I am here," she says in a voice like the wind. I feel the vibration of it go through me as she bends down to gather us both up, and then we are moving again towards the line of trees at the far side of the field. I'd been afraid she might leave me there in Aunty Marjorie's garden, to find my own way home or face endless questions from my family, but relief makes me weak, and I just want to lean against her and hold on to every precious moment. It could be the last time.

Now, though, it's the changeling's turn to peer into my face, and poke her pudgy little fingers into my eyes and nose. Annie, that's what she's called. Or was, once. I'm trying to remember that as I fend off her overgrown nails from my face. Aunty Marjorie cuts Christine's nails carefully, while she's asleep, but no one has tended to Annie's for some time. It comes to me that Aunty Marjorie must have known, somehow, that this was not her own baby. I hope she can recognise Christine now.

The rushing of the wind around us suddenly dies down. For a moment, I am looking around through the branches of trees, like a bird or a squirrel, but in the next instant I am lowered to the ground, and Elfrida is standing beside us, no longer treetop-tall but her own self again.

At once, I let Annie slide from my arms, and she starts picking up handfuls of leaves and crushing them in her fists. There might be acorns, she might put one in her mouth and choke, I think—and then realise that those are Aunty Marjorie's words. I can't keep her safe, whatever I do now. Pity is rising in me, a huge pain in my chest trying to get out, and I crouch down to hug her.

"Goodbye, little Annie," I whisper. She squirms and pushes at me, and then I feel Elfrida's hand on my shoulder.

"You see?" she says. "There is no right way, only one choice after another."

"It's not fair," I say again, looking down. I hate the childish whine of it.

"They call us the Fair Folk," she says, with a laugh in her voice. "Because they hope that will make it so."

I stand up, then, and try to meet her eyes. "But you can make it so! You're magic. You're fairies. You can do anything you like, can't you? If you choose to."

She laughs outright, then. "Why should we so choose?"

Because you're kind, and good, I open my mouth to say. And then I close it again, thinking of all the times we've played tricks on people, and led them astray, and frightened them. She watches me remembering all this, and smiles.

"You see?" she says. "And now we must go." She picks up the changeling, turning her face away as it—she—tries to stuff leaves into her mouth.

"Wait!" I know I'm pushing my luck, as my father would say, but I don't think there's anything left to lose, now. "When shall I see you again?"

She pauses, half-turned away. Of course, she won't answer. And then, with that laugh in her voice, she says,

"When you are ready."

And she's gone.

Chapter 22

I stood there among the trees, and the wind gusted suddenly, sending a shower of leaves pattering down all around me. It was that time in late autumn when the afternoon light seems to get thicker as night approaches. It would be full dark before I got home, and spatters of cold rain were finding their way through the gaps in the leaves overhead. No time to stand and feel my loss; other sensations crowded in, and maybe that was a kindness on Elfrida's part, or maybe she simply didn't think about it at all.

She had given me no answers, as usual, or only answers that begged more questions. Stumbling my way home through the woods that evening, I had no idea whether I would ever see Them again. Would that be the price I paid for returning Christine to her family, or was there some other forfeit I didn't yet know about? And underneath all the worries and heartache, a small constant warmth, like the baked potato that my mother sometimes slipped into my pocket when I set out for the school bus on winter mornings. *I did it!* I stood up to them, and I brought my little cousin home. Whatever the price might turn out to be, I could not regret that outcome.

I had realised along the way that if I didn't do something about the changeling, I myself would be changed. What I hadn't foreseen was that I would be changed anyway. Before that, I think, nothing I had done had made any real difference to anything. When does a child begin to realise that her actions have consequences?

Days went by. I caught the flu, or something like it, and had to stay in bed for several days. It was almost a relief. I was in no hurry to go back to the woods and find that they had shed their magic with the falling leaves. More than that; I didn't want to see Them again, or not just yet. Even after I recovered and went back to school, there were always reasons not to go. It was too dark, too cold. I had more homework now, preparation for the 11-plus exams next term, and I found that I really wanted to pass them. And what if I did? My schooldays would get longer with the journey to and from town, and the workload would get bigger. I shied away from thinking about what that might mean.

In the end, it was more than three weeks before I ventured into the woods again. Bonfire night had come and gone, and it was always dark now when I left for school and when I came home again. Weekends were the only time, and then there were chores and homework to be done. Or so I told myself.

The day I finally went back, it was almost by accident.

Hard frosts had brought down the last of the leaves, made delicate patterns on the inside of my bedroom window overnight, and hung in the air, veiling everything as though there were secrets to be hidden. It was time to pick sloes for the sloe gin that my mother made every year, and so I went out mid-morning in scarf and gloves, wearing two pairs of socks inside a hand-me-down pair of Angie's wellington boots that slopped around as I walked, making the journey across the icy barnyard even trickier than usual.

Sloes grew here and there in the hedgerows, but they were often out of my reach, and I worked my way from tree to tree, staying inside the field boundaries, until I was in the high field where the two ponies grazed. Their coats were shaggy now, and they came to me eagerly for the windfall apples I had stowed in my pockets. Their manes, I saw, were knotted and snarled into elflocks, and I wondered whose mischief that was. Their breath hung in clouds around us, and I leaned my head against

Goldie's neck for the solid living warmth of her. In that silent, white world, she seemed the only vivid thing. I left them reluctantly at last, and they followed me to the top of the field and then drifted off about their own business.

Thinking there might be more accessible sloes on the other side of the hedge, I climbed over the gate into the top woods. I went on up the hill, crunching through the leaf litter under the beech trees, until I reached the highest point, where I could look down across the sweep of fields to the roof of our house, almost hidden among the trees and half-swallowed by mist.

On the far side, the hillside fell away to more farmland and a road in the distance, but when I turned to face that way, all I could see was thick fog filling the valley like soup in a bowl, and the peak of a hill rising out of it, crowned by a ruined tower. That was not the everyday world; that was the tower I had glimpsed from below, by the dark water, the day I had awoken—what? Without knowing it, I had crossed the border.

I stand there, uncertain whether to turn tail now and head for home. But it's already too late, of course. Through the bare beech trees they come, a tumble and flurry of goblins like naughty boys, stuffing leaves down each other's backs and trying to trip each other up. No Elfrida, no tall and beautiful ones this time, only Hob and his friends, jostling around me like the ponies eager for apples. What do I have to give them?

One of them sweeps off his leather cap and makes me a low bow. I'm not sure I've ever seen him before, though it's hard to be certain when they change their appearance as they please. His ears are huge and misshapen, and his nose is a blob that almost hides his mouth.

"Fungus, I am, Lady Felicity," he says, and then the cap is snatched from his outstretched hand. He dives to retrieve it, and it is tossed high into the air, where it takes flight and flaps like a bat around his head while he tussles with the one who stole it. Another leaps to catch it, twisting aside to avoid the wrestlers, and comes to meet me with an odd, sidelong gait, like John Cartwright at school who has a club foot.

"They call me Adder," he says, grinning lopsidedly. "But that is not my name."

I look from one to the other. "You're the ones who came hunting those men at the twisted oak, aren't you?"

There is laughter. Adder tosses the cap to Hob, who peers into it, screeches, and flings it away as it takes flight again. It looks like a crow now, a black and tattered thing that darts and pecks at the hands upstretched to grasp it. They scare me, these misshapen creatures; they are like wild boys, capable of anything.

"Where is Elfrida?" I don't expect an answer, and I'm half hoping to slip away while they are at their rough-and-tumble, but at once my hands are seized and they begin to hurry me along. I'm tripping over tree roots and getting whipped by branches, and yet they flow on around me without pausing, and no one falls or bumps into anyone else. They remind me of the acrobats at the circus that came to town last year, except that they look more like the clowns, or even animals dressed up in human clothes. The acrobats were lithe and graceful, dressed in glittering costumes, though when I saw some outside the big top smoking cigarettes, I could see that some sequins were missing and their make-up was smeared with sweat. Not like Lord Ember or the other lordly ones; not like Elfrida. Not like the real thing.

I'm sure I haven't seen some of these faces before, and that could mean one of two things. Either there are new ones in the group—and in all the time I've known them, that has never happened—or they are the same, but play-acting. *Shapeshifting.* I've seen them do it before, after all, from goblin to monster, from boulder to living creature. I don't feel safe among them; I don't like it when there are none of the tall and beautiful ones. Are they here, tumbling and somersaulting around me? I wish they'd show me their real shapes, but I know better than to ask.

While I've been trying to keep my footing and keep track of

the moving figures all around me, we've moved into another part of the woods, from the tall beeches on the hilltop to the scrubby birches and rowans that fringe the lower-lying heathland. The paths here are sandy, and gorse and heather grow between the trees. *If you don't feed the soil, it turns to sand,* my father would say, and every year he spreads the muck from the barn and the pigsties, and the rooks follow in a great clattering cloud.

The next moment my father is forgotten, as we come to a sudden stop. We have arrived at the door in the hillside.

I'm expecting them to take me in, but instead they drop my hands and begin tussling and roughhousing again, splashing each other with the water from the stone basin and gathering fallen leaves to push down each other's jerkins. I'm standing by the door, looking at the curving patterns carved into it and wondering how old they are. Old enough for there to be green lichen growing in the fine grain of the wood, and fringes of moss along the lower sill. Who made this place? It could be hundreds of years old, and yet the ones who smoothed the wood and shaped the handle could still be here. *Time runs differently.* Maybe I will ask, even if I get no answer. And then I remember what may be awaiting me.

"Will you not go in?" Hob is at my side, looking up at me sidelong.

"I was waiting for you." It's not entirely true, but close enough.

"Oho! The choice is yours to make, Mistress Felicity. Open the door, cross the threshold, take the step. Or have you done that already?"

I turn away. Something in me opens its eyes, and rises; something born of all the choices I've had to make in the last few weeks. Not *had to make.* I chose, and now I hardly know this Felicity, who's tired of riddles and games. Who grasps the door handle, and pulls the door open, and goes in.

Chapter 23

The long room seems deserted, and I have time to look around. Hundreds of candles are burning in sconces on the walls and in tall holders along the tables, casting a wavering light that is never quite at rest. Sometimes I catch glimpses of the ceiling, but it's hard to tell how high it is, and whether it's made of ribbed stone or carved wood, or even the living roots of trees. On the hearth there is a fire, and by the fire there is a great oak chair, like a throne for a king or queen. It's not for me, I'm sure of that, but it stands empty.

I wander slowly between the tables, picturing them laden with wonderful food, the room full of laughter and music and talk. And magic, of course; always magic. Is it my fault that there is no one here now? Have I spoiled things for ever? I thought the price would be mine to pay, but what if it cost Them, too? *It's not fair!* Not fair to have to make decisions without knowing where they might lead. I look towards the door. Almost, I want to slip away, hide in my everyday world and pretend it's all fine, Christine is home again and that makes everything all right. But I don't move. As I stand there, tears in my eyes and desolation in my heart, I hear a sound behind me.

"Turn again, Felicity."

She must have known what I was feeling. Elfrida is standing by the hearth, facing me. Not tall as a tree now, or little and twisted like the goblins outside, but just herself. A sound comes from me, a gasp that is almost a sob. I want to run to her, but I don't move, waiting for whatever comes next.

"Come," she says, and gestures to the empty chair. "Sit with me."

I go over to the chair, and run my hand along the ancient wood of its arm. How many other hands have done this? Enough to work dark seams into the grain, and polish it to a dull gleam. I glance at Elfrida, but she gives no sign, so I climb up onto the seat. I have to use both hands to do it, and I can either lean against the back with my legs stretched straight out in front of me, or sit on the edge with my feet dangling. Today, it seems, there is no transformation for me. In the end, I choose to curl with my knees up, so I can lean my cheek against the carvings on the back of the chair, and gaze at the moving firelight.

There is no sound for a while, except for the small noises of the fire. Elfrida can wait for ever, but I can't; and now that I'm here, I want to get it over with, to know my fate.

And then something occurs to me.

I raise my head, and turn to look at her. Standing so still, she looks almost like a carving herself.

"Where is Alys? And—and little Annie?" Always, when I've visited this place, they have been here.

She doesn't move, doesn't look at me. "Gone."

My stomach clenches inside me, and I shudder as though a cold wind had blown in. My voice won't work properly, and then it comes out in a sort of croak.

"Gone where?"

Now, at last, Elfrida stirs. She looks towards the door, as though she is seeing through it and far beyond.

"Onward. Where else?" she says. I have a vision of Alys, trudging across that bare moorland in the dark, bent-backed against the winter wind, carrying her not-child into the unknown. Tears spill from my eyes.

"Oh, but why did she have to go? Couldn't they just go back to how it was?"

Elfrida smiles, but her eyes are deep in shadow. "It came

home to her," she says softly. "There is no going back. And so she went Onward."

I can't bear it. It's all my fault. "What will she find there?"

"Who knows? Strange things cross the border from time to time, but they don't speak of whence they came, if they can speak at all. And no one comes back." There is something in the way she stands now, head bowed and voice low, that makes me think: *She is afraid.* Then in a flicker of candlelight that thought is gone. Elfrida is never afraid. And just now, I am too full of my own fear and despair to give it attention.

"But I didn't mean for that to happen! I just wanted to make things all right again . . ."

Now, at last, she looks directly at me, and the firelight gleams in her eyes.

"Such a child," she says. "But not for much longer, I think."

To that I have nothing to say, but the unfairness of it burns inside me, and my eyes hurt as the painful tears force their way out. Surely, now, she will say the words that will bar me from this place forever. And I will deserve it.

Abruptly, without thinking it through, I uncurl and slide down from the chair. "I'm going home now," I say, though I can't bear to look at her. "Goodbye. And—thank you. I'm sorry I spoiled things. Goodbye."

She makes a sudden movement, as though I've startled her, and then she laughs.

"My brave Felicity!" she says, just as she did when I bargained for Christine, down by the bourn. But I was someone else then; I really was just a child, and it's true, you can never go back. So I start to walk away.

"Stay!" she says, and I don't want to turn around, but somehow my body moves of its own accord, and I'm facing the fire again, and the tear tracks are cold on my hot cheeks. Looking at her, as she takes my chin in her hand, and turns my face up so I have to meet her eyes.

"This is your doom," she says. "Your heart is turning towards the things of the world. You will come less often to the woods, and you will begin to forget. We shall watch you, and sometimes we shall summon you, but you will not always hear. Soon enough, you will think it just a dream."

"I won't!" I am angry now; she's treating me like a child again. "I never would, I swear it!"

"It is the way of things," she says.

"But it doesn't have to be. I will remember. I promise on my honour," I say, standing up straight and solemn. I'm not sure what that means, but I read it in a book about the olden days, and it feels somehow right. I look up into her face, but strangely, it is she who turns away.

"If you do," she says, aside, almost as though I were not there, "great gifts may await you. But we shall see, my little warrior. And now, how does your cousin?"

Great gifts, I think. I'd love to know what they might be, but of course I will never ask. "All right, I think. She had an assessment at the doctor's, but they think she's fine now. She got a new tooth last week."

"So." I don't think she's really interested in Christine; she's just trying to distract me, the way grown-ups do. And now I really do want to go home. I want to curl up under the blankets in my bedroom, and think about all that's happened. Is this "doom" a punishment for what I did? I've learned that I'll never understand everything They say and do, but it feels as though I'm missing something. Something very important, just beyond my reach.

"I need to go home now," I say. "It's dark, and they'll be worrying."

Elfrida smiles. "You see?" she says. "Already it begins."

I know what she means; I've never thought about my parents while I'm here, or wondered whether they get anxious about me. Since that one time when my father punished me, he's never spoken about the woods again. I suppose he's given up. I don't really care what they think, I just said that as an excuse. Does that mean I'm changing?

"I'll come next weekend if I can."

"If you can."

It's all coming out wrong. Maybe I really will forget, in time; maybe she's right. Maybe I'll never be able to come here again. But when I rescued Christine, I thought that was the end for me, and wasn't I just a little bit relieved? My thoughts go round and round, and Elfrida is watching me, silent in the firelight.

In the end, I just walk away and don't look back. I don't know how to get home from here, and there is no sign of the goblins when I get outside, but as I start down the path, a shadow breaks free from the darkness under the trees, and there is Lord Ember. Without speaking, he offers me his hand, and we walk together between trees that shift, and sigh, and seem to open the way we must go. At the edge of the last field before the barnyard, he stops.

"A gift for you, Felicity," he says, and my heart is in my mouth. Surely there can't be *great gifts* already, so soon? I've done nothing yet to deserve them. But he holds out my own basket—where did that come from?—and it is full to the brim with sloes, so that I have to take it in both hands.

"Thank you," I say. He bows, and then is gone. I pick my way across the frozen yard, and the light from the kitchen window guides me for the last few steps on my journey home.

Part Three: About the Shine

Fairy Ointment

Once upon a time there was, in the town of Tavistock, an old woman who was a midwife.

One night, she had just got into bed when rap, rap, rap came on her cottage door. The summoner was a strange, squint-eyed, ugly little fellow, but she dared not resist the command to come and attend upon his wife.

A large coal-black horse stood at the door. The ill-looking old fellow whisked her up on a high pillion in a minute, seated himself before her, and away went horse and riders, as if sailing through the air, rather than trotting on the ground. How she got to the place of her destination she could not tell; but it was a great relief to her fears when she found herself set down at the door of a neat cottage, saw a couple of tidy children, and remarked her patient to be a decent-looking woman.

A fine, bouncing babe soon made its appearance, and the mother gave the nurse a certain ointment with directions that she should rub it on the child's eyelids.

The nurse performed her task, though she thought it an odd one. She wondered what it could be for; and thought that, as no doubt it was a good thing, she might just as well try it upon her own eyes as well; so she made free to rub one of them, and when, Oh! ye powers of fairyland, what a change was there!

The neat, but homely cottage, and all who were in it, seemed all on a sudden to undergo a mighty transformation; some for the better, some for the worse. The new-made mother appeared as a beautiful lady attired in white; the babe was seen wrapped in swaddling clothes of a silvery gauze. It looked much prettier than before, but still maintained the elfish cast of the eye, whilst two or three children more had undergone a metamorphosis into a couple of little flat-nosed imps.

The woman got away as fast as she could, saying nothing about the magic ointment.

On the next market day, when she went to sell her eggs, who should she see but the same, wicked looking little fellow, busied in pilfering sundry articles from stall to stall.

So up she went, and inquired carelessly after his wife and child, and hoped both were as well as could be expected.

"What!" exclaimed the old pixy thief, "do you see me today?"

"See you! To be sure I do, as plain as I see the sun in the skies; and I see you are busy into the bargain."

"Do you so!" cried he. "Pray with which eye do you see all this?"

"With the right eye to be sure."

"The ointment! The ointment!" exclaimed the old fellow. "Take that for meddling with what did not belong to you—you shall see me no more."

He struck her eye as he spoke, and from that hour till the day of her death she was blind on the right side, thus dearly paying for having gratified an idle curiosity in the house of a pixy.

Anna Eliza Bray, *Traditions, Legends, Superstitions, and Sketches of Devonshire on the Borders of the Tamar and the Tavy* vol. 1 (London: H.G. Bohn, 1838) (Abridged)

Chapter 24

Newnham College, Cambridge
October 1967

Felicity leaned back in her chair, and sighed. She hadn't been aware, until then, that she was holding her breath. Holding out, perhaps, for a different outcome. Safely home. That was how it had felt; and there was the nub of it. Elfrida was right, of course. Already, even before what had happened with baby Christine, ten-year-old Felicity had begun to turn towards the everyday world. Or no; not the everyday world of the farm and the village school and her parents trudging through their daily routines, but the promise of a wider world, at the grammar school in town, and maybe even beyond that.

Did that happen to all children? The answer was clear even as she asked the question. Poor Alys must have been barely out of childhood herself when she bore her lost baby, and turned her back on her miserable little life forever. But what about children who never found their way into the woods, as she had done? Felicity pinched the bridge of her nose. For most of us, she thought, there is no final choice, no "This" or "That." Sometimes we choose, usually with no idea what we're really choosing, but mostly we just keep going, and life happens, and we more or less go along with it.

That was enough for today. She had two essays to hand in by Friday, and a heap of reading to get through. But caution made her gather up what she'd written, and fold the pages inside one of her more boring-looking textbooks on social psychology, just in case. She was almost sure that neither Elfrida nor Hob could read, but what could magic do? If they appeared while she was writing about them, or when she still had the pages in her room, she was sure that they would know, somehow. Fairies could get away with not quite delivering what they had promised; in fact, in almost all the stories, that was exactly what they did.

When humans tried it, it usually led to disaster.

“Are you coming, Fliss?” Never one to knock, Steph leaned in the doorway, half in and half out. Felicity pulled the top page of her essay over the drawing. Would she have seen?

“In a bit. I really need to finish this. It’ll only be the warm-up acts in the first half, anyway.”

“And one day, when they’re mega-famous, you’ll be able to say, ‘I saw them at the Clare folk club, when they were nobody.’ Only you won’t.”

“I’ll take my chances. You go on. I need about half an hour, tops.”

Steph went, leaving the door ajar. Felicity got up to close it, crossing her fingers and closing her eyes for luck. If they sensed her annoyance, they’d be there, no question, and then the essay would never be finished. She squeezed her eyelids hard shut, and counted slowly to ten.

Hob was sitting in her chair. The desk drawer was open and he was rooting through it, muttering to himself. She knew what he wanted; the pencil sharpener was his favourite thing, and he could spend hours reducing her pencils—her lovely coloured crayons, too—to tiny fans and splinters. She’d hidden it yesterday in one of the mugs on the shelf, partly to see if they could somehow read her thoughts, and partly to save the new tin of Lakeland 2Bs from ruin. He looked up and grinned at her.

“It’s gone a wandering, it has, my little wood-eater,” he said.

"Off into the corners and the crevices, munching up spills and twigs, till the leaves stick in its craw and it dies of a surfeit of greenery. Poor little louse."

He held up the hole-puncher, and with the other hand picked up a sheaf of pages, watching her with a wicked widening grin.

"Give that here!" She snatched at the essay, but somehow he was crouching on top of the bookshelves, holding it just out of her reach as he tried to push the edges into the hole-puncher.

"No!" She just about dodged as he let it fall. You needed two hands and a flat surface to work it properly, but she wasn't going to show him how. He was peering at the essay now, holding it about two inches from his face, probably upside down.

"If twenty prating parrots were to preach for twenty years, would they bring forth the Word? O my brethren, it is certain that they would not! And Jack and Jill fell down the hill, all in a tumble, the naughty thieving wretches!" His voice was a perfect mimic of Dr. Barnes, her Mythology and Religion lecturer; deep and sonorous, in love with itself even when what he was saying was utterly trivial. Despite herself, Felicity laughed.

"Have you been sneaking into my lectures?" she asked, peering up at him, but for answer he sprang away, over her head, landing lightly and impossibly on the sofa ten feet away. The essay pages fluttered down around her, only slightly ravaged, and she hastened to gather them up before he could do any further damage.

"Go away, Hob. I've got work to do." She knew from experience that this usually had the opposite effect from her intention, but it was worth a try.

"Talking about us, he was." He pointed his finger at her. "The Fair Folk, he named us." He fell over, clutching his stomach, kicking his legs in the air. "Hee heee heeee! Maybe we'll visit him one merry moonlit night, and then he can write for fifteen years with his scratchy gold pen and still not be done with it."

"They wouldn't believe him, Hob. It would be the end of his academic career. He may be a stuffed shirt, but I wouldn't wish that on him." One thing she had learned was not to wish anything on anybody—or at least, not where They could hear her. But of course, that was why they'd come to the lecture this morning. Her heart had beat faster, hearing them named, out loud in the dusty lecture room, for all of six diligent students to hear. Maybe now, at last, she might learn something about them. Something true, not moonshine and poppycock.

"It was quite interesting, I thought. All that about the fairy mounds and everything." She'd stopped asking direct questions long ago, but just sometimes, if you were casual enough and looked the other way, you might glean something. A seed, a grain of wheat among the chaff.

"Pfff! Why live under hill when you can dance with moonbeams and ride the rainbow?" He peered at her sidelong. "What's your writing, then? All these little creeping words, falling out of your pen. What does it say?"

Hopeless, to try not to show her feelings. They might not read thoughts (without looking, she imagined the sharpener inside the blue mug on the shelf, but Hob did not seem to react at all), but They always, always knew when she was excited, or upset. As she'd discovered, to her cost.

She crouched down, to meet him eye to eye, but as usual he avoided her gaze. Gently, she said,

"You can't read. I could teach you if you like."

He spun away, over the back of the armchair, and a second later she ducked as a book came flying at her. "Idle, good-for-nothing scamp! Away with you, back to your dungheap!" Suddenly he was right next to her, twisting her ear painfully. "You, boy, how far is it to London town?"

Then on the other side of the room, in a tiny voice, cowering on the floor, "Threescore mile and ten, Sir."

"And never you forget it!" drawing himself up tall, stabbing at the air. "God's breath, what sins have I committed, to draw such a penance?"

Felicity, rubbing her ear, raised her voice to interrupt the charade. "But Hob, my dear, it's not like that now. Teachers don't hit children, or throw things at them. It's not allowed."

"How do they learn, then?" He looked up at her, head on one side.

"I don't know. They learn because they want to, because it's fun and useful—or at least, some of the time it is. And because there are rewards. Praise, and good marks, and—that sort of thing."

"Bzzz, bzzz, this house is full of bees!" He ran around, arms outstretched. "Be careful, they might sting."

She gave it up. At some point, like just before exams when she could least afford the time or the energy, he might remind her of her offer; not that he'd ever be able to sit still for long enough to learn anything. Her sympathies, on the whole, were with the teacher. But there was a thought . . .

"When did you go—I mean, um, your teacher doesn't sound very nice. No wonder you didn't learn."

He cackled. "Not mine, oh no! Not for the likes of me. Spying, I was, while Master Hugh learned his declensions. "Bellum, bellum, bellum, belli, bello, bella blah blah, and a bang on the head with a big book to make it all stick and not run out of his ears and away under the floorboards, food for mice and beetles. Oh, but we paid him back, we chased him out, the naughty moths made holes in his black gown, they crept into his ears and ate up the lovely long Latin words."

He paused, rocking to and fro, his eyes shining. "Only rags and tags he had left, in the end. No mortal use to anybody. Out with him!"

"If I don't get this essay done, that's what will happen to me."

"And if you do, you'll go to the smoky folky place, you and that one with hair like a ripe wheatfield."

"Oh, you heard that. Yes, that's the plan." Too late, Felicity saw where this was going.

"I'll come too!" And he vanished.

She sighed, and went to put on the kettle. Strong coffee was called for; her thoughts were scattered like the things strewn around her room. How long was it since boys had been taught that way? Hob might behave like a hyperactive child, but he was old, much older than he looked. Unless, of course, he was making it all up, which was entirely possible.

She got down a mug, then hesitated and lifted the blue one from its place. Inside was no pencil sharpener, just a pill wood-louse, curled into a hopeless dusty ball. Gently, she tipped it into her palm, took it to the window and dropped it into the flowerbed below. Far from home, probably, and utterly bewildered, but still.

"Off you go," she murmured, but didn't stay to see if it would uncurl. There were words to be written. Some of the pages were crumpled, and the ink was smeared in places. She saw herself handing it in:

"Sorry, Dr. Barnes, a fairy tried to make holes in it. But I stopped him!" The picture made her laugh out loud. Would she wish them away, despite everything?

It was a pointless question. That was one wish she could never have. Sighing, she picked up her pen.

Chapter 25

Nearly an hour later, Felicity slipped in at the back of the crowded cellar. It was indeed smoky, and the dank tang of real ale settled in the back of her throat even before she'd fought her way to the bar and got her half-pint. She couldn't see who was performing, or even hear much over the people talking around her, but then there was a wave of applause, and the crowd shifted a bit, people moving to the bar and greeting friends. While the singer was giving his patter, winding up to the next song, she made her way to the front.

There was no sign of Hob; but then, there wouldn't be. He wouldn't turn up here in his real form—if it was his real form, and not just another layer of make-believe. As the next song began, she scanned the crowd. He could be that dark-haired youth dressed like a Victorian gamekeeper, in moleskin trousers and a hat with a feather, or maybe that man with the huge beard sitting at the bar, smoking a pipe. Completely by accident, she had brought them to a place where all sorts of eccentricities could quietly flourish. As long as they looked moderately human, no one would bat an eyelid.

Or maybe not. She couldn't see Hob for the moment, but there, unmistakeably, was Elfrida. In full Queen Mab splendour, just as Felicity remembered from that first meeting in the woods. Not so very tall, her long dark hair caught back in a silver snood, and that marvellous brocaded green dress falling almost to her feet. Silver snakes wound about her arms and neck, and one hand was raised as she turned to accept a glass from someone behind her. A little space formed, as people drew back to get a better look. It wasn't the clothes or the jewels, or even the perfect heart-shaped face and those demurely lifted eyes. She shone. She glowed, somehow, in a way that caught your eye and made you never want to look away. It was the first time Felicity had seen her like this, out among people. It would not do, not at all.

The place was crowded now, except where Elfrida stood. Heads were turning away from the stage, and there was a growing buzz of excitement. The performers, acoustic guitar and Dylan-soundalike, halfway through some endless hard times number, began to falter. Felicity elbowed her way through to the inner circle, where the Queen was holding court. Elfrida knew she was there, of course she did, but gave no sign of recognition. So Felicity did something she had never done before.

Before she had time to be afraid, she went straight over and took Elfrida by the arm. In her ear, she whispered, "Tone it down!"

Her hand tingled. *Please don't turn me into a frog*, she thought. *Not here, among all these moving feet.* Urgently, she pressed on. "They'll think you're a performer or something. You can't attract attention like this!"

At last, Elfrida turned towards her. "Shall I perform, then?" She spoke loudly, playing to her audience. "What shall it be, gentlemen? A masque, a part-song? For sure, we can do better than that groaning fellow. Is he in pain, do you think?"

"Stop it!" Felicity hissed, under cover of the rising laughter. "Come away now!" She pulled at Elfrida's arm.

"Touch me not." It was said mildly enough, but Felicity snatched her fingers back as though they had been burned.

"Sorry. Sorry, I forgot. But really, you can't do this. If you're going to show up wherever I am, you must blend in. Look ordinary. Like me."

Elfrida raised her voice again. "Where's the fun in that? You bring me to this wondrous place, with more people than I ever saw in one room before, and you ask me to be ordinary?"

The audience was growing by the second. They laughed. Somewhere in the crowd, a young man's voice, barely broken, said, "Live the dream, babe!" and was cheered by his mates. Beer slopped as they clinked mugs. Elfrida raised hers, then sipped a little. She made a face.

"Pah! What's drowned in this piss water?" Under the next wave of laughter, she said quietly "Like you, you say?" The next moment, her face was changing, melting, and there stood Felicity herself; only not as she was now, in jeans and a grey smock, with her hair caught back in a ponytail. A child, wide-eyed, with a smear of dirt on her pale face and twigs caught in that crinkly red hair that would never let a comb through.

There was a gasp, and swearing from the crowd as the front rows stepped back suddenly. Only Felicity stayed put, gazing into those frightened, yearning eyes. *That's how I was, back then. That's how she first saw me.*

"How you still could be if you had chosen right." It had been no more than a few seconds. Queen Mab was back, and already people were doubting what they had seen, making jokes about the strength of the ale. Drinking deep, to wash away their fear.

"Please, we have to get out of here. I know you're having fun, but it won't be fun for me later. Look, there's my friend Steph, she's coming over."

"Hey, Fliss, what's going on? We thought you were never coming, and—who's this?" Steph looked around, taking in the uncertain mood. Queen Mab had faded in her turn, leaving a dark-haired girl in an unfashionable dress, too small to see over people's heads to the stage, where at last the next number was getting under way.

"Hi, Steph! This is, umm—this is Ellie from home. We kind of knew each other at school. She's come to visit, but she's not feeling very well. I think we'd better get some air. Come on, Ellie, this way. Here, let me take that pint, that's probably what's done it, I should have warned you. Sorry, Steph, see you later." And Felicity waved a hand as she steered Elfrida towards the stairs.

For a miracle, she came quietly. She said nothing until they were out in the quad, and then she stopped in the middle of the path, heedless of people shoving past. She looked up at the night sky, bruise-coloured and starless from the city lights, and goosebumps came up on her bare arms.

"Are you cold, Elfrida? You can borrow my coat if you like."

The fairy shook her head, and her eyes reflected the lights in the quad.

"Never cold, never hungry, remember? But the world is bigger than I knew, and full of marvels. I'm glad you chose this way, after all. We'll see them together, you and I."

"I suppose we will." *If I'd really known what I was choosing . . .* Her thought was cut off as Hob arrived from nowhere, tumbling at their feet.

"Why not inside in the warm? They wondered where you'd got to, all the silly mooncalves. You mazed them, my queen." And he was off again, doing handsprings across the lawn. Felicity opened her mouth to call "Not on the grass!" and then realised that of course, no-one else could see him. He had been there in the folk club cellar, but the people she'd suspected were just ordinary university folk with their everyday oddities. Hob hardly ever shapeshifted, or not that she'd seen. He was his usual goblin self, always.

She turned back to Elfrida. "If you're going to visit me, you need to be inconspicuous. Or invisible, like him. Otherwise, things just start happening around you, and then you won't see anything except your own ripples."

"Ha! Very clever. I shall do as I please, sweet Felicity, and you shall do it with me. Silly girl! The glamour opens the way to all sorts of pleasures, and we'll sample them all before we're done!"

Oh, you're hungry all right! Hob's mischief-making was simple by comparison. How was she going to get through the next three years, get a degree, get a life?

Elfrida was watching her. "Foolish, to worry so much," she said. "You'll be old and wrinkled soon enough. We'll ease your path, never fear."

And that's the problem. I just bet you will! Aloud, she said, "Not tonight. I'm going home now." *And you can't stay without me.* If they really could read her thoughts, too bad. Where was her pencil sharpener now?

By the time she got back to her room, they were both gone. All was tidy and quiet, just as she had left it, except for two things. On top of her essay there was a curl of pencil shaving. And next to it, the drawing she'd been doing when Steph arrived. She'd hidden it between the pages of writing, but now it lay there in full view. Hob, or as near a likeness as she could manage, with his ugly goblin face, the huge misshapen ears, the bow legs and twiggy hands. She hadn't quite finished it, but somebody had kindly done it for her, adding a huge bushy beard and a forked tail.

Chapter 26

If her companions were around in the next few days, Felicity never saw them. She was busy, going to lectures and finding her way about the city, working, and making the first tentative steps towards new friendships. Quiet happiness bored them; it was upsets and intensity that drew their attention.

And yet, coming around a corner sometimes in one of the older colleges, she would be stopped in her tracks by the sheer beauty of an ancient quad, or the sweet harmony of steep-pitched roofs, mellow mediaeval brickwork and the dance of leaves. There was intensity enough and to spare in her surroundings, in the flood of new ideas, in simply not being on the farm any more. She could feel herself growing, stretching, becoming something new, like a forest sapling when the sun breaks through. In all this seethe of novelty, there was almost no room for regret.

Together, she and Steph made a vow to sample every folk club and film society that the university had to offer. It looked as though three years would not be nearly enough to take them all in, but as Steph said, "We'll have a lot of fun trying!" Five weeks into their first term, they had sat through quite a few memorably terrible arthouse movies, had some delightful surprises, and grown adept at fending off advances wherever they went. Steph, tall and blond and confident, drew most of the attention, but Felicity got her share too.

"It's only because there are so few women to go around," she said as they escaped from the latest event. "Did you hear that idiot? He was even paying me compliments on my hair!"

Steph stopped, so that Felicity had to stop too. "Why do you always do that?" she asked.

"Do what?" Felicity stepped aside as a group of drunken rugby players barged past, celebrating some famous victory. One of them grabbed her and attempted a sort of waltz, bumping into the others until they managed to pull him away. Steph had not moved.

"Put yourself down. You've got lovely hair."

Felicity laughed. "You're the only person in the world to think so!"

"No, I'm not. That guy in the club was all over you. And he's not the only one."

"That was the booze talking! For goodness sake, he could hardly string two words together."

"Fliss, you're doing it again. Why can't you take a compliment?"

"Come on, there's another horde of barbarians on the way." They walked on, and Felicity concentrated on watching her step in the dark. Steph, for a mercy, said nothing more until they were inside the college grounds, suddenly quiet and peaceful after the midnight mayhem in the streets outside.

"Cup of tea?" Felicity was glad it was Steph who had spoken first. Although there had been no sign of fairy mischief for a while, she never quite knew what she would find when she opened the door to her room. Best to be alone for that moment.

Steph's window looked towards the gardens behind the college. Sometimes you might see a barn owl or a fox, but tonight it was utterly quiet, moon-drenched. Steph turned out the light as she handed Felicity her tea, and they gazed out at the sleeping garden.

"Is it really true that no one's ever said how gorgeous your hair is?"

"Do you know how many ways there are to make fun of red hair? Carrot top, coppernob, ginger nut; and those are just the nice ones. Maybe people were more polite at your school, I don't know."

"Where did it come from? Do your parents have red hair?"

Felicity laughed. "What about the milkman, do you mean? I've had that one, too, a few times. No, they don't, or not now. Mum might have done when she was younger, but she's never said. It's grey now. My Dad's hair was red when he was young, or so I'm told. He hasn't got a lot left."

"But surely they don't make fun of you? Not your parents? I mean, school is fair enough in a way, that's what happens, but . . ." Steph shook back her own hair, and fell silent.

Welcome to my world, Felicity thought. And she tasted the idea of a family who praised you, who comforted you when you were teased or bullied, and encouraged you to explore all the many ways you might grow. It lodged in her throat like a lump of gristle, and she could not have spoken just then, even if she had wanted to.

"Sorry," said Steph, and touched her gently on the arm. "Insensitive."

Felicity shook her head. *Just naïve, and utterly sure of your own sweet reality.* "Not your fault," she said. Wanting to make amends, she added, "Actually, there was one person once."

Immediately the words were out, she regretted them. Damn! The unforgettable moment came back to her. Elfrida, tall and dazzling, crowned with May blossom, reaching down with one white hand to touch her hair. "Welcome, little firefly." The wave of delight that surrounded her, bore her up and transformed her, no longer a tearstained child with dirty knees, but a beautiful young woman with flame-coloured hair. That night, enveloped in fairy glamour, she could have had the world at her feet. And nothing, she realised suddenly, not all the joy of learning and the warmth of friendship, could match that feeling. Maybe nothing ever could.

Steph was watching her, waiting for some revelation,

something that would create a little intimacy between them, a shared secret. And there it was; the barrier that got between her and the world. Her own doing; there was no one else to blame. The bargain she'd made, with no idea what she was bargaining away.

"Oh, just a teacher who was visiting, once," she said. And the moment passed. The door closed.

If Steph was hurt or disappointed, she passed it off gracefully. *So well brought up.* All she said was, "Well, you'd better get used to it from now on. But d'you know what, I actually quite fancied that guy who bought us drinks. Tony something or other, from Caius. We could try out their film club on Thursday. What do you reckon?"

Chapter 27

Thursday night, another crowded room, peering through a forest of tall young men, to get smoke-hazed glimpses of the flickering black-and-white images. It was four hours long, in Spanish, and the subtitles were at the bottom of the screen. Nothing but loyalty kept Felicity in her seat.

She glanced over at Steph and Tony. They were both seemingly immersed in the film, but their hands told a different story. Would they even notice if she left? Between her and the door were rows of closely packed seats, people in the aisles, people leaning against the walls. For the first time since coming to Cambridge, she missed her secret companions. They came and went as they pleased, and she'd been doing a good job of boring them lately. What if she tried to summon them now?

Summon. There was a dangerous word. You couldn't control or manipulate them, or only in very small ways. If they got wind of it, there'd be payback, as she knew from bitter experience. But they did turn up when there was excitement afoot, or when she was in distress.

She looked around again. No chance of excitement here! In a spirit of enquiry, she dug her nails into the web between her finger and thumb, but could not bring herself to the point of real pain. Biting her tongue was no good, either. *Take responsibility*, she told herself sternly. *Either put up with it, or just get up and go.*

The flickering on the screen faded to white, and there was swearing from the back of the room where the projector was mounted. The soundtrack droned on for another minute or two, before someone finally killed it. One or two people left the room, and a welcome blast of fresh air wafted in. Now! Before they could make an announcement about fixing it in five minutes, she stood up and made her way to the door.

Outside, the wind was blessedly cool for about five seconds, and then bitterly cold. She hesitated, wondering whether to wait for Steph to emerge, while its icy fingers found their way under her coat and down her neck.

"Straight from the Ural Mountains, wherever they are, or so everyone keeps telling me. Though being frozen to death is probably a more merciful way to go than slow torture." She couldn't see him very well, haloed by the light from the windows, but he was young, and muffled in a heavy winter coat that looked much warmer than her own.

"Glad I'm not the only one!" She was shivering. "Sorry, I've got to go."

"Let's try the bar. Come on, it's just round the corner."

Well, why not? Pulled along by his certainty, she followed.

"Are you at Caius, then?" she asked as they found themselves a table. He was a pale, fair-haired young man, not much taller than herself. She liked what she saw.

"Yes, doing History. You?" He set down the drinks.

"Newnham. Arch and Anth." She was getting used to the shorthand they used around here. No one ever asked where you were from, or what your parents did. They were all too busy re-inventing themselves. There was nothing else but here, and now.

"Oh, interesting!" He sounded almost as though he meant it, but Felicity was not yet adept enough to read the nuances in the well-modulated public-school voices around her, and always on the alert for mockery.

"Do you think so?" She picked up her ale and drank. Too much, too fast. *Dutch courage.* It worked; the alcohol went straight to her head, made her reckless, ready to take risks.

"Yes, of course! I might have chosen that myself if I'd known a bit more beforehand. But you can't really, can you? Unless you had a teacher at school that knew about it, or something. How did you choose?"

She hesitated. But that was fine, here. Instead of assuming you were figuring out a quick cover story, people just thought that you were thinking deeply before you answered.

"Well, I wanted to figure out what makes people tick, if that doesn't sound too pretentious. The ways we make sense of the world." He was watching her, listening intently, as though he really did want to know. "And especially, the stories we tell. Mythology, religion, all that sort of thing."

He was nodding now. "History is nothing but mythology, when it comes down to it. Good subject for an essay! I might suggest it to my supervisor; earn some credit. I could do with some of that."

Felicity wasn't sure she agreed with him, but she understood that he was trying to agree with her. It was pleasant, slowly getting warm again, in good company. He didn't intimidate her, this unconfident boy, and he wasn't afraid to let his guard down.

"Hey," she said, "I thought we'd left Deep and Meaningful behind."

He laughed. "God, that film was terrible! Do you think anyone was actually enjoying it?"

"Well, nobody's followed us in here. I think my friend stayed, but she wasn't exactly concentrating on the film."

"Sensible girl," he said, and then blushed, deep red.

"Were you watching us?"

"Well, er . . . Well, yes!" He picked up his mug, traced wet circles on the table. "To be honest," and suddenly he was looking directly at her, "you were the most interesting thing in the room."

Felicity stood up, a little unsteady. "Look, I'd better go.

My friend will be wondering where I've got to. Thanks for the drink."

"Please don't go! I'm sorry if I said the wrong thing. I'm always doing that. I wasn't trying to pick you up or anything, honestly. It was just the truth." She looked down at him, and saw that there were tears in his eyes.

"I'll see you around, maybe." And yet she hesitated. He looked so forlorn, in genuine distress. She sat down again, leaned forward.

"I don't like being watched, all right? Sorry if I over-reacted."

"God, no need to apologise. You must get so sick of men staring at you wherever you go. Fair enough; I promise I won't look at you ever again. Or maybe only sideways, when you're not looking."

Despite herself, she laughed. "It does get a bit wearing." *But it's not the men around here that are the problem. I've never played the flirting game, and I don't know the rules, but that's not why I wanted to run away. It's just that at home, being watched meant someone was about to tell you off, or make fun of you, or maybe something worse. Or it's the fairies, poking and prying, so I never have any privacy.* Of course, she couldn't say any of that to this nice boy who was trying so hard.

"Well, I know one thing about you," she said, trying for lightness to break the tension.

"What's that?"

"You can't keep promises. You're watching me again already."

Once again, the colour rose in his face. He started yet another apology. Felicity had the strange sensation that she was looking through a lens, something that distorted shape and perspective. After a minute, it came to her.

"Can I ask you something?" she said, interrupting whatever it was he'd been saying.

"Umm, yes, I suppose so."

"Did you get bullied at school?"

He went "Hah!" and then took a deep breath. "That wasn't what I was expecting."

"But did you?"

"Well, yes, of course. Doesn't everyone? Unless you get to be the bully yourself, I guess."

"But you didn't do that, did you?"

"No, actually, I didn't. It can be kind of hard not to—I don't know how it works in girls' schools—but it was a bit of a principle of mine." He was sitting up straighter, and his voice had taken on a different tone.

"I don't know about girls' schools either, but I'd guess the old rules apply." She picked up her ale, took a deep swallow.

Nothing ventured, nothing gained. "The thing is, I started to feel like a bully just then, like I could be cruel to you and you would let me. That's not a place I ever want to go to. It scared me a bit." She shivered. "And I got the feeling you were actually scared of me. It took me a while to work out what it was. I don't think anyone's ever been scared of me before, and I'm not sure I like it."

She stopped, appalled. What on earth had possessed her, to babble on like that? It was definitely time to leave, fast. But somehow, here she still was.

"I think I get what you're saying." He was excited now, his eyes shining. "You're saying that the way we approach people, if—for example—we expect them to be stronger than us or not friendly, then it's more likely they really will be like that."

"Sort of. And if you look confident and in control, people will let you be."

"Like your friend at Clare folk club the other day? She had all the men at her feet, didn't she?"

"Wait a minute. You were watching me then too?"

"Oh God, please don't go! Let me at least try to explain before you rush off. It wasn't like you're thinking, at least I hope you're not thinking that at all, but I wouldn't blame you if you did." He picked up his beer and tried to take a swallow, managing to slop some of it down his front in his agitation. Felicity waited. *I'm really not afraid of this guy. Interesting.*

"OK," he said, when he'd wiped up the spilt beer with the end of his scarf. "It was like this. I was somewhere near the back when I saw your friend come in—not the one you were with just now. It was another one, small, with dark hair. She stopped at the bottom of the stairs, looked around at everything as though she'd never been anywhere so brilliant in her life before, and then she—she sort of changed." He paused, feeling for the right words. Felicity could have helped him out here, but she said nothing.

"It was as though she got taller," he said at last. "And somehow so amazing that you just wanted to keep watching her. Like a film star or something. Although I've seen a few film stars, I worked in Harrods at Christmas once, and they're not like that in real life. But she was. I tried to get closer, but a lot of other people seemed to have the same idea, and the braver ones were talking to her. Someone bought her a drink, and then you were there."

He stopped again, took a deep drink, and didn't spill it this time. "I couldn't quite see what happened next, but everyone moved back suddenly and someone trod on my foot, and when I could actually see again, she just looked normal, as though she'd turned the lights down. I didn't know people could do that." Slowly, he came back from his story. "So when I saw you just now in the film club, of course I was watching you. You don't forget a thing like that in a hurry."

"Well, you probably should," said Felicity at last.

"Why? I know it wasn't just me. Or the ale. She did something. And you tried to stop her, didn't you?"

"Look. My friend's gone home again now. You probably won't see her again." *Or not if I can help it.* "She's a bit—unstable."

He laughed. "Is that what you call it?"

"That's what it is. She likes playing games with people, and she doesn't care if they get hurt." *And I hope to God she's nowhere near me just now.*

"Okay," he said slowly. "So why is she your friend, then? If you don't actually like her."

"It's not that I don't like her, not at all. It's just—" *What? What do I actually feel about Elfrida, and the rest? They've been in my life for nearly as long as I can remember, and I've got no choice about that, whether I like it or not. So I suppose I try not to think about how I feel.* Aloud, she said, "She's pretty much like a sister to me. And they say you can't choose your relatives. You make the best of what you get." *Elfrida, marvellous friend, forgive me.*

He was nodding again. "Oh, I know what you mean. I've got an older brother, and boy, could I do without him sometimes!"

You don't have any idea what I mean. There was the barrier again. With Steph, with this boy whose name she didn't even know, with all those other potential friendships. She had made her choice, and the gates to fairyland had closed behind her. At the time she'd thought that was it. She'd chosen the everyday world, and was free to immerse herself in it. Only she wasn't, of course. The things she couldn't say would always get in the way. *It's not that I don't like Elfrida. Sometimes, I come close to hating her.*

"Sure," she said absently. "Look, I'd better get back. It's been nice meeting you. Oh—I'm Felicity, by the way." She started to hold out her hand, then took it back again. What did you do next, here? She'd seen people hugging and kissing each other, but she hadn't hugged anybody—or been hugged—since she was very small, and she wasn't about to start now. Luckily, he didn't seem to notice.

"I know. I heard her call you that, remember? And I'm Sebastian. Please, can I see you again?"

"I don't know, yes, maybe." She was flustered now, just wanting to be away from here, to collect herself. She had said too much.

"Are you going to the folk club next week? We could meet there. If that's OK with you, of course."

"Yes, OK, fine. I'll see you there." In the end, all she managed was a half-wave as she worked her way through to the door. When she finally reached it, she looked back, and he was still sitting there, gazing after her. He raised his pint. *So much for not watching!*

Chapter 28

She set off walking fast, not back to the film club but heading for home, for safety. The flagstones were slick with ice, and her breath steamed, condensing in the wool of her scarf. By the time she got there, it would be frozen, and she thought with pure pleasure of the big old-fashioned radiator in her room, belting out heat like a tame obedient dragon. The winters might be fiercer here, but with central heating you could bear anything. And she realised that, already, she thought of her room in college as home.

"That was interesting." Somehow, there was Elfrida, keeping pace with her on the icy path. She was wearing little green slippers and a flimsy sleeveless dress, and looked completely comfortable. Felicity stopped so suddenly that she almost fell over.

"God, you made me jump! I wish you wouldn't do that."

The fairy only smiled. "You could have been more encouraging to that nice young man," she said.

"And I wish you wouldn't watch me when I don't know you're there! It isn't fair. If I'd known what it would be like, I'd have been more careful about what I agreed to."

"Foolish humans," said Elfrida. "Always trying to set terms." She looked sideways at Felicity. "You're getting cold, standing there."

"Huh!" Felicity walked on, shoulders hunched. After a few paces she stopped again.

"Were you listening the whole time?" she demanded.

As usual, Elfrida simply ignored the question. "You should see him again. You liked him. Why do you make things so complicated?"

Well, two could play the question-ignoring game. "For your information, he was more interested in you than in me! So why don't *you* go out with him if you think he's so nice?" As soon as the words were out, she regretted them. Elfrida was quite capable of doing exactly that if the fancy took her. Felicity shuddered to think where it might lead.

"Ah, jealousy already! That's good. You will meet him again, and then we'll see what we shall see."

"Elfrida, please go away. If I make friends with somebody, that's my business."

"Is it so? But you were glad enough when the stupid picture-maker broke, and gave you both a reason to slip out together."

For a third time, Felicity stopped suddenly, and the cyclist coming up behind her had to swerve off the path. He swore at her as he skidded on the frosty grass, barely avoiding a fall.

"Was that your doing? Why are you so keen for me to see Sebastian again?"

Again, she got no answer. She gave up and walked on, but just as she reached the college gates, Elfrida spoke.

"It's time you went with a man. How old are you? Nineteen summers? Would have been long married with a babe in arms and another beneath your belt, before the world turned topsy-turvy."

"That's none of your business! Leave me alone!" There were other students waiting for the porter to let them in, and some turned to look at her, hearing the vehemence in her voice. Felicity lowered it to a furious whisper.

"You've no right to interfere in my life like this! When I agreed you and Hob could visit me, I didn't mean you could push me whichever way you fancy. It won't work, don't you understand? If I can't make my own choices, it'll all go wrong. Please, Elfrida, even if you think I'm making a mistake sometimes, you've got to let me. Surely you can see that?"

"Are you going to stand there all night, talking to yourself? Some of us would quite like to get our beauty sleep." The porter stood in the doorway, waiting. Everyone else had gone in, and Felicity stood alone on the frosty path.

"Sorry!" She hurried past him, head down. It was after two o'clock in the morning, and she had an early lecture tomorrow, an essay to write before Monday, and her bike saddle had been stolen so she would have to walk everywhere until she could get a new one. There was no time to think about Elfrida, and certainly no time to think about Sebastian. And yet, even not thinking about him made her smile.

A new friend, perhaps.

For the first time, Felicity missed the nine o'clock lecture. She got there at 9.15; there was ice on the pavements and walking was a treacherous business. Inside, Dr. Barnes was holding forth to three dedicated followers, and she could not bring herself to walk in and become the focus of attention. She hesitated by the noticeboard, debating whether to go to the library or pick her way down to the bike shop, half-listening to the two older students standing there.

"Oh, you should go!"

"What for? It's not on the syllabus, and I've got enough on my plate already."

"He doesn't do many lectures, and he is completely bonkers. Talks about fairies as if he actually believed in them. Kind of sweet, in a slightly creepy way."

The second girl gave a mock shudder. "I think I'll pass on that, thanks. Let's get a coffee while it's quiet."

They moved off. Felicity scanned the notices. Which one

had they been looking at? Then she saw it. "'The Fair Folk: What are we to them?' Professor T. Edgerley, 10 A.M. Tuesday November 19th, Sidgwick Lecture Room."

She stood very still. What are we to them? It was probably just a way to pique the curiosity of his audience, but if so, it had worked. That was a question she would very much like to answer. In theory, students could attend any lecture they chose, in any subject, although she had not yet tested that in practice. Now, it seemed, was the moment. There would just be time to get there.

In fact, she arrived a good five minutes early, surprised by her own sense of urgency. In her sensible, thinking brain, she knew that of course this elderly don would not have the answers to any of her dilemmas. It was her heart's yearning that drove her; a simple longing not to be alone with what she knew. If she could not speak the words, maybe there might just be someone else out there who would know without the need for speech. Surely she could not be the only one?

The lecture room was like a small theatre, with tiers of seats, so that although she chose a seat at the back, she was easily visible. That could not be helped, but when the professor went to the podium, he cast a brief glance around at his audience, and did not seem to notice her at all. There were about twenty students there, and none she recognised. She began to relax a little.

"You will all be familiar, I assume, with the folklore of our native isles," he began without preamble. "Or if you are not, you should be by now." There was a brief ripple of laughter, and Felicity guessed they must be third years or even postgraduate students. "You will know that the stories gathered from the length and breadth of the country have a great deal in common. The appearance of the Fair Folk, it is true, varies a great deal, from diminutive to giant, and from beautiful to hideous, but that is of no account if we recall that they can change their shapes at will. In short, what we see is what they permit us to see."

In the group of young men sitting two rows below her, someone snorted, and they all began elbowing each other and sniggering. The professor paused for a moment, and then continued as though nothing had happened. "The fact that we call them 'Fair Folk' or 'Fairies,' sometimes corrupted to 'Fairises' or 'Pharisees' in the southern counties, reflects our own human desire to placate them and so avert disaster, rather than a reference to their physical beauty; rather as the ancient Greeks named the Furies, who wrought such terrible vengeance on humans who offended the gods, the 'Eumenides' or 'Kindly Ones.'"

Felicity watched him as he spoke. A slight man, probably in his mid-sixties, in a shabby academic gown, with a shock of white hair, a sharp nose and a slightly crooked mouth. He stood there, apparently completely at ease, his hands resting on the lectern in front of him. He must be used to ridicule, she thought. Studying folklore is one thing; actually believing in it is quite another. But probably he was just playing with his audience, having a quiet joke at their expense. That would be it.

His next words made her sit up straighter.

"One of the common factors in the stories is that the actions of the Fair Folk—for so we may as well call them—are not to be trusted. They give wishes that never quite deliver what they promise. They grant aid, but always with conditions, and sometimes with a terrible price. They play tricks on us; they steal babies, children and sometimes full-grown men and women, and if they ever return, they are changed, or so much time has gone by that their loved ones are long dead and the world has left them behind.

"Now, the usual and most obvious question to be asked is, 'What does this tell us about the psychology of the people who relate these stories?' Note that I did not say, 'The people who made up these stories.' Whether they were made up or not, they were repeated again and again, and passed down the generations. Here and there, in the more isolated and rural parts of Britain, they are told to this day. It is obvious that they serve some purpose to those who tell them.

"However, that is not the question we are addressing today. My contention is that there may be a great deal to be learned by turning the question around. In short," and here he paused, looked around at his audience, and permitted himself a small smile, "I am proposing that we consider what their behaviour may tell us about their motivation. Or to put it another way: what do they want from us?"

With one part of her attention, Felicity was aware that he had gone on to address this question in general terms. But that was a distraction, just like the whispered comments from the group below. How could it be that in all the time she had spent with Them, she had never thought to ask herself:

What do They want from me?

Or to be even more specific: *What does Elfrida want from me?*

I was a child. I never questioned why they should be interested in me at all. I took it for granted that they had allowed me in just because they wanted to.

It's obvious, now, that Elfrida is hungry to experience the world through our connection. That's what brought me here, to this lecture hall. But what about in the past? What have they asked of me?

There's only one request they've ever made. That was on the night when they came into the farmhouse. The night Alys took Christine. Her skin prickled, thinking of that.

Had they planned it all along?

She shivered, rubbing her arms that had come up in goosebumps. Even now, her mind shied away from the thought of that night like a nervous pony spooked by its own shadow. Automatically, she began to doodle a margin of flowers and leaves along the edge of her notes. Some weeks ago, she had discovered by accident that it helped her to empty herself of emotion, and so avoid attracting Hob and Elfrida to her. But it was already too late.

That flicker of movement on the far side of the lecture hall was not somebody getting up to leave, or raising a hand to ask a question. It was Hob, crab-walking along the desktops, peering over people's shoulders or even into their faces as they wrote. As she watched, he took hold of the pen in the hand of a girl sitting a few rows to her left, so that her writing trailed off into spider-squiggles across the page. Felicity dug her fingernails into her own palm, as though by not moving and making no sound, she could somehow make this not be happening. But the girl simply shook her pen impatiently, flapped her hand to shoo away an imaginary fly, and went on writing.

Felicity breathed again. They could not see him. Their notes might fall to the floor or their shoelaces come undone, and it would be no more than a nuisance. He would get tired of the game eventually, and vanish as abruptly as he had arrived. But even as she turned her attention back to the lecture, she became aware that the professor had stopped talking. Around the room, people were beginning to look up, to wonder what was going on, but Professor Edgerley paid no attention to any of them. His eyes were fixed, unmistakably, on Hob.

Hob's back was turned to him, and he was scanning the rows of faces, as more and more students looked up. Some were whispering and nudging each other. One, sitting alone, simply sat with his mouth slightly open, staring. Hob took a sudden flying leap and landed right in front of him, shouting "Boo!" into his face, scattering papers to the floor. He gave a start, and dived under the desk to retrieve his notes, but he did not react to Hob at all. He sat there shaking with laughter, and then he looked up directly at Felicity, and winked.

She stared fiercely at him, willing him to disappear. Useless, as ever. There was only one thing to do. She stuffed her notes into her bag and slid out of her seat, thankful to be near the back. A few heads turned as she left, and she felt sorry for the professor. He would think she had walked out of his lecture—and just when it was getting interesting, too. She hoped he might pick up the thread again when she and Hob were gone. Perhaps there would be another opportunity to hear him speak; she would have to look out for that.

She walked fast, not checking to see if Hob was with her; watching him would only encourage more antics. The sun had come out, and frost sparkled on the roofs around the market place. It was in full Christmas swing, with music and coloured lights and a choir singing on the far side. Nearby, chestnuts were roasting on an open brazier, warming and scenting the air. She took a deep breath, and prepared to wade her way through the crowds.

"Excuse me, Miss—?" A hand on her arm, and there was Professor Edgerley, a little out of breath. Without intending it, she took a step back, and his grip tightened.

"I'm so sorry. I didn't mean to startle you." He let go, and she rubbed at her arm as though he had hurt her. "You were at my lecture just now."

Felicity tried to collect herself. "Yes, I was. It was very, um, very interesting, but I have to go now."

"Wait a moment, please. You're not one of my students. Why did you come?"

She took a deep breath, trying to ease the tightness in her chest. "I'm a first year. I just thought it looked . . ." She could not say "interesting" again, that was ridiculous. He was watching her, smiling a little now.

"'Entertaining?' Or possibly 'relevant?' Maybe even 'a potential source of vital information?' She stared down at the ground, clenching her fists. He spoke very softly. "You have a follower, Miss—?"

"Turner," she said automatically. "Felicity Turner. I'm at Newnham."

"So, Miss Turner," he said, speaking even lower, so that she had to come closer to hear him. "Are you in need of help?"

Now she did look up at him, wide-eyed. That was not what she had expected, and nor were the tears that suddenly threatened to fall.

"Ah," he said. "I see. No," and he held up a hand as she started to speak, "do not say anything." He was searching his pockets, looking for something, and then he gave up and grinned at her. "Do you by any chance have a pen and a scrap of paper I can use? I've left everything—and some rather bemused students—back at the Sidgwick room."

He waited, while she searched out a pen and her notepad. She handed them over, and then blushed as he looked at her notes, complete with decorative doodles. He made no comment, just scribbled something and then gave them back to her. "Come at three o'clock on Friday if you can, Miss Turner. Otherwise, leave me a note in my pigeonhole at Emmanuel College. And in the meantime . . . I hope you won't think me impertinent, but my guess is that you have given a promise not to speak about them. Am I right?"

After a long, long moment, she gave a brief nod. Even that felt dangerous, a betrayal. Was Hob watching?

"So," he confirmed that he had understood. "You may not speak. That's not uncommon. But perhaps,"—and he glanced down at the notepad in her hand, "you may be able to draw. Or possibly even to write?"

She stared at him. Her mind was whirling. Was that part of the promise? She knew they could not read, and they had never forbidden the drawings she tried to make, although Hob loved to deface them. Had Elfrida ever said that she must not write? And suddenly she remembered: *Those diaries, still hidden in a jigsaw box in my bedroom at home. I did write about Them, didn't I?*

He was watching her again. "When they make promises to us," he said, "There is generally a loophole so that things do not fall out as expected. But the converse may also be true. Try it and see. And if you would like to show me whatever recollections you have, I should be happy to receive them. Perhaps I may be able to interpret them for you, or assist you in some way. But we have said enough. I must go back, though I doubt whether any of my students will have stayed. Good day to you, Miss Turner." He inclined his head to her, and then began to move away.

"Wait!" she said, and he turned back at once. "I'm sorry about your lecture. And—thank you."

He smiled again. This time, he made her a proper old-fashioned bow, right there in the market-place. "On the contrary," he said. "It is I who should be thanking you."

Chapter 29

She stood there in the middle of the path, until a woman with several shopping bags barged her out of the way. Where was Hob? She could not see him, but that did not mean much. Did she dare to try writing? Her excitement rose as she pictured the dusty jigsaw box and the treasure inside. *I drew Them, over and over again. But I wrote about Them as well.*

Where could she go to be safe? The answer to that, at least, was clear. Nowhere was completely safe, but she had found that libraries were the best places to be if she wanted to work uninterrupted. Not the public library, where people moved around constantly, and even talked to each other, but the college library, or the faculty library perhaps. There was something about the combined effect of all those people studying, she thought, that acted like a sort of fog to dampen any emotion.

At any rate, it was worth a try. But first, she had an essay to write, and a bicycle to mend, and two more lectures to attend this morning. Too much to do; but she took another deep breath, and the rich scent of roasting chestnuts spoke to her of life, and warmth, and ordinary human desires. She bought a bag of them, to warm both her hands and her heart as she threaded her way through the crowded alleys in the marketplace. After all this time, she might just have found an ally. She was not alone.

Friday came, and still she had not tried to put anything down on paper. She had stayed up until three o'clock in the morning last night to finish her essay, and there was plenty more to do before the end of term. None of that really mattered.

I'm afraid. That's the truth of it.

On one level, it made no sense. Elfrida had never been anything but kind to her, had forgiven her when she chose, in the end, not to cross the border; had even given her a precious gift, though she had no idea what to do with it. And yet.

I've seen them change in an instant. I've seen that they can be cruel.

Professor Edgerley was right; people did not call them the Fair Folk for nothing. If you broke the rules, there was always a price to pay.

So what about the professor? What's in it for him?

Well, the answer to that was easy, at least in part. He had built his career on his study of British folklore, so of course he'd be interested in a first-hand account. But she suspected there was more to it than that. Perhaps his interest was driven by some first-hand experience of his own. She might not be able to speak, but she could listen, and if he knew anything that could help her to understand, she was ready to hear it.

Midday found her in the faculty library, sitting in a corner with a blank notepad in front of her. Even now, she held back. In the margin she drew Elfrida as she had appeared at the folk club, tall and beautiful with flowing black hair crowned with white flowers. That was fine; she had done that many times over the years. Underneath the drawing she wrote in her best Celtic script: *ELFRIDA*.

She looked around, and everything was as it should be, as far as she could tell. Next, she closed her eyes and tried to summon up the memory of the night when she had first stepped into their circle: the sights, the sounds and, most important of all, the feeling of joy and awe and thankfulness that had coursed through her when they had finally let her in. It brought tears to her eyes now; all those feelings were still there, as strong and fresh as ever.

Again, she checked, getting up to walk the length of the library so that she could see every desk. Nothing. Lately, she had begun to notice that when they appeared, it was usually in response to some excitement or upset that she was feeling in the here and now. Thinking about the past did not interest them, it seemed. It wasn't much to go on, but it was all she had.

Now or never, she said to herself. But where should she start a story that had no real beginning, and certainly no end? Should she explain about her family, her home? No. This was not really about making things clear for the professor. If she did this, she had to do it for herself. And with that, she picked up her pen and began to write.

Chapter 30

She stuffed the book into her bag, though it was heavy to carry around, and slipped out of the library. Professor Edgerley's rooms were a short walk away in Emmanuel College, and she had come to love that moment when she left the busy street to step through the great gates, past the porter's lodge and into the first quadrangle. It was a kind of magic all of its own, as though everyday life fell away and things became simpler and clearer. Probably, if she had lived here all the time, it would simply have become part of her everyday life, but for now it worked for her. If she had crossed the border, would she really have escaped? Or would she have been like Alys, lurking on the edges of her former life while it left her further and further behind?

No. If I'd crossed over, I wouldn't have stayed near the farm, watching my parents get older and sadder, until it was sold and strangers moved in. I'd have done it properly. I'd have gone Onward, whatever that might hold.

She shivered, pushing that thought away. Here was the entrance to the staircase where Professor Edgerley lived, up two flights of narrow crooked steps that were worn in the middle by hundreds of years of passing feet. The outer door was open. She hesitated.

Shall I push my writing under the door and slip away?

Curiosity won out. She knocked.

"Come in."

The inner door opened with a delicious creak. Felicity stood on the threshold, looking into the study of her dreams. A huge old desk with lots of drawers and compartments, a worn turkey rug whose colours glowed like dusty jewels, and a small fire in the fireplace, with a coal scuttle and a set of fire irons. That gave her a rush of homesickness, sudden and unexpected. She had come to love the enormous iron radiator in her college room, like a sleeping dragon keeping it always warm and dry, but this fire was bright and alive and made its own light. *A room should have a hearth*, she thought. *It's the heart of the place.*

"Ah, Miss Turner!" The professor stood and came to the door, holding out a hand in welcome.

"Sorry to disturb you, sir." Was that the right way to address him? "Only you said . . . So I've brought you this." She fumbled in her bag, pulling out the heavy textbook, almost spilling out pens and tissues across the lovely carpet. He looked quizzically at *Sociology: a New Perspective*, and waited.

"No, it's not that!" She tried to open the book one-handed, and her notes slid out. They both bent to pick them up, and almost bumped heads. She stood up, red with embarrassment, and felt for the door.

"Wait a moment." He held up one long-fingered hand, not looking at her. He glanced down through the sheaf of papers, and his whole body went completely still. She held her breath, and her heart bumped in her chest. No one, no one in the world knew where she had been and what she had done, and she had just given her secret to a perfect stranger, simply because he had asked. What had she been thinking?

"Well now." He looked up at her at last. "Neither of us has turned into a toadstool, it seems. Or not yet, at any rate. Come in, please. Come and sit down," and he indicated a chair by the fire. He looked out onto the staircase, and then closed both doors, outer and inner. Next, he leaned across the desk to close the curtains, and the glow of the fire became the only light until he switched on the reading light above his own armchair.

When he sat down, the light made dark pools of his eyes under those white eyebrows. His nose was a curved blade. He saw her staring.

"My apologies, Miss Turner. No cause for alarm; the wards are to deter unwanted guests, not to keep you in. You are free to go, of course, at any time."

She shook her head, one hand at her mouth. "It's not that," she said again. What could she say? For a moment, there in the moving firelight, he had looked like—but what was the point? She had just entrusted her life to him, and it was too late now to snatch it back and bolt for the door. Whatever he had seen in that brief glimpse, it had been enough.

He was watching her now, with those shadowed eyes. Suddenly he got up and turned on the main overhead light. Electric light, harsh and clear and unambiguous. "Better?" he asked, and his eyes were smiling now.

She nodded. "Thank you," she said. Her voice sounded small and shaky.

"It is I who must thank you. You have given me a pearl of great price, and I shall do my best to safeguard it. More than that. You have given me your trust, as once you gave it, long ago, before you were old enough to know what you did. Am I right?"

She nodded again, mute this time.

"And now you are wondering whether you have just been ensnared again. Or if you are not wondering, you should be. Where the Fair Folk are concerned, almost nothing is as it seems."

He leaned back in his chair, steepling his fingers and looking at her over the joined "V" of his two hands. "So it is entirely pointless for me to assure you that your words are safe with me. But I see that you have a need to trust someone. Something has happened, or you have come to a point where the burden of your secret has become too great. No, don't try to speak," and he held up one hand as she opened her mouth to respond. "The less said, the better. I shall talk, and you may indicate where you think I am straying from the path. How does that sound?"

Felicity just looked at him. *My heart is in my mouth*, she thought. *That's exactly how it feels. I couldn't speak even if I wanted to.*

"Good," said Professor Edgerley. "Now, does this account bring us up to the present day? No? No matter. If there is more to tell, and you feel able to tell it, I shall be happy to receive whatever you have to offer. Please be assured, Miss Turner, that this will not find its way into anything I may write for public consumption. Not in recognisable form, at any rate. Although if we are correct in our assumption that your—followers—do not read, it is very unlikely that it would ever come to their attention." He smiled, then, and suddenly looked two decades younger; a man in his prime with the light of mischief in his eyes. "But of course, the unlikely is the very essence of fairytales, is it not?"

She was only half-listening. All her senses were awake, drinking in her surroundings: the sound of his voice rather than the words, the smell of old upholstery and burning applewood, the dust-motes dancing in the slant of sunlight where the curtains were not quite closed, the warm and living feel of the leather armchair under her hands. Then a sudden jolt of alarm and a rush of terror, and all those lovely safe things counted for nothing.

Something was tapping at the window.

Professor Edgerley looked up. "Don't worry, Miss Turner. The wards will hold. And besides," and he got up, walked to the window and flicked the curtain aside. She almost cried out, her hands to her mouth. There on the window ledge was a pigeon, walking sideways, its claws scratching on the stone. It did not take flight at the sudden movement inside, but peered in and then tapped again at the glass.

"My fault, I fear," he said. "I put out crumbs for them. The porters do not approve." He drew the curtain again, and turned to face her.

Felicity forced in a deep breath, and blew it out. "Wards?" she said, and her voice came out husky. She wanted to curl up in the big chair.

"Well," he said, and came to sit down again. "There are ways to avert their notice, as I'm sure you know. The power of the threshold grows with age. These rooms were built for humans, by humans, more than six hundred years ago, and that intention—to separate inner from outer—is renewed every time a door or a window is closed. Beyond that, there are charms, there are herbs and sigils. It's all in the literature. Some of them have some efficacy, or so I've found."

Felicity cleared her throat. "I don't think that would work for me," she said. "I made a bargain. They—I mean my two 'followers'—can come to me whenever they choose."

"Ah." He looked at her very intently. "But here, in this room, you should be safe." He glanced over at his desk, at the piles of papers and open books. She had interrupted his work; she should go. But as she started to move, he held up a hand.

"They may notice that you were beyond their reach, and you will find it difficult to lie. I think," he said, picking up the diary that lay on the corner of the desk, "we should arrange for you to have the occasional supervision with me. I do not usually teach first years, but They will not know that, of course." She noticed that slight emphasis when he said "They," as though it were an actual name. It was exactly how she thought of Them herself; and as simply as that, she trusted him.

"Let's see," he said. "Would next Friday at three o'clock suit?"

She didn't need to check. Whatever might be on the calendar, it could be moved.

"Excellent. I shall look forward to reading this first instalment, then." He stood up, moved to the door, and bowed slightly as she passed by. "Good day to you, Miss Turner."

Chapter 31

Outside in the empty quad, Felicity felt lighter on her feet, as though she had been carrying a heavy load. Even when she emerged from the college onto the busy street, she wove and dodged between the slow-moving crowds like a dancer. Later, perhaps, there might be time to write the next instalment. Then, from across the road, someone called her name.

"Felicity!" As she looked up, Sebastian began to cross, side-stepping bicycles as he went. In a town where there were more bikes than cars and no one paid much attention to traffic lights, she had learned that you had simply to step into the flood and trust that you would fetch up on the other side, but it was always a test of nerve. In a few moments he stood before her, slightly out of breath and smiling.

"You looked as though you were in a world of your own," he said. Just by stopping, they had created a boulder in the stream of pedestrians on the pavement; people spilled into the road to get around them. "Come on," he said, "let's get a coffee in here." He pushed open the door to Fitzbillies café. She hadn't been in there before; she'd assumed it was a place for tourists rather than students, and in any case her weekly budget was too small for such things. But today she felt expansive and carefree. She followed him in.

Once inside, the moment of decisiveness seemed to have passed. He blushed, and even stammered a little. "I—I mean if you're not in a hurry or anything? Sorry, I should have thought. You're a woman on a mission, aren't you? Have you got time?"

Again, she had that odd sense of power. She wasn't afraid of him; there was no need to be wary. And he had called her "a woman on a mission." She stored that away, to take out and enjoy later.

"Sure. Well, not really, but enough for a cup of tea."

"And a Chelsea bun. You have to try them, they're legendary." He saw her hesitate. "My treat," he said. "I accosted you, so I pay."

It was gracefully done. As she slid into a seat at one of the tiny tables in the window, she banished the anxious voice in her head: *Do I look poor? Can he tell from my accent I'm not middle-class?* When she went to Cambridge, one of her teachers had assured her, it wouldn't matter where she was from or what her parents did for a living. She had already discovered that although this was very far from true, you could get quite a long way by acting as though it were.

There was barely room to struggle out of her coat, but he managed to be in the right place to help her get her arms out, and hang it up on the coat stand by the door while she was settling herself at the table. Another first: no one had ever helped take her coat on or off before. She saw that he did this not to demonstrate his command of the situation, but because it was a simple courtesy that he took for granted.

The Chelsea buns, when they arrived, were cinnamon-fragrant and oozing with sweet stickiness, completely unlike the dry and flaky things she had expected. Finger-licking was necessary, and wordless sounds of appreciation, and there was no room for nervousness.

"This is amazing," she said with complete honesty. "Dr. Barnes gave us his definition of a legend in his lecture last week: 'a traditional story sometimes popularly regarded as historical but not authenticated.' I think we've just authenticated these, so they can't be legendary any more."

"But when you go telling all your friends about them, then

they will be again." He looked serious for a moment. "I wish I'd done anthropology. So much interesting stuff!"

"Trust me, Dr. Barnes manages to make it pretty boring most of the time." *Not like Professor Edgerley,* she almost said. Somehow, she felt wary of talking about him, as though all the things she couldn't talk about might leak out if she spoke his name. "You're doing history, aren't you? You know, you can go to lectures in other subjects if you want to. I went to one the other day."

He made a face. "No time," he said. "I'm already behind with coursework, and I've signed up to be in a play next term." He looked away, wiped up a trail of sweetness with one finger. "You could come too if you like. They're always short of women." He gave her a quick sidelong glance. "It'll be fun!"

Felicity saw that he was trying desperately to mask his eagerness, to play it cool, but that was several steps too far for her. "Sorry," she said, hoping to let him down gently. "I'm no performer. I'll come and watch, though, if you like."

He brightened. "You can be my muse!" Then he blushed as the implication of that sank in. "I—I mean, it would be great, obviously. I'll need all the encouragement I can get."

"Have you done any acting before?"

"Oh yes! At school, you know. But this would be a real step up. People notice you here. I'm hoping to join the Footlights. It can really open doors."

"Do you want to be an actor, then?"

His eyes were alight. He looked, in the sunlight now burning its way through the steamed-up window, absolutely beautiful. *Of course they'll notice you*, she thought. *How could they not?*

"Well, it would be amazing, don't you think? It's not what my parents have in mind," and he laughed, looking aside for a moment, "but if I got offered something, I'm sure they'd come around in the end."

In the last few weeks, Felicity had got used to handling

several thoughts at once, and editing as she went along. *No, it wouldn't be amazing, it would be horrible, being stared at on stage.* And at the same time, *What would it be like to have parents who cared about what you do, apart from not wanting you to be a farmer?*

Out loud, she said, "Gosh. Well, good luck with it. I'd love to come and watch. What do your parents want you to do?"

He made a face. "Civil service, probably, since I've shown no aptitude for anything else."

"That can't be true! You're here, aren't you?" She thought about the choices open to most children, to the ones who'd excluded her from their playground games, knowing an outsider when they saw one. Most of them would live their whole lives in that small place, doing much the same as their parents before them. But it did no good to think that way, not here.

"Well, yes, sure. But what about you?" She could see he felt rebuked, and a little part of her was glad.

"I don't know," she said; nothing but the truth, for once. "Right now, it's enough to cope with my course and everything. I can't see that far ahead."

"Right, right. I should probably be doing the same, but this is too good a chance to pass up. I expect you think I'm a time-waster, don't you?" He looked anxious now, as though he really cared what she thought.

"No, of course not." *You remind me of myself, chasing after fairies because nothing else in my life came close to that beautiful intensity.* "I think if you don't try for this, you'll always be wondering what might have been. The civil service must be full of people like that. If you'd rather be an actor, I'm sure they can spare you."

"Where did you learn to be so wise?" That startled her. Wise? Wisdom belonged to Elfrida, along with beauty and glamour and magic. It was flattery, that was all, because he wanted her to like him. Perversely, she liked him a little less.

"It's just common sense," she said. "Give it a go. As long as you don't fail your exams, it won't stop you getting a degree, after all."

"You're right," he said. "Thanks!" As though she really had given him valuable advice. And she knew a moment of desolation: *I'll never really belong here. I don't speak the language.* What would Steph have said? Something light and teasing, a little flirtatious. Oh, well. They probably wouldn't have become friends, anyway.

Sebastian had summoned the bill, and she looked tactfully away until he had paid. "Thank you," she said. "That was really lovely."

He was standing up now. "Don't mention it," he said. "Listen; would you like to have a meal before the folk club? There are loads of places I haven't tried yet. My treat; no, really, I mean it. If you're going to be my muse, you'll need food for the body as well as the soul. And it's the last one before the Christmas holidays. Please?"

Suddenly, just like that, she liked him again. He looked so eager and so hopeful, and what could be the harm? It would be too boring for Hob and Elfrida, so she might get to go to the folk club without her—what had Professor Edgerley called them? Her "followers."

She smiled up at him. "I'd love to."

Chapter 32

After that bright and busy first term, it was very strange to go back to the drabness and slow decline of the farm. More chunks of plaster had fallen in the back porch; more sagging gates had been repaired with baler twine, bright orange against the rotting wood. Her parents seemed smaller, older. They asked her very little about Cambridge, and she did not volunteer much information. What could she tell them that they would understand?

It was several days before she went walking in the woods. There was holiday reading to be done, clothes to sort out, plenty of small tasks to keep her busy, but none of those things really mattered. When she finally did go, on a dank and lightless day just after Christmas, it was just as Elfrida had promised. The hoofmarks of deer in the half-frozen mud by the stream, and drifts of sodden leaves choking the entrance to her den. Somewhere in there was her tin box; had she left any biscuits inside? Maybe there was a blanket too, she thought with a lurch of guilt. In the year to come, it would be nesting material for mice and birds. If her mother had missed it, she had never said.

No sign, anywhere, of Them. That way was closed to her now. They might be watching, and she would never know. In the clearing where they had danced, on the day she had been a dragon and had claimed back her cousin, she stood in the centre and spoke aloud. "Lovet. Ember. Adder. Fungus." And there was only wind, and a spatter of icy rain.

It was a kind of answer to one of her many unasked questions.

Elfrida had said that she was not the queen, that she could not make the others do anything they did not want to do. In this matter, then, perhaps they were all agreed. Or—and here she stopped dead in her slow trudge back to the farm—perhaps they were all gone? No. That could not be it. Her mind shied away from that thought, and she walked on, pushing through the leaf drifts and cracking ice on the puddles as she passed. There had to be fairies. Their story was much bigger than her own.

It was a relief to get back to college, to greet other girls in the corridors, to unlock the door to her own clean, warm room, and to be home. This was home. Every day, learning and understanding more, and the bright fierce collision of minds that was a normal part of any conversation. Here, people did not look at her askance when she used long words. Instead of mocking, they offered new ones, and new ways of thinking. She drank it all in, and her world grew larger and more wonderful.

Life began to fall into a pattern. Lectures in the morning, reading and writing in the afternoon. In the evening, time with Steph and other friends, sampling music, films, talks. Sometimes Sebastian would be there, and sometimes it would be just the two of them, trying out a new place to eat or going to a play. She looked forward more and more to those times. He and she together, building a place in the world that held shared understanding, mutual regard, and the strange undercurrent of sexual desire. They didn't go the whole way, whatever that meant, and he said he was happy to wait. For what? Steph had slept with Tony almost straight away, and they had gone out together for a while, and now she was seeing someone else. That was fine, really it was, but Felicity wanted there to be more.

She found herself checking for the signs of love. Did she think about him all the time, draw pictures of him in the margins of her notes, write his name in curly letters? In all the books she had read, being in love was unmistakeable, and she distrusted it for that very reason. It was a glamour, she thought; a spell born out of a yearning for magic, for something more than ordinary.

And I, of all people, know what glamour can conceal.

But yes, she did look forward to seeing him. When they kissed, it did wake fire in her belly. The thought of a future together, taking their first steps hand in hand into the world beyond university, was a warm and steady glow that felt very different from her childhood yearning for magic. And yet, was it too good to be true? Did it even matter?

Yes, it matters. I turned away from magic, so the choices I make must be real, and true.

Whatever that means . . .

When her thoughts reached this point, she would laugh, and give herself a little shake. Right now, real and true meant finishing the current essay on time, preparing for a supervision, looking again for one elusive book in the library. And the most important thing, more than Sebastian, more than Steph and her other friends, more than her course itself, was her weekly visit to Professor Edgerley.

It wasn't just the hour or so that she spent in his study. The whole of Friday afternoon, from leaving her bike outside the porter's lodge, to crossing two quads and then climbing the winding stairs, had become part of something else, set apart from everyday life. It wasn't like going to the woods as a child, and leaving the everyday world behind. In fact—and she almost laughed aloud as she thought of it—it was the opposite. Time out from magic. Ever since she had made her agreement with Elfrida, on that sunny day before her first term at Cambridge, They had been there.

Whether visible or not, making mischief or simply watching, Their presence had affected everything in ways she couldn't fully understand, and certainly could not control. When she had invited Them into the farmhouse, on the terrible night when they had taken Christine, that had only been for a few hours, although it had seemed then like a lifetime.

Now it really is a lifetime. They will always be able to find me, whenever They choose.

I didn't know how precious it was to be able to return to my everyday life, until I'd given that possibility away.

Not that Professor Edgerley knew that, not yet. There was not enough time to write more than a few pages each week, and somehow she was reluctant to tell him about that last bargain. Partly because it was the end of the story so far, and she was taking it step by step, trying to recall every detail as she went along. He was interested in all of it, even—or perhaps especially—in things that had not seemed important at the time: how they dressed, how they spoke, what they could and could not do. But it was more than that.

Felicity was reluctant even to think about it, let alone to make it real by setting it down in writing. She had opened the door to Them, and that would shape her life in ways she could not begin to imagine.

And then there was the gift that Elfrida had given her, unasked for: that was another thing altogether. How she could use it, she had no idea. What would the consequences be? If she had learned anything, it was that getting what you wanted could lead to things that you did not want at all. It frightened her, so she tried to hide it away behind the growing pile of new things in her life.

But it would not stay hidden. She had brought her account for the Professor up to the point, after Christine had been restored to her family, when Elfrida had promised her *great gifts.* She had told him about Their presence at Cambridge. What she had not told him, though, left a great gap in the story; the writing was finished except for that one last encounter. If she did not write it, it would be a deliberate omission. It felt wrong; if this were a fairytale, it would be the one lie that undid everything.

So what can I do?

I should write it down, she decided. *I don't have to show it to the Professor if I choose not to.*

Yes, that's the answer.

Chapter 33

Felicity picked up her pen, and then hesitated. She had come here, to the University Library with its brutalist straight edges and looming dark tower, armed only with pen and paper. Here, rather than to any one of the beautiful gothic and mediaeval libraries she could have chosen, because it was as far from the domain of the fairies as it could be. "Logic rules here," it proclaimed. Logic, and reason, and the works of man. No room for glamour, or things that turn into other things, or are not what they seem. She could not imagine Hob or Elfrida following her here.

For this last part of her story, she needed to be as safe as she could be. She felt reluctant to begin; telling it would make it more real, somehow. She had put aside the memory, almost forgotten it for long periods of time. Now that the time had come to look at it directly, it was like looking at an old black-and-white photograph, foxed and faded almost to obscurity. Had it all really happened? Perhaps the best way was to tell it as one more piece of make-believe, and not try to clarify what it might mean. The Professor could do that, if she ever showed it to him.

If she showed it to him. There was the source of her reluctance, at least in part. She didn't understand the gift Elfrida had given her. It scared her, but it was also her special secret, her one piece of magic, and she feared to expose it to his scrutiny, in case it turned out to be nothing but moonshine and cobwebs after all, as magic so often did.

She needed to know, to understand. Elfrida was right; she

was very young, and one thing she had learned from Them was that there were very few things that stayed true over the passage of time. What she thought was right and proper, at the ripe old age of eighteen, was not at all the same as what she might think if she lived to be old. Or even, if she stepped beyond time and never grew old at all. Elfrida's idea of "wisely and well" would be very different from her own, or—more likely—she would not think in those terms at all.

The Professor, at least, could give her a human perspective. But she didn't need to decide whether to show him, not yet. The first thing to do was to write it down, and then she could make up her mind what to do with it.

I was fifteen, she began.

Chapter 34

It was almost the end of the summer holidays. I'd taken my O levels and was waiting for the results, but I already knew I was going back to school for the sixth form. My father had said only, "You're not getting a job, then?" And nodded, turning away.

He wasn't interested in what came next, in my choice of A levels and maybe beyond. It was outside his world. What it meant to him was what he already knew: I wouldn't be marrying a local boy and taking on the farm. Nor would I be bringing in a wage, contributing to my own upkeep. I'd half-expected arguments, complaints that they couldn't afford to keep me while I stayed on at school, but there was nothing. It was tempting to think he didn't care, that he'd given up on me long ago because I wasn't the son he'd hoped for.

But it was more than that. In an odd way, I felt that he was relieved. And I simply put that aside in my self-centred fifteen-year-old way, and thought no more about it. I'd got what I wanted, and that was that.

Elfrida and her companions were another story. On one of those dry, breathless days at the end of summer, when the leaves hang heavy and time seems almost to stop, I took a book and a sandwich and walked up through the woods. I wasn't expecting to see Them; hadn't seen Them for months, in fact. Just as Elfrida had predicted, as my everyday life grew a little larger, so my hunger for magic diminished. It wasn't by choice. I wanted both; wanted to be able to come and go at will, to tread the treacherous path along the border. But my will did not count for much.

I didn't pay much attention as I walked, thinking about what it would be like to be in the sixth form, and how I might get a Saturday job at one of the shops in town. Sixth formers didn't wear school uniform, and I would need some more clothes. The path climbed up through the trees, and then there was a gap in the greenery, and I lifted my eyes and saw them. Those distant jagged mountains, snow-capped, lying like clouds along the far horizon. But they were not clouds.

I come to a stop on the path, and all my skin prickles as though a cold wind is blowing, although there is no wind. Where are They? No good looking for them; they'll show themselves when they are ready. But as I take a step forward, I feel the change. I am no taller, or older, as far as I can tell, but my dress swirls around me, a soft translucent material that clings to hips and breasts, stippled and striped with green and yellow and red. I've seen that pattern before, though never on cloth; it's infinitely familiar. I catch a fold of my skirt and spread it taut between my hands, and then it comes to me. Ripe apples, like the Coxes in the orchard below that are almost ready for picking. And the way it caresses and shows off my body makes me want to curl up and hide, and at the same time to spread my arms wide to the sky and dance. I remember the black skirt and plain blouse I have to get for school. *Elfrida, you never give up.*

She is there, just beyond the bend in the path, looking Onward, and she is alone, as far as I can tell. I go to stand beside her, and see to my surprise that although she hasn't changed me, I am now a little taller than she is. Some changes happen of their own accord.

"Well, Felicity." She is not looking at me. "You are a woman grown."

Instantly, I bring my arms up to hide my breasts. "I'm not a woman!"

She laughs. “The men who came to help with haymaking think otherwise.”

I am blushing now. “They were just boys being stupid. I’m not interested in boys.”

“Not yet, perhaps. But you have chosen to stay in this world, and that means that other choices are now closed to you.”

Now it was my turn to laugh. “There are more than two choices! Elfrida, the world has moved on. I don’t have to find a boyfriend and get married.” *Not like Angie, working in town and “going steady” with Barry Elson the butcher’s son. Auntie Marjorie says he isn’t good enough for her, though she doesn’t say no to the chops and steaks that come their way.* “I’m going to take A levels and, if I can get a place, I’ll go to university.”

Elfrida looks straight at me now. “Grown women do not have choices at all. They are chosen, by men, and then come the children. That is how it has always been, and I do not think the world has changed so much.”

How would you know? I think but do not say. After all, I am her only window on the world beyond these few miles of woodland. That feels like a huge responsibility when I’ve hardly begun to explore it myself yet. *But I will,* I promise myself silently. *If I’m not staying here, with you, then I’ll do all I can to make that choice worthwhile.*

Aloud, I say, “I think it has. And I hope I’ll be able to prove it to you.”

She just looks at me steadily, and I cannot read her expression. Amusement, sadness, and perhaps a hint—just a hint—of respect. *My brave Felicity*, she’d called me, back then when I reclaimed my cousin Christine, and we made our—

Our bargain.

“Well, then,” she says. “I see that you remember. It is time to give that which you promised. Do you hold to that promise, Felicity?”

My mouth has gone dry, and sweat prickles under my arms. What will she ask? I've read the stories. The power of speech? My eyesight? My firstborn child? Whatever it might be, I know that although I may have many choices to make in my life, this particular choice was made long ago.

"I do," I say, and my voice shakes only a little, though I can't stop the tears that come to my eyes.

She smiles, and reaches out to take my hand. "Then this is your doom. The way to where we dwell is closed to you now, and you may come there no more. But wherever you go and whatever you do, I may come to you."

I am staring at her, open-mouthed, when Hob comes crashing between us. "And me, and me!" he yells, tearing around and around as though he would weave a web to bind us all together. "I'll come too! Never you without me!"

For an instant, Elfrida looks angry, and then she smiles down at him. "Be easy, flibbertigibbet," she says. "Of course, you too."

"Me too! We three!" he crows, seizing both our hands and whirling us around. "Where shall we go? The far Indies? Ultima Thule?"

Elfrida disengages her hand. "We go where Felicity goes. That is the bargain."

"But—" I say, and Hob tries to whirl me off again. "Promises are not piecrusts. You said, you said!"

"No! No, I know, that's not what I mean. But—" I say again, and turn to Elfrida, knowing I'll get no sense out of Hob. "But that's not a doom. I mean," and again, my eyes fill with tears. "I thought I was losing you forever, and there was some awful price to pay for—for what I did. Now you're telling me I can see you whenever I want?"

Elfrida smiles. "Whenever we want," she says. And waits.

"Ohhh." I can barely breathe. I've made myself not think about this moment, about the time when it would all come to an end, because I couldn't bear it. And now, suddenly, everything has changed.

At last, I look up. "Yes," I say. "Yes, of course!" Hob capers around us, shrieking for joy. A small whirlwind springs up in his wake, and in it a storm of leaves, green and yellow and red, so that everything is obliterated, dreaming woods and sunshine and those far-off white-fanged peaks. Everything but the touch of Elfrida's hands, holding mine.

After a time—I can't say how long—the wind dies down and the leaves settle gently to the ground, a carpet of rich autumn colours for our feet as we walk. I've no idea where we're going and I don't care. At this moment, I'm happy to be exactly where I am, with my two best friends in all the world, and to know that wherever the path takes me, I won't be alone.

At length, we come to a high place, where an outcrop of bare rock juts out above the valley below. With the woods behind us, we look down across fields and streams and gently rising hills. A small road, unpaved, follows the nearest stream for a way, before disappearing into a grove of trees. In all that beautiful landscape, there is nothing living to be seen; no birds wheeling, no cows grazing, no people moving. They must be there, though, and the thought comes to me that all it needs is for me to step into it, and it would spring into life. It's tempting, to journey Onward into that land of miracles and wonders, but my way lies elsewhere, for now.

Beside me, Elfrida says, "And now for the gift I would give you."

That startles me. "You've already given me so much. There's nothing else I need."

At this, they both laugh. Hob clutches himself and rolls around in the bracken, while Elfrida shakes her head and puts her finger to her lips.

"Do you know how many times a human has answered that question in that way? Think again, Felicity. There is always something. Riches, or health, or beauty, or power over others. You don't yet realise what any of those might do for you, but even so, you might wish for brilliance of mind, or prosperity and contentment for your parents while you make your way in the world."

She is watching my face, and I can't hide the truth from her: that I never gave them a thought, and that I am ashamed. "You see? The problem is not that there is nothing you might need, but how to choose between a myriad possibilities."

I don't know what to say. Could it really be that simple, to make me pass all my exams, or make my mother happy? To give my father peace of mind?

Before I can think of a reply, Elfrida continues. "But we must not tease you. This is not a wish, but a gift, and you do not have to choose. For all the years of your growing, we have watched over you, entertained you at our hearth, and shared with you our enchantments and glamours. And now, as you leave this place behind, you may take one thing with you. I cannot give you the power to cast glamours of your own, for you have chosen to remain human. But when the time is right, you may give the gift of glamour to one other person."

She stops, and Hob, too, pauses in his restless roving and muttering to himself. He is so seldom still or silent that I stare at him, but he does not look at me, only peering intently at something in the fine grass at his feet. Around us, the world holds its breath. Waiting.

"Thank you," I say at last, and my bewilderment must be plain in my voice.

"You do not understand, not yet," says Elfrida, and she smiles at me. "But when the time comes, you will."

She's right. I don't understand at all. But I feel she has already given me a gift beyond price, and that is more than enough. When the time comes, as she says, I'll be able to ask her, because she and Hob will be there. So I put it aside, to take out and wonder about later, like a wrapped parcel with a surprise present inside.

All that long summer afternoon, as we walk the boundary between here and Elsewhere, I am simply content in their company, and I don't give a thought to what may come next.

And I still haven't, she thought. Or rather, I have, but it doesn't make any more sense to me than it did then. So I suppose the time hasn't come yet. In which case, what's the point of telling the professor? It had been such a relief to write about Them; to feel that at last, there was one other human being who knew her story. She didn't quite understand her own reluctance to tell him this one last thing, and she didn't even want to look at it too closely. So she folded her writing and slid it between the pages of a textbook about human evolution. It could stay there for now. Until the time was right, in fact.

Sebastian's play was to be performed at the end of the Lent term, "so as not to get in the way of exams," as he put it. She didn't know how he could have time to revise, and could not bring herself to ask. She helped him to learn his lines and stood in for other actors when he rehearsed alone. At the final rehearsal, she sat alone in the theatre with a handful of other faithful followers. Afterwards, they dispersed quickly, without the usual late night chat over bottles of cheap wine. Sebastian was on edge, alternately alight with hope and optimism, and then plunging into the dark pit of despair, like a candle guttering in a draught. He walked her to Newnham, and then suddenly begged her,

"Stay with me! Just tonight, please. I don't mean for sex, really, I swear. I can't be on my own tonight. Please?"

So they walked back into town, arms around each other. She'd heard Steph and other girls laughing about the perils of sharing a narrow single bed with a lover, and they had not exaggerated. As it turned out, Sebastian fell asleep almost at once, while her arm underneath him went numb, and the edge of the bed dug into her thigh. He jerked and muttered in his sleep, and once cried out just as she had drifted off, jolting her awake again, to lie there not daring to move.

She was sandy-eyed and slow-witted in the morning, and slipped away as soon as she could. But the play was wonderful; he shone like a jewel, and at the after-party all the others seemed to revolve around him. Or perhaps that was just her exhaustion, as night gave way to early morning and still they went on celebrating, high on adrenalin and relief and wine and exhilaration.

It felt strangely familiar. How often had she stayed with the fairies as a child, long beyond bedtime, drunk on magic? And, then as now, she was a bystander, part of the group, and yet apart. It was a role she knew well, and there was a kind of comfort in the familiarity of it.

Chapter 35

The Easter vacation came and went, and the woods were full of birdsong and new growth; the everyday magic of springtime. But that was the only kind of magic, as far as she could tell. Even Hob and Elfrida were nowhere to be seen. She missed them, and yet it was a relief as well. Exams were looming, demanding all her attention, and fear of failure drove her to long hours of revision. She knew that Sebastian and Steph would not be taking work so seriously, but it seemed to her that this was just another step on the road she had chosen when she had turned away from what They offered. To make that bargain worthwhile, she had to do her utmost with what the world had given her instead.

And what the world had given her, so far, was full of wonders. As a child, she had sought out magic with a fierce hunger, and now that hunger was being fed in a different way. Already—if she passed the first set of exams—she had decided to carry on studying social anthropology. Next year, there would be more on mythology and culture. The focus was on other cultures rather than local folklore and customs, but her sessions with Professor Edgerley more than made up for that. Each time she came to him with a new "chapter," he would talk about the one before, telling her traditional stories that were like her own experience, and citing old country beliefs that bore out what she had seen and done.

She herself spoke little, but he encouraged her to write whenever she could. When she had questioned him about where the Fair Folk came from, he had said only,

"There are conjectures and suppositions in plenty, but I would urge you not to explore them. What you have is an unparalleled opportunity to discover the truth of the matter." Then he had smiled, and said, "Whatever 'truth' may be. I will interpret for you after the fact, but I will not venture to impose the theories of others upon you. And while you may not ask questions of your "followers," you may find out much that they will tell without realising it.

The professor stood before the little coal fire, and Felicity curled—quite at ease these days—in the big armchair. He never spoke their names aloud, for a name had the power to summon a person, or at least to make them aware of you. Only about Elfrida, he had said, "The name comes from the Old English 'Aelfthryth,' meaning 'Elf power.' Which implies that she gave herself that name in her dealings with men, probably a very long time ago."

Now, though, his attention was on Hob. "Take, for example, your friend's response when you offered to teach him to read. He said it was 'not for the likes of him' to go to school or learn from books. Of course, he may simply have meant that the Fair Folk have no need of schooling. But there might be another interpretation. He told you that young Master Hugh had to be schooled because he was of gentle birth. Perhaps your friend was referring to his own humble station in life, rather than to his position outside human society altogether. No," and he held up a hand as Felicity was about to speak, "don't think too much about it now. Take it away and ponder it when you have time. Draw Them out further if you can."

But there was no time for pondering. As the exams approached, Felicity's life shrank down to a constant round of revision, with short breaks as she cycled between libraries and college, from lecture to supervision, and back to the books. Sometimes, in the evening, she and Steph cycled out of town and along the lanes, where great fragrant drifts of cow parsley grew almost across the road, glowing in the last light of the day. And sometimes she passed the evening with Sebastian, talking about anything other than exams, or trying out a new place to eat. They did not spend the night together again. For now, sleep was too precious.

She saw Professor Edgerley only one more time that term. They had not arranged a meeting, but there in her pigeonhole was a note, in his elegant backward-sloping handwriting, saying only, "Three o'clock. Bring no notes today." She hadn't written anything anyway, had not even thought about the fairies for some weeks. She put her revision plan aside.

Ten to three found her climbing the winding staircase to his room, with a mixture of annoyance and anticipation. To her surprise, she could hear voices beyond the half-open door, and when she went in, she found two other students standing about. There was no sign of the professor.

"Well, if you don't know, I certainly don't," one of them was saying. "But he does love to be mysterious." He glanced up as Felicity went in, but obviously found nothing to interest him about her. They were both final year students, she thought, or maybe postgraduates; no one she knew.

"I could do without this," said the woman, who had not taken off her coat and bicycle clips. "If he doesn't show in five minutes, I'm off."

Felicity felt a tiny thrill of something—could it be jealousy?—as she looked around the room. What connected each of them to the professor? Might there even be others like herself? Conversation died, and no one felt quite able to sit down, so they all stood there uneasily, avoiding looking at each other. Even so, when they heard the sound of slow footsteps on the stairs, they drew closer together, watching the door.

Professor Edgerley came in sideways, pushing the door open with one shoulder. In his arms, he carried a cloth-wrapped bundle, cradling it as though it were a baby.

Carefully, he set it down on the bookstand on his desk, and went at once to close both doors and draw the curtains. The young man looked around with raised eyebrows, but nobody spoke. In silence, they watched as the professor took a box of matches out of a drawer, struck one with a small flourish, and lit the two tall candles that stood at either end of the shelf above the desk.

The effect was dramatic. It was a sunny day outside, but the closed curtains had created a twilight gloom. When the candles were lit, moving shadows sprang into existence, as though crowds of unseen people stood behind the little group, whose faces were thrown into sharp relief. Professor Edgerley looked around, and beamed.

"Forgive my little piece of theatre," he said. "The necessity will become clear. I have something to show you. And there is one thing I must ask. You may look, but not touch." As he spoke, he was putting on a pair of white cotton gloves. He drew aside the cloth wrappings, and the group moved in closer. It was, of course, a book. But not just any book; a great heavy tome, with thick leather covers worn down by many human hands. It invited touch, somehow, but Felicity clasped her hands together and stood a little back.

The tall girl cleared her throat. "That's one of the chained books, isn't it?" *What's it doing here?* was what she really meant. And judging by the sudden stillness among the students, that question was on all their minds.

"One of the privileges of rank," said Professor Edgerley. He ran one finger down the front of the book, with such reverence that no one could have challenged his right to do it. "Not even the Queen herself may take a naked flame into the chained library. Therefore, the library—or, at least, one of the books—must come to us."

A naked flame? Surely he couldn't be about to set fire to the book. There was a gleam of excitement in the young man's eye, and he moved a little closer. That one wasn't about to save the book, Felicity realised. He wanted to see it burn.

But Professor Edgerley did not hold a match to the thick, densely written pages he was turning. He leafed through until he found an illustration, and Felicity craned to look at the beautiful, intricate painting. It was a capital "H," almost filling the page, so encrusted with animals and flowers that the shape was hardly discernible, and the gilding raised so that it caught the light, a shifting gleam that made the pictures move as though life were stirring in them.

They had all crowded in closer to see, and Felicity could feel someone's breath warm on her neck. To her right, the tall girl said "Wow!" It sounded silly, completely inadequate, as though by speaking she was trying to take the tension out of the moment. A sacred moment: the work of human hands inviting spirit to descend into matter. She couldn't see why she had been summoned for this, but it made a little respite from the ever-present preoccupation with revision and exam timetables, and for that she was grateful.

Abruptly, the electric light was switched on. Harsh and unambiguous, it flattened the painting. It was still beautiful, but the life had gone out of it. Felicity glanced round at the professor, standing now by the light switch, but he only stood there as though waiting, smiling a little. She looked back to the page, tilting her head to and fro, trying to reawaken the gleam in the gold. One of the others reached out a hand towards it, and then drew back.

When the professor spoke from behind the group, she jumped. "Do you see what you are all doing now?" he asked.

They looked at each other then, of course, but no one ventured an answer. As they turned their attention back to the book, Felicity kept watching. After a moment, she saw it.

"We're all moving our heads," she said. It was true; small random movements, this way and that, while their eyes stayed fixed on the book.

Professor Edgerley inclined his own head. "Indeed. And why do you think that might be?"

This time it was the young man who answered. "To see the shine on the gilding, I think. At least, that's why I'm doing it."

"Ah!" said the professor. "And what happens now?"

Once again, he switched off the overhead light, and wavering candlelight played over the faces of the students, and along the gold illuminations in the book. There was no need to move any more; the light was doing it for them, picking out a glint here or a line of soft fire there, and again the pictures themselves seemed to stir a little.

"Until very recently, firelight was the only way to see in places or at times when the sun was not shining. That is the way these manuscripts were designed to be seen, by an inconstant, ever-shifting light. The pictures are called 'illuminations' for good reason. Precious metals will capture light. They shine. If the light itself does not move, you will find yourself moving, as Mr. Kemp has observed, to see the shine."

He paused, looking around at them all, and now he had their absolute attention. He picked up another book that lay on the table, a modern one with coloured photographs, and held it up to show them the same page they had just been looking at.

"Do you see the gold and silver illuminations in the photograph?" he asked.

The tall girl answered straight away. "Well, yes, but it's flat," she said. "I mean, you can see they're meant to shine, but really they just look brown and grey."

"Precisely so," said Professor Edgerley, and shut the book with a snap. "And the illuminations are raised, with layer upon layer of gold and silver leaf, in order to maximise the shine. That can never be reproduced in a print or a photograph. Our eyes and our memories must do the work of bringing the picture to life."

He placed the book back on the table, and moved toward

the little group, who parted to let him through. With one cotton-gloved finger, he did what they were all longing to do, and followed the line of gold along the stem of a grapevine that twined its way up around one vertical of the letter "H."

"We have brilliant colours to choose from, made from ground up stone or plant extracts," he said. "Some, like the blue of the Virgin's cloak, were more costly than gold. But it is the metals that we call 'precious.' Gold and silver, too soft to make tools from, but infinitely valuable to us. Why is that, do you think?"

This time, no one said anything, and the answer hung in the air between them, wavering in the candlelight, almost but not quite visible.

"It's not the metal that is precious, not really," he said quietly. "It's the shine. It's all about the shine."

Chapter 36

At last, it was done.

No more work, no more crabbed and aching fingers. Suddenly, the world opened up again, to a round of parties and picnics, concerts and excursions and, of course, the play. Sebastian was full of plans, for this play and the one after that, for travelling during the long vacation, and for trips to London to see plays and exhibitions. Felicity had a job lined up in a shop in her home town, and had expected to work there for most of the summer, but his enthusiasm was so lovely that she took warmth from it herself. Perhaps, if she budgeted very carefully for the rest of the year, she could manage a small holiday. And of course, his friend's parents had a villa in France where they could stay rent free. How could she refuse?

They lay together in the tall grass by the river on an endless golden afternoon, drinking wine and eating strawberries, reading from the script, and pausing, more and more often, for long, slow kisses. Gently, almost worshipfully, they explored each other's bodies, and the fire in her belly grew stronger, more insistent.

"You're my Felicity," he said in a low voice, and they drew apart a little, to gaze into each other's eyes. The playscript lay forgotten in the crushed grass.

"And you're mine, even though that doesn't make any sense." *Go away, Elfrida. This is my life now.*

He laughed. "You really are my muse," he said, and his voice was reverent. "If I'm any good at anything, it's because of you."

"Shh," she said, and kissed him again. "Don't stop." She moved against him, urgent with desire. Beyond, on the river, there was a burst of cheering from a group of young men in a punt. As Felicity scrambled to pull down her skirt, they cheered again. The one holding the punt pole was trying to hold the boat in place against the current, and all of them were sitting up to watch.

"Head down!" Sebastian hissed at her. He made a rude sign at the watchers, and then said "No, wait. Look!" and pulled her up again. They looked on as, in slow but inevitable motion, the punt slewed around. The punter had driven the pole in too deep, and now tried hopelessly to pull it out, while his passengers jeered and swore and shouted advice. Just in time to save himself a dunking, he let go, and the punt drifted slowly downriver, leaving the pole sticking up at an angle.

"Oh, god," Felicity said when she was able to speak again. "We'd better move. We don't want to cause a multiple punt pile-up. And this isn't quite the atmosphere I was hoping for, my first time."

He looked at her, eyes streaming from laughing so hard. "Me neither. I mean, me too. Whatever. You're amazing! I love you!"

"I love you too. Do you think we should do something to help?"

"They're going to go aground in the mud by the bend," Sebastian said, shading his eyes to watch. "Serves them right. There's not a lot we can do. And we have more important things to attend to."

He kissed the back of her neck, and she shivered. "Let's move. We're causing an obstruction."

He laughed as he kissed her shoulder. "It's fun being obstructive." He was threading his fingers through the curls in her hair, turning them to admire the way the sun made them gleam. "Like copper wire," he said, dreamily. "Like you're on fire inside, and it's exploding out of you."

"I am," she said. "And so are you. I want you, Sebastian. I'm ready now. I think—I think I'm in love with you." She waited, gazing up at him, holding her breath, and he did not look away.

"My Felicity," he said again. She shivered again, but not from desire this time. Her mother would have said, "As though someone walked over your grave." But she knew who it was. Years had passed since Elfrida had spoken those words, but they had burned themselves deep into her heart. *Whose Felicity am I now?*

"My Sebastian," she said, and they both smiled, a little self-conscious, a little shy.

"Listen," he said, when the silence grew too full and deep, "I've got tickets for the May Ball. Yes, I know it's a lot of money, but I want to give you this. No, I'm not just being noble." He held up a hand as she half sat up to protest. "I want you to be there with me. I want to show the world what a fabulous, amazing girlfriend I've got. I love you too, and I'm not going at all if I can't go with you. And that would be a shame." His eyes sparkled as he looked at her. She had read that in books and thought it was just a poetic fiction, but it was true; they really did sparkle, as though tiny shooting stars were moving in their depths. *This is real,* she thought. *Not magic.*

"Of course I'll come," she said.

His smile lit up his face. He jumped up, pulling her to her feet. Holding her a little away from him, so that he could look down into her face, he said, "And something else. I want you to be my lover. Right now, I want you more than anything. But let's wait a little longer. If it's all right with you, let's wait until the ball. It feels right, somehow. A rite of passage, or something. What do you think?"

She laughed. "Like a fairytale, you mean? As long as I don't have to wear glass slippers."

"Yes, exactly! You are a bit magic, you know. I think you have fairy blood in you. Maybe I should call you Fay."

She tried to draw back, then, but he hugged her close. Over his shoulder, she could see the river flowing by, and the fronds of willow trailing in the current by the far bank. Were They watching? She half expected to see Hob perched in the tree, or Elfrida standing at the water's edge, but there was only the sunlight purling on the water and the distant sound of voices.

It was only talk, after all. That was how people talked when they were in love. Reaching for magic, for ways to describe this wonderful feeling of connection, deep and strong, like a secret shared by the two of them and no one else.

And there it was. She couldn't see Hob and Elfrida because this was nothing to do with them. If it was a kind of magic, it was a kind that they knew nothing about. She had been afraid that there was no part of her life where they could not intrude, but now she knew better. And with Sebastian at her side, she could do anything. This magic was stronger than theirs.

She drew a long, slow breath, and let it all out. "You can call me anything you like," she said, "as long as it's not Fliss."

He made a face. "Is that what your family calls you? They have no poetry."

"Do families and poetry ever mix? Yes, that's what they call me. So did the kids at school. Flossy Flissy." She lifted a strand of her hair. "I'm definitely leaving that behind."

"Definitely! I'm not even going to tell you what they called me at school. The past is another country. This," and he took her hand and swung it high, "is the future!"

Chapter 37

Steph, I can't afford it, and that's that." They were standing in front of the mirror in a shop Felicity had never even considered going into, a shop full of tulle and satin, sparkles and shimmer. The shop assistant was about their own age, and she watched them knowingly, pretending to flatter. Later, in the pub with her friends, she would cut them down to size. Felicity knew her as though she had been one of her classmates at school, or even her cousin Angie, who worked now as a secretary and made snide remarks about brainy people with no common sense, whenever they happened to meet. Under that gaze, it was impossible to enjoy this properly.

"Fliss, you can't go in that old blue smock of yours. I mean, you look lovely in it, but this is a May Ball. This is black tie and pull out all the stops. You won't regret spending the money, I promise."

"I haven't got the money! It's as simple as that. Honestly, Steph. And we're supposed to be going to France in the summer." She put her head closer to Steph's as they gazed into the mirror, and whispered, "Can we get out of here? That girl is listening to every word we say."

Steph stared for a moment, and then something changed in those clear grey eyes. "Sorry," she said. "Come on, let's get a coffee."

They didn't speak again until they were out on the street. Then Felicity said, "No, I'm sorry. You should go shopping with Jane, or Tessa. I'm no good at this."

"Don't be daft. You've got a good eye for clothes, even if you mostly get yours from charity shops. It's just—well, I forget, sometimes, how different things can be."

Let it go, Felicity thought. *Is it that obvious? She doesn't mean it as an insult. Let it go.* Aloud, she said, "It's OK. I'll help you choose, and it's fun trying things on, but I'm really not going to buy anything."

Steph put a hand on her arm, so that they both came to a stop. "What if I lend you the money?"

"No, you don't get it. I couldn't pay it back. It would make a difference between us, and I really don't want that. I'll find something, don't worry." *And it's not just a dress. It's shoes, and a handbag, and a wrap to wear over the top. It's hair and makeup and jewellery and all of that. But never mind.* "We haven't tried this shop yet. What about that one in the window? That would really suit you."

Steph sighed, and followed. "It makes a difference anyway. You know it does. You're my best friend here, and I want to help. Why can't I?"

"Let's talk about it later, all right?" The assistant in this shop was an older woman, but her gaze was no less supercilious. Just by being able to buy what she was selling, you condemned yourself in her eyes: privileged, spoiled. For Felicity it was like wearing someone else's glasses that gave her double vision. All those comments had been made about her, back in the village when she was offered a place at Cambridge, and now she found herself thinking them about other students, even her friends. Even Sebastian. She wanted to protest to this woman with the tired eyes and too much makeup, "It's not like that! You don't understand!"

Instead, she helped Steph pick out two or three dresses, and even tried one on herself, just for form's sake. This one was simpler, made of pale blue satin, with borders of embroidered flowers at the hem and around the cap sleeves. It was pretty, and it cost more than her budget for the entire term. But that was not the only reason for refusing them all. She held up the hem for a close inspection. Here a thread had come loose, and there was a flaw in the weave of the satin. She had worn the real thing, and none of these confections came close by comparison. When she thought about the dresses in which Elfrida had clothed her, these looked cheap and ill-made. It was easy to walk away.

Later, alone in her room, she tried to find that clarity again, and failed. The blue smock had come from a charity shop, and would have been quite expensive when it was new, but it had seen a good deal of wear since then. Perhaps a beautiful shawl to go with it? She had some silver and moonstone earrings that Sebastian had given her; they would have to do. And what about shoes? She met her own eyes in the wardrobe mirror, and sighed.

"Why so sad, sweet Felicity?" Elfrida stood behind her and a little to one side. *I'm two inches taller than her now,* she noted with part of her brain, even as she gasped in shock and whirled around.

"Don't do that! You scared me!"

Elfrida did not reply. She picked up a fold of the smock, feeling the fabric between her fingers. "You dress like a penitent. When there are such riches to choose from, why do you go garbed in sackcloth?"

"It's not sackcloth! And you can't just choose whatever you fancy. You have to pay for things, you know."

"I do not."

Don't know, or don't have to pay? Both, probably. Aloud, Felicity said, "Well, I do. And remember what I told you at the folk club? If you attract too much attention by the way you look, it can cause problems."

Elfrida ignored this, too. "But this is for a grand occasion, is it not? Is it a masquerade, perhaps? Do you go in disguise?"

Felicity sighed again. "No. May Balls happen once a year, and I'm going with Sebastian. But I expect you knew that already."

"And you will surrender your maidenhood. Past time for that, but no matter. You will go to your lover like a novice about to take her vows. Let us hope that his eye is not dazzled by the spectacle."

"Don't be so mean!" She was far from reconciled to the fact that Elfrida knew all of her business, no matter how private. But since there was no choice about that, she had given up trying to hide her feelings about it. "Elfrida, this means a lot to me. I want it to be special, but that doesn't depend on the clothes I'm wearing or what other people think. We love each other, and that's all that matters."

There was a silence. Perhaps Elfrida had got the message? Then she said, "You are very young." They had been looking at each other in the mirror, but at that, Felicity had to look away. Then she looked up again, and said, more loudly than she intended,

"Yes. I am. You've seen it all before, I know. But I haven't. Please don't take this away from me."

At that, Elfrida laughed. "Oh, lackaday! Here you stand on the brink of a new adventure, and all I want is to help you make it as wondrous as possible. I can make you shine, so that all the young men will forget their partners and wish to dance only with you. I can make your swain fall down and worship you. Do not tell me, Felicity, that in your heart of hearts you do not yearn for that. This modesty is indeed a masquerade."

As she spoke, and Felicity watched her in the mirror, their reflections were changing. They seemed to stand straighter and taller; their eyes shone and their faces, though recognisably their own, seemed to grow more beautiful and somehow more compelling, in a way that the most skilful of makeup could never have achieved. And the clothes, of course, were marvellous to behold. It had been many years since Felicity had been so transformed, and the wonder and joy of it brought tears to her eyes.

"You have missed this," Elfrida said softly. "And it can be yours again. Only say the word."

Felicity turned to face her. She made a movement to take Elfrida's hands in hers, and then drew back, remembering. *Touch me not.*

"I know it can," she said. "And don't think I didn't consider it, believe me. But I don't want all the other men to fall in love with me, and I certainly don't want all the other women to hate me! I only want one man, and I want him to love me as I truly am. Without magic, or expensive clothes. I want it to be real."

"Is that all?" Elfrida's gaze met her own, just for a second, and Felicity could not begin to read her expression. "And that's a thing beyond my power to bestow. Beyond the power of any being, mortal or otherwise."

"You know what I mean. Please, just let me be myself."

"As you will, sweet Felicity." And she was gone. *My fairy godmother,* Felicity thought, and laughed. *But I shall go to the ball anyway. And it will be fine.*

Chapter 38

On the evening of the May Ball, Sebastian came in a taxi to collect her. "You can't arrive on a bicycle, not for this," he said, and it was a relief not to have to gather up the folds of her long dress in case it caught in the chain, or to walk in uncomfortable heels all the way to Clare College. Fine clothes are not for doing anything in, she thought. Unless you're a fairy, of course.

When they arrived, their coats were whisked away, and Felicity found that Elfrida had not quite honoured her wishes after all. She was wearing the blue smock, but over it was a shimmer of fine netting, in a colour that moved from purple to green to blue, shot through with silver thread. Tiny flowers were embroidered on it here and there, and when she moved they seemed to catch the light somehow. There was no time to examine it more closely. Sebastian was standing back, staring at her.

"Wow," he said. *What has she done to my face?* Felicity wondered, in something close to panic. *What do I have to do to get her to listen to me?* But then he came close, seized her hand and said, "You look fabulous! Come on, let's get some drinks." So at least he had not fallen at her feet, overwhelmed by her beauty and magnificence. She stole covert glances at other couples as they walked, but none of them seemed to be particularly overwhelmed either. She began to relax a little.

Champagne in hand, they began to explore. Lights were strung in the trees and along the paths, and waiters circulated with trays of food and drinks. They had tried for a magical effect, and if she hadn't known what real magic could do, she might have been overawed by it all; but here on this beautiful summer night, with her soon-to-be lover by her side, she felt ready for anything. In one room there was soft music and low lights, in another a stand-up comedian was performing, and in yet another there was a band playing dance music. More than one band, Sebastian told her, "Let's visit them all, and then we, can take our time. We have the whole night, and then a champagne breakfast tomorrow morning."

"Are we allowed to sleep at all?"

"Nope. Anyone found sleeping will be thrown in the river. Oh look, there's James with Tessa. Hi, James, have you seen what they've done to the Master's garden? Tessa, you look lovely." Sebastian bent and kissed her hand, but she didn't seem too impressed. She was staring at Felicity, eyes wide.

"You're a dark horse," she said. "Most of the time you try to be invisible, and then suddenly you're covered in diamonds. That must be worth a fortune!"

"What? Oh no, you mean the little jewels? They're not real. And it's only a loan." They were all staring now, and Felicity did not know what to say. She didn't know Tessa very well, and couldn't tell whether there was mockery or just plain curiosity in her voice. "I'll turn into a pumpkin at midnight," she said, trying for lightness. Nobody laughed.

"Nothing else sparkles like that," said Tessa. "Can't you tell? If it's not yours, I hope it's insured." She turned away. "James, let's find the dancing."

Felicity stood quite still. *She thought I was lying. Or stupid.* Out loud she said, "Did she mean to put me down, or am I being over-sensitive?"

Sebastian put his arms around her, and kissed the top of her head. "It doesn't matter. She was just jealous. You outshine them all, whether the diamonds are real or not."

Felicity felt sick. "I don't want to outshine people. I'd rather have friends." As she said the words, she felt the truth of them. Better to be looked down on by people like Tessa; better to be despised rather than envied. But somehow, tonight, she had managed to be both. She took a shaky breath.

"Seb, I didn't know about the diamonds—if that's really what they are. I want to take this off. Can we find the bathrooms, please?"

"Hey, come here!" He pulled out the carefully folded handkerchief from his jacket pocket, and held her as she cried, just a little, trying not to smudge her mascara. After a few minutes he said, "Come and sit down," and led her to a bench nearby.

"Listen," he said. "People like Tessa don't matter. No, really. You'd be more beautiful than her if you dressed in an old sack, and she knows it. And I'm not just saying that because I'm in love with you. Don't be afraid to outshine people. It's like when you're on stage. If you hold back, if you don't really go for it, you fall flat. Whoever lent you that wanted you to sparkle, and so do I. So should you."

You are so right, Felicity thought. *I bet she's watching somewhere.*

"And if you did take it off," Sebastian went on, "Where would you put it? Not in that tiny handbag. So wear it and be proud." He wiped away a smear of mascara from her cheek. "But we'd better find a bathroom anyway. You've got panda eyes."

"Oh, god!" She laughed then. "I'm not very good at this."

"Practice makes perfect. That's what my English teacher used to say when we forgot our lines. Once you know your part, then you can start to improvise. But first, you've got to learn it. And if you really didn't know—" he looked down at her, questioning, "then it's not surprising she upset you. But now you do know, you have to play the gorgeous girl who wears diamonds and doesn't give a toss what anyone else thinks. Do you see?"

"Sort of. But what if they're only paste after all?"

It was his turn to laugh. "Doesn't matter! That surcoat or whatever you call it is a stage prop. Act as though it were the real thing, and it will be. Here's the Ladies'. I'll loiter over there by the shrubbery. Keep the handkerchief." He kissed her cheek, said "Mmm, salty," and gave her a little push towards the door.

"I love you. Back in a minute."

In the bathroom, she repaired her makeup, and was relieved to see that she looked like her usual self, except that her nose and eyes were a little pink. But then, Elfrida could transform her at any moment, if the fancy took her. She examined the embroidered flowers, and the little jewels were indeed very sparkly. But Tessa had guessed right; she wouldn't know a diamond from a rhinestone. Another girl came in then, and gave her a curious glance. *Play the gorgeous girl who wears diamonds.* She smoothed her dress into place, gave a final glance at the mirror, and attempted a regal exit. It was only for one night, after all. Everything about the ball was designed to take people out of everyday reality, and if it wasn't quite as good as anything the fairies could conjure up, it was very wonderful all the same. She could do this.

And it was a marvellous time. With Sebastian at her side, she felt she could do or be anything, and if some people looked and then looked again at her dress, she ignored them with a proper disdain. They danced, and drank champagne, and towards dawn they crept up to Sebastian's room and finally, with some laughter and much tenderness, made love. *That is the truth of it*, she thought. Love had been made between them, and if technique and finesse were a little lacking, they had the rest of their lives to learn.

After stumbling back downstairs to enjoy breakfast with the other survivors, they fell into bed and slept until mid-afternoon. Felicity was the first to wake, and she tiptoed out to make tea for both of them. They had forgotten to draw the curtains, and sunlight was pouring in, far too hot and thick. Sebastian was sitting up when she came back, sleepy-eyed and squinting against the light.

"Sometimes tea is just the best thing ever," he said, accepting the mug and cradling it carefully. "Apart from you, of course."

She put her mug down and curled against him. "I won't make you choose. That was the best night ever, for all sorts of reasons. And now we've got the whole summer to play with."

"Mmm. Summer can wait. Come here. You're even more gorgeous without your diamonds, do you know that?"

Later still, as they gathered up clothes so that Sebastian could walk with Felicity back to her college, he picked up the flowered surcoat and said,

"Actually, now I can see them in full daylight, I'm not so sure these are diamonds, after all."

Felicity laughed; a full-bodied laugh that made him look at her in surprise. "You were right. It doesn't matter. Not one bit!" *And lucky it didn't turn out to be a heap of dead leaves. Thank you, dear Elfrida.*

Holding hands, they walked slowly through corridors and quads, where people were busy clearing away the remains of the ball, taking down garlands and strings of lights, collecting stray glasses and picking rubbish out of the flowerbeds. In full daylight, it wasn't just the diamonds that had lost their sparkle. She had hardly thought about Professor Edgerley since that strange afternoon with the illuminated book, but now his words came back to her.

"It's the shine. It's all about the shine."

CHAPTER 39

Going back to the farm was stranger than ever, now. Everything was smaller, drabber, and she was hardly ever there in any case, working all the hours she could get, getting up early to cycle the five miles into town, and home again in the evening. Once, she stayed after work for a drink with the other staff, but she had nothing to contribute to chat about nights out and boyfriends, who was going out with whom and who had got pregnant. She didn't go again, and thought they were relieved. Going to the grammar school had automatically earned her the label of "stuck-up," and Cambridge University was out of their universe altogether. It was too strange. She was too strange. And in any case, she needed to save every penny for the French holiday.

On the evening before the journey, she came down to the kitchen to forage for something to eat, to find her father at the sink. Her parents ate their tea early, but she had learned the habit of having "supper" or "dinner" much later, and now avoided mealtimes with them, coming and going like a ghost, unseen. Conversation with her workmates was awkward, but with her parents, a whole meal might be eaten with barely a word spoken.

"Off tomorrow, then?" It wasn't really a question, since her father knew perfectly well when and where she was going, and had even offered to drive her to the station. He half turned, holding something in his hand.

"I'm nearly packed. What's that you've got there?"

He hesitated, then reached over and placed the object on the table. She picked it up, and then froze. The blue webbing of the watch strap was almost rotted away, and the glass face was dull, but she could just make out the face of Cinderella behind the hands, forever stopped at ten to nine on a long-ago summer morning.

At last, she let out a long, slow breath. "Where did you find this?"

"In the hedge, over by the old coppice. We're grubbing out those stumps, draining that bit. Never was good for anything much."

She looked up then. "You're clearing that hedge. Why?"

He shrugged. "Grant's come in for improvement. We might get a plough down there, put it down to oats for feed. With prices going up the way they are, it all helps."

"But you can't just clear it away! That hedge must have been there for hundreds of years. Are you taking the trees down, too?" She stared at him. That hedge was the boundary. That's why the Cinderella watch was there, carefully placed in a hollow at a height an eight-year-old child could reach before passing through, and then forgotten, one endless day when she must have returned, probably long after dark, by another way.

"I'm sorry about the watch," she said now, trying to move back from attacking. She glanced down at the sad little face. "It never did keep very good time, though."

He made a noncommittal noise. "Neither did you."

Was he trying to make a joke? Even a short time ago, she would have taken that as criticism, but now she wondered. He had turned back to the sink, and she saw how his shoulders rounded, worn down like the pebbles in the bourn from a life-time of hard work. She felt suddenly tender towards him; an uncomfortable, itchy sensation.

"Did you ever want not to be a farmer?" she asked suddenly.

He went still for a moment, then shivered like a horse trying to shake off flies.

"You do what you have to do," he said, after a long pause, when she'd given up waiting for an answer. "Like the hedges. Times change. The new machines can't work in those small fields. You change, too. Or you go under."

She had never heard him speak so plainly before. But then, she had never asked.

"I'm sorry not to be more use to you," she said, lamely. *Sorry not to be the boy you longed for. Sorry not to take up the burden, and succeed where you've failed.* Because the farm was failing; the signs were everywhere. He couldn't change enough to keep up with the new ways.

"Don't you be sorry!" he said, suddenly loud and fierce. He turned round to face her, full on. "You get on out there, my girl. You'll go far. Far away from here."

She couldn't meet his eyes. It reminded her of what Hob had said, on a summer afternoon four years ago, when Elfrida had laid her doom upon her. "Where shall we go? The far Indies? Ultima Thule?" Her father wasn't talking about farming, or not only that. He wanted her to leave it all behind.

But it was too late; had been too late, probably, since the day she'd left the ruined watch in a hollow tree and never looked back. Wherever she went, They would follow.

Felicity had expected Them to be with her in France, for sure. Would they appear on the ferry, picking their way invisibly among the passengers sleeping in corners or drinking steadily in the bar? Or maybe at the villa, making mischief for Sebastian and his friends? She crossed her fingers and willed them not to come; and if they did, after all, she never saw them. It was all too new, too bright, somehow, and hard enough to deal with the flood of sensations while trying to seem as cool as everyone else.

The villa belonged to Chloe's parents, and she had been coming here for years. When Felicity came out onto the terrace beside the turquoise pool that first morning, dazzled by the glint off the water and the white intensity of sunlight, Chloe had turned those huge opaque sunglasses towards her and said, "Wow. You'll need some heavy-duty sunscreen with skin like that."

Felicity had not known what she meant, until later when she began to feel lightheaded, and not just from drinking wine at lunchtime. By the next day her whole body felt hot and tight, as though she had outgrown her old skin and was about to burst out of it, becoming—what? Not a butterfly, certainly, she thought, peering into the bathroom mirror on the following morning. More like something amphibious, that had crawled too far from the cool damp shadows and now was shrivelling and cracking in the sun. Chloe lent her an old straw sunhat of her mother's and told her to stay in the shade. Which she did, at some distance from the others, who were splashing and shouting in the pool.

Sebastian brought her a glass of wine. "Are you sure you won't come swimming? The water will cool you down a bit."

"I'd better not; the chlorine will make it worse. Sorry to be so boring."

"You're not boring." He pulled another sun lounger over and lay down beside her. "You look very fetching under that hat. A proper English maiden."

She made a face, feeling the skin on her nose pull tight. It was beginning to peel.

"I'm just not used to it, that's all."

"Didn't you used to burn at the seaside when you were a kid? I can remember my mother making me have a cold shower. I screamed the place down, but it did feel better."

She said nothing. How to begin? They had never taken holidays; it was not what farmers did. And until a few days ago she had never had a shower either. Never been abroad, or on a boat, or eaten mango or drunk cognac. *Act as though you were a girl who wears diamonds.* If she asked, could Elfrida dress her up in designer jeans, silk sarongs and filmstar sunglasses like the other girls here? The thought made her smile, and somehow that made her feel a little better.

"I'm a woodland creature, really," she said. "Don't get me wrong, it's lovely here. That village we went to yesterday, and the church in town; that was really special. I'd like to do some more exploring." *Just you and me*, she wanted to add, but did not. When they went out in a group, the others always wanted to go to a bar or a café, where they ordered food and drinks and said, "Let's just split the bill, shall we?" She could not afford it, and knew that they saw through her. Sebastian always offered to pay her share, but that just made it worse, somehow.

"Tell you what," he said. "The others want to go out for a meal tonight, but I vote we walk up into the hills this evening when it's cooler. The view from the top of the *causse* is spectacular at sunset. Unless you'd rather join them?" He was watching her, head on one side.

"Oh, I'd love to go walking!" she said. He was laughing now. "What? What's so funny?"

"You are," he said, and kissed her peeling nose. "You were right; you'd be a terrible actress. Your face when I suggested going with them! You're right about them too, by the way. I've known Chloe forever, but when she's with her shouty friends it can get a bit much. She's trying too hard, is all. She doesn't know what to make of you."

"I could make a good guess. She thinks I'm strange, and mean with money, and you'd have much more fun with someone like Harriet, if only she'd stop mooning over that guy Adam who couldn't come because he had to go to Venice with his boring parents." She stopped, not liking the sharp note in her voice. *Poor Felicity.*

Sebastian laughed outright, and some of the others glanced over at them. "Harriet? Never in a million years. She's got a good backhand at tennis, but she can't string two ideas together. If you only knew . . . Sitting there so elegant in the shade, reading your book, you make them all feel a bit brash and stupid. You've got something magical, my woodland creature. I think you're a dryad, really." He reached over to put a finger through one of her curls, tugging at it gently.

Hob likes to do that, she thought, and suddenly missed Them terribly, sharply.

She caught his hand, nestling her cheek into it. "It would be nice to spend a bit more time with you. Just the two of us, I mean. Does that sound selfish?"

"Of course not. Most people are more interesting in ones and twos than in a mob, don't you think? And you," he was kissing her neck now, "are much more interesting all by yourself. Mmmm . . . "

She sat up, trying to push him away. "Don't. They're watching."

"Good. Let's make them jealous."

"I don't want them to be jealous!"

"I do. You're the most beautiful girl by far, and I want them all to envy me." He kissed her, and there was cheering from the pool. "See?" he said, pausing for a moment. And maybe the girl who wore diamonds did see; the girl who didn't care whether they liked her or not, who took it as her due that this lovely man should want to kiss her while the world looked on. But she wasn't sure she wanted to be that girl. Or at least, not all the time. For now, though . . . she put her arms around him, and gave herself up to the joy of the moment.

Chapter 40

That evening was the best time. They raided the fridge for cheese, tomatoes and olives—another new taste—and walked up the footpath, startling lizards from the rocks and a sharp, dry scent from the thyme and sage underfoot. They were walking roughly north, Sebastian said, up the side of one of the great *causses*, or limestone plateaux, which made up this region, like a huge broken mosaic with all the rivers and towns hidden in the cracks between. When they emerged at the top, he put his hands over her eyes, turned her westward and said, "Now look!"

Far, far away, at the edge of the next plateau, the sun was going down in smoke and flame. Up the nearer side, now in deep shade, a road wound to and fro, and all around them cicadas sang, like a celebration of the land itself. It reminded Felicity a little of the Onward view that Elfrida had shown her, but this was in the real world. If she travelled along that distant road, there would not be dragons and monsters, but only other people. And for now, that was strange and wonderful enough.

Hand in hand, they walked slowly, until they found a flat rock to sit on, and ate their food while the shadows in the valley gathered like rising water and, at last, the harsh light faded to something gentler, something her body understood. *Now*, she thought. *Now there could be fairies*. And found that although she had prayed for privacy for this adventure, a part of her wanted to share this with them. But then, they would be here if they chose to be. Probably watching her right now, and laughing. She threw up her right hand in a great wide gesture, encompassing earth and sky and everything in between. *Look at this!*

Beside her, Sebastian stirred and stretched. “We should be getting back. It’ll be dark soon.”

She sighed. “I suppose so.” She leaned back against him. “Thank you for this. Can we do it some more, please?”

She felt the vibration of his laughter inside her, almost soundless. “Your wish is my command. Only I can’t make it be sunset all the time.”

“Oh, why not?”

“Because I’m not magic like you. But I’m sure we can find things to do indoors. If we go down now, the others won’t be back for hours yet.”

She jumped up, pulling him to his feet. “Quick, then! Let’s make the most of it.” It was impossible to hurry on that uneven ground, growing darker by the minute, but they stumbled and giggled and slid their way down, sneaking like naughty children into the silent house, raiding the fridge again for wine, and the fruit bowl for apricots full of the sun’s warmth, and taking them to bed. They were deeply asleep by the time the others did come back, startling them awake with their cheerful drunken laughter, and they lay in each other’s arms listening to the shrieks and splashing as someone pushed somebody else into the moonlit pool.

That was the most marvellous thing of all, in some ways. Just the two of them, curled together in the wide bed, while the rest of the world carried on outside. *Even more marvellous than being with Them?* But the one couldn’t be set against the other, she thought, hearing Sebastian’s breathing grow slow and deep as he slid once more into sleep. This was grown up magic. This was real.

What if you could have the best of both? What if a night like this could last as long as you wanted? She remembered those fairy feasts that seemed to go on for days, when she'd stumbled out of the woods to find that a single night had passed, and the next morning had yet to dawn. But perhaps that wasn't about magic at all; perhaps it was just about being a child. And her last, fading thought as sleep claimed her: *Perhaps it's the same thing.*

Time moved on, of course. She was grown up now. And it wasn't so hard to let go of one precious moment, when so many more awaited them. They lay in bed the next morning, planning.

" . . . Maybe in the third year, we could move out of college and find a flat together."

She sat up in bed. "Really? Could we do that?"

"Of course! Why wait until we leave Cambridge? Once we're in London, we'll definitely want to live together. Unless you've gone off me by then."

She punched him in the shoulder, not hard, and he pulled her to him again. There was no more talking for some time.

At last, when they had showered and dressed and taken their breakfast out to the terrace, she said, "I can't think that far ahead. Getting a degree, finding a job. Moving to London! It's too much to take in. Why London, anyway?"

He shrugged. "It's where the work will be. Acting, I mean. And whatever you decide to do, London will have it."

Not if I were a farmer, she thought. But that was just perverse; a small rebellion against having her future mapped out, even with her beloved. She would never be a farmer, whatever else she might become. She had turned away from that path long ago, and brambles grew thick across the entrance now. What she might do instead, she had no idea. The path ahead was shrouded in mist. Her plans were all about the next term, and the two of them at Cambridge.

But it wasn't true that she couldn't think further than that. The truth was, she didn't want to. It scared her.

"London hasn't got this!" she said. "Where shall we go today?"

Chapter 41

It wasn't until the last evening but one that They came to her. Everyone else had gone into town for a *son et lumière* display at the cathedral. Which would also mean a restaurant meal, and drinking in a bar until very late. Felicity had pleaded a headache, and Sebastian had offered to stay with her, but for once she was glad to be simply by herself, to enjoy the deep peacefulness of this grand empty country. She had walked up the *causse* and found a shady place to sit and read, and it was there, raising her eyes to take in the long view, that she saw them. Hob and Elfrida, some way away on the edge of a steep scarp, gazing out over the valley.

It came to her that she had never seen them at such a distance before. Standing there with their backs turned, they looked like a woman and a child. Not hand in hand—Elfrida would never permit that—but linked, nonetheless. And she wondered, not for the first time, what the bond between them was. When she had finally been exiled, Hob had said, "Never thee without me!" And Elfrida had conceded that. Could he have come anyway, or did she hold the final power?

Briefly, she thought of Professor Edgerley. So many questions that could never be asked. And some that were answered without asking, as they turned and Hob bounded towards her like an overexcited puppy. She had just time to put down her book before he had bowled her over into the bracken. She came up flushed and laughing, with bits of bracken in her hair.

"You're here! I didn't know for sure. It's—I'm very glad to see you."

"Always in a crowd, you are. Great loud folk with no clothes, splashing in the blue water. Do they want to be frogs or fishes?" Hob was dancing around her, frog-hopping and mock-diving in an invisible pool.

"No! They do it for fun. You'd enjoy it."

He shrieked and hugged himself. "And all my skin would turn to scales and fins, and the pike would come after me!"

She laughed. "Well, your skin might, but theirs won't. And I'm sure there are no pike in the swimming pool." She looked up as Elfrida came up to them, smiling. "I wondered—well, some of the stories say you can't cross running water, but that can't be true or you wouldn't be here."

"Pah!" said Elfrida. "Nor can we abide the touch of cold iron, or the kiss of sunlight. We feel no hunger nor thirst, can spin straw into gold, and I know not what other nonsense may be spoken of us now." There was a question there, and Felicity was not sure how to answer. After a while she said, carefully, "People don't talk about you much, these days."

Elfrida lifted her narrow shoulders. "That's as well."

"Have you been here all the time? Did you see the town, and those villages on the hills? Isn't it beautiful?" Felicity did not expect a reply, but she found that she wanted to share these wonders with them, wanted to be able to talk about all these new things with friends who would find them as strange as she did. She had been lonely, even with Sebastian at times.

"Will you come here to live?" As usual, Elfrida ignored her questions.

"To live? Oh, no!" It was a startling idea. "We go home the day after tomorrow, and term starts in about two weeks' time." She was looking forward to it.

"More books, more study. Would you be a monk, Felicity?"

That was even more surprising; but after a minute, she

thought she understood. "It's not like that now. Anyone can study whatever they like, more or less. The Church isn't the only route to learning. I couldn't be a monk or a nun, anyway," she added. To her annoyance, she blushed as she said, "I'm not celibate, not now."

Elfrida made the "Pah!" noise again. "That never stopped any of them! Nor poverty, nor chastity, nor obedience, nor any other vow they might vouchsafe. Some things have changed for the better, perchance. But if a maid may choose her own path, why spend your time at a desk, always writing? Or travel all this way, only to return again?"

Felicity had been expecting teasing about that coy statement, "I'm not celibate," and found she was a little disappointed. "Well," she said, thinking it through, "Spending time at a desk, learning and getting a degree, will give me more options later, when I look for work. Though I don't know yet what I want to do. Coming here is just a holiday, a little break before the next thing. It's what a lot of people do now."

"Work? What need will you have of work, Felicity? Here is gold, if you want it." She reached up to strip the leaves from the branch of a small birch tree that grew by the rock where Felicity had been sitting. They were still mostly green, but when she opened her hand, they poured to the ground in a shower of bright gold. The coins struck the rock, rolling this way and that, and Hob clapped his hands with delight.

Felicity did not move. After a long moment, she said, "It's not real. You know that. If I paid for something with that—even if I could, these days—it would turn back into leaves by the next day. And anyway, I want to earn my living. I want to do work that matters. I chose to stay in the world, so I think I need to play by the rules." She had not known that until this moment, but she felt the truth of it as she spoke.

Elfrida gave her a long look. "And so you shall, then."

Felicity had picked up one of the coins that lay at her feet, and now looked more closely at it. The edge was milled like a real coin, but the faces were plain, as though it were waiting to be imprinted with whatever design she chose. She made a sudden motion of her hand, as though to throw it from her, and then stopped.

"I don't want these," she said slowly. "But what about my parents? The farm is failing. My father is grubbing out hedges; he might even sell some land for houses. Your woods are not safe, not any more. Maybe you could help him, if you chose."

Elfrida stirred the coins with her foot, not looking up. "A hoard of gold unearthed by the plough, do you think? Or a wondrous treasure wrapped in sackcloth, hid in an old barn? Such things have been managed."

"Yes!" Felicity had expected prevarication, some clever twisting of her request. "Yes, that would work. Could you really do that?"

"I could. If I would."

"Oh." Around the coin, her hand closed into a fist. "But you won't."

Elfrida turned away, and began to walk back towards the cliff edge. Over her shoulder, she said,

"If your father had one wish to spend, what would it be, do you think?"

"I don't know! He doesn't talk to me. I only just found out about the farm." But in her mind's eye she saw him, heard the sudden urgency in his voice. "You go, girl. Go far away from here." Would that be his wish?

"And your mother?"

Felicity stood there on the path amid the fool's gold. The day before she left for France, her mother had come up to her bedroom as she was finishing her packing. She had hovered in the doorway, watching, and then asked,

"Have you got everything?" She didn't really expect a reply, but after a few moments Felicity had looked up and said,

"I'll send you a postcard."

Her mother had made a little brushing gesture with her hand: *No matter.* Felicity, filled with a kind of irritable pity, had asked suddenly, "Mum, if you did have to sell up, what would you do?"

Her mother had looked up at her, just a quick furtive glance, and said, very quietly, as though someone might overhear,

"Well, we'll cross that bridge when we come to it. But I wouldn't mind a nice new bungalow somewhere. Easy to keep clean . . ." Her voice had trailed off, and then, more briskly, she said "We'll just have to see. I'm doing macaroni cheese for your tea."

Elfrida had turned and was watching her. "You see?" she said. "Your father had his one wish long ago, and has lived with it all his days. And your mother has no care for farm and fields. It is all used up. If untold riches came their way, it would simply bring the end that much closer."

Felicity stood, fists clenched, fighting back tears. *A nice new bungalow.* On the edge of the village, or even in town. Easy to keep clean, convenient for the shops. Elfrida was right, of course. Her parents wouldn't save the farm even if they could. They were all used up. Maybe her father had seen it coming; maybe he'd turned her away from farming to give her a different life, different choices. What might he have chosen, if his path had not been mapped out for him from the day he was born?

She looked up at last. "You said my father made his one wish. What did he wish for?"

"Ask no questions, get no lies!" Hob had been scrambling to gather up the coins, and now he threw them at her. They flashed in the sunlight, and Felicity cowered away, hiding her face. But instead of the stinging impact of sharp metal, there was just the gentle flutter of leaves settling to the ground. When she looked up at last, her eyes were wet.

"It never comes to anything, your magic," she said. "Does it? The wishes never come right, somehow. Whatever he wished for, it didn't make him happy. So you'd better keep your gold."

She turned away, and began to walk unsteadily down the path. But before she had taken more than a few steps, she heard Elfrida say, "It is not our story to tell."

At the same time Hob caught up with her and spun her around, so that she almost lost her balance. Somehow instead they were spinning and spinning, and her feet no longer touched the ground. He was shouting something, whipping up a whirlwind, and she drew breath into her lungs and screamed, wordless, a cry of defiance and despair that shredded in the wind and became birds, wheeling, shrieking, until at last the storm subsided and she found herself back on the path, alone. Her book lay face down on the rock, and on top of it lay one round blank coin, glinting in the sunlight. She picked them both up and set off for home.

CHAPTER 42

There was less than a week to spend at the farm, after they'd stopped off in London for two nights with some of Sebastian's friends who were actors, or hoping to be. Felicity found the late nights and brittle nervous energy exhausting, and was glad to step out of her father's battered old car in the farmyard, to be greeted by the cackle of geese, and under that, the deep quiet of late summer fading gently into autumn.

There was a new gentleness, too, in the way she and her parents were together. They asked very few questions about her time away, as though they had no framework within which to understand her answers. And she drew back from asking questions, too, so that they simply chatted about how Christine was growing up and what news there was of neighbours. There was a kind of healing in that.

About the farm, they did not speak, and she put off going to see for herself until three days had gone by. And then, abruptly, she could bear it no longer. As though going early might soften the blow, she went out straight after breakfast, promising to come back with blackberries. Her mother looked up as though to say something, and then shut her mouth and bent to clear the table. Her father had gone out with the dogs long ago, and she made her way through the barnyard alone, stopping to greet the cats who came to wind their way around her legs. Some of them went with her up the slope; the nearest hedge was a favourite hunting ground. Or it had been.

At the top of the rise, she stopped.

Her eyes, her whole body, simply could not make sense of what she saw. Each field had its own name, its own character, and the hedges between had been there for hundreds of years. There were thorn trees, blackthorn and hawthorn, and hazel and bramble, sloes and bullaces. There were the homes of mice and birds, the nests of ants and bees, the larger trees where owls perched at night. The hedge was a highway for foxes and badgers, hedgehogs and weasels. She could not begin to count the number of creatures, the flowering plants, the grasses and bushes she had listed in her nature books over the years, all carefully dated, sometimes with a dried leaf or a careful drawing pressed between the pages. It was a place of its own, as complicated and many-layered as a city, and as immutable.

All gone. Instead, a long slash of deeper-coloured soil ran across the ploughed field like an old scar. Up by the top hedge—at least that was still there, so far—were piles of ash where the burning had taken place, and the twisted stumps of larger trees that had resisted the fire. Two fields had become one, and Low Meadow was no more; it was all ploughed across, and new winter wheat was already pricking through the turned earth.

One of the cats bumped at her leg, and she bent automatically to stroke it, then knelt suddenly and pressed her face into its fur. That was an intimacy too far for a barn cat, and it slid away. No help there.

It sounded so simple: grubbing out hedges to make room for the modern farm machines. There were grants; yields would increase. You had to keep up with the times. It was a business, after all. But would business tear down cathedrals, build across roads? It was a violation. She dug her hands into the earth, clenched them into the ground, shaking as though it was bitterly cold, feeling the sun's warmth on her hair and fury in her heart.

Useless, to rage against the inevitable. Small mixed farms were on the way out; agribusiness was the future. Farming was an industry like any other, and if it did not adapt to changing times, it would fail.

Deep in her core, she felt the lie. No one could truly own the land they farmed, even if they had lived there for generations. They were custodians. The welfare of all the living things in that place, and of the soil itself, was in their hands. And if Felicity herself was no farmer, she was something deeper-rooted, more primitive. She had read about the Aboriginal songlines, and how each rock and pathway and river had its own story that would be told and retold, added to and handed down, by all of the people who passed that way. She could do that for these fields and woods, hills and trees and hedges and ditches. There was a long and complicated song just for that one hedge, and it shimmered in the air now where the living pulse of it had been.

And yet, Elfrida did not seem to care. Surely she, who had been here for who knew how many hundreds of years, should be feeling it far more deeply than Felicity herself? Hadn't she said once that all of the woods were under Their protection? If they chose, couldn't they weave some great magic that would save this place from destruction?

Felicity had raised her head, but she was not looking now at the absence where the hedge had been. Some of her rage, she realised, was directed at Elfrida herself. What if she had said yes to the offer of treasure? Perhaps she could buy the land herself, have a bungalow built for her parents and let the rest be reclaimed by nature. But she felt the truth of her own words to Elfrida.

"The wishes never come right, somehow. So you'd better keep your gold."

If there was a way through all this, it could not be found by scattering fairy gold. She got up, looked at the black soil driven deep under her fingernails, and walked on. Walked right across the place where the hedge had been, and felt only the yielding where the ditch had been filled in. It would settle, in time. Walked to the far edge of the field, where her entrance to Their world once was, and now was not. Looked, for a time, dry-eyed, at the raw edge of woodland held back by barbed wire, and then walked on, fast, up the hill and over the gate at the top, and so into the high woods.

She found her father with the sheep in one of the top fields, sitting and smoking, the two dogs watchful at his side. Coming down the field from above, she saw that he had grown almost bald, his shoulders rounded from a lifetime of heavy work. Again, that irritable pity rose up in her, but she could not afford to feel it now. Almost before she was within hearing range, she began to speak.

"Will it be enough, what you've done?"

He squinted around at her, but did not get up. When she got no reply, she sat down beside him. The grass here was short and fine, peppered with sheep droppings and prickly beechmast thrown down by the trees. Not comfortable, but dry at least, and you could see clear across to the next rise of hills, and hear the distant clatter of tractors at work. She had been afraid to have this conversation, but somehow, out here, it seemed easier.

"Will you be able to save the farm, Dad?"

He cleared his throat, looked down at the cigarette held between two fingers, and took a deep pull on it before stubbing it out beside him. Felicity heard the tiny dry crackle as the spark went out.

"There's new grants and subsidies coming in, all sorts. We'll see."

She paused, gathering herself to ask the bigger question. Her chest felt tight, as though she had not enough breath to form the words. "But do you want to?"

He looked down again, but his hands were empty now.

Even as she asked the question, she knew there was no useful answer he could give. It went too deep. If he had an answer at all, it was deep underground, buried beneath a lifetime of putting one foot in front of another, doing what had to be done.

"Dad," she said suddenly. "You knew Them, didn't you?"

His whole body went still. After a few moments, he began to pluck the blades of grass that grew near his right hand. He looked at them lying in his palm, and picked out two of similar length, laid them one against the other, and fitted them between his two thumbs. Raising his hands to his lips, he blew gently through the gap. It took a few tries, but then a sound emerged: a low, buzzing note, like a hunting horn heard far away. He blew again, more strongly, and then laid the grass aside.

"Bob could never manage that," he said. "Drove him mad, trying."

Felicity was watching him. "So you went on your own," she said. "Or They let you in, but not Bob. And you've never spoken about it. I'm not supposed to, either. But I think with you, here, it's all right. Because we both know, don't we? And they told me it was your story to tell. What did They give you in return?"

He was shaking his head. "No gift," he said. He made a harsh sound in his throat, something between a laugh and a sob. "If I'd known . . ."

She was on her knees now, trying to see his face, not quite daring to touch him. "What? If you'd known what?" But he only drew into himself, fumbling for tobacco and papers. His hands shook as he tried to roll another cigarette.

"No gift," she said slowly. "But they asked something of you. That's it, isn't it?"

He stumbled to his feet, letting the half-rolled cigarette fall. "Cap! Jess!" he said, and the two dogs rose silently. "Got to get on," he said as he turned away.

Felicity stayed there, watching as man and dogs went down the field, and all the sheep crowded across to the far side. When she finally moved, grass stems and twigs were printed red into her knees and feet, and she had no answers, only more questions.

Part Four: The Gift

Once upon a time, and be sure 'twas a long time ago, there lived a poor woodman in a great forest, and every day of his life he went out to fell timber. So one day he started out, and the goodwife filled his wallet and slung his bottle on his back, that he might have meat and drink in the forest. He had marked out a huge old oak, which, thought he, would furnish many and many a good plank. And when he was come to it, he took his axe in his hand and swung it round his head as though he were minded to fell the tree at one stroke. But he hadn't given one blow, when what should he hear but the pitifullest entreating, and there stood before him a fairy who prayed and beseeched him to spare the tree. He was dazed, as you may fancy, with wonderment and affright, and he couldn't open his mouth to utter a word. But he found his tongue at last, and "Well," said he, "I'll e'en do as thou wishest."

"You've done better for yourself than you know," answered the fairy, "and to show I'm not ungrateful, I'll grant you your next three wishes, be they what they may." And therewith the fairy was no more to be seen, and the woodman slung his wallet over his shoulder and his bottle at his side, and off he started home.

But the way was long, and the poor man was regularly dazed with the wonderful thing that had befallen him, and when he got home there was nothing in his noddle but the wish to sit down and rest. Maybe, too, 'twas a trick of the fairy's. Who can tell? Anyhow, down he sat by the blazing fire, and as he sat he waxed hungry, though it was a long way off supper-time yet.

"Hasn't thou naught for supper, dame?" said he to his wife.

"Nay, not for a couple of hours yet," said she.

"Ah!" groaned the woodman, "I wish I'd a good link of black pudding here before me."

No sooner had he said the word, when clatter, clatter, rustle, rustle, what should come down the chimney but a link of the finest black pudding the heart of man could wish for.

If the woodman stared, the goodwife stared three times as much. "What's all this?" says she.

Then all the morning's work came back to the woodman, and he told his tale right out, from beginning to end, and as he told it the goodwife glowered and glowered, and when he had made an end of it she burst out, "Thou bee'st but a fool, Jan, thou bee'st but a fool; and I wish the pudding were at thy nose, I do indeed."

And before you could say Jack Robinson, there the Goodman sat and his nose was the longer for a noble link of black pudding.

He gave a pull, but it stuck, and she gave a pull, but it stuck, and they both pulled till they had nigh pulled the nose off, but it stuck and stuck.

"What's to be done now?" said he.

"Tisn't so very unsightly," said she, looking hard at him.

Then the woodman saw that if he wished, he must needs wish in a hurry; and wish he did, that the black pudding might come off his nose. Well! there it lay in a dish on the table, and if the goodman and goodwife didn't ride in a golden coach, or dress in silk and satin, why, they had at least as fine a black pudding for their supper as the heart of man could desire.

Three Wishes: Traditional tale, British Isles

Chapter 43

It was a relief, in the end, to go back to Cambridge, to throw herself into the second year's work. No longer a newcomer, she greeted the city just as she greeted old friends. She and Steph had rooms next door to each other this year, and together they shopped for posters to put on the bare walls, covering the marks left by other students who had come and gone. Steph bought cushions too, and a giant beanbag that took up half the floor, but Felicity was content with a picture or two. Sebastian laughed when he saw it.

"It's like a monastic cell," he said. "Most girls would have stuffed toys and dried flowers, but not you. If I didn't know, I wouldn't be able to guess who lived here at all."

"Good," was all she said. It seemed too hard to explain that she had no money for such things, had never put her own stamp on her surroundings, and did not want to be judged by her possessions. It didn't matter, anyway. Her inner life was vivid and filled with marvels; who needed all those things? *I've seen the real thing,* she thought, not for the first time, and wondered whether They had killed her appetite for what the world could provide. But she didn't wonder for long. She felt rich and full of blessings, cradled by love and wide open to all that Cambridge could offer.

She was glad that she and Sebastian had not moved into lodgings together. Living out, as it was called, was more expensive and more time-consuming, and she had precious little of either money or time to spare. Besides, he was up and down to London nearly every week for auditions or plays involving one friend or another. He had not done well in his first-year exams, and he really did not seem to care. "It's a distraction," was all he said about his college work. "They made me choose history, but they know it's not going to lead anywhere." He wanted Felicity to go with him, but after that first time before term began, she refused. Even if she had no idea what to do after university, doing her best mattered enough to make that decision an easy one.

On one of the last warm days of the autumn, he took her to the top of one of the towers in his college. The street below was already in shadow, but up there the sun shone golden on old stone, and on the jumbled roofscape below. Along the low walls, generations of undergraduates had scratched their names. Sebastian produced a penknife and began to carve in a blank space just under the parapet.

"What are you doing?" Felicity was scandalised. "That's vandalism!"

"See that one there?" Sebastian pointed with the knife, then returned to his scraping. Felicity looked closer, and made out "P+T" in an attempt at Gothic script. "That's my brother, Piers. He was here two years ago. He showed me that in my first term. And my father did one somewhere too, though he won't say where, probably because it wasn't my mother he was with at the time. It's a family tradition." He had carved out the rough shape of a heart, and now began to add an arrow through the middle.

Does it make it all right if your father did it? And Felicity wondered again what it was that her father could not or would not say. But that was a world away, another story. She watched as he finished the "S" on one side of the arrow, and began on the "F."

"I didn't know you were capable of such vulgarity," she said, trying for lightness.

"If you're going to be a vandal, you might as well be a vulgar one," he said. "There! Now we're set in stone, you and me. It's official."

"Hmm," she said. "Is your brother still with 'T,' whoever she was?"

Sebastian frowned. "Teresa, I think. Or was it Tricia? I only met her the once. But he'll never settle with anyone. Whereas we two . . ." He shut the blade of the penknife and flipped open the corkscrew. "We are celebrating!" From the inside pocket of his waxed jacket—the "poacher's pocket," as he called it—he drew out a bottle of wine.

"What are we celebrating?" She sat down beside him against the parapet, out of the wind. He took a swallow from the bottle and handed it to her.

"Two things. Actually, both next week, but this is close enough. Do you know what happened a year ago next Tuesday?"

"Oh, wait." She was beginning to guess. "You remember the exact date?"

"Of course I do! Clare folk club, and your friend making that scene in the middle of some act. Are you still in touch with her, by the way?"

"Yes, sort of." She did not want to talk about Elfrida now. "But that's not when we actually met, so it's not really our anniversary."

"It's my anniversary; the first time I saw you. We can celebrate yours later."

"Idiot!" she leaned over and kissed him, tasting red wine. A gust of wind whipped her hair against both their faces, and he gathered a handful of it and kissed that too. She snuggled against him, and he pulled one arm out of his jacket so that he could wrap the coat around them both. They sat there, feeling the sun on their faces and the warmth of the wine inside them, passing the bottle back and forth. After a while she said,

"So what's the other thing?"

"What?" He was kissing her neck, letting the cold fingers of the wind in under her collar.

"You said there were two things."

"Oh, yes." He sat up, and she felt the sudden tension in his body. "Well, you remember a few weeks ago I went for an audition in 'Much Ado?'"

"Sort of." She had lost track of auditions. There were so many, and always so urgent, so important, coming to nothing in the end.

"They want me to come for a second go." He turned around to face her, gripping both her hands, so that the coat was suddenly pulled away.

"Oh!" She wasn't sure what to say. "That's a good thing, is it?"

"It's a brilliant thing!" He leaned in to kiss her, on the mouth this time, then pulled away to look earnestly into her eyes. "It means much better odds. And—" he paused to take a swig from the bottle, "it's for a better part, too. In London! If I get this, I might be seen by agents, reviewers, anyone! This could really be the start of something." He waved the bottle around, sloshing a little wine against the sandstone, across the carving he had just finished. Dull red on honey brown; a strange combination. Would it leave a stain? She realised she had stopped listening.

". . . But you could come down at weekends," he was saying, and of course, she had been listening after all. She just hadn't wanted to hear.

"Maybe. Sometimes. But it wouldn't run for weeks, surely?"

"Not this play, no. But if they asked me to join the company . . ." His eyes were shining, the fire in him burning so brightly she could hardly bear to look. He took her by the shoulders. "Felicity, I really, really want this. I've been working towards it ever since I was eight years old, and I got to be the Angel Gabriel in the nativity play. It's all I want. Apart from you, of course. I can't do it without you."

"I can just see you as the Angel Gabriel." She could, too; a blond-haired, sweet-faced boy, glowing as he delivered his tidings of great joy. "How could they possibly resist you?"

And yet, once he had given her the news, it seemed that there were all sorts of reasons why they might resist him after all. He would be up against established actors, even famous ones. There would be strings being pulled, favours called in; that was how it worked, and he was cut off here in Cambridge. Even if you were in the Footlights, no one would take you on without an Equity card. On it went, as they went back down to earth and finished the wine with some take-away Chinese food, until by the time they went to bed, he had talked himself into a kind of despair.

Later, much later, she lay beside him as he muttered and tossed in his sleep. *I am your muse*, she thought. *You can't do it without me.* And whether or not that was true, she did have one thing that might help, more than all the love and listening, all the sharing of food and sex and conversation. One gift to give.

Well, who else would I give it to? Carefully, she eased herself out of the narrow bed, and went to stand naked at the window. The quad below was utterly silent at this time of night; moonlight bleached one side and threw the rest into black shadow. She opened the window, though the icy air raised goosebumps all over her body, and spoke into the waiting darkness.

"Elfrida. I claim my gift. It's time." She waited a moment, but nothing stirred, and she was shivering now, her muscles clenching in the cold. When she closed the window and got back into bed, Sebastian murmured something and turned to face her, wrapping arms around her, pouring warmth back into her body. She lay rigid for a while, and then turned on her side, fitting herself against him; the only way two could fit with any comfort into a narrow student bed.

She was on the edge of sleep, thoughts drifting into dreams, when she felt it pass from her body into his, gently, softly.

Something she had not known she possessed until it was gone. Part of her reached after it, mourning, but with the last shreds of consciousness she told herself: *I chose this. It's done.* And fell into a deep sleep without any dreams at all.

Chapter 44

If Sebastian looked any different the next morning, she could not see it. *But then,* she thought with a small, private smile, *I look with the eyes of love.* What had she expected? A golden glow around him, like the risen Messiah in a Renaissance painting? Or perhaps he would be so beautiful no one could bear to look at him? The smile grew broader as she watched him pack his valise, choosing and rejecting the same shirt for the fourth time.

"What are you laughing at?" he asked. He claimed not to have slept at all, and she knew for certain that was far from true.

"Nothing. Just you," she said. "It'll be fine, whether you wear your best shirt or that old t-shirt with the CND symbol on it. If not this audition, then this will lead to something else. I'm sure of it." She was sure of nothing, of course, but that was what he needed to hear.

"Come with me?" he asked again.

"You know I can't. But call the Porter's Lodge and leave me a message when you can."

"They won't tell me straight away, unless I'm hopeless. It could be days."

"Then come back tomorrow!" She tried not to sound too desperate.

For a moment, he paused. "I should be on the spot. Just in case. If they did want me and couldn't reach me, they might choose someone else. You know how it goes."

Felicity did know; had learned from experience. "What

about your coursework?" would have been the next question, but experience had taught her to swallow that one. So she stood up and said, "I'm just getting in your way here. I'm going to go now."

She held out her arms, and he went into them. He held her, hard, and then a shudder went through him and he let go.

"Love you, my Felicity."

"Love you too."

Do mothers feel like this when they wave goodbye to their children? She wondered. Her own mother was no guide; she never seemed to feel anything much.

At the same time, as she ran down the stairs and across the quad, her thoughts were already moving on. *If I hurry I can get back to college to change, and still make my first lecture.* She had chosen not to go with him, and there was no sense in repining like a lovesick maiden.

But she could not help looking back before she went through into the next quad. His window reflected the early morning light, and she could see nothing but the hard white winter sky.

Over the next few days, she wondered a great deal about the gift. Elfrida could appear magnificent, larger than life, more than human, but ordinary mortals could not. How did glamour work? She looked at the stills from films outside the cinema, at the women with their perfect hair and makeup and the men with slicked-back hair and what Steph called "bedroom eyes." No one looked like that in real life; if they did, you couldn't possibly take them seriously. But then, if Sebastian did succeed with his acting, it could be his picture up there; his face in the magazines, and people—women—would fall in love with him. Or their idea of him, at any rate. *Is that what I did with Them?*

Almost a week went by, and she stopped going into the Porter's Lodge. He had begun to expect her, and she felt his eyes on her when she checked in her pigeonhole. But today as she wheeled her bicycle under the archway, he came out of the lodge calling, "Miss Turner!"

She stopped. He was holding something in his hand. A small yellow envelope.

"A telegram for you," he said, and held it out to her.

Felicity's stomach clenched; she felt sick. She had never seen a telegram, but she knew what they meant. *It's my father.* She stared down at the envelope, gripping the handlebars of the bike so hard that the binding, she saw later, had made red ridges in her palms. Slowly, one of her hands uncurled, reached out and took it. She said, "Thank you," tucked it into her pocket, and walked on. Not until she was safe in her own room—*safe!*—did she unstick the envelope and slide out the thin folded paper inside.

"GOT IT!" The message read in blurred, uneven type. "THEY WANT ME STOP COME DOWN STOP LOVE S."

Her eyes read the words, but she was shaking, dry-mouthed, expecting the hammer blow. COME AT ONCE STOP FATHER—but she could not complete the sentence. It hadn't happened. It was all right. There was a sudden stab of anger at Sebastian. How could he frighten her so? But for him, she guessed, a telegram might be just a quick way of sending news; the expense wouldn't matter. He must be beside himself with excitement; couldn't wait to tell her. He must have heard just this morning. She sat down suddenly on the bed, fighting back tears.

What now? It was out of the question to rush off down to London, leaving an essay unfinished and a seminar to prepare for. She had the phone number of the friends he was staying with, but he wouldn't be there, not now; he'd be out somewhere, a pub probably, celebrating. She'd have to keep going down to the Porter's Lodge to try the number until she got through. It would be fine, he was with friends, he would understand. He'd be back in a day or two, surely.

It came home to her, then. Rehearsals, performances. How

many? A play could run for weeks, months even, with maybe more work to follow, if he did well, if they liked him. And they would like him, of course. They would love him, because she had given him the gift. She saw herself catching the London train, weekend after weekend, finishing essays in other people's houses, spending money she did not have.

She had wished this for him, had paved the way for him to have his heart's desire. And she had done it for love.

Her mind was racing, snatching at possibilities. She could leave Cambridge, find work in London. It wouldn't be the end of the world. Or maybe he would decide, after all, to finish his degree. He had the gift; the world would be at his feet. There was plenty of time to become a star. But all the time, in some deeper place, the truth waited.

"So you have bestowed your gift."

Elfrida stood at the window, looking down at the quiet garden. Felicity knew what she would see: bare plane trees fringing the path, a touch of frost lingering on the plants by the high wall. No magic there; just a frozen November afternoon, already waning into darkness.

"Can I take it back?" She hadn't meant to say that, knew it was foolish, and yet she looked up at Elfrida like a child beseeching its mother to make everything all right. That made her smile, though not for happiness. Elfrida had been many things to her over the years, but motherly was never among them. The tears welled up again.

"Ah, now." Elfrida sounded almost kind. "It's a wondrous thing you have done for your beloved. Why so sorrowful?"

Felicity shook her head, willing the tears away. "It's fine, I'm all right, really. I'm just—" she stopped, took a deep breath, tried again. "It's going to be difficult to see him, that's all. I wish I'd waited a bit longer."

Elfrida smiled at that, and it was not a kind smile. "You humans and your wishes," she said. "You never learn."

"That's not fair!" Despite herself, she rose to the bait, the anger and desperation in her clamouring for outlet. "People do learn. That's what so many of the stories are about: getting it wrong, and then learning how to get it right. Living through and taking responsibility. It's part of how we grow up."

"Such a clever one. Do they tell you that in your books?"

"Please. Please don't make fun of me. It's just a lot to take in." She held up the telegram, crumpled in her hand. "It's good news, it's wonderful, really."

Elfrida waited.

"And I'm scared, all right? I'm scared of what it might mean for—for us." She looked down, twisting her hands in her lap, beginning to shred the fragile paper.

"But true love always finds a way. Isn't that what the stories tell you?" Elfrida had turned from the window, and now Felicity stood up, facing her.

"But you don't believe that, do you? You've seen too much."

For a long moment, they held each other's gaze, blue eyes and hazel, very young and immeasurably old.

Then Felicity said, "If you don't mind, I think I'd like to be alone now."

She went to the window herself, stared down at lamplight gleaming on the wet path below. And when she turned around, Elfrida was gone. That wish, at least, was granted.

Chapter 45

Felicity!"

She stopped, half-turned, and then Sebastian crashed into her, open-armed, and they both slipped and staggered on the icy path, almost falling, laughing and talking all at once.

"Why didn't you come?"

"I tried to call you, but you were never in. Three days!"

"It's been mad, it's been amazing. I missed you!"

"Oh, tell me all of it. Tell me now." Through layers of wool and thick cloth, he held her, kissed the cold tears on her cheeks. Around them the flow of walkers and cyclists parted and re-formed, moving on to the next thing, while time stopped like a boulder in the stream. *If only.*

They were not far from college. He had been there already, had just missed her on her way to a ten o'clock lecture, so they turned back, and she made tea in the quiet morning kitchen while he spilled out his news. *Missing one lecture won't hurt.* And then the traitorous thought, *If you got back last night, why didn't you come then?*

"You were right, you're always right," Sebastian was saying. "They loved me! They've offered me a bigger part, and a place in the cast if it goes well." His eyes shone. She could see that he was tired, had probably hardly slept for the last few days, but he was alight, glowing.

It's all about the shine.

"So what does that mean? Will you have to be in London for a while?"

"Well, yes, of course. I've been kipping on James's sofa, but there might be a room going soon. Or we could even look for a place of our own, in time. I'll get paid!"

"Wait. Wait a minute." She was afraid to speak her thoughts aloud, in case that made them true, but she had to know. "Does that mean you'll have to defer this year?"

"What? Oh! God, no." But she barely had time to breathe before he went on. "I'm on course to fail this year anyway. This is it, Felicity." He took her by both hands. "This is what I've been waiting for."

She pulled her hands away, wrapped her arms around herself. Her faithful radiator was pulsing out waves of heat, but she felt cold to the core. *I did this. My fault.*

"You're not even going to finish the year? You'll just—leave?"

He laughed. "Of course! What's the point of stringing it out? I'll get a lecture from my parents about the money, the waste of opportunity, all that, but this *is* my opportunity. You can wait a lifetime for a chance like this. They'll come round in the end. They know this was always where I was heading."

"But what if you don't get offered anything else after this?" Even as she asked the question, she knew the answer. There would always be parts for Sebastian. Maybe more than he wanted. Because he had the gift.

"All actors take that risk, you know that. They do bar work, adverts, all sorts. And you'll find a job, no problem. London's the place for everything." He was looking at her now, really looking. "What is it, Felicity? I thought you'd be happy for me."

"I am," she said at once. "I'm really happy for you. But I'm not so happy for us."

He stood up, paced across the room, turned back. "What do you mean?"

"Think about it." She looked up at him, willing him to understand. "You'll be in London, working evenings, weekends, staying up half the night. Even if I did come down, get a job, all that, I'd hardly see you."

For the first time since he had found her on the path, he stopped his restless movement. She saw him thinking it through, working it out, and she braced herself for anger, even tears. There was something familiar here, something she understood. Every time she had defied her father's orders to stay out of the woods, disappointed her mother with her lack of interest in cooking and sewing and pretty dresses. She had never been able to be what other people wanted her to be, and perhaps she never would. And then he did something that surprised her utterly.

He came back to where she sat on the bed, went down on one knee, and took her hands again.

"I'm sorry, my love," he said. "I'm a selfish pig. Can you forgive me?"

"What? What for?"

"For being a beast. For assuming you'd be ecstatically happy to give up your degree, when I know how much it means to you, and come and support me in London in a dreary little bedsit at a dreary little job, while I swan around with my actor friends, drinking in the adulation and never being at home."

She was staring at him, speechless. "I'd roll in drunk at four in the morning, stay in bed most of the day, eat all the food you bought and get cross when you complained. And probably tell you that you were lucky to share your life with such a genius. Am I right?"

They were both laughing now. "Yes!" she said. "And I'd turn into a little grey mouse, while you went spinning off with your wonderful fans, and everyone would pity you and wonder what you were doing with me."

"No, not that bit," he said. "You could never be grey or mousy. But listen. We can make this work. I'll come up when I can, and you'll come to London when you can, and you'll finish your degree, and then we'll see. How does that sound?"

"Give me my hands back. I need to blow my nose," she said. "You are amazing, and I forgive you completely. It's me that's being selfish. But yes, let's make it work, somehow." *And if Elfrida is watching us now, too bad. Being hundreds of years old doesn't mean you're always right. If we love each other, we'll find a way.*

And it did seem, after all, that they would. Auditions were continuing, and Sebastian did not need to be in London for the next week or so. Time to make arrangements with his college, and time to visit his parents. He wanted Felicity to meet them, but they agreed that now might not be the best moment. It would be difficult; there would be an atmosphere. She went to the station, expecting a serious and subdued returning traveller, but he seemed, if anything, bemused. They got coffee in the station café, and Felicity noted how the waitress glanced at him, and then looked again. She was not the only one. They sat at a corner table out of the way, but every time she looked up, someone would be watching them.

"So what happened?"

He made a face. "To be honest, I don't really know. It was as though they'd had some kind of Damascene conversion, or someone had made a prophecy about me or something. I don't remember them being so positive about anything since I won the hundred yards race at school."

"That can't be true!"

"Well, almost. I've got used to being a disappointment and a worry, and being compared to my brother who can do no wrong. But this was weird. Just before I left, Ma took me aside and said, "I've always believed in you, darling." She had tears in her eyes. And Dad slipped me some money "to be going on with," and said he admired my determination and to let them know when the play is on." He stopped, frowning a little.

"Even my tutor in college didn't give me a lecture. When I said I was leaving, he came out from behind his desk to shake my hand. 'You have a very promising future ahead of you, young man,' he said."

She laughed. "Well, there's your prophecy. Let's hope it comes true."

"Yes, but . . ."

"What?"

"I can't quite explain it. It's as though they'd put on rose-coloured glasses, you know? Instead of worrying about my shortcomings the way they usually do, they could only see the good points. I mean, it's great, I'm not complaining. I'm just not used to it, I guess."

"Maybe you'd better get used to it," she said. "When you're a famous actor, it will happen all the time."

He laughed, then. "Yes, but you don't expect your parents to fall for that, do you? And definitely not your college tutor. He'd more or less written me off until now." He shrugged. "Well, I've got until the end of term to clear out my room, and then it's goodbye, Cambridge." Seeing her face, he added quickly, "Though I'll be back whenever I can, of course."

"I know. It's OK."

"You are amazing, you know that?" He helped her into her coat; she was used to that now, but as she stood up, several pairs of eyes followed the movement, and in her embarrassment she missed the second sleeve. There was some awkward fumbling, and the couple at the next table shared a private smile. *Well, I suppose the gift will affect the way people see me, too. And probably not for the better.* That was another thing she hadn't foreseen.

There were two days of cold winter walks, making love under piles of coats and blankets, and long, comfortable silences. There were so many unknowns ahead, and it seemed important simply to enjoy each other's company. Then he was off again, and Felicity did her best to settle back into work, catching up on the last assignments before the end of term.

She wondered, though, about the gift of glamour. To her, Sebastian seemed no more or less beautiful than he always had, but in the eyes of those who watched them in the street, there was a look that was very familiar. Those students at the folk club, paying court to Elfrida in her splendour. Herself as a child, gazing in incredulous joy as They whirled and danced around her. It was the lordly ones her eye was drawn to, of course; she'd found Hob and his friends too strange, too unnerving, even though she had learned over time that they were one and the same. When they chose to be lovely, to put on the glamour, were they doing it for themselves, or for her?

Professor Edgerley's lecture came back to her. "What do they want from us?" She had not seen him this term, had sent him no more writing and received no stories. When she thought about the gift, she still felt reluctant to tell him about it. He, like Elfrida, rarely gave direct answers. As in all the old tales, he seemed to feel that she had to work it out for herself.

So, she decided; it was time to try.

Chapter 46

She began, not with the stories, but with her own memories. She did not know how many of Them there had been when she first stumbled into their circle, but by the time she had taken her leave for the last time, they had been far fewer. New faces had come and gone over the years, but never any children like herself, though they had talked about others from time to time. Certainly never any adults. Where did they come from? She had no idea, had never thought to ask. She knew where they went, though. Onward, into stranger and more magical places, where dangers and marvels waited.

I know, too, that Elfrida fears those places.

Elfrida had questioned Felicity about how humans lived, tried to persuade her to leave Cambridge and travel the world, experience all that it had to offer. There was a hunger in her that could be frightening at times, but she did not yearn to travel Onward, although others did. What was it that made the difference?

For the moment, Felicity could go no further along that path, but re-reading the accounts she had written for Professor Edgerley threw up another mystery. Before They had stolen Christine, she would have accepted without question, but now she wondered.

Why did they promise, many times, that I could join them one day? Why not simply let me stay?

It was time to turn to the old stories. Fairies kidnapped people on a whim, it seemed, or lured them with enchantments, or persuaded them with rewards. Nowhere could she find an example of someone permitted to come and go unless They gained something by it.

So what do I have to offer that they could not get otherwise?

Again, a dead end, though she resolved to put these questions to Professor Edgerley—in writing, of course—and see whether he could come up with a story that might shed light on it. She need not say anything about the gift, after all, and she had missed those sessions in the firelit study, listening while he retold the old tales. Now that Sebastian would not be around so much, it was time to return. She had neglected her friendship with Steph, too. After Christmas, it would be time to put that right.

Felicity left her questions for the professor at his college that afternoon, together with an account of what had happened in France. She did not expect an answer before the end of term, but there was a note in her pigeonhole the next morning reading: "One o'clock if you can." The distinctive copperplate handwriting, in the dark blue ink that faded to violet, told her instantly who it was from. And so she found herself climbing the worn wooden stairs again. The outer door stood open, and before she could knock, the professor himself opened it to her.

"Miss Turner. How very good to see you." He stood aside to let her in, closing both doors carefully behind her. Winter sunlight slanted across the room, making the fire in the hearth look pale and insubstantial. Its warmth was real enough, though, and she went gratefully to one of the big armchairs while Professor Edgerley made tea for them both. She had missed this, she realised: a little oasis in her life where only truth mattered.

"Thank you," she said, when he handed her a mug of tea. "I didn't think you'd have time before next term."

"Ah," said the professor, coming to sit in the chair on the other side of the fire, "for me, end of term means an end to teaching and more time for other things. You travel home within the week, I take it?"

"Yes." She cradled her mug in both hands. "It's not urgent, but I haven't seen you since June, so . . ."

"Indeed. It is good of you to keep me informed. And one never knows when something significant may emerge, often quite by chance, it seems."

Felicity felt guilty. *Does he know there's something I haven't told him?* To cover her unease, she asked, "Is there anything in what I've written this time?"

He steepled his fingers in that familiar gesture, leaning forward a little, musing. "Oh, there's a great deal. It's the throwaway remarks that are so telling. It has often been said that fairies are not able to cross running water, and that they cannot abide the touch of cold iron, but your friend has given the lie to that. Indeed, the supposed aversion to iron has been taken by some scholars to mean that the 'little people,' as they were sometimes called, were a remnant of some folk who inhabited Britain before the iron-wielding Celts pushed them out into the margins of the habitable lands."

"But they speak English, more or less." Felicity tried to think back. "Sometimes I found them hard to understand, but I don't think they were ever speaking a different language."

He smiled. "From your notes, I'd say that while some of their speech mannerisms are antique, they are always recognisably English. And they are not 'little,' either." He sat back, watching her.

"I don't know," Felicity said slowly. "They can be tiny if they want to be, or giant. It's hard to tell what they're really like, if 'really' is even worth anything. But some of them—Hob, especially—never change. I've seen him be a bird or an animal, but his human form—if you can call it that—is always the same. Either he can't change, or he doesn't want to."

She stopped, and then something else occurred to her. "When I first met them, he was a little taller than me. Now, he only comes up to my waist. The others, when they're being 'goblins,' they vary a bit but none of them are full height. So they could be little."

"Well. And clearly, they are not simply products of your own imagination, as other theorists have claimed." He glanced over at the bookshelves that lined the walls, leaving space only for windows and the hearth where they both sat. "A great deal of energy has been expended in trying to explain them away, but that need not detain us now. We know that they are 'real,' whatever that means, but they are not always 'here.' Their home is not accessible to us unless they choose to make it so. They can come and go at will, but we cannot. And we also know that they dwell in a kind of borderland between here and what they call 'Onward.' If they go too far onward, they cannot come back. Am I right?"

"Yes, but things from there can come through; maybe into our world, too." Felicity thought of ripples on black water, and shuddered. "Elfrida talks about being a guardian, as though they kept us safe, somehow. Although they love to play tricks on us themselves." She fell silent, sipping her tea, remembering.

"As so many of the stories testify. If they are not seeking our help, they are up to mischief of one sort or another." He held up one finger. "To return to your first question. Where do they come from? We have established, at least, what they are not: neither a remnant race of little people nor figments of your imagination. Question two, as I recall, was about your friend in particular. She appears very interested in the human world, and not at all willing to move Onward, as several of her troupe have done over the years. Correct?"

Felicity nodded, watching him over the rim of her mug.

"Your question was 'Why?' It seems to me, however, that your third question might contain the key. Why did they not let you stay? Or to be more precise, why did *she* not let you stay?" He seemed to have forgotten his tea, and the question made a little silence around it. *As though,* thought Felicity, *we were in a room where music was playing in the background, and it suddenly stopped.*

Now, we are coming to it.

"I don't know," she said at length. "I've been round and round that one. I used to think it was a punishment for bringing Christine back, but I don't think it was only that. I wonder whether she always meant to refuse me. Every time, when I was younger, I'd beg to stay, and she warned me that as I got older, I'd want to live in the 'real' world. She said I'd forget, or think it was all make-believe. And then, when I thought I'd have to leave Them behind forever, she said that she and Hob could come to me instead."

Felicity looked up. "I was so happy! I couldn't go to them in the woods any more, but it meant I wouldn't lose them altogether. Well, just Elfrida, really. I don't think she meant Hob to come too, but he always does." She smiled. "He is a burr, or so he says."

He held up a hand. "You are speaking more freely than before. While I am fairly sure that the wards will hold, it would perhaps be wiser not to use their names aloud. Names have a summoning power that has existed, I believe, for as long as we have had language. Perhaps even longer."

She glanced involuntarily at the window, but there was nothing to see but pale winter sky and a wisp of cloud. "Sorry. I've never talked about Them with anyone before. Oh, except for my father, this summer. Nothing bad happened then, and I suppose—well, I suppose I do feel safe here. It's quite a relief." She looked down, suddenly shy.

Professor Edgerley was leaning forward, intent. "Tell me about your father. It may well have a bearing on your questions."

Felicity frowned, remembering beechnuts underfoot, the plaintive sound of the grass whistle. "It was after France. He's had some hedges taken out, including the one at the edge of the wood, although that land is no good for ploughing. I asked him if he knew about Them. After what El—what my friend said—that it was his story to tell. He didn't say anything, but when I guessed that they had made some request of him, he got up and left."

"Ah." The professor was silent for a moment, thinking. "And yet They have requested nothing of you."

"Well, only that I don't speak, and that they can come and go as they please."

"Are you happy with that bargain?"

She laughed. "I was, at first. They didn't ever turn up at school, or in friends' houses, or anything like that, so it was like a wonderful privilege. I can see now that it probably stopped me making close friends, because I didn't need any. But since I've been here, it's been more of a nuisance, sometimes." She felt disloyal, even thinking it. "I'd hate to lose them, but they have no sense of privacy. In fact, they seem to know when they're not welcome."

"I can imagine. So tell me, if it's not a further invasion of your privacy: have they tried to shape the direction of your life in any way?"

"Well, yes, of course. I wrote about it in my notes last year."

He nodded. "You did indeed. But humour me, if you would. What exactly has your friend done to influence your decisions since you started here at Cambridge?"

Felicity put down her mug, drew up her knees and clasped them with both arms. "It started before Cambridge," she said slowly, thinking it through. "She couldn't see the point of going to university. She said with her at my side, I could do anything or go anywhere. She likes it when I go out or see friends, but she gets bored with me working or just talking with people. They both do. And actually, now I think about it, she's not that interested in my college friends. It's mainly Sebastian. That's my boyfriend," and she blushed as she said it. "She wants me to have, um, experiences. All sorts."

"Well, that might go some way towards answering your question about what they want from you," he said, pretending not to notice her embarrassment. "They, or rather she, is hungry for some of the things our world can offer. It might also explain why she teased you, as it were, with the promise of joining them one day, only to withhold it until it was too late. You have given her a window on the world."

"She wants me to shine," Felicity said abruptly. "I asked her not to, but she made me look beautiful at the May ball. What you said when you showed us the illuminated book keeps coming back to me: 'It's all about the shine.'" She had only half-listened to the last thing he said, intent on her own thoughts. "She wants me to attract attention and admiration. She's not really interested in whether people get jealous or feel hurt," remembering Tessa and that flash of dislike in her eyes, "or whether I have friends at all. She doesn't understand about wanting to learn, or that I'll need to earn a living after university. I think if I let her, she'd use magic to make me rich, make men fall in love with me, all that sort of thing."

"And you do not want that?"

"No!" The strength of her own response surprised her. "If I do well in the world, I want it to be because I deserve it." *And yet I bestowed the gift on Sebastian.* "I suppose that might sound naïve, or silly. I think it's because I've already experienced all that. When I was a child, I mean. They made me beautiful, and grown up. We flew together. You might say that it was all make-believe, but it was the most real and vivid thing in my whole life. So I know what magic feels like, and I'm not interested in using fairy gold or glamour to get what I want in real life." She laughed. "Whatever 'real life' may be."

The professor smiled. "So young, and so wise," he said. From Elfrida, that would have carried hidden mockery, but from him, she could not tell for sure. He went on, musing, his eyes on the fire, "And perhaps beyond your friend's comprehension. Being what she is, how could that make any kind of sense to her?"

"You mean, if you could get whatever you wanted by magic, why would you bother doing it the hard way?"

"Certainly that. But also this: if you could use magic to get whatever you wanted, how do you think it might shape your character?"

"Oh." Felicity had never thought about Them in quite that way. "Well, I suppose it would be hard to take things seriously. You'd get bored easily, and you might be quite inconsiderate of other people . . ." She stopped. Now, he definitely was laughing at her. "No, wait! Yes, they are like that. They love playing tricks on people, leading them up the garden path. It's all in the stories, isn't it? But if magic can get them whatever they desire, how come they're so interested in us stupid humans? Why do they steal people, or entice them away?"

"Or to put it another way, what do we have that they cannot simply conjure for themselves?"

Felicity was silent, thinking. The Professor got up to attend to the fire, adding more coals, giving her space. When she spoke, it was to herself, following her train of thought. "They can run rings around us, but they can't just leave us alone. It reminds me of something . . ."

She gazed into the pale flames, searching for the memory. Then she had it; she sat up straight, suddenly animated. "Every year, in summer, there's a fete in the village. Everyone goes. Usually there's a fair, lots of stalls, a dance in the evening. Children run loose all day, and there are always a few—boys, mostly—who spend their time being a nuisance. Stealing things off stalls, getting in the way, barging into other cars on the dodgems, that sort of thing. They behave as though they want to wreck it for everyone, even though they know their fathers will punish them for it later. And they can't just go somewhere else and let people enjoy themselves. If anything's happening, they have to be there, disrupting it."

He was back in his chair, looking at her directly now, his eyes catching the firelight. He said, very softly, "And if there were no fathers to punish them later? If they could withdraw beyond the reach of retribution? What then?"

"Children with magic powers, living free from adult constraints, but still wanting the adults to notice them. Needing them for some things, perhaps, but wanting to annoy them as well." She got up and went to the window, gazing out left and right, as though Hob might be lurking on the roof tiles, listening. But there was nothing, just the fading gleam of winter sunlight on wet tiles, and a tiny rivulet of ice in the gutter below.

As she turned back, the professor said, "Tell me, if you can remember. Which children was it who ran wild at the fair?"

"Some of them were in my class at school, when they bothered to turn up. Just boys who didn't care if they got punished. Ones who didn't do well at school, or had awful parents, like David Mace whose father got drunk all the time and beat the children. Or Johnny Grant, who couldn't sit still for five minutes. And older ones I didn't know very well." A sudden memory came to her. "One time, They mentioned a boy who used to visit them, and then found himself a girlfriend in town and stopped coming. Dick Miller, that was his name. He was one of the worst when he was at the village school. We smaller ones were all afraid of him. I was glad he was never with them when I went; he was bad news."

"So. The misfits. The damaged ones, and the just plain wild. The lonely, like you."

"Well, yes, I suppose. But not the girls. They weren't children, were they? Alys had a baby."

"She did. But does that make her an adult?"

Felicity tried to think back into her own child self. At eight or nine, teenagers had seemed like grown-ups to her. Her periods had not started until she was fourteen, and she could not even begin to think about having children for years yet, but she knew that some girls began bleeding when they were as young as ten. The professor was right: you could become a mother before you became a woman.

"They took the baby away, to give to the lord's wife," she said. "His wife couldn't have children. I don't know whether Alys slept with him willingly, or not."

"The lord's wife," he repeated. "That implies that it happened at least two hundred years ago. Whether she was willing or not, she probably had very little choice in the matter. And we know that both boys and girls were often married as children. No reliable means of birth control, remember? If a girl was sexually active, she would become pregnant unless there were something preventing it. Of course they tried to preserve their virginity, but all too often they did not succeed."

"Oh, that's horrible," she said. And then neither of them said anything for a while. Outside, the white sky had leached to no-colour, and snow had begun to fall.

"Miss Turner," he said at last. "I advise you to think carefully about these matters. It may be that we are, as they say, barking up the wrong tree. After all, They are famously good at misleading the unwary traveller. But watch, and listen, when you see them next. Do not ask leading questions. And—" he paused, looking as she had done at the window, where gathering darkness pressed against the pane, "Be careful."

CHAPTER 47

The words stayed in her mind, through the business of packing, the feverish parties in overcrowded rooms, the last-minute scrum to secure useful library books before the vacation. She looked for books about fairies and folklore, without much success. Her courses this year were all about other cultures, or sociology, and there had been no mention of home-grown mythology. When she had mentioned this to Professor Edgerley, he had laughed.

"Folklore is out of fashion," he had said. "Most of my colleagues consider it to be the province of country vicars and Victorian spinsters. The very word is pejorative. I am an eccentricity, I fear."

So that brought her back to the stories the professor had given or told to her. Stories collected from all over Britain, told by ordinary people about extraordinary happenings. She had a file full of them by now. Her own stories, of course, were in his keeping, but her memories were not. On trains between Cambridge and home, and—after Christmas—between home and London, she tried to review everything she knew. Did They really behave like children? Felicity had no chance to observe any children in college, and did not know any at home either. Except, of course, for one.

It had become the family custom to have Christmas dinner with Aunty Marjorie and Uncle Bob. Various polite reasons were given for this, but in private, Angie was as forthright as ever. "The beds are damp and it's freezing cold at your house," she had said. "And there are mice and spiders. Last time we went to see Uncle Ray, there were mushrooms growing out of the mould around the kitchen sink." All of which was true.

Instead, they would sit around the table in what Aunty Marjorie called the "dining area," in a kitchen so clean "you could eat your dinner off the floor," as Uncle Bob liked to say. Felicity suspected he said it simply to irritate his wife, but she liked to imagine him doing it, perhaps at night, in secret, leaving feathers and smears of blood on the pale linoleum for Aunty Marjorie to find in the morning.

"And what about that boyfriend of yours, Fliss?" She came back with a start. Christmas pudding was looming, after an enormous lunch "with all the trimmings." Paper hats had been unfolded from Christmas crackers, and were already askew. Aunty Marjorie was looking at her. "When are we going to meet him, then?"

"Oh, he's in a play in London just now. He's very busy. I'm not sure." She had not told them that Sebastian had left university. Had told them as little as possible, in fact, but the mere existence of Sebastian made an excellent topic of conversation over dinner.

Aunty Marjorie sniffed. "He gets about, doesn't he? All right for some." The trip to France had also been much discussed. In fact, her aunt and uncle had also been to France, on a day trip organised by their caravanning club. They had disembarked in Calais, been driven to a supermarket to buy duty-free wine, beer and cigarettes, and returned laden with spoils. It was French wine they were drinking with their roast turkey, as Aunty Marjorie had informed them more than once. In her opinion, that was quite enough Frenchness for anybody.

"I'm going to see him next week, before term starts," Felicity offered. This was Tommy's cue to scrape back his chair, making his mother wince.

"Thanks, Mum," he said. "Just off to see Maureen. Back later."

"But you haven't had any pudding!"

"I'm stuffed," said Tommy. "Save some for me."

"And you'll miss the Queen's speech. They haven't got a TV, I know."

Tommy grinned. "Yeah, they have now. Got one just before Christmas. That's why we're off out for a bit."

"Where are you taking her? You'll freeze on that motorbike."

"Just out. See you," and he was gone.

The room seemed to be larger once he was out of it. People cleared their throats and shifted in their chairs. "Well!" said Aunty Marjorie. "All the more for us. She's a nice girl, though, Maureen. Her father's an accountant."

"It won't last," said Uncle Bob. "You know what young Tommy's like. A heartbreaker, that one," he confided to the table at large. "Then they come round in tears and Marjorie has to clean up the mess. Kids, eh?"

"That was only one girlfriend," Angie said, looking up from her pudding. "Penny Myers. I liked her. Too good for my beastly brother though."

"And what about you, Angie? Are you seeing your—John, is it?" That was Felicity's mother. There was always a faint stirring of surprise when she spoke, as though one of the tall candlesticks had come to life. They were new this year, three of them along the centre of the table, getting in the way. The candles were unlit because they were a fire hazard.

Angie smiled, and her sulky face was transfigured, just for a moment. "Tomorrow. 'My John' is back at work the day after."

"I can't keep up with you lot, dashing around all over the place." Bob leaned back in his chair. "Anyone for a Tia Maria with your mince pie?"

"At least Christine's here at home, where she belongs. Aren't you, sweetheart?" Aunty Marjorie leaned over and tucked a stray curl of Christine's hair behind her ear. Christine kept her eyes down, and smiled.

"Can I have some Tia Maria, please, Dad?" She gave him a quick glance, and he winked at her.

"'May I have,' and no, you may not, young lady," said her mother, just as her father said "Well, maybe just a taste. Oh go on, Marjorie, it's Christmas."

"That's not fair. She's only nine! You never let me have stuff like that when I was her age. She gets away with murder, just because she's small and looks like a china doll." It was a fair description, Felicity thought: blonde curls, blue eyes, and Aunty Marjorie insisted on dressing her in frocks with sashes and patent leather shoes, unlike most girls of her age. Angie herself had not grown into a beauty, although you could hardly tell what she really looked like beneath the thick foundation and black eyeliner. She was a disappointment in more ways than one; you could see it in Aunty Marjorie's eyes whenever she looked at her elder daughter.

"Right," said Uncle Bob, getting to his feet. "That's my cue to start the washing up. You with me, Ray?"

"Glasses first, and rinse them afterwards. Be careful with the good plates!" All part of the Christmas ritual. Twelve days of misrule, when the natural order of things was overturned, dwindled to this: the men do the washing up on Christmas day only, and the women roll their eyes at each other and clean up properly later. Felicity wondered whether Professor Edgerley would be interested, and decided probably not.

"Christine," she said, "Would you like to go for a walk? There's ice on the pond, I bet."

"Oh no," said Aunty Marjorie at once. "You'll catch your death, and you can't go out in your best dress."

"I'll help her get changed," said Felicity. "We won't stay out long." Christine was already out of her chair and almost at the door.

"Christine! What do you say?"

She turned, gave her mother a demure smile, and said "Please may I get down?"

Felicity felt a little guilty, leaving her mother to make conversation with Aunty Marjorie, but not for long. Even before she and Christine had closed the bedroom door, the sound of the television came up from the front room. They would sip their Tia Maria and watch in silence, while the men, in a more companionable quiet, managed the washing up. And Angie, in her own bedroom, turned up her radio and hated them all.

Chapter 48

They waited until they had climbed the stile into the fields, and then held hands and ran, stumbling over tussocks and stubborn thistles. The colour came up in Christine's cheeks, and her eyes sparkled as she showed Felicity where she had found a wasps' nest hanging from a tree in the autumn. Boys had thrown stones to knock it down and then run away screaming, but she had salvaged a piece of the nest and kept it until it dried out and fell to dust. Felicity told her how traditional Japanese houses were sometimes made of paper, easy to replace and less likely to hurt people when earthquakes happened. Together, they wondered whether humans had ever made paper by chewing wood pulp, as wasps did.

The mud around the field gates, a deep and potent porridge of dung and urine, had frozen into a miniature mountain range of peaks and crevasses, creaking beneath their boots. Shallow puddles froze into strange shapes, some geometric with holes between the razor-straight sides of triangles and squares, and others all curves and layers, white and grained and clear as glass, with bubbles sliding beneath the ice. Neither of them knew what made the difference. Felicity knew that Christine would believe anything she told her, and so she was careful. It seemed important, though she could not have explained why, that for this child, only the truth would do.

At the pond, reeds stood clotted with ice, but the centre was clear. Where the stream flowed in through overgrown grass and watercress, icicles had formed, fringing the water. They took off their gloves to dip fingers in, feeling the secret current move beneath the surface, and gasping at the cold. Their fingers turned white, and then burned as the blood returned to them.

"There'll be frogspawn here in spring," said Christine. "I'm not allowed to take it home, but I come and watch the tadpoles grow."

"I know," said Felicity. "If you can manage to be here when there's a full moon in January, you might see the frogs coming to lay their eggs. There used to be hundreds of them. Toads, too."

Christine wrinkled her nose. "Not likely," she said, "if it's after dark. Unless Dad comes with me."

It surprised Felicity, though it probably shouldn't have done. Christine was nine now, and by that age Felicity had been making her own way to and from school, not to mention spending most of her time in the woods. Sometimes she had stayed out all night. She remembered Elfrida saying something about how children did not come alone any more, and wondered whether that could be why the troupe was dwindling. If some of them, at least, had once been children . . .

"And Mum wants to move into town," Christine was saying. "She says there are more opportunities there. Dad doesn't, though. They argue about it a lot."

"That's not much fun for you," Felicity said. Christine, squatting at the edge of the stream, twisted to look up at her cousin.

"You get used to it," she said, matter-of-factly, and Felicity wondered whether it was better to have parents who argued, or a mother and father like her own, existing side by side in silent unhappiness.

"I wish I could live on the farm," said Christine, as though she had heard Felicity's thoughts. "Uncle Ray and Aunty June don't mind anything, and they never tell you off. I like collecting the eggs. Angie says they're pooey, but I don't mind." She pushed her fingers into the soft mud at the water's edge, then held them up, threatening to smear them on Felicity's coat.

Felicity scrambled away, laughing, and then they both held their hands in the freezing water until they couldn't stand it any more, and flicked icy droplets at each other.

"I wish you were my sister and not stupid Angie." They had reached the edge of the woods now. It would be dark soon, time to turn back, but that was not why Felicity hesitated. This child had been taken once, and she was never alone; surely she was safe now? They would not appear if she herself was there; she had seen none of them but Elfrida and Hob for four years or so.

And yet . . . At Christine's age, she had longed to stay with Them forever, had thought them the most wonderful thing in her whole life, and now here she was, trying to protect her little cousin from those wonders. Did that make her a grown-up? She smiled at the thought, and took Christine's hand, damp and gritty and very cold.

"I wish you were, too," she said. "I hope you don't move to town, but if you do, I'll come and see you when I can. And maybe it's better, being cousins. We'd probably fight all the time."

"No, we wouldn't! You're nice, and you let me do things. At school they always say, 'You take after your cousin.' Except for not having red hair, of course."

"Do they? I wonder what they mean by that?"

"Just liking lessons, mostly, and being interested in animals and things." Christine gave a little skip. "And then they say, 'How is she getting on at Cambridge?' and I have to say, 'Very well, thank you.' Though I don't know, not really. What's it like there?"

"Maybe you could come and visit. In the summer term, after exams." Her parents had been, once, trailing around the colleges and standing around awkwardly when she introduced them to her friends. She could not imagine Aunty Marjorie there.

"It's beautiful," she said. "And really, really cold just now. When I cycle in to lectures in the morning, I get frost in my eyebrows!"

Christine giggled. “You could wear a balaclava,” she said, “Like the boys at school. Only people might laugh at you.”

“People wear all sorts of things, and nobody laughs,” said Felicity. “There’s a boy who comes to some of my lectures, and he wears this sort of pink tablecloth thing. And nobody takes any notice at all. You can be whoever you like.”

That was a step too far; she could see that Christine did not quite believe her. Felicity would have liked to take this beautiful child and show her how much bigger the world could be. She had read somewhere that if you save someone’s life, you are responsible for them forever. That was how it felt. What would Christine have been now if she had stayed with Alys? She pushed the thought away.

“You’ll see, one day,” she said. Angie worked in a shop in town, and was going out with a boy who was a bank teller. “I’m sure they’ll be engaged soon; I don’t know what they’re waiting for. He’s got good prospects,” Aunty Marjorie had said, when Angie was out of the room. Getting married and having a home of her own was the height of Angie’s ambition, as far as anyone could tell, but it did not seem to make her happy. If Christine grew up to have wider horizons, Felicity would feel that at least part of her responsibility had been fulfilled.

Christine read her thoughts again. “I want to see now!” she said.

“Well, maybe you could ask Uncle Bob if you could all come up for a weekend, or something.” Felicity’s heart sank at the thought, but it would be the only way. “But summer really would be better. I’ll have lots of work to do this term, and I might be in London quite a bit. Sebastian’s in a play there.”

“Is he a famous actor?”

Felicity laughed. “He might be, one day.”

“Can you get me his autograph for my book?”

“Of course I can. I could take your book with me, and give it back to you at Easter.”

They had almost reached the stile into the last field, the one where Elfrida had stood while Felicity returned Christine to her family. She could not help glancing at the spot, though there were only docks and nettles there now. You couldn't see into the garden any longer; Uncle Bob had put up a tall wooden fence because Aunty Marjorie said the cows brought flies with them. Only the bedroom windows were still visible. Christine looked up, and frowned.

"We've been a long time, and I got dirty. Mummy will be cross, and she'll have to take an extra pill."

Felicity stopped. "I didn't know Aunty Marjorie was on pills."

"Oh yes. She takes them to help her cope. It's my fault."

"What? How is it your fault?"

"I was ill when I was a baby, and they thought there was something wrong with me. Angie says the doctors were baffled, and they talked about putting me in a home. When Angie's being mean, she says she wishes they had. And Mummy had to go on pills for her nerves, and Daddy went to the pub a lot, so Angie had to do everything at home. She says that was all my fault."

Only truth will do for this child. How much of the truth is another matter . . . Felicity sat down on the stile. "Come here," she said, and Christine came to lean against her.

"Listen," she said. "None of it was your fault, I promise you. Remember this; it's important. Something happened to you, and you weren't well for a time, and then you got better. I didn't think you knew anything about it, or I'd have told you that sooner. I should have thought, of course, I might have known Angie or Tommy would tell you things."

"People at school do, too. Mandy Reed says her mother thought I was dull-witted. I'm not, am I?"

"It's Mandy Reed's mother who's dull-witted!" said Felicity, and Christine giggled again.

"It's funny how you can't remember stuff that happened

when you were a baby," she said. "Do you remember anything from that far back?"

Oh yes. Leaves and laughing faces, and the blue sky beyond. "Not really," said Felicity aloud. "What about you? Do you remember anything at all?"

"I'm not sure. It's all muddled up, like dreams or stories. Things that couldn't be real. And you can't tell how old you were, can you?"

"Well, this would be from before you could walk or talk, so that might be a clue." *Surely the memory is there, somewhere? She just doesn't recognise it for what it is, I suppose.*

Then Christine said,

"I still see my imaginary friends, sometimes."

Felicity stopped breathing. After a moment she said, carefully, "What are they like?" The questions were buzzing around them like a swarm of bees. *Be careful.*

"We used to play together sometimes, down by the stream when Daddy was fishing. He said my little fingers were better at tying flies and undoing knots. He never caught anything much. Angie said he did it just to get away from Mum."

"So who were your friends?"

"They only came when he was asleep," Christine said, in a dreamy voice, seeing them in her mind's eye. "I haven't seen them for a while now, though."

"What were they called, Christine?" Felicity's mouth was dry. She had not known, until this moment, how much she had missed the others: Lovet and Ember, Adder and Fungus, and the rest. The woods were full of their absence, and it hurt, knowing that they might be just out of sight, watching her, laughing.

"Well, that's the thing. They never looked the same, and I didn't know their names, but somehow I knew that they were the same people, even when they were small as beetles or all twisty like the roots of trees. That's funny, isn't it?" She looked up at Felicity with those wondering blue eyes. "When kids at school have imaginary friends, there's usually only one. They always have a name, and you sort of know they're really making it all up."

"Did they—" Felicity had to clear her throat and try again. "Did they ever want you to go with them?"

Christine did not seem to understand the question. "We played at being tiny, and at tickling the fish, and tying Dad's shoelaces together. I don't think we ever went far from the stream, though. We'd better go in now."

"Just a minute." Felicity tried to think. What could she ask that would make sense to her cousin? "How did you know they were imaginary?"

Christine just stared at her. "Well, they couldn't be real, could they? And if anyone came along the path, they couldn't see them. Only me." She hopped down off the stile and started across the last field, towards the house.

Felicity followed slowly. She was remembering how Elfrida had touched her eyelids; one of the few times they had actually physically touched. Perhaps, when they had taken Christine, they had done the same to her. Would it last for a lifetime?

She thought of Professor Edgerley. He could see Them, and she had never thought to ask how that could be. He must have his own story to tell, but she was much too shy to ask. And Christine, too; she had thought, when she placed her back in her own playpen, that that would be the end of it for her. As if she didn't know by now that bargains made with Them never quite turned out the way you might expect.

Christine had almost reached the far side of the field now. At the corner, she turned to wave, and then climbed over the gate. Daylight was fading, and Felicity was alone.

"Keep her safe," she said to the empty air. She waited for a moment, half-hoping, before starting her own trudge across the frozen grass.

Chapter 49

The few days in London were a blur of faces, endless talk, and not enough sleep. Felicity and Sebastian were sharing a sofa bed in someone's living room, so there was nowhere to retreat until the last wine glass was emptied and the last cigarette smoked, and the last friend finally left before the underground trains stopped running, if they were lucky.

The play was doing well, and the run had been extended. There was talk of Sebastian taking a bigger role if it continued, and certainly in the next production. People brought newspapers and exclaimed over the reviews. Sebastian had been approached by an agent; should he accept the deal, or might something better come along? There was talk, and talk, and talk, and always, he was at the centre of the group. To Felicity, he looked pale and a little tired, but that was clearly not what others saw when they looked at him. When she managed to persuade him to go out for a walk in daylight, heads turned as they walked along the street, and one young woman stopped them and asked for his autograph.

This wasn't just about the play; that was obvious. Or rather, the play itself was part of what was going on. She couldn't tell how good he really was at acting, if "really" had any meaning at all here, and she was sure that one play in a small theatre meant very little to most people. It was the gift that made them turn in the street and forget they were in a hurry to be somewhere else. In his chosen profession, the gift might catapult him to the starry heights. She saw that, and began to be afraid.

There were rehearsals for a new play. She sat, almost alone in the empty theatre, watching the dustmotes move in the lights trained on the stage. Outside, there was gentle afternoon sunshine, and she was thinking about how the professor had drawn the curtains and turned off the electric lights to show them the shine. It seemed that if you lived for the shine, as the actors did, you had to spend most of your life in darkness.

Felicity slipped out of the theatre and went walking, with no particular aim in mind. The sunlight and fresh air were like a blessing after the frowsty gloom of the theatre, and after a few minutes she came to a park. There was a pond, with ducks who came cruising towards her though she had nothing to give them, and she had the place to herself in the post-Christmas sleep before the world started up again. Out of the shade, it was warm enough to sit for a while on one of the benches that fringed the pond. She got out her sketchbook, and began to draw the patchwork patterns on the trunk of the nearest plane tree.

She was thinking of Christine, and the pure pleasure of being with just one person at a time, when a shower of something pattered down on her head and made her look up with a start. High on a branch of the tree sat Hob, raining crumbled bark upon her.

She jumped up, shaking bark from her hair and clothes. "That could have gone in my eye!" she said.

"Then you would see what the trees see, leaf and root and tunnelling beetle. Though these are strange trees, all dressed in motley like fools."

"They're plane trees. They shed their bark, and that means they can survive in cities with all the pollution." She wasn't quite sure how that worked, but Hob wasn't interested. He aimed another handful of flakes at her.

"I've been at home. I thought I might see you there," she said. "You haven't been around so much lately."

"Here and there and there and here," he chanted. "Why stay at home when the wide world awaits you?"

Together, they watched Elfrida walking around the far side of the pond, saw the ducks arrowing across to gather around her feet like little courtiers, scrambling over each other to get close. She stopped, then threw out one arm in a wide arc, scattering something. Not bark, Felicity hoped. Whatever it was, the ducks fell upon it joyfully.

Hob sprang about like a squirrel in the branches, showering her with twigs, so she got up and went to the edge of the pond. The ducks ignored her, quarrelling noisily over who could get closest to Elfrida, and she watched the group drifting slowly around until Elfrida came to a stop, a few feet away. Today she looked almost ordinary, just a girl in a long dress, wearing silver earrings and bracelets that rang together as she moved. Felicity had seen plenty of girls like that, wearing far more outlandish clothes. Ordinary, until she looked up and met Felicity's gaze.

"This city is full of souls," she said. "How can there be so many, all in one place? The lands must be stripped bare for miles around."

"There are bigger cities in the world," said Felicity. "Food can be kept fresh and brought from a long way away." This was not the conversation she wanted to be having. "I don't like London much, but this is where Sebastian needs to be."

"This is a place of marvels."

"It's dirty and smelly and noisy, most of the time." Felicity looked around at the peaceful winter park, and laughed. "There are places like this, more than in a lot of cities, but not enough. I might have to live here for a while, but I don't want to, really."

"Foolish girl," said Elfrida. "Your path could be broad and straight like that road yonder, if you so chose. Your pretty lover and his friends yearn for the world to fall at their feet, but I can give you that and more. Why does it always have to be books, and words, and more books? You are afraid to live your life, and your youth will not last for long."

"People live longer, these days." It was the least of the many things she could have said. She turned away, walked a few paces, and came back to stand by Elfrida, looking out over the pond. The ducks were following Hob now, climbing over him without fear when he lay down in the muddy grass, chattering quietly to each other. "Elfrida, my life is full of riches. I get to live in a beautiful place, to study with the brightest people. And you're right. It won't last long, and I want to treasure every moment." It was true. "Even if I could go into fairyland now, I wouldn't. Not if I had to choose."

Elfrida stared at her, and Felicity could not read her expression. "Well. So be it, for now. Who would have thought such a child could spring from Turner stock?"

"It's not the family, Elfrida. It's the times. People have more choices these days. I'm sure I'd have been a farmer's wife if I'd been born even twenty years earlier." *Though not, perhaps, a happy one.* "I'd have grown up, as you predicted, and forgotten about you, and been afraid to let my own children play in the woods without quite understanding why. Just like my aunt and uncle now, with Christine." She spoke the name deliberately, wanting to see where it might lead.

Elfrida smiled. "That one," she said. "She is not bold enough to fly. Not like you. They hold her on silken reins, and she does not seek to break them."

Felicity took a deep breath, and let it slowly out. *Careful, now.* "I think that's because they lost her once," she said. "And although Christine doesn't really remember, I think it's made her cautious."

She waited. For what? An explosion of anger? But all Elfrida said was, "Just so. That is why she will never find her way beyond the border now. Her eyes are open, but she will forget how to see." She watched Felicity for a moment, and then said, "Why so sad? It is the way of things."

"Yes, but . . ." Felicity looked away, not wanting Elfrida to see the tears in her eyes. She had made her own decisions, and there was a kind of peace in that, even though the contradictions in her life sometimes seemed impossible to manage. But Christine? She had never had a choice. She would forget her not-so-imaginary friends, grow up and become ordinary. Elfrida must have seen it happen so many times in her long, long life. Did she never feel sad, or was there only mockery left?

"Elfrida," she said suddenly, "don't adults ever remember? I mean, I can't be the only one, surely. There must be other people, here and there." *Like the professor.* She would not speak his name, but still it felt dangerous. *Be careful.*

"Oh, now and then, here and there. Poets and dreamers, drunkards and desperate men. More than you might imagine. Usually only for a little time, and then they tell themselves a story to make their lives bearable again, and on they go. You humans have a great talent for lying to yourselves."

"But where does make-believe end and lying begin? I can remember being told off for lying when I was small, lots of times, when I was just making up stories about the cats having a party or my dolls talking to me. I never said anything to anyone about you, though," she added quickly. "Somehow, I knew that was secret and precious, and much more real than my everyday life, a lot of the time."

"For a child like you, my Felicity, that knowing came to you without any need for words. Not all children are so fortunate, and grown men and women, almost never." Elfrida turned in a circle, including all the houses on the boundary of the park with one wide sweep of her arm. "How many live behind those windows, do you think? There must be many hundreds, surely. Among them all there might be one, perhaps, who might look this way and see something more than just a girl by the water."

As her hand moved, colour seemed to flow from her fingers as though she was painting on the air; a bright ribbon that became a river, and then a torrent, and a storm of butterflies, blue and crimson and orange, whirling around them. Felicity felt the wind of their passing, heard their wings beating, and then the whole cloud lifted into the air, higher and still higher, until it dwindled into the pale blue of the winter sky, and was gone.

"If perchance someone did look this way at just that moment, what do you think they are telling themselves now?" Elfrida was watching her, smiling.

"Yes, of course, I get it. If I saw that myself, and didn't know you were here, I'd probably explain it away somehow. But you touched my eyelids. You gave me the ability to see. That must have happened to other children from time to time. I can't be the only one."

"Perhaps." Elfrida did not seem to be much interested in the possibility. "Those ones you are staying with, the ones your beloved spends his time with: they talk about making magic with their lights and costumes and words and music, but would any of them know it if they saw it in the plain light of day? Pah! I do not think so." She bent to stroke the head of one of the mallards, and it looked sideways up at her, quite still. "It is much simpler for these little ones."

"You've been watching us." It was not a question.

"Of course. I will tell you what is in plain sight before your eyes, and yet you choose not to see. If you go back to your books and your beautiful rich life of study, you will lose that young man. There are others around him who are hungry for what he has, and they will take him from you."

Felicity laughed. "Oh, I know who you mean!" *Rowena with her eyeliner and purple lipstick, or Sophie who looks fabulous in a leotard.* "We've talked about that; those girls who eat him with their eyes and think everything he says is amazing. Sebastian loves me. I know he does." It felt dangerous to say so, right out loud, as though some malignant providence might be listening. But there was only Hob, crawling among the reeds with the ecstatic ducks, and Elfrida, crouching down now, stroking the mallard's smooth feathers, over and over.

"You are his one true love; I do not doubt it. What difference does that make?"

"Elfrida." Felicity felt on safer ground now. "You are my dearest friend, and wiser than me in so many ways." She paused, choosing her words. "I don't know whether you have ever been truly loved. I know that people adore you—even that duck there—because you are gorgeous and magical, and marvels happen around you. I started out from there, when I was small and lonely and you invited me into your circle. And I understand that that's what people see in Sebastian. They want a part of it, and they think that by getting close to him, they can somehow share it. Whether that's only because of the gift I gave him, I don't know. But it's not the same as love, not at all."

She stopped, fearing she had said too much; said things, indeed, that she had not even known she knew until this moment. Elfrida said nothing; did not even look up at her. After a moment Felicity went on. "We've made promises to each other. We trust each other. Of course girls are going to be attracted to him. Men, too. But the glamour is all about potential and possibility; it's all about shine. And the thing about shine is that you can't see through it; it just reflects you back to yourself. What we have is down-to-earth, and often not shiny at all. But it's real." And then she felt suddenly foolish, talking to the top of Elfrida's bent head, talking into thin air. "I'm going to see what Hob's up to in those reeds."

She had gone just a few paces when Elfrida spoke behind her. "And I say again: what difference does that make?"

Felicity swung round, exasperated. "All the difference in the world!"

Elfrida was standing now. No longer a young girl in a faded

green dress, but a tall and majestic woman. Jewels flashed at her throat and wrists, in her hair and sewn into the fabric of her clothes. She was all shine. She looked down at Felicity, and smiled.

"You are young," she said. "You will learn how much your true love is worth. Humans have always been dazzled by firelight and starlight and the glitter of gold. They always want that one thing more. They put out their hands to the fire, even when they know it will burn and destroy. The only reason you think you know better is that you do not believe it can be yours. Your 'down to earth' is not wisdom, but fear. You turned away from what we offered you out of fear, and you refuse my help now because you are afraid. But you will see, in time. And sooner or later, you will lose him."

The light around her grew more and more intense, dazzling, until Felicity could not bear it any longer. She closed her eyes, and even then it was too much, brighter than looking into the summer sun at midday. She put her hands over her eyes, weeping with the pain.

When at last she could see again, there was nothing to see but the empty park, and her sketchbook fallen on the muddy grass, and the wandering ducks, forsaken.

Chapter 50

Elfrida's words trembled inside her like an annoying piece of music, playing over and over again until all its meaning is leached away. *It's rubbish,* she thought as she and Sebastian stole some precious time alone, away from the overcrowded flat, always full of people smoking, or sleeping, or talking. By night it had a kind of glamour, with its strange collection of posters and curios; everything from a stolen street sign to a vase full of peacock feathers to a human skull, complete with lopsided trilby hat and cigar. Candlelight, low lamps draped with scarves, and the leak of yellow street light through drooping curtains, all lent their small magics, just like the spotlights in the theatre. But by day, it was simply squalid. No one emptied the ashtrays or cleared away the stained coffee mugs. Felicity had done it herself once or twice, wanting to be friendly, and then realised that if they noticed at all, they despised her for it.

It's not true. She just likes to needle me. They were sitting in a café some streets away, having a very late breakfast. She had a train to catch. For Sebastian, it was time stolen from sleep.

"I'll come down again in a couple of weeks," she said. "I've got no supervisions on Fridays, so I can get an afternoon train."

Sebastian frowned. "There might be a meeting about a new production then; I can't remember what's in the diary." He yawned. "But we'll make time, don't worry."

"Maybe we could go to an exhibition. I haven't been to the Natural History Museum since we had a school trip when I was ten. There's loads I want to see."

"Maybe. We'll have to play it by ear." He took her hand, kissing each knuckle in turn. The waitress, in the act of serving food at the next table, forgot what she was doing. So did the couple seated there. Sebastian, in a woollen scarf and fingerless mittens because it was always cold in the flat, looked utterly endearing to Felicity, but hardly glamorous.

The shine reflects you back to yourself. Out loud, she said, "I wonder why we're so keen to see other people as more special than we are?" The waitress gave her a pitying look, so she leaned over and kissed Sebastian, right on the mouth. *So there.* "I don't care what we do, as long as we manage a few hours, somehow. When can you come up to Cambridge?" She moved her chair around so that she could lean her head against him, and he put his arm around her. *Asserting ownership now,* she thought, and smiled.

"Don't know yet. It'll have to be midweek, in any case." He yawned again. "Sorry. More coffee?"

"Not for me." But the waitress was already there, filling his mug, leaning over him, too close. She smelled of bacon grease and deodorant, hairspray and stale human. Felicity recoiled. Sebastian, ever polite, thanked her, and avoided Felicity's eye until she had retreated back behind her counter.

Felicity watched him take a sip of the fresh coffee. He made a face. "That's been brewing too long."

"I thought vampires only came out after dark."

"Shh. She might hear you."

"I don't care, much." She looked at her watch. "I have to go. Watch out for her fangs."

He held the coffee mug against his face, enjoying the warmth. "You're my garlic necklace. How shall I manage without you?"

"So romantic." She kissed him again, and he put down the mug and held her close. "Love you," she whispered into his ear, and then was up and moving to the door, not looking at any of the audience, and out into a biting January wind. They were all right. Now, in this moment, they were fine, and Elfrida's prophecies meant no more than the cloud of butterflies. *Are you watching now, Elfrida? We're fine.*

Her own room awaited her, quiet and clean and warm. She eased the heavy rucksack off her shoulders, shut the door and just stood for a moment, taking possession. *I'm home.* Other people were arriving; she could hear doors banging and voices raised, but here was her sanctum, and no one could come in without her permission. She had not realised how precious that was, until now.

Well, almost no one. Upon the pillow of the freshly made bed lay a single feather, soft grey to black, and then the gorgeous intense blue, shading back to black and then white at the tip. A wing feather from a male mallard. *We may come to you wherever you are.* She picked it up, smoothing it through her fingers. There were no exams this term, and no Sebastian to distract her. Time, she thought, to do some serious research. *Who are you, Elfrida?*

Once more, she read through the stories the professor had given her. They came from all over the British Isles, and the fairies themselves came in all shapes and sizes. Not much help there. Hob never changed, but whether he could not, or would not, was another question. Alys had not changed, either, and Felicity knew that she, at least, had once been human. She, and her poppet. How long had it taken for that creature—*Annie,* she corrected herself. *Her name was Annie*—to become something so far from human that her own mother, if she could have seen her, would have recoiled in horror?

If the professor's theory was correct, then some at least of the troupe had also once been human. Human children, to be exact; children who had stepped out of their own time and found refuge in the borderlands. What was it he had said? "The daring, the desperate and the just plain wild." Children like herself, eager and willing to shed their everyday lives, to live in a world of make-believe where they would never want for anything again. Or like Alys, fleeing horror and persecution. By their clothes and their speech, Felicity judged some of them to be many hundreds of years old, and she knew that the life of a child back then must have been unimaginably different. Hard work, hunger, physical abuse and worse must have been commonplace. And if, now and then, a child disappeared, what could be done about it?

She thought about her own times, and the stories people told to keep children close. Gypsies were said to kidnap children, or they might run away to join the circus, perhaps. They were warned against talking to strangers, but she knew from her sociological research that when a child came to harm, it was usually at the hands of its own family. And perhaps that was a clue. How many disappearances were blamed on the gypsies, when the truth was buried somewhere far closer to home? And if, once in a while, a child found its way to a place of sanctuary beyond the reach of adults and their cruelty, who would ever know?

This feels right.

Some of Them, at least, had once been children. Children who had taken refuge, but still remained on the edge of the world they had known, watching their families grow and change, and new generations taking their place. Watching their age-mates getting older, and having children of their own, and dying. Were they never tempted to try to return to the life they had known? There were stories about grown men and women stolen by the fairies, who yearned to escape. They could only be rescued by their loved ones, at great risk to themselves. Felicity did not think anyone would have tried to rescue her, if she had crossed the border and disappeared from her human life. Not even her father, although she was sure that he had known Them, long ago.

So. Damaged or desperate children, who found that whatever they imagined could become real, just like that. Together, they could create and sustain wonders beyond anything they could have managed on their own. If there was a leader, perhaps a little older or more daring than the rest, they could become a force to be reckoned with. But with the values and judgment of children, of course they would be mischievous, capricious, not to be trusted. And if they sought revenge for the wrongs done to them, they would be capable of great malice and thoughtless cruelty.

Felicity was unpacking as she mulled over what she knew, or thought she knew, putting away books in their places, stowing clothes in drawers. Time to go out and buy milk later, and maybe some food to eat in her room. She had overspent her budget in London. There were pieces of the puzzle missing; some things did not make sense. If the way Hob looked was his true form, he was certainly no child.

The knock at the door made her jump. There was Steph, in a new jumper that must have been a Christmas present. She sang out "Happy New Year!" and hugged Felicity. Hugs were still not easy to handle gracefully; she smelled of shampoo and warm wool and, after a moment, Felicity lifted her arms and hugged her back.

"When did you get back? I've just finished unpacking. Listen, my parents drove me up with a carload of food. You must come and help me eat some of it. If I put it in the fridge it will just disappear by magic. Hurry up and sort all this, and I'll arrange a picnic. Fifteen minutes? Brilliant." Steph waved a hand and was gone.

Will it ever be easy to accept Steph's generosity, knowing I can't repay her? It was a useless question. If she didn't go now, Steph would be hurt. And she did want to catch up with all the news. This term's book of meal tokens would be waiting in her pigeonhole, and she could get milk and breakfast at the buttery tomorrow. Really, it was silly to invent problems where they didn't exist. She picked up the feather again, held it against her cheek for a moment, then tucked it behind one of the postcards on her noticeboard. It would be safe there. She had nothing to contribute to the feast, but she could offer to cook a meal another day.

Chapter 51

For the next few weeks, whenever she had a spare moment, Felicity found herself going over and over everything that she could remember about Them. There were not many spare moments, stolen from a busy schedule of lectures, supervisions and essay work. Once or twice, she laid her work aside and tried to summon Hob and Elfrida, but that had never worked before and it did not work now. If they came, they were not visible to her. But she knew that her quiet life bored them, and they were unlikely to turn up of their own accord.

She was hesitant about visiting Professor Edgerley again, with nothing new to say. Although Elfrida did not seem to know that she had spoken about Them in the sanctuary of his study, still it felt dangerous, not to be done lightly. And in the meantime, there were other things to think about. She went into the Junior Common Room one afternoon to check the noticeboard for the time of a meeting, and was hailed by Steph, who was reading the Observer.

"Have you seen this?" Steph held up the paper. "Your boyfriend is making waves."

Felicity sat down and took the paper, opened to the reviews section. The review was supposed to be about the play, but most of it seemed to be devoted to Sebastian. "Astonishing young talent"; "rising star"; "mesmerising performance," she read. She looked for the by-line. The writer was a critic known for his acid tongue, but this time he had found nothing to be critical about.

"Wow," she said. Steph was watching her expectantly. "I mean, he's very good, but this is amazing."

"You must have seen the play. What did you think?"

"Oh, it's great. Brilliant, actually. They're working on the next production now."

"So he's definitely left Cambridge for good?"

"It's looking that way, yes. This is what he wanted." She could see that Steph felt her response was inadequate. "He'll be really excited about this. I wonder if he's seen it yet?"

"Exciting for you, too. Is it working OK, being apart most of the time?"

"Well, you know." *I'm going to be answering that question a lot in the next few days.* "Even if he was here, actors seem to work at night and sleep most of the day. I'm going down again in a couple of weeks. We're taking it day by day. What else can you do?" The picture next to the article showed Sebastian with a girl on either arm, dazzled by a camera flash. That must have been at the party after the first play finished. She took Steph's meaning, even though she had been more diplomatic than Elfrida. "That sort of thing happens all the time. They are actors, after all."

"Good luck with that! He's a hot property, that one."

"Yes, I had noticed." They both laughed, and Felicity was turning away when a thought struck her. "Steph, when you're researching something historical, how do you go about it?"

"What's your time period?"

"No specific time, really. Anything from the recent past to way back. That's not very helpful, is it?"

Steph ignored the question. "What do you want to find out?"

Felicity took a deep breath. "Would there be any records of missing children?"

There, she had said it.

Steph looked away, thinking. "Nowadays, you'd have police reports, articles in local and national papers. Lots of stuff. But

I don't think that would go back very far. Even a hundred years ago, say, the coverage would be very patchy. It would depend on whether the child was from a wealthy family, I should think. Does that help?"

"Sort of. What about when you go further back?"

"I don't know where you'd start. Parish records only have births, marriages and deaths, and sometimes occupation. Court records survive for some places, but there would only be a court case if there was a dispute over custody or something. In feudal times, serfs weren't allowed to move around freely, but if you just went missing and changed your name, I don't suppose it would be easy to track you down. So I guess children could have gone missing without any official paper trail. Parish records of births often don't survive from that far back, so you'd have no documentation of a child's existence in the first place." For the first time, she came back from her scholarly examination of the question. "Are you looking for someone in particular?"

"No, not exactly." Felicity thought fast. "We've been looking at the stories people told about children being taken by the gypsies and so on, and I wondered if there was any way to check, one way or the other."

"Well, I guess the short answer is, 'no.'" Steph laughed. "And actually, people can drop out of their lives and reinvent themselves quite easily, even nowadays. Countries like Germany have identity cards, but we don't. Though if a child disappeared, an adult would have to be involved."

That's all you know. "Thanks. That's really helpful, even though it doesn't answer the question. It saves me going through old records looking for something that isn't there."

"What the records leave out can be as revealing as what they say. That's what Dr. Armitage keeps telling us, though it's not very useful when you're trying to research something. It all comes down to money and power, according to the Marxists.

But I'm not sure that would apply to missing children. They were workers, but not very valuable ones. The mortality rate historically was shocking, but no one would have been much interested if a child just disappeared, I suppose. Except its parents, of course." Steph looked thoughtful. "There might be a dissertation there, if you were doing history. I'll see what I can dig up if you like."

"Well, thanks, Steph. Only if you come across anything; don't waste time digging on my account."

"No problem." Steph held up the paper again. "Do you want to keep this?"

"Oh! It's today's, isn't it? No, better leave it. There was a row last term about someone cutting out the crosswords. And I'm sure Sebastian will have all the reviews." Felicity left her to her reading. She had been almost reluctant to look at the paper when Steph offered it, because she knew already what it would say. This was not the first, and there would be more, and more.

I gave this to him, but it's out of my hands now.

Chapter 52

The days fell now into a familiar pattern: lectures in the morning, supervisions and essay-writing in the afternoon, and going out to meetings and folk clubs in the evening with Steph and other friends. Hob and Elfrida did not appear. Sebastian came up once, midweek, slept for most of the day and went back to London for a television interview. As far as it could ever be, Felicity's life was normal. She was almost halfway through her time at university now, and it felt more precious than ever. As for what would come next, she still had no idea, and did not want to think about it.

She had put aside her questions about fairies for the time being, and so the next clue came as a complete surprise. She was not studying physical anthropology this year, but a reference came up to variations in human bone growth, and she turned to her anatomy and physiology textbook from the first year of her course. Alongside the section on bone formation was one about cartilage. She read:

"Structures such as the nose and ears are composed largely of cartilage, which continues to grow throughout life."

Is that why very old people seem to have bigger ears and noses than when they were young? It struck her as amusing; what would you look like if you could live to be two hundred years old, say?

Then, as understanding dawned, she shivered all over as though a cold wind had swept through the quiet library.

For a few moments that seemed like a very long time, she

sat quite still, as if not moving could slow down the flood of her thoughts. She glanced around, but no-one seemed to have noticed anything. Very quietly, she turned to a blank piece of paper, got out a soft pencil, and began to draw.

The first face was that of a child, round-faced and large-eyed, looking up from under a tousled head of hair. Girl or boy? For the moment, it made no difference. Then, on the lower half of the page, she drew the same face, but this time she gave it grotesquely enlarged and misshapen ears, and a hooked nose that almost hid the mouth. Then she sat back as though the thing had suddenly come to life and leered at her. With a few small adjustments, it could be Hob, or Adder, or any of the ones she thought of as goblins.

What other changes might there be? Would they have bent backs, knobbly knees? They would stay the same height as they had been when they crossed the border, but they would not stay the same. In a hundred years, two hundred, their own parents would not have known them. Maybe the magic itself changed them, too, in subtle and gradual ways. They did not grow up, certainly, but they did grow.

All at once, Felicity could not bear to sit still any longer. There was not enough air in the library; she wanted to sweep her books onto the floor, turn the table over, lift her head and scream into the exquisite oak-beamed ceiling. Of course, she did none of those things. Instead, she gathered up her books and crept out, found her bicycle, and rode back to college. But that was no good either. Back on the bicycle, she rode out into the lanes west of the city, between hedges already thick with cow parsley, not yet in flower but leaning into the road on both sides. She rode until she came to a field, bordered by oaks with the first signs of budding leaves, and there she came at last to rest in the fragile spring sunshine.

She lay down flat, closed her eyes and felt herself sink into the earth, the way she used to do when she was a child herself.

It felt like a long, long time ago; another lifetime. How would it feel if you had left your childhood behind hundreds of years ago? And if that childhood was just a distant memory of pain and misery? Would you want to linger on the border, getting your revenge on the people who had mistreated you? Or would you want to move Onward, putting more and more distance between yourself and your old life?

Before she opened her eyes, she knew that Hob was there. Hob's arrival generally involved leaves down the back of her neck or even ants in her hair, but not this time. She had been listening to the tiny sounds of insects in the grass, the buzzing of early bees, the urgent spring calling of birds, and the soft background murmur of wind in the trees. Gradually, she became aware of another sound. Almost a song, but not quite. Stopping and starting, a few notes at a time, low and soothing like the bourn slipping over stones in the shallows. Carefully, she turned her head towards the sound, and opened her eyes just a little, just enough to see.

He was squatting a few feet away, crooning his almost-song. Beyond him, just where the stalks of last year's docks stood, where in summer the leaf-shade would not quite reach, there was a stoat. Sitting upright, her bright black eyes fixed on Hob, motionless. The vivid russet of her fur stood out like fire against the drab winter grass. It was as though the life force of the awakening spring had concentrated into one form; not moving, but brimful of possibility.

Something was beginning. Hob was moving his head from side to side, just a little at first, and the stoat mirrored him. Her gaze never wavered, but her body began a kind of sinuous dance, swaying like the tall grass, but out of step with the wind. Hob's form was changing, slipping long and low, close to the earth, holding up one paw and looking over his shoulder at the waiting stoat. For a long moment, the world held its breath.

Suddenly, they were off. Leaping and twisting, over and

under, too fast to follow, but the red streak of their passing lingered on the air, weaving a kind of cat's cradle that held all the fierce joy of spring flowers and nest-building and sun returning. *Once*, Felicity thought, *I would have been dancing with them.* But somehow, now, the thought did not bring pain. *There is joy in witnessing, too.*

As abruptly as it had started, the dance was over. The two stoats darted off into the grass. For a few seconds longer, the cat's cradle remained, and then it too was gone. But Felicity was on the watch now. When the robin appeared, looking at her with its head on one side, she held out her hand.

"Come on, then." The bird watched her for a moment or two, and then took flight, as Hob's strong arms hugged her from behind and they both fell sideways into the grass. He let go and went into a series of handsprings, finishing up a few inches from her face. She sat up, brushing dead grass from her clothes.

"You were a tumbler. A good one." She had thought about what to say. "And Lovet travelled with you."

Hob shook himself, like a dog after a swim. "Not he! That one came from north a ways, with a troupe that had a fire-eater and a dancing bear." He chuckled. "We understood but one word in three, he spoke so strangely. But his pipe spoke for him, oh yes." He mimed playing the pipe. "And he found us more to his liking than his old master, for all he could not speak to us. And even now does not, mostly."

"But the bear stayed behind." Not a question.

For a moment, Hob looked almost sad. "We opened the cage and out he came. No more dancing; but he had forgot the right way for a bear to live. The hunters took him in the end." He hugged himself, then went into a forward roll and came up several feet away. "There have been no bears for many and many a year, when the troupes come by. Where have they all gone?"

"They don't have bears any more. Lions and tigers and elephants, but not bears. I don't know why." Felicity thought quickly. "But they do have jugglers and tumblers and fire-eaters when the circus comes. I expect you've seen them. None as good as you, though."

Hob chuckled again. "And do they have cutpurses and pickpockets? That trade brought in more coin than the tumbling, most times. But only on the last night, mind. Then we would be off and away next morn, before they thought to speak together and take it up with the leader of the troupe."

"But you stayed."

"Stayed? I was caught with my fingers in Farmer Cartwright's pocket, and he swore he'd cut them off for me next day. Would have done it, too; he'd taken off two fingers from his stable lad for eating bread meant for the pig's mash."

"Oh, that's awful. How—" Felicity checked herself. "You've still got all your fingers, though."

Hob held them up for inspection, then made his knuckles crack. "That lad let me out of the kennel where they chained me, just before dawn. A good lockpicker, he was, but he wouldn't come with me. Said the troupe would have no use for an eight-fingered boy. Turned out they had no use for me either. They'd packed up and gone with the dusk, and no telling where to seek."

"Poor Hob; you must have been so lonely. And then you hid in the woods, until you found the way through." She could hardly believe it was this easy. The whole story, untold for so long, flowing out of him with scarcely a pause. Was it because she had, at last, found the right question, and the right way not to ask? Or was it—she could not help glancing over her shoulder—because, for once, he was alone?

He was hugging himself again. "They came with dogs, but they could not spare too much time; it was haymaking, and fine weather. In the dark, I was sure they would find me. I could hear the dogs baying, men shouting. A merry dance! By and by, there was cursing, and then, oh! The howling and screaming." He put back his head and howled like a dog. "At the last, when all was quiet, I crept out of the thicket where I was hid. It was then They came to me."

She was nodding, understanding, reliving her own path into Elsewhere. "And Elfrida was there."

"Elfrida and Thomas and Dickon, Adder and many another in those days. A merry dance, indeed. We made that farmer pay, all down the years. His cows were barren and his crops failed, and no one would work for him for fear of ill-wishing. A sorry pass, he came to, in the end."

Felicity did not want to find out what that end might be. A rope over a beam; that was the way for a farmer who saw no other way out. There were Cartwrights in the village still, but they were labourers, with no land of their own.

And what became of the stable boy? Aloud, she said, "You looked after the boy who helped you, though."

Hob looked down, intent on a beetle that was laboriously climbing up a stalk. It was almost at the top when the stalk bent suddenly, and the beetle disappeared among the grass roots. "That farmer did not learn kindness in his misfortune. The boy came to us in the end, but he lost more than fingers. He went Onward ere long, and we saw him no more."

"I'm sorry." What else was there to say?

"Oh, lackaday!" Hob jumped up and seized her by both hands. "Who knows what lies Onward? Mayhap he found great blessings, or mayhap he turned into a butterfly and flew into the mouth of a toad. It is all one, in the end."

Felicity leaned back, holding his hands, feeling their warmth and the calluses on his palms. He wanted to pull her to her feet, but she stayed put, trying to meet his eyes.

"Why don't you go Onward, Hob? Why do you stay?"

Of all the possible questions, "Why?" was probably the

worst one. In the kind of life where things simply happened to you and you did as you were told, "Why?" was no use at all. Dangerous, even. She knew her mistake as soon as the words were out of her mouth.

Hob flew straight up into the air. His hands were torn out of her grip, and the next moment she cowered as huge white wings swept down and then up again, and the bird landed not two feet away. It looked at her sidelong, angling its dagger of a beak to one side, and lifted one backward-hinged leg and then the other. After a few seconds, she realised that it was not about to attack her, and uncurled a little. *Not a heron; much bigger, though not unlike one. Nothing I've ever seen before.* Breathless, she watched as it stalked about the flattened grass, peering down from time to time at things she couldn't see. *A water bird, a wader.*

Then it lifted its beak to the sky and called; a strange, rattling sound, not a song but a kind of melancholy music like the movement of dry branches in winter, so full of yearning that tears came to her eyes. It sprang into the air, once, twice, infinitely graceful, and then with another rush of wings it lifted away, long legs trailing. Felicity watched until it was lost to sight and her eyes watered from gazing into the bright sky.

Slowly, she unclenched her fists, made herself breathe deeply, looked around and brought herself back to this quiet field, this late afternoon in springtime. There was her bicycle leaning against the gate; there, if she stood up and looked in the right direction, the spires of the city still gilded with sunlight. The trees cast long shadows now, and it was growing chilly. One question had been answered, only for another to present itself.

Part Five: No Birds Sing

O what can ail thee, knight-at-arms,
Alone and palely loitering?
The sedge has withered from the lake,
And no birds sing.

O what can ail thee, knight-at-arms,
So haggard and so woe-begone?
The squirrel's granary is full,
And the harvest's done.

I see a lily on thy brow,
With anguish moist and fever-dew,
And on thy cheeks a fading rose
Fast withereth too.

I met a lady in the meads,
Full beautiful—a faery's child,
Her hair was long, her foot was light,
And her eyes were wild.

I made a garland for her head,
And bracelets too, and fragrant zone;
She looked at me as she did love,
And made sweet moan

I set her on my pacing steed,

And nothing else saw all day long,
For sidelong would she bend, and sing
A faery's song.

She found me roots of relish sweet,
And honey wild, and manna-dew,
And sure in language strange she said—
'I love thee true.'

She took me to her Elfin grot,
And there she wept and sighed full sore,
And there I shut her wild wild eyes
With kisses four.

And there she lullèd me asleep,
And there I dreamed—Ah! woe betide!—
The latest dream I ever dreamt
On the cold hill side.

I saw pale kings and princes too,
Pale warriors, death-pale were they all;
They cried—'La Belle Dame sans Merci
Thee hath in thrall!'

I saw their starved lips in the gloam,
With horrid warning gapèd wide,
And I awoke and found me here,
On the cold hill's side.

And this is why I sojourn here,
Alone and palely loitering,
Though the sedge is withered from the lake,
And no birds sing.

John Keats, "La Belle Dame sans Merci," 1819

Chapter 53

I *think I know who They are.*

The words looked dangerous on the blank page. As though they might catch fire, or lift away and fly out of the window, getting larger and louder as they went. Before there was writing, what could you do with a secret that was bursting to escape? After she had delivered a piece of her story to Professor Edgerley, it felt almost as though she had buried it or burned it and given it to the wind; it was not hers any longer, or not hers alone. But here, in her A4 file marked "Social Psychology," in her room where Hob and Elfrida might turn up at any time, it was not safe at all. What would they do if they knew?

Abruptly, Felicity pushed the page between the notes for the essay she was working on. "The Authoritarian Personality: the root of fascism. Discuss." She paused, running her finger over the words. Not such an unlikely place to hide them, after all. If They had once been children, taking refuge from violence and abuse and hardship in a world where such things were commonplace, they were living proof that a brutal childhood did not necessarily produce a brutal adult.

But they would never be adults. However many hundreds of years old they might be, they were just children, playing at make-believe in their unlikely refuge. Some were even haunting the places where they had once lived, as though hoping for something from the families who had failed them so long ago. She thought of Hob's story about Farmer Cartwright, whose descendants were still paying the price, after all this time, for that man's cruelty.

Sometimes, in the stories, fairies were said to help people; it was not all trickery and revenge. But they were always capricious, not to be trusted or relied upon. Like children, in fact. Children who knew that they had to look after themselves, who had survived unthinkable horrors and would never grow up, never develop a wider perspective on the world.

No wonder they had made her crawl through bogs and briars before they welcomed her to their company. She had got off lightly. And yet. And yet. Sitting at her desk in her comfortable room, looking out across well-kept lawns and borders full of daffodils, she was seeing a very different scene. That wonderful company, when finally she had stumbled into the circle for the third time, and it had not gone up in a flurry of sparks and ashes. Those faces, lit by firelight and moonlight and magic, turned towards her in welcome.

Or was it something else? As a child, she had thought only of her own yearning to belong. Now, looking at those faces with new understanding, she saw wistfulness, wariness. Hunger. They had all once been where she stood, bruised and battered and desperate for sanctuary; or maybe just wild, ready for anything and careless of what they might lose as they stepped across the border. And they needed new recruits. Even during the few years that she had known them, the band had dwindled. Some went Onward, and were not replaced. It brought her back again to the question she had revisited so many times.

Why had they not let her stay? After Christine, of course, it was out of the question. But before that, when she had pleaded with Elfrida so many times, why, in the end, was she always sent back to the farm? It made no more sense to her now than it had back then.

She put the file back on the shelf. There were more immediate questions to deal with right now. The essay had to be finished before meeting Sebastian at the station at six, and then there would be three whole days when she would have him all to herself.

Her heart was light as she locked up her bike outside the station at ten to six. *That's how it feels,* she thought. *Light and jumping in my chest like a balloon in a high wind.* It was so much better when Sebastian came up to Cambridge, away from the people who surrounded him, the febrile atmosphere of the theatre, the cigarette smoke and late hours and lack of privacy. It was a while since he'd been able to get away, and she had borrowed a bike for him so that they could get right out of the city and enjoy the spring flowers and the wide views. Strange country for a girl who had more or less grown up in a forest, but she had come to care for this grand landscape where everything seemed to be visible, and yet it kept its secrets well. If there had ever been fairies in the fens, where would they find shelter?

The train was coming in. She craned to catch a glimpse of Sebastian as it slowed, but could not see which carriage he was in, so she waited while the crowds cleared and then, at last, there he was, stepping out of the train and turning, turning to lift a suitcase down and carrying it for the woman who emerged behind him, who was walking along the platform next to him now, looking up and laughing at something he was saying.

Harriet. Last seen in France, doing her dancing exercises by the pool in the mornings, or hanging on to the arm of her boyfriend—Adam, that was it—while they gazed out from the top of the plateau above the house. Harriet, who had swum and sunbathed and drunk wine with the others, and mourned when Adam had to leave early. Harriet, here in Cambridge, with Sebastian.

He put down the suitcase and gave her an awkward, one-armed hug, still encumbered with his rucksack. Harriet had started talking even before they reached her—"So lovely to see you! London was unbearable. I'm really looking forward to"—but Felicity heard only the one word that Sebastian murmured close to her ear. "Sorry."

She drew back a little, looked up at him, but Harriet was still talking, filling up the space. "And darling Sebastian said of course I must come up to Cambridge with him. Wasn't it sweet of him? You must show me everything while we're here. Look, there's a taxi. Quick, before those people grab it."

"I'd better go with her," he said. "I'll explain later." Then they were gone, leaving Felicity to cycle back to Newnham alone, nursing the faint hope that Harriet might be staying with friends somewhere, or even in a hotel. But there they were, waiting outside the porter's lodge as she arrived. She led the way up to her room, so full of all the things she could not say that she made no response at all to Harriet's chatter. Until they stood at last in her own precious space, and Harriet cast herself at once upon the bed and said,

"How quaint! 'A room of one's own,' just like Virginia Woolf. Though it didn't turn out so well for her in the end, of course."

"Where are you going to stay?" Felicity hadn't meant to sound so blunt, but there it was. Harriet sat up.

"Oh, I'll sleep on the floor, don't worry. I can sleep anywhere. I don't want to put you out."

Felicity almost laughed aloud. She was no actress. Her one talent was concealment, but something must have shown on her face. Harriet's eyes filled with tears.

"Oh god, this was a mistake," she said. "I thought it would be a relief to get away, but I've only gone and made things worse, haven't I?" Her eyes, always tragic because she used far too much eyeliner, brimmed over, and dark trickles began to run down her face. Sebastian produced a handkerchief. To Felicity, he said,

"Adam's finished with her. That's why I"—but then Harriet began to sob in earnest. For a long, frozen moment, no one did anything. *Like a play,* Felicity thought irrelevantly. *Only not a very good one.* Then she opened the door and said, too loudly,

"I'm going to make some tea."

She marched down the corridor, straight past the kitchen and along to Steph's door. Steph looked up from her desk, saw her face and said at once,

"What? What's happened? Did he not turn up?"

Now she did laugh, although it came out as more of a growl. "Oh yes, he's turned up all right. With an entourage."

Steph listened. She had a way of doing this that Felicity had never met before; simply listening, with no thought of how it might affect her.

"Anne next door is going home for a few days," Steph said when she'd finished. "I'm sure she wouldn't mind if horrible Harriet stayed in her room."

Now it was Felicity's turn to cry, just a little. "Steph, you are a true friend."

Steph shrugged. "It's just what friends do. I'll ask her in a minute. But tell me: are you sure she's after him, and there's nothing on his side?"

"As sure as I can be. He doesn't fancy her; we talked about it in France, actually. And she was all over Adam then. This is new."

"Hmmm." Steph looked up. "You do know he's gorgeous, don't you? I should think he's fending women off all the time, though he doesn't usually bring them here to meet his girlfriend."

Felicity blushed. "Of course I know he's gorgeous!" *And there's not much I can do about that, seeing that it's partly my fault.* "But I trust him. Really, I do. Well, I've got to, haven't I?"

"That's true. But if he did fancy her, I don't think he'd have brought her along. So, all we have to do is find a way to keep her occupied so you can spend some time with your beloved."

That's what Elfrida calls him. Distracted by this, Felicity missed Steph's next words.

". . . So a group of us are going punting tomorrow afternoon. Do you think she'd like that? You could come too, of course, if you want."

"I'll ask her. No, I'll tell her that's what's happening, and then we can duck out at the last minute and go off for our picnic. If she's having Anne's room, we'll get some time to ourselves later. You are a lifesaver! I'm supposed to be making tea. D'you want some?"

"Coffee for me, please." Steph glanced down at her desk and made a face. "This might be a late one. But I'll go and ask Anne now."

Felicity ran back to the kitchen to put on the kettle. *It's just what friends do,* Steph had said, but that was a kind of friendship she had never had. There was no question that her friendship with Elfrida—if you could call it that—had ever been a meeting of equals. As a child, she had been the humble supplicant, yearning for the touch of magic. Lately, the balance had tipped the other way, and it was Elfrida who seemed to be hungry for what her life had to offer. What Hob got out of it, she had no idea. She thought again about that strange bird; when she had time, she would work more on the sketches she had made. Somewhere in the college library there must be a bird book, and unless it was something completely mythical, she might find out what it was.

When she carried the mugs of tea back to her room, Sebastian and Harriet were sitting side by side on her bed. Harriet was leaning into him and her hair hid her face; over her head, Sebastian gave Felicity a beseeching look. She put the tea down on the desk and, as Harriet raised her head, caught the unmistakable gleam of triumph in her eyes. *This is all an act.* She hadn't been completely sure before, but now she was in no doubt.

A few moments later, Steph appeared in the doorway. She went to hug Sebastian, saying, "Hey, Mr. Successful Actor," and nodded to Harriet. To Felicity she said, as she picked up her mug of coffee, "All sorted. Anne's room will be free after eight o'clock, so Harriet can move in after you've had supper. Where are you going to eat?" Neither of them missed the look of dismay on Harriet's face, before she rallied enough to say, "Oh, that's so kind of you. You shouldn't have bothered."

As Felicity sipped from her own mug of tea, she and Steph exchanged a brief conspiratorial look. *It's what friends do.* Listen with no agenda of their own, help each other out without thought of payment, just because they are friends. This weekend was going to be fun in ways she had never anticipated.

Chapter 54

As soon as Felicity's bedroom door was shut and locked, they were in each other's arms. Between kisses, Sebastian drew back a little to cup her chin with his hand.

"God, I've missed you!" He began to kiss her face, tiny dry featherlight kisses on eyelids and temples, cheekbones and jawline, along the side of her neck to her shoulderblade, unbuttoning her blouse as he worked his way downward. Taking his time, waking shivers of delight as his lips brushed her nipples, her belly, teasing her until she begged for release. They had come a long way since those first fumbling attempts at lovemaking, and both had learned the joy of taking things slowly.

At some point there was a tentative knock at the door, and Harriet's voice, pitched so as to be heard while apparently trying not to disturb.

"Seb? I can't sleep."

Both of them were naked by now, and not at all inclined to stop what they were doing. Felicity put a finger to his lips and they listened, wide-eyed, until they heard her footsteps padding away down the corridor. Laughter bubbled out of them, a little hysterical, a wellspring of clear bright water washing away all the tension of the past few hours. *It's all right,* Felicity thought. *It's going to be all right. And if Elfrida and Hob are watching now, let them. I don't care.*

The next morning they took Harriet down to meet Steph and her friends at the punts. She emerged from Anne's room in full makeup, wearing high-heeled boots and a miniskirt that caused everyone to stare at them as they walked along the backs. Felicity felt almost sorry for her as she clambered into a punt with James and Stephen, but they seemed more than happy with their share of the bargain. The last they saw of her was her face, staring forlornly back at them as they waved the party off, and then that was that. The rest of the day was theirs.

"I do feel a bit guilty," Sebastian said as they walked back to Newnham to fetch the bikes. "Those poor guys might be in for a disappointing time."

"They might even manage to distract her a bit, you never know." *Does the charm wear off after a while?* "She's not really that heartbroken about Adam, is she?"

Sebastian laughed. "She hardly mentioned him when we were on the train. To tell the truth, I think he got fed up with this—obsession, infatuation, whatever it is. It's so strange. She's one of my oldest friends. We met at a children's party, or so our mothers never tire of reminding us. They used to joke about us getting together some day, but we never took it seriously; we were always just good mates, and then suddenly this. It's as though she's bewitched or something."

Felicity carefully did not look at him. "What, she's drunk a love potion meant for somebody else?"

He was frowning. "No, more like Titania in 'A Midsummer Night's Dream.' Which makes me the ass, I suppose."

"You're not an ass! You've done nothing to provoke this, have you?"

"Of course not. Well, not knowingly. But she's not the only one." He stopped on the path. "There's this girl in the cast who more or less threw herself at me after a rehearsal last week." He laughed. "Even Charles's friend—you remember Charles, where I was staying when I first went down to London?—this guy made a pass at me and now he keeps writing me letters. What are you supposed to do when people won't take no for an answer? It's not as though they're really interested in me, myself. Why should they be? It's something to do with getting successful, I think. People seem to believe that if they get close to you, it will somehow rub off on them. Like that woman in the Bible who touched the hem of Jesus's robe." He laughed again, but it was not a happy laugh. "And I know I'm not the messiah either."

Now she did look at him. "You're just you. I love you for that, not for your great acting or your good looks. That's all surface, don't you see? It's what one of my professors calls 'shine.' It just reflects your own projections back to you, so you can't see what's underneath at all. That's why people want to get close to you. But it's nothing to do with who you really are."

"So I am really Bottom after all? Ugly and bad at acting?"

"You know that's not what I mean."

"I wish we could be together," he said, suddenly grave. "I need you to keep my feet on the ground and my head out of the clouds. We're going on tour soon, all over the place. I've got an offer of some television work. All the people I meet, they're not interested in seeing through what you call 'shine.' It's the opposite; they want to make more of it. That's fine in performance, it's what's supposed to happen. But I don't want it when I'm walking down the street, or I'm tired after a late night, or I'm looking forward to a few days alone with the girl I love. Lately it's as though the spotlight is on me all the time, and I can't turn it off."

They had reached the college, and Felicity came to a decision. "We were going to Grantchester Meadows," she said, "but it will be full of people on a day like this. I know a better place."

She took him to the meadow where she had met with Hob, away from all the popular picnic spots, and there was no one there at all. They spent the rest of the day there, eating and drinking and talking about anything other than the theatre or the future. Cushioned by lush spring grass and spangled by sunlight dancing through the young oak leaves overhead, they made love; and if Felicity imagined, for a moment, that there were laughing faces among the leaves, she closed her eyes and gave herself up to her beloved.

It was growing dark by the time they returned to Newnham. At the lodge, the porter came out, diffident but determined, and presented Sebastian with a small book full of pastel pages to sign "for my niece, you understand, sir." Felicity had been given an identical autograph book for a birthday many years ago, although the only signatures in it were those of her family and classmates. She went ahead to put away the picnic food.

Harriet was there in her room. She was sitting on Felicity's bed, paging through her sketchbook, and she looked up without a hint of apology as Felicity stopped in the doorway.

"These are really quite good," she said. "You could be a set designer if you wanted."

What else has she seen? But no; surely she would never think to look inside a sociology textbook. And if she had, she'd be talking about mental institutions rather than set design. Felicity took a deep breath.

"That's private, actually. And no, I don't want to."

Harriet went on as though Felicity had said nothing. "Where did you see these? You said you'd never been abroad before France."

"Where did I see what?" *Pictures of Hob and the other goblins?* She crossed the room to look over Harriet's shoulder at her rough sketches of the dancing bird: standing on one leg, calling into the wide blue sky, rising with a huge sweep of wings. "Oh, just in a field somewhere."

Harriet stared at her. "There haven't been cranes in England for hundreds of years."

"How do you know it's a crane? You're not a birdwatcher."

"Definitely not!" Harriet made a face. "We did the crane

dance as part of a performance last year. We had to watch a film about them. They're a symbol of fidelity in Japan because they mate for life, and they dance together." But cranes, and how Felicity might or might not have seen them, were not what she was really interested in. "You're not right for Sebastian; you know that, don't you? You're not really part of his world, and you don't even want to be." Those kohl-rimmed eyes gazed earnestly up at her. "He's been on the path to stardom ever since I can remember, and he needs someone who'll be by his side and support him to achieve his potential."

"Someone like Felicity, you mean." Sebastian came to put an arm around her shoulders. "She will be by my side, as you put it, when she can be. But she's got her own life to live, and I want to support her in that too." Together they stood looking down at Harriet, and Felicity had never loved him more than in that moment.

Harriet sniffed. "How modern," she said, sounding very probably like her own mother. She pushed the sketchbook away and stood up. "Anyway, luckily you have good friends who will stand by you when you need them. Like the other night when those people came backstage and wouldn't leave you alone. Who was there to fend them off and call a taxi home? Or the time when someone had taken your shirt and I had to go and buy you a new one? Or—"

"Harriet," said Sebastian. "You are my dear friend and I hope always will be, but I don't need you or anybody else to be my bodyguard or secretary or personal assistant, or whatever else you may have in mind. I brought you along this weekend because you seemed so miserable about Adam, but if you are going to be like this, then we won't be able to spend time together at all. I'm sorry, but there it is. Please, can't we just go back to the way things used to be?"

"I'm going to bed," said Harriet. "I know when I'm not wanted. But you're making a mistake, and one day you'll realise that." She went to the door, straight-backed and proud, but spoiled it by pausing in the doorway to say, "And I'm not the only one who thinks so, either. You should listen to your real friends." Then she made her exit.

Felicity, who had been feeling sympathetic—and guilty, of course—now surprised herself by saying a very rude word. She picked up her sketchbook and held it to her chest, reclaiming it after Harriet's invasion. But as she did so, she glanced again at the crane pictures. Another piece of knowledge, and this time from an unexpected source. It should be possible to find out how long it was since there had been cranes in Britain, and that would tell her how old Hob might be.

And there was more. The dance, Harriet had said, was a mating dance, and cranes mated for life. Perhaps, after all, it was a kind of answer to the question she had asked him. *Why do you stay, dear Hob? I think perhaps I know.*

"Don't mind Harriet." Sebastian interrupted her thoughts. He came over and took her in his arms, with the sketchpad between them. "She'll get over it in time, I hope. Sounds like an illness, doesn't it? Perhaps I'm a sort of plague infecting everyone I get close to."

Felicity shuddered. "Don't say that." *I made a mistake,* she was thinking. *I started this, and I can't take it back.* Aloud, she said, "You've got to use your charisma—the shine, if you like—to get what you want. Good roles, good reviews, the recognition you need to succeed. Somehow you've got to separate that from this illness, or whatever it is, that infects people around you. Do you think you can do that? Surely it should be possible, at least some of the time." *Listen to yourself,* she thought. *Elfrida has made you into one of Them, but without any glamour. You're an unfair fairy. But then, the whole business is unfair.*

"I don't know," he said, speaking low. "But I don't have much choice, do I? I've got to try. Just keep reminding me, won't you? I can't do it alone."

Chapter 55

The next day, feeling sorry for Harriet, they began by taking her around some of the colleges, but they had to give it up before long. Wherever they went, people stared at Sebastian, and some even took photos. Tourist season was under way, and there were crowds everywhere. Sebastian tried to be gracious, but the second time a woman took his arm, saying, "Don't I know you from somewhere?" he brushed her off irritably.

Harriet, meanwhile, was basking in the borrowed limelight. "You will do soon!" she said to the woman as Sebastian strode away. To Sebastian she said, "Don't be so grumpy! You'll have to get used to this; it's the price of stardom."

He grimaced. "I'd rather not be a walking cliché, thank you. Let's find somewhere quieter to go."

"I know," said Felicity. "What about that horrible pub we found with all the old men, where they wouldn't serve us wine? It's not far from here. I bet there won't be any tourists there, or anyone who might recognise us. Come on."

They went. The Ancient Druids was, as she had hoped, empty except for three or four men propping up the bar, who looked over their shoulders, stared for a few moments too long at Harriet's legs, and turned back to their pints. The table was sticky, and there should have been sawdust on the floor. Harriet tugged at her skirt as she sat down, but of course it didn't help. She was looking around, wide-eyed.

"Gosh," she said. "This place would be really trendy in Soho. Why hasn't it been discovered yet?"

"It has, sort of," said Felicity. "But now is too early in the day, and they don't like students, or women, or foreigners. Or anyone much, really."

"That's kind of cool. Do you think those really are ancient druids? Shall I ask them?" Her voice, the product of stage training and an expensive education, rang out in that empty place. The men shifted on their stools.

"Not unless you want to get us thrown out. Maybe try a little louder next time. I don't think they all heard you."

Sebastian laughed. "I'll get the drinks. Let's see if my magic charm works on this lot."

Harriet was quiet for a bit, but as soon as Sebastian came back with the drinks, she returned to her theme.

"You know, you really should be grateful for your success. Loads of people would give anything to be where you are now."

"Don't I know it." He put the drinks down and began to play with one of the beer mats, trying to make it spin. "That's the other thing; people sort of hate me as well as doing the shiny-eyed act. There's all this praise and gushing going on, and underneath is something else that's not nice at all."

"Oh, for goodness sake!" Harriet grabbed the beer mat from his hands. "You've wanted this your whole life. Just ignore them. It's jealousy, that's all."

"Jealousy is not a small thing," he said, very serious. He took Felicity's hand. "You're the only one I don't get this from. If I didn't have you, I don't know where I'd be."

Before Felicity could say anything, Harriet was off again. "Onward and upward, that's where you'd be," she said. "This is all part of the deal, isn't it? What every actor yearns for. What's the problem?"

He was frowning, not looking at either of them. "It's just—too much, too soon. I don't feel I've earned it. You're supposed to have a hard time at first, work in bars and have no money, all that. That's where most of my friends are."

"Then make some new friends!"

He didn't look up, pursuing his own thoughts. "I think I'm going to say no to the television work."

Felicity had nothing to say. All she could do was to hold his hand in both of hers, while Harriet protested and argued and even produced a few tears. *Too much, too soon. What have I done?*

Of course, Harriet talked him round in the end. "You're committed to the season anyway, and then filming takes months. The series won't be aired for a year or two at least, and by that time you'll be used to being noticed everywhere."

"And by that time," said Felicity at last, "I'll be finished here. I'll find a job in London, and we can be together."

"That depends where the series is filmed," Harriet said at once. "It could be anywhere, even abroad. You can't be there to hold his hand all the time." *But I could,* was the implication. Harriet had an allowance from her parents and could do as she pleased until she found herself a husband. Felicity had discovered that most women, even at Cambridge, still expected to be married and give up their own work eventually. A husband's career came first, and children came before everything. A true bluestocking did not get married at all. She didn't know yet what sort of work she might do, but she wanted at least a chance to find out for herself. And if Sebastian's work did not bring in a regular income, they would be reliant on what she could earn. But of course, he would rise fast and far. Her gift had seen to that.

They stayed there, giving the regulars something to be grumpy about, until hunger drove them out in search of somewhere to eat. Felicity found it hard to keep up with Harriet's chatter, and Sebastian simply downed his first beer and went back for another. By the time they got back to college she had lost count, and it was a relief to pretend that she had some urgent work to do. Not altogether a lie, but she would certainly have put it off until Sebastian left for London. She didn't care anymore that she would be leaving him in Harriet's company, although he was not so happy about it. She shut her door behind them both, closed her eyes and leaned against it, suddenly exhausted.

"Giving up so easily?" Elfrida stood at the window, looking out over the garden. "Shall I give her pimples or crossed eyes, or turn her into some uncouth creature? A mayfly, perhaps, or a moth. What do you think?"

"Don't bother," said Felicity. "You'd have to turn half of London into uncouth creatures. It's the gift, isn't it? I only thought of how it would help him to get work as an actor, but it makes everyone fall in love with him. I wish I'd waited. In just over a year, I'll have finished my degree. He'd have been all right, working in a bar or something and going to auditions like all the others. But it's all happening too fast. Isn't there any way he can sort of turn it off sometimes?"

She knew the question was hopeless even as she spoke it, and Elfrida did not even turn around. "Poor mortals," she said softly, as though to herself. "Always wishing and wishing, and never an end to it."

Felicity pushed herself away from the door. She went over to her desk, where the sketchbook lay. Hob might be somewhere nearby, but she was getting careless now, wanting answers. "I drew these of Hob a few days ago," she said, taking the sketchbook over to the window. "This creature isn't uncouth."

Elfrida glanced sideways at the pictures. "I have not seen the cranes dance for many and many a year," she said. "Strange, that he should remember that."

"I think I know why." She waited. Elfrida did not like having to ask, but she was always intrigued by a mystery. They all were, Felicity thought; curious, eager to pry and meddle. In that, at least, they were still human, still childlike.

"Tell me."

Felicity crossed her fingers. *Here goes.* "He told me how you helped him, when he was a little boy and Farmer Cartwright was cruel to him. You were probably the first person to be kind in a long time. That's why he doesn't go Onward when the others do, and why he always wants to be with you. He loves you, Elfrida, in his own strange way."

Again, she waited, but not for long. Elfrida laughed. "Well, there's no great secret! Tis very plain to see. Did I not know after all this time, I'd be in poor case indeed." Felicity held her breath, crossed her fingers even more tightly. *She didn't challenge what Hob told me.* Aloud, she said "I tried to draw a picture of what I thought he might have looked like back then." She turned back a page or two, and held out her drawing of a small boy, snub-nosed, freckle-faced, not smiling. No question, or none spoken out loud. Elfrida looked down at the sketchbook, and raised her eyebrows.

"His ears stood out like the handles of a pitcher," she said, "but that is not so very far off." The next moment, there was the child himself, looking up at Felicity with wary eyes, light blue. And now he did smile, a gap-toothed grin that lit up his dirty little face. Felicity dropped the sketchbook and sank to her knees, staring. She wanted to gather him up and hold him close, but of course this was not Hob, who loved to rough and tumble. This was a semblance. *Are you just showing me what I want to see?* But every detail was there, down to the bare brown feet with their black toenails, the roughly mended shirt that was too big for him, a bit of bracken caught in his hair. No shine about this piece of make-believe, except the natural shine of a child.

Abruptly, he was gone, and Felicity knelt before Elfrida, empty-handed. She looked up and said, "Thank you," though that seemed entirely inadequate. Elfrida said nothing, only waited until she was on her feet once more. Felicity also held her tongue, trying to think of the right thing to say next. Buying time, she picked up the sketchbook and leafed through the pages.

"Hob did that," she said, stopping at the one he had embellished with horns and a long beard. "He never changes how he looks. But the others—Lord Ember and Lovet and Tom—they're really like him as well, aren't they?" *And you?* she thought; but that was too dangerous to think, let alone to say.

"What is this 'really' that you find so interesting? You, who so hungered for glamour when you first came to us that you begged to stay forever? You want your lover to see you 'as you really are' and still find you desirable, and yet you bathe, you tie up your hair and try on any number of clothes before you go to meet him. It seems to me that 'real' moves around according to your whim, and that humans spend most of their time trying to get away from it."

There was so much there that Felicity could not begin to answer, and of course it would make no difference to Elfrida. She was paging through the sketchbook, pausing here and there, lingering especially at the many drawings of herself in all her guises.

"You make a good likeness," she said eventually. "Yet every one of these has something of yourself in it. How could it be otherwise?"

"I don't know," said Felicity, with simple honesty. Even photographs, she knew, were a product of light and shade, angle and exposure. She thought again of the gilded illuminations in the chained book in Professor Edgerley's study: flat brown, or shining gold? Was one more real than the other?

She put that aside for another time; for now, she did not want to lose this precious opportunity to find out more. Not looking at Elfrida, she said,

"So they were all children when they came to the woods. Alys was old enough to have a child herself, but still not grown up. I can see that. The stories say that grown-ups sometimes do find the way, but not often, and only when they are allowed to. You must have been older than Hob was, unless you came by a different route."

She should have known better. Elfrida could recognise a question, however disguised it might be. She said only, "Cranes were good eating, back then," laid down the sketchbook on the windowsill, and vanished.

Chapter 56

Early the next morning she said a hurried goodbye to Sebastian, shivering on the train station while Harriet looked on. "I'll write when I can," he promised, and that was that. He would be on tour until the late autumn, and then the television series would begin filming, mostly on location "somewhere in the north." If the contract was finalised; but it would be, of course. In a few years' time there would be films and interviews, and it would be his face up there on the posters outside the Odeon. There would be an entourage. And there would be Harriets, an endless stream of them.

Felicity had been amazed, at first, that he could love someone like herself. Amazed, and then joyous in the growing confidence that it was true, that it was mutual, that they both wanted a future together. Now, as it seemed likely that he would become a household name before too long, she found herself picking up the papers that lay around in the Junior Common Room and reading the interviews with famous actors. Who were they married to? Some married each other, of course, but she took comfort from one woman, whose husband of twenty-five years was a civil servant, who said, "It works best when one of you has something like a normal life. He's my anchor." She could be that for Sebastian, she thought. Since she had bestowed the gift upon him, it was surely the least she could do.

In the meantime, there was plenty of other work to be getting on with. That was the excuse she gave herself for not talking to Professor Edgerley about what she had learned. There was always an essay to finish, a book to read, and a new round of revision as exams loomed once again. After all, what could he add to what he had already said? And so, like black ink dropped into clear water, her silence about the gift spread, creating shadows where there had been light.

She did, however, go to the town library and consult a very large book on birds, where she discovered that the common crane had been extinct in Britain for at least four hundred years. Good eating, indeed. And Hob must have seen them when they were still plentiful, which placed the time of his birth in the early sixteenth century or before. If Elfrida, too, had once been human, that made her even older. Somehow, that came as no surprise. It also meant that Steph would be unlikely to turn up any useful information about missing children. She put the book back in its place and returned to her studies.

Life was simpler without Sebastian. She loved him, but now that contact had dwindled to the occasional postcard, with no more than a few rushed sentences from a different town each time, it was a kind of relief to have no expectations. Her friends were all in her year, all on the same journey, and understood the demands of work. She did not visit the Professor, and for the most part, Hob and Elfrida kept their distance. Nothing disturbed her focus, except for one thing.

She was coming out of the Museum of Archaeology and Anthropology, her thoughts a million miles away, when someone blocked her path. She muttered "Sorry" and tried to sidestep, but he blocked her again. At that, she looked up.

"I thought I recognised you," said the young man, standing squarely in the way. "It is her, isn't it, Jen?"

His companion, a tall girl with long hair blowing across her face, gave Felicity a brief glance. "Maybe. Come on, we'll be late."

"Hold your horses. So," he said, leaning one hand on the wall and looking down at Felicity, "What did the old man want with you, eh? You're not one of his supervisees."

"I think you've got me mixed up with someone else." He was standing too close, looming over her.

"Oh, no. I remember you. You were there when he did that weird stunt with the book. I thought he was going to set light to it; wouldn't put it past him. I know why we were there, but why were you?"

Felicity stared at him, and then at the girl who stood a little way away. Slowly, understanding dawned. That strange episode in Professor Edgerley's study, a brief interlude amid the intensity of revision. Something made her wary; he was too eager, like a hound on the scent. "I don't know," she said. "I'd forgotten about that."

"No, you hadn't." He was watching her face. "What did he want with you?"

"Adam, give her a break. She doesn't know anything." The girl was American; too tall, with beautiful even teeth.

"I think she does." Handsome, self-assured, and used to getting what he wanted. Felicity's resistance hardened; *I wouldn't tell you anything even if I did know what you're after.* She looked up at him, all bland innocence. "It was a demonstration of how your expectations change your experience, wasn't it?"

"Ha!" He leaned closer, not smiling. "It was a demonstration of glamour," he said, watching for a reaction. "And you were there for a reason. There's always a reason."

"I'm sorry, I have to go." Felicity slid past him, and he actually took hold of her arm. "Come on," he said, "We're after the same thing here. What do you know?"

"Adam, for God's sake!" The American girl stepped closer. "I'm sorry about my friend. Look, the Prof has a bee in his bonnet about Faery, and we think there might be something in it. That's all."

Now, Felicity was really alarmed. "I can't tell you anything about that," she said, entirely truthfully. "You'd better ask the Professor. I really must go." And she walked off. Her bike was locked to a lamppost a few feet away, but she went straight past it without looking back. Any moment, she expected to hear him shout, feel his hand on her shoulder, but it seemed he had given up, at least for now. She rounded the corner and leaned against the wall, breathless, her heart jumping. *What was that all about?*

She twisted her hands together to stop them from shaking, but she could not stop her thoughts skittering about like frightened mice. *What do they know? Have they seen what I wrote?* The Professor was right: fairies and fairy lore were unfashionable and looked down on by academics, but there were students who were eager for anything mystical or magical. She had avoided them when she could, because having actually been there created a divide that could not be crossed, but now it seemed they had caught up with her. And if those two had seen something, they were not going to give up in a hurry. Adam, in particular. She remembered the gleam in his eye as he watched the professor bring a lighted candle to the illuminated book. He was eager for sensation, that one. What could she do?

Her mind was still racing. She imagined setting Hob and Elfrida onto them, causing havoc until they begged for normality. When the fairy troupe had set upon those three young men at the twisted oak, all those years ago, the path of their lives had been turned. But Hob and Elfrida were not hers to command. She did not know how far they might go, and very much did not want to find out. No; the only answer was to talk to Professor Edgerley himself. If he did not already know about Adam and Jen, he needed to be warned. And he might have some idea of what to do about them.

She was already walking in the direction of his college, and she realised with some surprise that she would be glad to see him. A few minutes ago, she had decided yet again that there was no need to talk about her findings, but now she saw that for what it truly was. Avoidance. That one all-important secret she had kept back had created a barrier that stopped other things from passing through as well.

And that, she thought, was the story of her life. There was nobody with whom she could share everything: not her family, not Steph and her other friends, and especially not Sebastian. When she had said "Yes" to Elfrida, it had been a "No" to a host of other things; things she could not possibly have predicted or understood at the time. What she did understand was that Elfrida never truly shared things with her, not as a real friend would have done.

Felicity had traded glamour for intimacy. That was what it came down to; and the trade off, once made, could not be undone. She could never talk to anyone about Them; had never even tried to break her promise, for fear of what it might mean. A fantasy sprang into being as she walked: she would ally herself with Adam and Jen, and together they would find a way—to what? Those two wanted to meet fairies, not be rid of them, and her life was complicated enough already.

Chapter 57

As she approached the Porter's Lodge at the Professor's college, she glanced behind her, but saw no one following. She went into the first quad and began to write a note to put into his pigeonhole, crouching awkwardly at the side of the path with her notepad on one knee, but got no further than the first words. "Dear Sir" sounded much too formal. In the past, she had simply left the latest piece of writing, and he had replied with an appointment time. "I need to see you" sounded the opposite of formal, as though they were having an illicit affair. That made her smile. Students had affairs with their teachers all the time, but Professor Edgerley was always utterly correct in his dealings with her.

"Miss Turner?" He was standing on the path in front of her. She looked up, blushing as though he could read her thoughts.

"Oh! I was just writing you a note. I wanted—I mean, could we book a supervision when you have the time, please?"

He said nothing, only studied her as she scrambled to her feet and gathered up her things. Then he said,

"Would you like to come up now, if it's convenient?"

She gave him a quick, grateful glance, then dropped her gaze. "Yes, please."

Neither of them said anything more until he had closed the door to his study.

"I don't know what you can do, really, but I thought you ought to know," she began. He held up a finger, then motioned her to sit in the big chair. She waited while he poured sherry for both of them into two tiny crystal glasses. Then he turned the desk chair to face her, seated himself and said, "Tell me."

She told him about her encounter with Adam and Jen, and he listened without comment, steepling his fingers in that familiar gesture. When she described how Adam had looked when the professor lit the candles to show them the gilding in the book, he inclined his head a little, but did not speak.

"And so I came straight here," she finished. *It will be all right now,* she was thinking. *He'll tell them to leave me alone, and that will be that.* The Professor took a sip of his sherry and set down the glass. He turned on the desk lamp, and the faceted crystal glowed like rubies.

"Ah, Mr. Kemp," he said softly. "You are right. That young man is convinced that I hold the key to marvels which I am unfairly withholding from him, while believing at the same time that I am not of sound mind and probably not fit to be teaching." He sighed. "They are both working on dissertations in the field of folklore, which is why they come to me for supervision, but their motivation springs from very different sources."

She waited. After a moment, he went on. "Miss Booker is a romantic, who yearns for the world to be more than what we see. She came here to study because this is the Old Country, and there should be mythical beings lurking in every corner. So far, she has been disappointed." He smiled. "There is no harm in that, of course. It is, more or less, where both you and I started from. But Mr. Kemp is interested in the power that such beings might give him. From various things that he has said in supervision, he has attempted contact through ritual, fasting, and other methods which I am sure you will have encountered in your studies."

Felicity nodded, and he continued. "However, as we know, such contact can only be achieved if 'They,' as you call them, are willing. And so far, They have found no use for either of these two. Why should they? One has simply to study the stories to know that what they want from us is help, from time to time, of a very specific sort. A midwife, a labourer, a lover. Their gifts, moreover, always come with conditions, or at a price."

What did They want from me? Aloud, she said, "But they take children. You were right." She told him what she had learned about Hob and Lovet, and about the crane dance. "I don't know whether they were all once children. Sometimes they appeared to me to be tall and beautiful, and I thought those were the true fairies. That's what I wanted to believe, I suppose. But now I think most of them, or maybe all the ones I knew, had once been human children."

He was watching her. "Once upon a time," he said. "And a very long time ago it was, for some of them. They are dwindling now, or so I understand from your recollections. Perhaps children do not go out alone these days, or perhaps they are less eager to find fairies. What do you think?"

"I don't know." *What about Christine and her "imaginary" friends?* "Very young children wouldn't have the preconceptions about fairies and magic, would they? But they wouldn't be out by themselves, either; not these days. If I had to guess how old the ones I knew were when they crossed the border, I suppose they'd be between about seven and maybe twelve or thirteen. Alys might have been a little older, but I don't think she was quite 'all there.' My cousin was just a baby, but she didn't choose to go with them." *And what about Elfrida?*

"And your particular friend? She seems to be a leader of sorts. Would she have been older, do you think?" He had a knack for picking out the thing she had not said. She had the feeling that there was not much the professor failed to notice; that if he did not remark upon something she had left out, it was because he respected her choice to keep it to herself. That made her wonder: *Does he know, or at least suspect, about the gift?*

Now, though, he was waiting for an answer. "I don't know,"

she said again. "But I think she could have been maybe fourteen at most. When do you stop being a child?"

He smiled. "To that there is no definitive answer. But when you look at the stories of adults meeting with fairies, they are often either drunk or dreaming or in love. A state of altered consciousness seems to be necessary, whereas to a child—or to some children, at least—there is no barrier."

"That sounds right. It's frustrating that I can't ask direct questions. I find things out by making assumptions, mostly, and they correct me if I get it wrong. I'm sorry it's so haphazard."

"On the contrary, Miss Turner." He looked steadily at her. "Your testimony is invaluable. To have spent time among Them, and to have returned with your memory intact: that is very rare, I think. Mr. Kemp is right to be jealous of you."

Not for the first time, she wondered: *What about you? What's your story?* Today he had talked about "You and I"; had said that they had a common starting point. Beyond that, she knew nothing about Professor Edgerley. How had he come to be so interested in fairies? He could see them, of course; that was why he had introduced himself, after Hob had invaded his lecture. He had ways of keeping them out, too. She glanced up at the window. *There must be more.*

He followed her gaze. "Did your companions come with you this time?"

"If they were there, I didn't see them. But they often seem to turn up when I'm upset about something, so they might have been."

He considered this. "Would they approach Mr. Kemp or Miss Booker, do you think?"

She laughed. "You said just now that they only allow themselves to be seen if they want something. But sometimes what they want is to play tricks on people, to scare them or shock them. I've seen them do that lots of times. So yes, I think they might."

"If our two seekers get a glimpse of what they seek, it will make them all the hungrier. When next you see your companions, it would be wise to warn them."

"They won't care. In fact, it might make them more likely to do something, just out of mischief. They get bored with me and my quiet life. I expect those two—Adam and Jen, I mean—would be much more interesting for them." And she wondered suddenly, *How would I feel if They left me?*

"Ah, but if they could simply choose anybody to follow, or change allegiance as they pleased, we would have a different set of fairytales, don't you think? They would be drawn to the sensation-seekers, the risk-takers, and they would urge them on to greater exploits. If that were the case, I doubt that their chosen subjects would stay silent about it for long." He fell silent, musing. "Absinthe, *la fée verte*, was the key to visions and transcendent experiences for poets and dreamers in my youth. Always temporary, alas, and ultimately fatal."

"Are their gifts always dangerous?" Felicity asked abruptly. "In the stories, there's hardly ever a happily ever after. The old stories, I mean, before they were tidied up and only read to children. It never works out right in the end." She paused, thinking it through. "Usually because the human breaks the rules or asks for too much."

"Who sets the rules? A fairy bargain contains the seeds of its own destruction. They set conditions, knowing that they cannot be met, and so they always come out free and untrammelled by their promises to us. It's as though," and his voice changed as he spoke, becoming softer, the professor giving way to the wondering human being, "having once been children hurt beyond endurance, they will never trust us again. They set snares, they take what they want and lead us into the mire, and then they leave us, like La Belle Dame Sans Merci, 'alone and palely loitering.'" He looked up. "You know that poem?"

"Yes! Except that they haven't left me, not yet. So there

must still be something they want from me. I'm not going to start partying and taking drugs, so there's something else, isn't there?"

"Time will tell." The professor got up to draw the curtains, and then paused at the window. "I think it would be wise, Miss Turner, to leave by the back entrance to the college grounds. It seems our friends are eager to talk to you again."

She came to look. At first sight the quad seemed empty, but then, under the archway, there was movement. Two people were standing there, half-concealed behind the wall. A face, pale in the evening light, turned towards the professor's staircase, and then withdrew again.

She took a deep breath. "I know you can't stop them, but perhaps if you tell them I was here for some other reason, they might believe you. Unless—" she could hardly bring herself to ask, but she had to know. "They haven't seen my writing, have they? You didn't show it to them?"

They were standing side by side at the window, almost touching, so she felt the sudden stillness in him. After a moment he turned his head towards her, but she kept her eyes down.

"Miss Turner," he said, very gravely. "Unlike the fairies, I keep my promises."

Chapter 58

Felicity went home by a roundabout route, out onto the Backs and then back into town to fetch her bicycle, and out again to Newnham. It was full dark by the time she got there, and she was looking forward to curling up in her big chair and forgetting about all of it with a good book, but the porter stopped her as she was passing the lodge.

"Telegram for you, Miss Turner." It always made her nervous, but she had learned to accept the way Sebastian used them, sometimes just to say hello. This one read "Sorry can't come next week stop extra days stop will write love S."

She stood there, holding it in her hand. Yellow paper under yellow lamplight, with the typed words very black and spiky, and all the words in between, the words that were not there, clamouring to be heard. Next week's visit would have been a fleeting one, just one night midweek and back to Norwich, where the company were appearing next, the following day. But still. What did "extra days" mean? More performances, presumably. It must be going well. But he had promised! It was four weeks since his visit with Harriet, and much longer than that since they had had any real time to spend together. *It's not fair!* said the childish voice of hurt in her head, and tears came to her eyes.

"Anything wrong, Miss?" The porter was standing in his doorway, watching her. His eyes under the harsh lamplight were black pools in a white face, but his voice was kind. She could not deal with kindness, not just now.

"No, thank you. I'm fine." Clutching the telegram, she walked on towards her room, a little unsteadily, feeling his gaze on her back. "Will write," he had said, and that was all there was to hold on to. That, and "Love S."

Not for the first time, she wished there were some way she could reply, but she didn't have the addresses where the actors stayed on tour and, in any case, by the time a letter could be delivered, they would most likely have moved on to the next town. "Will write" was all very well, but when? She was walking fast now, hurt giving way to frustration and almost to anger. It wasn't his fault, of course, but knowing that didn't make the feelings go away. Head down, fighting back tears, she turned the corner into the corridor leading to the shared kitchen, and almost ran into Steph, coming out carrying a mug of tea.

"Hey, steady!" Some of the tea splashed onto the floor, but Steph managed to rescue most of it. "What's up?" Then she saw Felicity's face. "Oh, what is it? Hang on, let me put this down."

They both went into the kitchen. "Sit down, I made a pot. There should be enough for you too. I've got biscuits as well." Steph found a clean mug and got milk out of the fridge. "You missed a good folk club tonight. I thought you were coming?"

"I was." She'd forgotten all about it, of course. "Sorry, I got sidetracked with this essay I've got to hand in on Friday." That would have to do. She could not tell Steph about her encounter with Adam and Jen, nor her meeting with Professor Edgerley. So many parts to her life, and there was no one with whom she could share all of it. "And now there's this."

She held out the crumpled telegram, and carried on talking as Steph smoothed it out. "It's stupid to get upset, I know. We knew this might happen, and it's a good sign as far as the play's concerned, of course. But I kind of wish he hadn't been coming at all, and then I wouldn't feel so let down. We hardly have any time these days."

Steph cradled her mug in both hands, looking at the telegram. "Well, you could always go there."

"What?"

"You know, go and see the play, spend the night, or maybe just go in a day. Norwich isn't so far."

In all their planning, they had never considered this possibility. "But he'd be busy anyway with setting up and all that. I'd just be in the way. Believe me, I've done that a few times too often."

"Not if you stayed after the performance. They never go straight home to bed with a cup of hot cocoa, now do they? We could look in the local papers tomorrow, find out where the theatre is, and there should be a phone number for the box office."

"I'd have to miss lectures the next day."

"Felicity, when was the last time you missed a lecture?"

"I don't think I've missed any so far this term."

"Well then, you can afford to copy someone else's notes for once. Honestly, just get on a train and go. If you don't, when are you likely to see him next?"

Felicity looked down at her mug of tea. "Not for a month or so, I think. They're moving around every few days, and there aren't many gaps when he can get away."

"So take the chance while he's so close. What are you waiting for?"

"I don't know!" She felt cornered. "It's hard to explain. I just feel they—his acting friends, I mean—don't want me there. I don't fit in. And he has to try to bridge the gap between them and me. It's fine when it's just the two of us, but we can never be alone when he's in some production or other. It'll be better when we can live in the same place and not in some overcrowded house share."

Steph gave her what her mother would have called an "old-fashioned" look. "And by that time you'll have forgotten what he looks like, at this rate. Tell me to mind my own business, but do you really love him?"

"Yes! Yes, I do. I don't know why he loves me, though. Sometimes I don't quite believe in it. Why should someone like him take any notice of someone like me?"

"You really don't need me to answer that." Steph put down her tea. "Or maybe you do. Because you're gorgeous and utterly faithful and would do anything for him. And that's just for starters."

"Oh God, you've made me start crying again." She dug in her bag for a tissue. "But you know, Harriet spent the whole time she was here telling me how unsupportive I was being because I won't give up my degree and follow him around."

"Harriet has her own axe to grind. Anyway, he doesn't want you to do that. Does he?"

"He says not, but I'm not sure sometimes. Of course it would be great if we could be together all the time, and it might stop him being pestered by people like her, but we'd have nothing to live on. If I had an allowance from my parents like she does, I could do what I liked. I'm sorry; I don't mean to sound bitter, but I've got to make a living somehow."

"And you love your degree, and you're very good at it. Don't forget that."

Felicity laughed. "No danger! But I do feel guilty, not being there when he needs me." It was true, although she had never admitted it out loud before. Wasn't the man's career always supposed to come first? Didn't love mean giving up everything for your loved one?

"Look," Steph said. "If he's successful, acting will take him all over the place, often for weeks at a time. You two are going to have to weather that, aren't you? There will be an endless stream of Harriets wearing very short skirts and making smudgy eyes at him, and saying anything they can think of to get between the two of you. If you can't cope with it now, I wouldn't give much for your chances. Sorry to be so brutal, but there it is." She gazed at Felicity over the rim of her mug, her blue eyes very far from brutal. "You're sweet together, you two, but you're like the babes in the wood, wandering along with no idea how to get to where you want to go."

Felicity looked away. *You can have too much of fairytales,* she thought. Aloud, she said, "We have talked about it. And in the end, I've just got to trust him, haven't I? If I go rushing off to Norwich, won't it look as though I'm spying on him?"

"Does it matter, if what you both want is to be together?"

"I suppose not. I'm just so used to fitting myself around his work. You know, I never thought of going to see him on this tour."

"Sleep on it," said Steph, and got up to rinse the mugs and empty the teapot. "See you in the morning."

"Steph?"

"What?" Steph turned in the doorway.

"Thanks."

Alone in the kitchen, Felicity sat on for a few minutes, suddenly so exhausted that the idea of getting up to go to bed was almost beyond her. Without looking around, she knew when Elfrida was standing behind her. *By the pricking of my thumbs . . .*

"Not now," she said. "I'm too tired to think about anything, whatever it is. I'm going to bed." She put her hands on the table and pushed herself to her feet. And was halfway through the door, just as Steph had been, when Elfrida said,

"Your friend is right. You should go to your beloved."

For an instant, she paused. There were any number of replies she could have made, from "All right then" to "Mind your own business."

In the end, without looking back, she said simply, "Goodnight."

Chapter 59

It wasn't hard to arrange, after all. There would be a matinee performance on Thursday at the Theatre Royal in Norwich. She would have to meet Sebastian outside the theatre, because without the addresses of the places where they were staying, there was no way to let him know that she would be there, and no other way to be sure of finding him. Then she could either catch a train back in the evening, or stay until the next day.

Steph was right about the distance; it was only about an hour and a half's journey by train. She could not prevent the small, disloyal voice that said: *He could have come, even just for a few hours.* It didn't matter now. Once they were both in the same place and able to have a proper conversation, all the doubts and fears and hurt feelings could be laid to rest.

She had never been out of Cambridge during term time, except to London. Beyond the city, a huge sky and huge fields stretched away to eternity. One crop, no animals, almost no trees. It was a kind of farming so different from her own experience that she could not begin to imagine what life might be like in those isolated farmhouses, standing naked and exposed amid their endless acres. Even if all the hedges in Surrey were grubbed out, it would never look like this; the land itself was too folded and curved, the soil shading from sand to loam to clay, the lanes winding and the woods too stubborn, surely, ever to be eradicated. She felt a pang of homesickness and, at the same time, a sense of unfolding, an awakening into a wider and more spacious world. *Are you with me, Elfrida? Hob, do you see this?*

The journey was over too soon. Another city, this one completely unfamiliar, but there was the usual human landscape of people and taxis, the horizon suddenly bounded by roofs and telegraph lines. It was not far to the theatre, she discovered, and there was time enough to wander around, even to sit by herself in a café and study the street map she had picked up at the station. But she was too nervous, now, to go sightseeing. Sebastian and his fellow actors would probably get no sense of the places they passed through. They would carry their community with them and barely look beyond it, she thought; it was no wonder he would find it hard to get away.

Long before the performance was over, she had found the stage door and was waiting a little way away. She had considered going in to see the play, but the risk of missing Sebastian was too great, and there was something about the bright clear light in this eastern place that made the idea of going into that dark, stuffy auditorium almost too much to bear. It was possible, of course, that they wouldn't come out at all before the evening's performance. Someone—often Felicity herself, when she sat in on rehearsals—would be sent out for sandwiches and coffee, and the rest would make themselves at home backstage, chatting or dozing or practising lines. If that happened, she would have to wait until after the evening showing, and hope they weren't planning to party in there until the small hours.

She had a book to read, but it was hard to concentrate, and when, after a long, long time, the audience began to trickle out through the main entrance, whatever she had been reading fled instantly out of her head. She watched people move off in ones and twos, stopping to chat or to look again at the posters outside. They seemed cheerful, animated, going off to have tea somewhere nearby and talk over what they had just seen. It must be possible, she thought, to enjoy glamour and its effects without being burned up by it like a moth in a flame. Normal people did it all the time. There would be a way, somehow, for Sebastian to come to terms with the gift, and to accept the blessings it offered. Together, they would find a way.

At last, the stage door opened, and out they came, their faces shiny from creaming off the make-up, blinking in the sunshine. She recognised some of them, but the one she was looking for was not there—and then, suddenly, there he was.

Sebastian had his arms thrown over the shoulders of two people, a man on one side and a woman on the other, and his head thrown back, laughing. As he looked down again, his eyes passed across her without seeing her, and he bent to kiss the woman at his side.

That was fine, of course. They were actors; they did that sort of thing all the time. And she watched as the kiss went on and on, and Sebastian put both arms around the woman and lifted her right off her feet. A couple of the other actors cheered and applauded, and the rest moved on, talking loudly, away down the street and off into a side road. The kiss broke off at last, and he swung her around, both of them laughing. They came to rest, gazing into each other's eyes, and then she arched her back and stood on tiptoe to kiss him again.

Felicity simply sat there. She knew that gesture, felt it in her own body. She had done it herself, many times, and he had responded just as he was doing now. This was no celebratory kiss borne out of exhilaration after a good performance. She saw it in the way his arm went around her shoulder as they finally began to walk on, the way she leaned her head against him, the way the others had left them to themselves. They were lovers, or very soon would be.

After a time that could have been minutes or maybe many hours, she looked around as though waking from sleep. Her hands were shaking, and she had to lean on the arm of the bench before she could stand. Her whole body was vibrating like a plucked string; it seemed impossible that she could stay upright, let alone put one foot in front of another. It was evening, or beginning to be, the colour leaching from the street while the tops of the taller buildings still glowed. Slowly, she walked back down the way she had come, until she came to the bridge across the river. The station was a little way further, but there was no train due for a while yet. There was a path by the bridge that went along the riverside, and so she went to find another bench, and sat to watch the river flow, her mind almost empty. A few mallards came questing for food, but soon lost interest and drifted away. When someone sat down at the other end of the bench, she did not even look up.

"Would you give up so easily?"

She had no answer to that. Some way further down the path, there was a splash and a flurry of ducks as Hob threw a scatter of something into the water. With part of her mind, she hoped it was actual food and not simply dust or twigs. Eventually, she said,

"This river is called the Wensum. Some of the land between here and Cambridge is reclaimed from the sea; that's why it's so flat and rich. Imagine living in a place that really shouldn't be dry land at all. Wouldn't you feel like a trespasser; as though you had no right to be there?"

"Who holds the rights?" Elfrida was watching her, smiling. "You make up these wrongs and rights in your own head, and then live as though they were solid walls that hold you in. You could go anywhere and do anything. All you have to do is to step over them, and pfft!" She snapped her fingers, creating a small explosion that sparked and was gone.

"You're wrong." Felicity turned to face her. "You can't just go anywhere and do anything, not in the real world. Not even with magic. There are other people, and what they think and feel matters. Maybe you'll come to understand that in time."

"And maybe you will come to understand how you keep

yourself small, and safe, like a woodmouse trembling beneath the leaves. You have but to say the word, and I will make you just as gilded as your beloved. You could have walked up to them and every eye would have turned to you. One glance, and he would have forsaken that company and followed wherever you led. They all would; or you could have dismissed them as you chose."

"I don't want that!" Tears sprang from her eyes, all the pent-up feelings of the last few hours rushing up inside her, pushing for outlet all at once. "I want this to be real, don't you see? I want him to come to me freely, because he loves me, not because he is dazzled by my beauty. Do you think it makes him happy that everyone falls in love with him? It doesn't. But it's hard for him to separate being praised for his acting and being admired because the gift makes him seem 'gilded,' as you just said. He wants the praise, but he doesn't want the constant adulation. If I could take back the gift now, I would. It's hurting him, and I'm afraid it will destroy us."

She was sobbing now. A couple passing by turned to look at her and looked quickly away; just a girl crying on a bench, talking to herself or to her absent lover. Hob, on the other hand, came running. He leaped onto the arm of the bench and hugged her, hard, and then began to lick away her tears, making little whimpering noises like a distressed puppy. That made her laugh despite herself.

"Get off! Stop it! Oh, I need a tissue." She reached for her bag, and Elfrida handed her a handkerchief: beautiful delicate silk edged with lace, far too fine to blow her nose on. But she did anyway, knowing it would disappear before long.

"The gift, as you call it, is a part of him now," Elfrida said. "It cannot be given back or taken away. He has what he yearned for, and now he must learn to live with it. So must you, else you will lose him." She spoke the words formally, almost as though she was telling a story; solemnly, but without feeling.

And perhaps she was. Perhaps, thought Felicity now, she had played out this scene before, down the long centuries as she lived alongside the world of men. Perhaps in the end you would outlive all feelings, seeing people make the same mistakes over and over again. It was a cold thought.

"I know," said Felicity in a small, desolate voice. She huddled into herself, still clutching the handkerchief, rocking a little. Hob sprang down from the arm of the bench to crouch by the river. He stretched out his arm and beckoned to the ducks, and they came crowding and jostling up onto the riverbank, around her feet, nibbling at her shoes and talking to each other, a gentle continuous murmur with occasional sudden squawks. Despite herself, she smiled.

"I'm going home now," she said. "Will you come with me? Please."

Elfrida smiled. "Always," she said.

Chapter 60

The next day in her pigeonhole there was a long letter from Sebastian. He must have written it before the troupe had arrived in Norwich, probably right after sending the telegram. It was full of apology, news about the play—it was going well, of course—and promises to visit as soon as he could. Little character sketches of his fellow actors and of the theatres he had seen, the awful guest houses they had stayed in and the hours on the road, dozing uncomfortably, drinking too much coffee, playing endless games of cards. Then, almost as an afterthought: "It's just occurred to me. We'll be in Norwich for a few days, and it's not far on the train. Why don't you come and see the play? There won't be time for me to get away, but maybe you can." And there was the address of the place they would be staying.

Too late. She had seen for herself, there was no room for her there. Better to wait until the season was over, when there would be a week or two before the television work began. Sebastian had talked about renting a cottage somewhere in the country, far from London, just to walk and talk and be together for a few precious days. "You'll have to wear a fake wedding ring," he had said, laughing. "It may be the era of free love in London, but it hasn't yet found its way into the provinces." She had liked the idea of being seen as his wife; their relationship sealed and legitimised in the eyes of the world. As it would have been, in due course, with a wedding in the village church and her father to give her away, and all her old classmates no doubt looking on. Her heart had quailed a little at that thought, and then she had laughed at herself. *Better get used to it.* By that time he might be a household name. She had almost wished they could just get married now and be done with it, but it was not that simple. After her degree: that was when their life together would truly begin.

In the end, she said none of what she was feeling. Not in a letter, which he would read over breakfast with the others talking and laughing around him. She wrote him a short note, explaining that she could not get away before next weekend, and by that time he would be in a different town, playing to yet another audience. The thought of taking that train journey again, walking up through the town to the theatre, was too much to bear.

Something in her had hardened. She still loved Sebastian, no question, but she would not go to spend time with the crowd, drinking too much and talking endlessly about the performance they had just put on, and the one to come, and people she did not know, and everyone constantly revolving about him like planets around the sun, drinking in the light of his presence and wishing that she, Felicity, simply did not exist. If they were ever to build a life together, it would be set apart from all that and as normal as she could manage. She had given him the gift, and it was up to her to protect him from it.

And yet, it was so hard not to go. Despite herself, she imagined those kisses turning into something else, those hugs on shadowy landings in strange guest houses after too much drink, everyone fizzing with nervous energy after a performance, ready to do anything that would keep the adrenalin flowing. Sooner or later, Sebastian would be seduced away. Probably it had happened already; perhaps that was the real reason why he had sent that telegram. Thoughts like these were a constant undercurrent as she went through her day, always present unless she and Sebastian were actually together. Always, until now, she had pushed them down, not even allowed them to come to the surface. *If I don't let myself imagine it, it won't happen.* That might be true for Hob and his fellows in their never-changing world of make-believe, but in the real world, here and now, she finally brought it into the light of day and saw it for what it was. Moonshine. Smoke and mirrors. Wishful thinking.

Time to miss the morning's lectures yet again. Getting her bike, she cycled fast out of town, riding along empty lanes into the teeth of a brisk east wind. Not right out into the vast fields of the fenlands, but back, without giving it conscious thought, to the meadow where she had seen Hob dance the crane dance for Elfrida; where she had taken Sebastian on that last lovely day when they had given Harriet the slip.

Now, in early autumn, the hay cut had been made long ago, and weeds stood tall with their cargo of seeds: rusty-looking docks, rampant nettles on the site of an old manure heap, an army of willowherb along one side. She saw them and read the meaning of this field without thinking about it. Horses had been pastured here, not cows or sheep. After rain, there might be field mushrooms to harvest. To Sebastian, it had just been a good place for a picnic, but to her it was somewhere with its own life, its own layers of history, and far more welcoming than a house or any building. It was also, as she recognised with a rueful smile, familiar, like the fields surrounding her home; small, bounded by hedge and woodland, unimproved with fertilisers, and so probably completely outdated and useless to a modern farmer. Were all such places to be swept away? That was another thought too painful to contemplate. This was no sanctuary. Getting back on the bicycle, she let the east wind push her back towards Cambridge and what awaited her there.

Second year exams were due next week; she really did have a good excuse not to go anywhere. In the autumn she would start the final year of her degree. Not quite a year, really, and it would all be over. Some people already had jobs to go to; there were careers interviews to attend. Life was getting serious. This was what she had wanted, had planned for. For this, she had let Sebastian go alone to London, and for this she might have lost him. And right now, she could not remember why it had mattered so much.

There was still time to get to the last lecture of the morning, but she sat through a discussion of ethnolinguistics without hearing a word. Later, she read through her notes and found them perfectly understandable and completely unfamiliar. This would not do. If she fell behind with work now, or did badly in the exams, it would all have been for nothing.

All the time she could not be with Sebastian, the thread of connection between them was drawn out more and more finely. Perhaps it was already broken. *Felicity Turner, you have been a fool.*

She got out the writing she had done for Professor Edgerley. Quite a thick sheaf of pages, now. He was right, of course. As a child, her longing for colour and magic—for *shine*—in the drabness of her everyday life had turned her path towards Them long before she knew for sure that They were out there. But why would they not let her stay?

Was I not unhappy enough? Hob's story was surely far worse than her own, and Alys's too. About the others, Lovet and Ember and the rest, she could only guess. But in that case, there must be other people like herself, forbidden to speak of the wonders they had seen, shut out from fairyland and left to make their way in the real world.

What about the professor? Had he been exiled from fairyland, in his long-ago childhood? Or had he, perhaps, chosen to turn away? But that made no sense. He could not only speak about the fairies, he had made them his life's work. If he had taken a vow of silence, he must have broken it thousands of times, and nothing terrible had happened to him. She had often wondered about him, but there was a gap between student and professor that was too big for her to bridge. There were people who made friends with their teachers; she had seen it in action, and marvelled at their self-confidence from afar. Thinking about that now, she shrugged her shoulders like a horse trying to get rid of flies. *You're a fool. Silence and not asking questions. Those might be the rules where They are concerned, but they don't have to govern your whole life.*

Sitting still was hopeless. Before she had time to consider it, she was halfway down the stairs again, back to the bike sheds and away, heading into town this time. Outside his college, she hesitated, then got out her notepad to write a message. Even armed with her new-found boldness, she could not bring herself to risk knocking on his door.

While she was writing, someone stopped in front of her. The last time, it had been Professor Edgerley himself. She looked up, ready to be pleased and grateful. And Jen Booker looked back at her.

"Hi. Look, please don't rush off. I'm not here to hassle you, I promise. Actually, I wanted to apologise."

What had the professor said about her? "She yearns for the world to be more than what we see." *Well, who doesn't?*

Impatience made her brusque. "Go on, then."

Jen recoiled a little at her tone; clearly, she had not expected the mouse to show its teeth. "Hey, I really am sorry. Adam's not exactly a friend, you know? We just share supervisions sometimes. He shouldn't have spoken to you like that. Is there somewhere we could go have coffee?"

"I told you, I don't know anything." Felicity held the note in her hand, but she did not want to put it into the professor's pigeonhole while Jen looked on. What if she read it, or even stole it?

"Yeah, I got that, okay? But I'd like to buy you a coffee. It's the least I can do. And I promise Adam's not hiding round the corner." Jen smiled with those perfect teeth. It was meant to dazzle, and it might have worked on someone who had not experienced *the real thing.* At that, she smiled herself. *I've got no idea what that means any more.*

Jen took the smile as encouragement. "Hey, I know a place. They do a great lunch too. You hungry?" And Felicity found herself following.

Chapter 61

The prices were out of her range. The old Felicity would have gone along with it, hoping that Jen had been serious about paying, but in her present hard-edged mood she was taking no chances. "Are you buying lunch too?" she asked as Jen sat down.

"Sure, why not?" The waiter greeted her by name, and she flirted with him while they ordered, in a natural, easy way that made Felicity like her more. She had seen some of Sebastian's acting friends trying to charm people like waiters and bar staff, but this was different, as though for Jen it was simply good manners.

While they waited for the food to arrive, Jen poured water for them both. She sat back, turning her glass around and around on its placemat, making finger-trails in the condensation, not looking at Felicity. Having got this far, it seemed that it was up to Felicity to make the next move.

"What's your subject?" she asked. Along with "Which college are you at?" this was the standard first question, and always a safe place to start.

"I'm a postgrad. Working on European folklore and how it translates to the States." Jen paused, and then looked up. "It's funny. Back home they're really into all that stuff, but here people mostly see it as a bit of a joke. I had real trouble finding a good supervisor."

Felicity said, "In anthropology, remote tribes with complicated kinship structures definitely score highest. If your subject is local to Britain, it has to be about the urban working classes or migrants. 'Folklore' isn't academically respectable unless it comes from another continent."

"I know, right?" Jen leaned forward, pushing her long hair back behind one ear. "But the Prof is okay, though he does have a bit of a screw loose. Seems like he actually believes in fairies and all that, the way he talks." Under that direct gaze, Felicity felt herself getting hot, and then fiery red as blood rushed to her face. Jen continued to stare at her.

"The thing is," she said, still staring, "when he did that weird thing with the candles and the book, that wasn't the first time I'd seen you."

Felicity grabbed her glass of water and pressed it to her forehead, as much to hide her face as to cool herself down. This had been a mistake. She looked past Jen to the window and the street outside, and Elfrida looked back at her. Lower down, Hob squashed his nose against the glass, making his goblin face even more hideous. Definitely the wrong move.

She stood up. "I'm sorry. I'm going to go now."

Jen had risen too. "Oh, hey, no, *I'm* sorry. Look, our food's coming. I can't possibly eat it all myself. Please stay. I promise not to hassle you. Please?"

Behind her, Elfrida raised her eyebrows; a warning, or a challenge? As Felicity sank back into her seat, she nodded slightly. *All right, then.*

"I really can't tell you anything," she said, a little too loudly. "You'd better ask Professor Edgerley if there are things you want to know. He's helping me with my dissertation, so you've probably seen me at his college."

Jen shook her head, and that shiny hair slid forward again. *Honey blonde,* thought Felicity irrelevantly. *She could do with a hairslide.*

"He won't say. But I didn't see you at his college. You came to a lecture he gave, and then you walked out halfway through, and he went after you."

"Oh, that. I wasn't feeling well. I didn't mean to cause a fuss though." *Maybe I'm not so bad at acting after all.*

But Jen had not finished. "And there was someone else in the room. Wasn't there? It's okay, you don't have to say anything. There's just this, and then I'll shut up. There was someone I couldn't see. People's pens and paper and stuff were going on the floor, all along my row, for no reason." She was talking very fast now, as though that might somehow make it all right, leaning around the waiter who was placing their food and pouring more water. "And he could see whatever it was. The Prof, I mean. He stopped talking and just watched, and that was when you got up and left, and he dropped his notes and everything and followed you. So that's how I know."

She stopped suddenly, and they stared at each other over the plates of food. Hob reached around from behind her and removed a chip from her plate, and she did not react at all. He bit off a piece, and his eyes began to grow as though it was the most astonishing thing he had ever tasted. And somehow, although the situation was fraught with danger, Felicity found that she did not care any more. If They were not taking it seriously, why should she?

She picked up her knife and fork and began to eat. Chips and moussaka, and maybe even a dessert afterwards. Why not? Jen, on the other hand, had not touched her lunch yet. She said, "I'm right, aren't I?"

Felicity gave her a sideways glance as she chewed. "You said I didn't have to say anything. This is lovely, by the way." Hob, meanwhile, was roaming around the room, sampling various dishes that took his fancy. And Elfrida still stood outside on the street, looking in, while tourists and shoppers flowed around her. She seemed to be smiling a little.

"Okay, okay." Jen held up her hands in mock surrender. "Let's just eat." She picked up her own knife and fork. "You've never tried this place before?"

"I came here once with my boyfriend, but that was in the evening. The menu's different. So how are you getting on with Professor Edgerley?"

Jen waited until she had finished her mouthful, then took a sip of water before answering. "He's good at analysing things. The messages and morals hidden in the folktales; that sort of stuff. And he's interested in how the stories changed—or didn't change—when people took them to the States. But although he lectures about fairies as though they really existed, he gets all cagey when you ask him about actual proof." Behind her, Hob put up his arms and wiggled his hands, as though they were growing out of her head. His fingers grew longer, sprouting twigs and leaves. Apple blossom began to appear, and petals floated down, catching in Jen's hair and falling into her food. She carried on eating, oblivious.

"That could be because he doesn't have any." They were only drinking water, but Felicity felt light-headed and reckless. *This is out of my control, so what have I got to lose?* Aloud, she said, "Maybe he just wants them to exist. Wouldn't it be wonderful if they did?"

Tiny apples were growing now. She could hardly bring herself to look, but still Jen seemed unaware. "But they do!" she said eagerly. "It's like they're just out of sight, teasing us. There have been times, like when I visited some ancient woodland in Hampshire—the New Forest, I think it's called, for some ironic British reason—when I got this really strong sense of being watched. You must have felt that, surely?"

Felicity pretended to ponder this, while above Jen's head the little apples hung like Christmas baubles. Crabapples, they were, small and hard as bullets, with flesh that would suck all the moisture from your mouth. Good for nothing but making jelly, her mother would say. The first one fell with a solid thunk onto the table and rolled away under their feet.

"I don't know," she said, when she could trust herself to speak without laughing. "When I was a child, maybe." Another apple fell, and this time it hit Jen on the shoulder before bouncing down to the floor. Jen pushed back her hair and speared another chip with her fork. "Anyway, you probably were being watched. By deer, for one thing. There are lots of them in the New Forest."

"Huh! Trust me, this was not wild animals. I wanted to go back after dark to see if there were lights or anything, but my friends had to get home." The third apple landed squarely in the moussaka, where it began to glow green, more and more brightly. It was impossible to look away; was it about to explode? Felicity watched, transfixed, as Jen stuck her fork into it, lifted it and put it in her mouth.

There was no explosion; Felicity found she had been holding her breath, readying herself—for what? Jen screwed up her face, said, "Too much salt," and swallowed. Then she glanced up at Felicity and said, "What? Have I got sauce round my mouth?" and reached for her napkin.

Before Felicity could say anything, Jen stopped, napkin at her lips. Her eyes went wide, staring at something just over Felicity's shoulder. She made a sound in her throat, something between a gasp and a moan. Then she shrieked, as apples began to rain down on her head, far more than could have grown from just one branch; a torrent like stinging hail that tumbled and scattered all around them.

Other diners had stopped eating and turned to stare. Someone said, "Is she choking?" Someone else leapt up to thump her on the back. All they could see, Felicity knew, was a girl in some distress; not Hob's face, alight with glee as he conjured apples from nowhere, nor Elfrida, standing now at Felicity's shoulder, gazing calmly at Jen. She made no move until Hob began pelting the other diners. And then, at last, she said, "Peace now,' and the tumult stopped. The apples vanished, and there was only Jen, cowering in her chair, her eyes fixed on Elfrida while everyone else in the room stared at her.

Felicity stood up. "It's all right," she said. "She's fine now. Thank you for helping. Something went down the wrong way, I think." She handed Jen a glass of water and said quietly, "Drink this."

Jen took the glass meekly, and stopped twisting the napkin between her hands; if it had not been made of real linen, it would have shredded by now. The man who had thumped her looked rather disappointed. He hovered nearby, until his wife hissed at him, "Come away, John!"

"Jen," said Felicity in the same low voice, "Let's pay up and get out of here." There would be no dessert after all; a pity, but it could not be helped. Jen fumbled for her purse, put down far too much money, and they left. Hob gambolled around them like an excited puppy, and Felicity steered them into the nearest quad, where at least they could be out of the flow on the pavement. Jen was moving like a drunk person, stumbling along, trying to keep track of Hob and Elfrida both at once.

She stopped suddenly. "I ate something," she said. "Didn't I?"

No one answered. Only Elfrida began to grow, tall and magnificent in a long robe embroidered with mystical symbols picked out in gold thread. Felicity recognised some of the signs of the zodiac, and what looked like runes although she could not read them. Jen seemed about to sink to her knees, so Felicity grabbed her arm and steadied her.

Her voice came out in a hoarse gasp. "Who *are* you?" she said.

Elfrida ignored this, of course. Hob bent over and peered at Jen from between his legs, then went into a forward roll. He landed in the flowerbed at the centre of the quad, picked a rose and ran back to present it to her. As she took it, the flower changed from pink to deepest red. She gave a little shriek, and blood welled from one fingertip where she had clutched the stem too tightly.

Felicity felt almost sorry for her, but the next thing she said was "Damn! I knew I should have brought my camera," and the feeling vanished before it had time to grow. She let go of Jen's arm.

"You can't take pictures," she said.

Jen did not take her eyes off Elfrida. "Sure I can. How else am I going to prove this?"

"You're not going to prove anything." Felicity looked to Elfrida for guidance. Was she just going to stand there looking imposing? Back there in the café this had seemed like fun, but now she was beginning to be annoyed. Annoyed and, yes, *jealous.* Why had they appeared to this stupid girl out of the blue, when she had done nothing to deserve it? They belonged to her, Felicity, and to nobody else. Then she recognised this for what it was. However much she might wish it, she had no control over what they chose to do. She took a step away from Jen, and waited for whatever came next.

Elfrida spoke, and her voice, although it was not loud, seemed to reverberate around the quad. "No pictures," she said. "No words."

Jen just looked at her, and then started as Hob leapt from the ground and flew at her face, a great winged thing that veered away at the last second and soared up high above their heads. It was not until he dropped down to land on Elfrida's shoulder that Felicity could see what he was: a peregrine falcon, fierce-eyed and deadly. She had seen one only in one of her bird books, never in real life, in the wild. They must have been more common, once.

Elfrida reached out one hand, one finger, and touched Jen on the lips. "You have what you sought," she said. "Now go. And tell your friend to beware. The power he reaches for is a will-o-the-wisp. It will lead him into the marsh, and he will drown."

To Felicity she said, "Come." And turned to leave. The falcon launched itself into the air and gave a piercing cry that was clearly audible to everyone nearby; they stopped whatever they were doing, looking in all directions to find the source of the noise. Elfrida walked through them all and Felicity, after one glance back at Jen, followed. Jen was just standing there, gazing after them, and silent tears welled from her eyes.

Chapter 62

Elfrida moved swiftly, and Felicity had almost to run to keep up with her. She did not stop until they were on the Backs, where there were fewer people and the trees along the river made a little quiet space in the busy town. She went up to a tall lime tree, laid her hand on its bark as though exchanging greetings, and then moved to the edge of the river. She did not look round when Felicity caught up with her, only said:

"So. Out with it, then."

"What?" Felicity was out of breath.

"If words were flies, they'd be buzzing around you as though you were a horse on a hot day."

Despite herself, Felicity raised her hand, waving the imaginary flies away. There were indeed plenty of words tumbling about in her head, but in the end she said only,

"That wasn't very kind."

Elfrida smiled, watching the ripples on the water. "I gave her her heart's desire, did I not? What has kindness to do with that?"

"That's what I did to Sebastian," said Felicity. "And now I've lost him."

She had expected something along the lines of "I told you so." Instead, she found herself enveloped in a cloak of fur. It was deep and soft and dark, and with it came such a sense of loving protection that she wanted to curl down inside it and be held all over. She had no memory of being held in that way by her mother; where it took her was to that strange journey, cradled in Elfrida's arms, as they restored baby Christine to her family. That journey had closed the doors of fairyland to her, and marked the end of childhood.

The grief of those immeasurable losses swept over her, mingled with the new loss of her first love. She did not weep aloud. It was all too big for that; but she crouched there at the foot of the tree and buried her face in the fur, and with that gentle cradling came such a feeling of acceptance and compassion that she wanted to stay there forever.

After what seemed a very long time, she sighed, and uncurled at last, and stood up. Elfrida was watching her now, a little way off.

"Thank you," she said, in a voice that shook only a little. "Can I keep the cloak?"

Elfrida laughed aloud at that. "Were you beyond the border now, you could fashion it for yourself whenever you chose. But I think that even in this world, there is some faint echo of magic, from time to time. You have only to bring it to mind."

"I suppose that's true." She remembered Jen, alone and desolate on the path where they had left her. "But Jen won't look for magic inside herself, not now. She'll spend the rest of her life hoping for another glimpse of you or others like you, just like the Prof—just like anyone who's seen you in childhood and can't quite forget. Just like me, really."

"The Sight will not last long, not for her. There will never be another glimpse. Those who try to steal it do not prosper, as her friend will also find. She will have to make her peace with that. Or not." Elfrida turned away as Hob came rushing up to them.

"She tried to follow me, poor thing," he said. "And they told her she must not walk on the grass, and she wept and pointed to where I played in the fountain, and in the end they led her away." He turned a cartwheel and almost landed in the river, but at the last minute he became a kingfisher, disappearing under water and bobbing up a moment later with a small fish in his beak. Felicity had time to think, *But I don't think there are any fish here,* and then, *It probably isn't a real fish,* before he tossed it up, swallowed it whole and then was himself again, standing dry-clothed on the bank before them.

Felicity said, "I suppose it serves her right, though I think the other one—Adam—was worse. And she did buy me lunch."

"If they presume to trouble you again, there may be less pleasant things than crabapples to swallow. You have nothing to fear from them. Now, what would you have us do with your faithless lover? Afflict him with foul breath, perhaps, or an attack of the pox?" Elfrida walked a few paces, musing. "Something to mar his beauty. The gift cannot be taken away, but there are ways to make him an object of curiosity rather than desire. Shall we have moths fly out of his mouth when he speaks?" She glanced sidelong at Felicity, and her expression was impossible to read. *Simple mischief, or malice?* "Or shall we render him unable to perform?"

For a moment, Felicity thought she meant perform on stage. And then she realised.

"No! Please, Elfrida, I don't want you to do anything to him. It's not his fault, after all. It's mine. I've afflicted him enough already."

"Have you so? And do you not think this would have happened, soon or late, even without the gift?"

"I don't know," Felicity said miserably. "We made promises to each other. He wasn't lying when he made them, I'm sure of it."

"Sweet Felicity." Elfrida came very close, reached out one hand and touched her cheek; a featherlight touch, almost imagined, just for an instant. "Glamour is naught but a will-o-the-wisp. It flits hither and thither, always inconstant. Even we can assume it only for a time. Allow it to be your guiding star, and it will always leave you desolate in the end. Did you not hear my warning to yonder heartsick maiden? But no, of course, you could not. You humans reach for it like babies reaching for a candle flame, and then wail when it burns you. To cure that sickness is beyond my medicine."

With that, she was gone. Hob, too, and with them the beautiful fur cloak. Felicity stood there, shivering a little in the sudden wind, and tried to imagine it still enfolding her as Elfrida had suggested. For the first time since the border had finally been closed to her, she felt real regret, reaching for her heart like the cold wind playing around her ribs through her thin dress. *I wish I could go back. Walk away from all this, and never have to be hurt again.* But the brambles had grown over that path long ago, and there was no way back.

She could not summon up the will to trudge back into town, find her bicycle and go to the library for some revision after lunch, as she had planned. Like a wounded fox going to earth, she wanted only to get back to her room and curl up in her bed, shut out the daylight and hide from it all. She walked fast along the path, not stopping when she reached the porter's lodge to look for messages. Five minutes to boil the kettle in the kitchen for a cup of tea, and she would be safe.

He was there. Sitting at the kitchen table with a newspaper and a cup of coffee, cigarette in hand. Sebastian, and two of the girls who shared the kitchen, laughing too loudly and too long at something he had just said.

She stopped dead: Not *now. Not like this. It's too much*—and then he looked up and saw her.

"Surprise!" he said. He jumped up and came to hug her. He smelled of smoke and trains, and for a moment she searched for the old sense of safety and homecoming, as though he could enfold her in the magical fur cloak after all. But this hug was not for her; over his shoulder she could see one of the girls making a rueful face at the other. It was a performance for their benefit, and there was no safety to be had there.

She pulled away. "Let's go to my room. I need to dump these books." She felt their disappointment, all three of them, and did not care. These girls were not her friends, and Sebastian—what was he, now? Without looking back, she left the room and, after a few seconds, he followed.

Once there, it suddenly seemed very important to unpack her books and files and arrange them carefully in their right places. She did not look at Sebastian while she did this, but she was aware of him watching her. He sat down on the bed and lit another cigarette.

When she had run out of things to do, she seated herself on her desk chair, as far away as possible. It felt essential to keep distance between them, as though if she got too close, the gift might seduce her as it did everyone else. And so, although she yearned to be close to him, to hear him say that it was all a mistake, she summoned up the new hardness that had come to her aid with Jen. At last, she looked him in the eye.

They both started to speak at once. "I thought you were in Norwich," she began to say, at the same time as he said, "We had a few days before the next place. I could have gone to London but—" and then he laughed as their words got tangled up. Felicity did not laugh.

"Sorry! It was a last-minute thing," he said. "The theatre in St. Albans had an electrical fault, and we've got nothing booked until next week. Weird; like being becalmed at sea, or something." He ran a hand through his hair. "It's so intense, being on tour. You're with each other all the time, you don't know which town you're in and the rest of the world kind of fades away. I don't think I've been out in daylight so long for ages. I'm probably deathly pale, like a ghost." He stopped talking at last, looked at her properly for the first time. "What's the matter? You look as though you'd been crying. Felicity, what is it?" He came over, knelt by her chair and took her hand.

She shook her head, turning her face a little away. "I'm tired.

I've got my first exam on Monday, and I'm behind with revision. Not sleeping well." Somehow, it was impossible to say what really mattered, any more than she could tell him about Jen and the fairies.

"Oh, is that all? These exams don't count towards your degree, do they? You'll be fine, anyway. You always are. I bet you've done loads more work than you need to." He probably meant to sound encouraging, but in her fragile state all she heard was, *It doesn't matter. You worry too much. Forget your exams and focus on me.* And out of the fog of exhaustion, there was the sudden flare of anger.

"I won't be fine if I don't get the work done. You couldn't just go on stage without learning your lines, could you? I know you don't think they're important, but I want to do the best I can."

"Of course you do." He put his head on her knee and looked up at her sideways, still trying to coax a smile out of her. "Let me look after you today, at least. I'll take you out to eat tonight; somewhere new if you like."

Tears pricked at her eyes; it was easier to be angry. "No, I don't like! I'm sorry, but you can't just turn up and expect me to drop everything. All those times I've waited around while you rehearse or perform or talk about how it went and who said what. What if I said to you, 'It doesn't matter. It's just play-acting. Come and be nice to me instead.'" It wasn't entirely his fault, of course. It had been her choice all along, but she was past being reasonable now.

"Sebastian, in three weeks my exams will be over and there will be plenty of time for other things. You know that. Right now, I really need to focus." Abruptly, she ran out of steam again. "And yes, of course it would be lovely to go out to eat." *For the second time in one day.* The thought made her smile despite her wretchedness.

"Hey, hey." He got up, sat on the desk, and put his arms

around her. "You're exhausted, poor love. Why not sleep for a bit now? I've got good at taking catnaps, even in the most uncomfortable places. I can recommend it. You get your head down, and I'll make myself scarce for a few hours, maybe book us a table somewhere. How does that sound?"

"Don't be nice to me," she said, and began to cry in earnest. It would be so easy to let him care for her, to be grateful for this unexpected bonus of time together. To pretend that she had not seen what she had seen. And again, anger came to her aid.

She pushed him away. "You do what you like," she said. "I've got work to do. We can talk later, maybe."

He let go of her, stood up and paced a few steps, turned back. "What is it, Felicity? This isn't just about exams, is it? Has something happened?"

Where do I start? She took a deep breath. *After this, nothing will be the same. Except, of course, it's already changed, and there's no going back.* She looked up at him, her beloved, saw the bewilderment and concern in his eyes. Watched them change, becoming wary and guarded, as she said, "I saw you. In Norwich, with that girl."

Chapter 63

Sebastian went to the window. To look out at the garden, or so that she could not see his face? He stood, just as Elfrida liked to do, gazing downward. She had expected a torrent of words: guilt, justification, denial? The silence was unnerving. It stretched on, too long, so that to break it seemed impossible. But into it, she read acknowledgment of what she already knew. There was some relief in that, at least.

He stirred at last, just as it seemed he would never speak. Without turning to look at her, he said,

"I knew you'd know, somehow. I wasn't going to lie to you."

She laughed, then. "So this was the first time?"

At last, he turned to face her, and she saw hurt in his eyes. *But then, he is an actor.* "If you knew how many times I've said no! People are always throwing themselves at me. Well, you've seen for yourself, haven't you? Look, I'm not trying to excuse myself, honestly, I'm not." He crossed the room, knelt down and took her hands. "When you're there, it's easier. But I haven't seen you for weeks, and soon there'll be the television filming up north somewhere, and it's just going to go on like this. I'm not strong enough; that's the truth. Please shout at me or something. I can't bear it."

She looked down at him, at his hands clasped around hers. *It's all my fault* was the one thing she wanted to say, and could not. And maybe it would have happened anyway, even without the gift. That was something she could never know. But with the gift it was a certainty, and it would keep on happening, over and over again.

She took a deep breath, willing herself not to cry. "I know you're not strong enough. This might be the first time, but it won't be the last, will it?" She did not wait for him to answer. "The thing is, I'm not sure I'm strong enough to deal with it." And now the tears did come. She pulled her hands away, fumbling for a handkerchief, and he put his arms around her and held her as she wept.

How long they sat there, she did not know, but finally she pushed him away. "I won't sleep," she said, not looking at him, "and I can't work. Let's go for a walk." And he stood up, obedient, as though doing what she wanted now might somehow atone for what he had done. She led him into town to his old college, and neither of them spoke until they came to the staircase that would bring them out on top of the tower. Then, at last, he put a hand on her arm. He began to say something, but she pulled away and started to climb the stairs. After a moment, she heard him following.

When they came out on the top, he hurried to catch up with her.

"Felicity, don't. Please. I won't let you do this."

"What?" As realisation dawned, she almost laughed. "God! We're not in a play now, Sebastian. I'm not going to jump. Have you got your penknife?" And then she did laugh. "And I'm not going to do that either, don't worry."

She watched as he fished the penknife out of his jacket pocket; saw the grace in the way he moved, the self-consciousness in his actions, even now. Such a long way he had come, from the awkward boy she'd first met at the film club to the star of his own show, the centre of everyone's attention. And such a long, long way he had yet to go.

She took the knife and went over to the parapet wall. Crouching down, she felt along it, searching with fingers as well as eyes, until she came to the place where he had carved their initials in the sandstone. Not so very long ago; it was hardly weathered at all. Over her shoulder, she looked up at him.

"Do you remember when you did this?"

He shrugged a little, embarrassed now. "Of course I do."

"And what you said?"

"Felicity, please don't do this." He came over to crouch beside her, put his hand on her shoulder. "I meant it, all of it. I feel exactly the same now as I did then. You and me, together. I made a horrible mistake, and it will never happen again. Forgive me. Please." He cupped her chin in his hand, trying to make her meet his eyes. At first she pulled away, and then looked straight at him.

"I know you mean that, just as you meant what you said back then. But it doesn't change anything." She opened the knife and began to scrape at the soft stone. "You say I'm your muse, your anchor." Already the "F" was blurring, losing its shape. "You say you can't do it without me. And I can't explain this to you, but you've been my anchor too. Being with you, loving you, it's part of what makes me real."

She stopped, took a deep breath, willed the tears away. "But I can't be with you, not like this. Watching from the audience while you stumble through, making one 'mistake' after another. Because you will, so please don't try to make promises you can't keep." She began on the "S," following the curve of it, taking it down to bare stone as though it had never been there. "You say I help you keep your feet on the ground, but you've started to believe what they all keep telling you, haven't you?"

A quick glance at his face told her that she had struck home. She put down the knife and turned to face him. "And I can't be there to be your reality check. Somehow, you've got to work it out for yourself, or it's no good. We'd just end up hating each other, don't you see?" She went back to work, scraping away the heart shape now, leaving the stone fresh and clean, waiting for someone else's promises.

When it was all done, she handed him the penknife. "I release you," she said, formally, as though freeing him from a spell. *Undoing a love charm. Elfrida, are you watching? Are you proud of me now?*

He took the knife and the hand that held it. "You're cruel," he said quietly. "I never thought you could be so cruel. I don't deserve this."

"Yes, you do. And so do I." Felicity could hardly believe it herself. *If you're watching, Elfrida, you should be proud. I've learned more from you than I knew.*

After a moment or two, she drew her hand away, and got to her feet. Not quite steadily, she said, "I'm going to go now. I'll put your rucksack in the kitchen so you can collect it without—well, anyway. Please don't try to see me."

"How do you know I won't try to jump?" he said. "If you're right and I'm bound to make a mess of things, why not just end it now?" His colour had come back and his eyes looked very blue. *It's easier to be angry than to feel pain.*

"You won't," she said. "You'll go away and be a brilliant actor, if that's what you want. You'll learn how to live your life. Use your gift, but don't let other people use you because of it. If you can do that—and I really hope you can—then maybe one day we can see each other again. But I don't think it will be for a long time yet."

She had run out of words, and was suddenly so tired that she could barely stay on her feet. Without even a goodbye—*well, what would be the use of that?*—she went to the stairwell and began to descend, one foot after the other, holding on to the handrail as though without it she might just fall, all the way down. He did not follow, and for that at least, she was grateful.

There was no rest to be had that night, only a succession of nightmare images that jolted her awake every time she dozed.

She longed for Sebastian to come to her door, and dreaded it at the same time, and wept when, after all, he did not come. Monday morning brought her first exam, and she sat through it with no idea of what she had written, or whether it made any sense at all. She almost did not care. She had given herself heart and soul to her relationship with Sebastian. With him went the future they had planned together, and she could not begin to imagine a new one without him.

After the exam she left without talking to anyone, wandered the streets among the crowds of tourists, and finally slipped back into college late in the afternoon, when most people would be revising or sitting exams. She went to bed and slept like a dead thing, beyond exhaustion, and did not wake until after eleven the next day.

Chapter 64

She had forgotten all about her note to the Professor, and her meeting with Jen seemed very small and far away, like an old photograph of someone she did not know. But there in her pigeonhole was the invitation: "Come tomorrow at 2.30 if you are free." It seemed irrelevant now, but then so did everything else. Her next exam was tomorrow, and she was already a long way behind with her revision plan, but she could not find it in herself to care very much.

It seemed she might just as well do this as anything else, and so half past two found her climbing the stairs to the Professor's study. What had she wanted to see him about? Just now she could not actually remember; only that this place was a refuge of sorts. Like a fox going to earth, she wanted to burrow away from the demons that pursued her. And yet, while the fairies could not pass this threshold, it was no barrier to her own thoughts.

Professor Edgerley was smiling as he opened the door, but the smile faded quickly. He stood aside to let her in, and when she turned to face him, said,

"Forgive me, Miss Turner. Are you quite well?"

Mutely, she shook her head. She started to speak, but he held up a hand and said, "Tea first. And there are biscuits today. Only malted milk, I'm afraid." He made a rueful face. "I was over-enthusiastic with my thanks when the housekeeper first brought them, and now she thinks they are my favourite."

He kept up a flow of talk while making the tea, not looking

at Felicity. She took a biscuit, running her finger over the raised picture of a cow on the surface, and thought of the milking parlour, the patient cows standing in line while early birds sang outside and the cats wove around her feet, waiting for their share. Suddenly, unexpectedly, she longed to be there.

The Professor brought tea and settled himself at his desk. Looking away, he said,

"Miss Booker has already been to see me, in some distress. But that is not what you wanted to talk about, I think."

It was the faintest hint of a question. She could still back down. She thought, *I like you very much. But it's time, and past time, as Elfrida would say.*

She took a deep breath. "There's something I haven't told you."

And so, at last, she told him about the gift. A strange and unexpected blessing, kept close to her heart and never opened, like a locket containing a beloved picture, until the morning when she gave it to Sebastian. And how, almost at once, it had begun to work to tear them apart, and maybe to tear him apart as well. She talked, and the Professor listened, and the tea grew slowly cold.

When she ran out of words, there was silence. Somehow, she had no need of a response, as though the listening itself had been enough. It changed nothing; the Professor had no magical solution to offer, and yet she did feel a little lighter. *All my life, I have kept secrets,* she thought. *I never realised how heavy they could be.*

At length, the Professor stirred. He looked directly at her for the first time, and there was such a depth of sympathy in his eyes that it almost undid her. Not a trace of judgment; just kindness, and a kind of recognition. She did not understand that, until he sighed, got up from his chair and crossed to the bookshelves on the far side of the room. For a moment he stood there, his back turned, and then he came over to the fireside where she was sitting in the big armchair. In his hand he held a small photograph in a silver frame.

"Time for a secret of my own, I think," he said, and handed her the photograph. "You have never asked, but I am sure you must have wondered."

She looked down at the picture in her hand. It was old and faded, so that the faces were hard to make out, but she could see that there were two girls, one perhaps eight or nine years old and the other much smaller, dressed in the voluminous clothes of the Edwardian era. Both were facing the camera, unsmiling, and something about the posture of the elder child suggested defiance. She had her hand on the shoulder of the younger child, whose face was screwed up against what must have been bright sunshine.

"Myself and my elder sister Marigold," the Professor said quietly. "In those days, small boys were often dressed like girls until they were six or seven. I would have been five years old when this photograph was taken, and Marigold was eight. It is the last picture I have of her."

Felicity waited. After a moment or two he went on. "Our parents were away a good deal, and this was taken to be sent to them on their travels. You cannot imagine how different things were then, before the Great War. We had a governess and a nanny, and servants to keep us clean and fed. We had a park to roam in and ponies to ride." He glanced at her. "And if you are thinking that this sounds like a life of extraordinary privilege, then consider how vulnerable a young child could be, in the hands of those who have power but not love."

He fell silent, and Felicity looked again at the picture; at the girl, Marigold, staring at the camera with one hand resting protectively on her brother's shoulder, and the other curled into a fist at her side.

The Professor followed her gaze, and after a moment he said, "She took the brunt of it, my brave sister. They did their best to break her. To 'tame that ungovernable wildness'; 'to beat those demons out of her.' Those were the sort of things I overheard. Of course, I realise now that they were stupid as well as vindictive, and perhaps that was a saving grace. Their cruelties were commonplace, though that did not make them any the less terrifying for small children with nowhere to turn. She protected me when she could, took the blame and was beaten for it, freed me from locked cupboards and smuggled food from the kitchen when they starved me. Perhaps she could not have done it on her own behalf; perhaps I was what made her keep fighting. I was too young to understand then, and I cannot ask her now."

He stopped again, turned away and went to the window. Felicity understood that his story was too difficult, too loaded with emotion that had gone unexpressed for a lifetime, to be spoken face to face. She understood very well.

With his back turned, the Professor said, "And then They came to her."

Of course they did.

"She met them in the wilder part of the parkland. She had hiding places there, just as you did in your woods, and sometimes she would take me with her, until They came. They swept her up with them, and she asked—or so she told me later—to bring me too, but they laughed and said I was too young. So she would whisper to me in bed, telling me stories of where they had been and what they had done." He half turned, smiling. "And after that, she truly was ungovernable. Nothing they could do could take away that shining secret from her. And they soon learned not to follow her! I never did hear the whole of it, but I saw the beginning of fear in their eyes when they looked at her. It changed everything."

He took a deep breath. "One night she crept into my room with muddy feet and twigs in her hair and made me lie very still while she touched my eyelids with what she said was magic ointment, stolen so that I, too, would be able to see them. Soon after that she hid me deep in a thicket, covered with leaves, and left me for what seemed like a very long time, alone. When, at last, They came, I saw—well, you know what I saw."

He turned now, met Felicity's gaze, and they both smiled. No need of words. "Of course," he added, "I am sure they knew I was there. They probably knew what Marigold had done, too. But it did not matter to them. I watched, and I saw how they transformed my sister, how she became truly herself in that company. I yearned to join her, to be accepted by them just as she was. But I was afraid that if I stood up and revealed myself, it would spoil everything. So I stayed hidden, cold and uncomfortable and bitten by insects, until she came back to find me just as dawn was breaking."

"She said that they had asked her to go with them. I will remember her face until my dying day, transfigured, glowing with joy. I cried, then, and clung to her. I may have begged her not to go. I don't remember all that was said; only that, in the end, she made me a promise. She would stay as long as they held the way open for her, but if she had to go, she would come back for me."

Now it was Felicity's turn to look away. Knowing what the end of the story must be, and the lifetime that lay between then and now. She bent her head, looking again at that long-ago photograph. At the girl, so young and so resolute. Unlike herself, with the promise of a wider life ahead, Marigold had had only her brother to stay for. And it had not been enough.

The Professor was speaking again. "We made our way back to the house and crept into our beds. We were only children. We never thought about footprints in the dew-wet grass, about mud on our boots and clothes. They beat her, and they locked us both in. She would be sent away to school, they said, where she could no longer lead me astray. I was let out at suppertime and told that I was not to see my sister again. She would be kept in her room until my parents had written to give their consent, as they surely would, and there would be no more going out alone, by day and certainly not by night."

He smiled, and when he spoke again, his voice had a new tenderness. "I remember thinking it was my turn to be brave. I made myself stay awake that night until I was sure they were all in bed, and then I went to my sister's room. I was afraid to call out to her in case it woke someone else, and I could not turn the key in the lock. But she heard me there. She came to the door and told me to slip the key underneath, and a few minutes later we were out in the stable yard."

"At the edge of the lawn, we stopped. She told me I had to stay. Then she threw the key into the hedge, and she hugged me. 'I'll come back for you. I promise!' she said, and then she was off, running across the grass towards the distant trees. I watched until she disappeared under the shadow of the woods, and she never looked back."

There was silence for a while, until at last Felicity cleared her throat and said, "Thank you."

He looked round at her and smiled. "Well. Her story is also my story. There was a search, of course, and there was nothing to be found. The other servants spoke up about things they had witnessed, and the nanny and the governess were given notice. Not long after that the house was shut up, and I was taken to live with relatives until I was old enough to go to prep school. The war began, and the house became a convalescent home for the wounded. It was many years before I was able to return. I don't know what I was hoping for; some sign that she had come looking for me, at least. But there was nothing. No trace."

He turned from the window now, restless, and walked over to his desk, where books lay open and a pile of written sheets awaited his attention. "For a long time I went on hoping that somehow, she would find me. Now and then, I have caught glimpses of Them. But I could only watch from a distance, just as I did all those years ago. You know what the stories say about those who steal from them, and the punishments they can mete out if they so choose. And so all I had were the stories, gathered from all over the British Isles over many hundreds of years, and no doubt changed in the telling. It's been my life's work, as you know, to find out as much as I could about the Fair Folk and their ways. But until you came along, I had never met another living person who had met them, and remembered, and was still here in this world."

Felicity glanced up at that. "I always hoped," she said. "I thought there must be others like me. Surely there must be? I can't be the only one."

"Who knows? You have your whole life ahead of you. Perhaps one day you will find out."

Felicity let that go, following another train of thought. "You know," she said, "I'm sure your sister would have come back if she could. I think they must have gone Onward, and then she couldn't come back."

"Ah yes," he said, "That was my thought too, when I read your account. It was a great comfort to me. In fact," he went on, crossing once more to the window, "Our meeting has brought me more joy than I can possibly say. Miss Turner, I am deeply in your debt." He turned and made a little mock bow.

Felicity blushed red, and to hide her embarrassment she bent her head low. "And I'm in yours," she said. "You've helped me so much. To understand, and—just to be able to talk about it all. I'm glad if it's been useful to you too, and not just for your work. Thank you for telling me about Marigold." *You must have been so lonely, all those years. Is that how my life will be?*

"Well," he said, "I hope she found happiness beyond the border. I daresay if we were to meet now, we should be so changed that we should not know one another. I by age, of course, and she by stranger things."

Felicity looked up at him. "Professor," she said, suddenly

brave. "If you did meet again; if she did come back for you now, would you go?"

In an instant, he became completely still. It reminded her of time spent in the woods looking for wildlife, and the way that, if you saw a deer or a stoat or some rare bird, you had to be utterly motionless, to erase yourself as much as you could, in order to receive that particular kind of magic.

At last he said, very quietly, "Would I go? Ten years ago, perhaps even five, I might have stepped out of my life, as she did, without a second glance. But I do not think that place is kind to the old. Some of your friends may be hundreds of years old, but at heart they are just children. There would be, I think, another kind of loneliness."

He paused, thinking, then turned to her. "But you, Miss Turner, you are young. What would you do if the way were opened to you after all?"

He was smiling as he spoke, but his words brought all the events of the last few days rushing back, and her voice came out raw and fierce with emotion.

"What would I do, right now? I'd go. I've made a mess of everything. I've ruined Sebastian's life and I'm going to fail my exams. The world beyond the border looks a lot more inviting than my prospects here. So yes, if I had the chance, I'd take it."

His face changed. "Oh, my dear," he said, and his voice was so kind that she could hardly bear it. She thought, *he's going to tell me I'm very young and it'll all be fine,* but instead he just stood there for a long moment. When he finally did speak, it was not to try to comfort or dissuade or even respond to her words at all.

"I wonder," he said. "I believe that what you have told me today is the missing piece of the puzzle, but I don't yet understand what it means. When you were given the gift, and told that your friends would continue to come to you, it seemed to you a marvellous blessing, and far more than you deserved." He glanced at her for confirmation and continued. "And of course, both of those blessings have turned out to be very mixed. Their presence in your life is not just incidental. It shapes how you think and what you do, just as their absence in my life has shaped mine. And I am sure that your friend would have known what would happen. In fact, I suspect that may be exactly what she intended."

Felicity looked up, startled.

"Remember the stories!" he said, beginning to pace the room as he followed his train of thought, animated now. "Wishes are granted, and who benefits from the consequences? Remember the subject of that lecture you came to when we first met? They do not bestow magic upon us out of benevolence. There is always a reason. They know it is what we crave, and they use it to get what they want from us."

Felicity was shaking her head now. "So you're saying," she said slowly, "You're saying that El—that she meant this to happen? But she's my friend. She's been so kind, in her own way. I don't see what she could get out of it."

"No more do I," he said. "But I would advise you to be very careful in your dealings with her. Weigh up any suggestions she may make, and consider things from her perspective. And," he turned to her again, "Make no decisions while you are heartsick. Believe me, you will heal, and you can have a bright future here at Cambridge, if that is what you want."

Suddenly, Felicity was impatient. She did not want to be consoled, reassured that everything would be fine. She knew that the Professor did not mean his words in that facile way, but she had had enough of intensity and she was very tired.

"I should go," she said, looking down at her empty cup. "If I'm ever going to catch up with revision, I really need to get on with it. Thank you for the tea."

If he was hurt by her abruptness, he did his best not to show it. "Miss Turner, please come again when your exams are finished. We should talk further."

Felicity got up to go. She was halfway to the door, but instead of coming to open it for her as he usually did, he remained by the window, looking down into the quad below. He held up a hand, and then turned at last to face her.

"I do not know whether you will get much work done this evening," he said. "Your friends are waiting for you."

For a moment she thought he must mean Jen and Adam, and her heart sank. When she realised what he did mean, she was afraid. *Have They found out about the Professor?* She did not want him to be punished in some way, not after all his kindness. What if they took away his ability to *see*?

"I'd better go," she said. "I'll come again when I can." Before he could move, she had opened the two doors herself and was hurrying down the stairs. She was sure he was watching from his window as she crossed the quad, but she did not look back.

Chapter 65

Hob was spidering from window to window, two floors up on the opposite side of the quad, peering in, sometimes tapping at the glass, then jumping away whenever someone came to look. Of course, they could not see him. He spotted Felicity and, instead of climbing down the Virginia creeper as she expected, he launched himself into the air. She gasped, even though she knew he would not hurt himself, and the young man at the window gave her a stern look, as though she was somehow to blame, and shut it with a loud bang. Hob landed on the path in front of her, already talking.

"Sticks and strings! Measuring and marking!" he said, seizing her hands and trying to dance her off the path. She pulled away; the man was still watching. "Painting signs on trees and notices on gates with tiny little words like black ants!"

"What? Slow down. What are you talking about?" But he could not slow down. From somewhere he produced a catapult and a pebble, and took aim at the man in the window. Felicity said, "No, don't!" but the pebble was already in flight. Above them the glass starred with a loud crack, and the face behind it disappeared. This time, when Hob tugged at her hand, they ran.

They did not stop until they were out on the Backs, and Felicity was breathless with laughter. Running with Hob was like wearing seven-league boots; every stride took her several yards further, and her feet barely touched the ground. No one paid any attention, and she realised that as long as he held her hand, she must be invisible too.

She collapsed on the grass by the river. "That was wicked," she said. "Promise me you'll never do that again. But it was brilliant!" She felt weak from released tension. For a few blessed minutes there had been no room for worry or heartache, and a part of her was reluctant to take it up again. *If only I could be like Hob, and move fast enough to leave it all behind.*

Elfrida spoke from behind her on the bank, and Felicity sat up, twisting to look at her. "Stakes and squares," she said. "In the field by the brook. And men go among the barns and sheds, taking stock and numbering everything."

"What do you mean?" But dread was already taking hold, her laughter forgotten. "What are you talking about?"

"Will they sell the woods too, do you think? Will they cut down the trees, Felicity? Where shall we live?" Elfrida, who was never upset about anything, looked stricken.

"What woods? Where?" But a part of her already knew. It had been coming for a long time, and she had refused to see, to believe that it would actually happen one day. But now, when she was far away and could do nothing about it; now, in the middle of exams and without her knowledge. How could they? In Elfrida's face, she saw her own anger, her own outrage, mirrored and amplified. And Hob, beside himself, put back his head and howled.

She was on her feet. "I'll get a train. I can be there tonight; I just need to pack a few things."

"There is no need of things. We will take you. Will you come?"

Elfrida reached out a hand; she, who never wanted to be touched. Felicity, without hesitation, took it. Hob grasped her other hand, and at once the world fell away. It was not at all like flying, moving far above the landscape and seeing familiar things below. Rather, it was as though they stood still while the world moved around them. It reminded her a little of the one time she had been to the seaside with her aunt and uncle. Standing at the edge of the waves, watching the sand being sucked from under her feet as the tide withdrew, feeling as though she was moving backwards, out of control. The only constant thing was the strong grasp of those two hands, and she held on for dear life. If she lost them, where would she be?

The onrushing movement stopped all at once, and she staggered and almost fell; without realising it, she had been bracing herself—against what? Elfrida was already moving away, but Hob kept hold of her hand until she had her balance. She turned to ask him where they were, but he was tugging her along after Elfrida. They were moving between trees, the ground soft with new grass pushing between last year's leaf litter, and then, as they came out at the edge of a field, she saw.

Chapter 66

Low Field had never been ploughed, as far as she knew. It was rough pasture, with a damp corner where marsh grass and kingcups grew. Frogs lived there, and sometimes a heron visited, looking for easy prey. There was no heron there now. Up at the drier end, there was a digger and a cement mixer, and a caravan with steps up to the door, and all around them the grass was trodden down to mud. The field gate, that was always closed, stood open, and two cars were parked just inside it. And down here near the trees, there were stakes driven into the ground with string stretched between them, just as Hob had said. She moved out into the field, following the line of string from one stake to the next, around a right angle and another and another, until she was back where she started. Beyond it, more rectangles were marked out, almost to the hedge.

Felicity knew what she was seeing. The memory came back to her, clear and sharp. She must have been four or five years old, being shown around the footings of her aunt and uncle's new house to be, on the edge of the village. It was further on than this; concrete had been poured and three or four courses of bricks laid, enough to show the ghost of the house before it had yet come into being. She remembered the strangeness, that inside the brick outline would be a living room, a kitchen, and above in the empty air would be the bedrooms where people would sleep; where children who would never go alone into the woods would live their private lives. "And here we'll have

French doors opening onto the patio," her aunt was saying proudly, already taking possession. Would these houses have French doors? Where would the frogs go now?

Hob was still tugging at her hand. "And in Well Mead too, where they used to cut the reeds before all the water ran away into the new ditches and down to the bourn. Shall we uproot their stakes and plant saplings instead? Shall we make dodder and bryony grow over their machines overnight?"

Felicity was shaking her head. "It's no good," she said. "They would only bring more stakes, and the village boys would get the blame. These will be houses, and people will come to live here. This must have been planned months ago, and they never told me."

She looked again at the gate and saw that it was not just open but off its hinges, lying askew against the hedge. Probably that would soon be gone, too. And underneath her exhaustion and wretchedness there was another feeling, deep and visceral, rising as though from the land itself and filling her until she could hold no more. She clasped her shaking hands together and took a deep, ragged breath. Rage coursed through her, and everything else fell away.

"I'm going to talk to my father," she said. She started across the field, but Hob pulled her back. "You must come!" he said. "They will not bide for long. We must away!"

For the first time, she realised that it was close to nightfall; the shadows were long across the field, though it had only been mid-afternoon when they left Cambridge. It was still early summer; that much she knew without thinking about it, but was it even the same day? Hopeless to wonder now. Elfrida was speaking.

"Go, and tell them we shall come soon," she said to Hob. "I would talk with Felicity."

In an instant he was gone. Felicity stood there, waiting once again to be told what to do, and then she put back her head and screamed through bared teeth at the indifferent sky. And Elfrida, who had seen every possible human emotion and probably more, simply waited.

"It will do no good," she said when the startled rooks, grumbling to each other, were settling again to their roosts in the nearby trees. "They are resolute to leave by dawn tomorrow."

"Who? Who is resolute?"

"Lovet. And Adder, he whom you knew as Lord Ember."

"What about the others?"

"All gone, by ones and twos. They have stayed only for us, and now will wait no longer."

Felicity stared at her. Of all the blows she had taken in the last few days, this was one that she had not foreseen.

"But you promised!" she said, childlike. "You said you'd always be with me, you and Hob. You can't leave me now when everything's ruined. I need you!"

"We cannot stay," said Elfrida simply.

"But they can't be cutting down all the trees, surely. I'll talk to my father. He can't have sold everything. He can't! Please, please don't go now. I can't bear it."

"Bear it you must, sweet Felicity. You will forget us in time."

Felicity shook her head. "Of course I won't forget you. How could I?" She thought of the Professor, and a life shaped by loss and longing for what could not be recalled. There was nothing left to lose, now.

"Elfrida, please answer me this one question. Why would you never let me stay, back then when I begged you, when I was a child? And now, when I'd give anything to come with you, how can you leave me behind here?" Rage and desolation made her careless of consequences; what did it matter now?

"We go Onward," said Elfrida, as though that were an answer. "There is no turning back. Would you choose that?"

"Yes!" Felicity clenched her fists, took a step forward. "Yes, I would. I know you're scared. I can see it in you when you talk about it. And I guess the others have only stayed so long because of you, and you'll go because you don't want to be left alone. I know all that. But I'll tell you this now, because it doesn't matter any more. Right now, I'd give anything to be able to go where you're going. I wish with all my heart that I could come with you."

Part Six: Across the Border

"But tonight is Hallowe'en and the faery folk ride
Those that would their true love win at Miles Cross they must buy
So first let past the horses black and then let past the brown
Quickly run to the white steed and pull the rider down
For I'll ride on the white steed, the nearest to the town
For I was an earthly knight, they give me that renown
Oh, they will turn me in your arms to a newt or a snake
But hold me tight and fear not, I am your baby's father
And they will turn me in your arms into a lion bold
But hold me tight and fear not and you will love your child
And they will turn me in your arms into a naked knight
But cloak me in your mantle and keep me out of sight"

Extract from "The Ballad of Tam Lin." Scottish borders.

The ballad was popular in the Middle Ages, and there were many versions, but they all tell how a young girl, Janet, falls in love with Tam Lin. She becomes pregnant, but when he finds her picking herbs to abort the child, he tells her that he was kidnapped many years ago by the Queen of Faerie. However, these verses reveal that there is a way for Janet to win him back, if only she can be strong enough.

Chapter 67

Through her tears, she stared at Elfrida, willing her to hear, to understand. Elfrida's eyes met hers, just for an instant, full of a light so fierce that Felicity had to look away.

"My brave Felicity," she heard Elfrida say. And then, as though musing to herself, "So. Maybe there is a way, after all. With all your heart, you say?"

"With all my heart. Just tell me what I need to do. Anything! If there is a way, I'll take it."

Elfrida turned away, her head bent, and took a few steps into the edge of the woodland. "And so, and so," she murmured. "Now we shall see."

Once more, Felicity waited, but now she was filled with hope. Just when everything seemed lost, it seemed there might be a solution; and not some wretched compromise, but a wonderful bright road full of magic. She found she was holding her breath, digging her nails into her palms. She took a deep breath, willing her hands to unclench, willing her whole self to be open and ready for whatever came next.

Elfrida stopped, turned, and spoke more loudly, as though she had come to some decision. "Would you give up your life, Felicity? Would you go Onward and leave it all behind?"

She thought about it then. Her home, changed beyond recognition, with no fairies waiting in whatever woodland remained. Her parents moving to a new house, probably in town. Cambridge, lost to her without the exams it would now be too late to take. Sebastian, lost to his own kind of glamour and already changing under the influence of the gift. She thought about the Professor, and Steph, and her heart ached. Perhaps the people she loved mattered more than anything.

She thought about Christine. Her little cousin, for whom she had given up this chance long ago. Whatever came next, she was proud of that decision. She might have ruined her own chances of happiness in life, but Christine was free to make her own way, make her own mistakes and—she hoped—find her own joys, her own dear friends.

But if I went Onward, I wouldn't be here to see it. I wouldn't be one of them. The people she loved would miss her for a while. Some of them would mourn her for a long time; but they would go on with their lives. They would survive the loss, as the Professor had survived the loss of his sister.

She lifted her head. "Yes, I would," she said. "I wouldn't want to linger on the border, watching my family get old and die. I'd go Onward. If there's a way, I'll come with you tomorrow. Only—only I'd like to write to a few people, just to say goodbye, and tell them I'll be all right."

She waited. Elfrida came a few steps closer, and as she moved, she changed. At first, it was like looking into restless water. Felicity could see that there was someone there, but she could not make out any features. The image shifted, broke and reformed, and she frowned, trying to bring it into focus. And then, as the ripples died away and the water grew calm, at last the figure in front of her became clear, just as though she were looking into a mirror.

Exactly as though she were looking into a mirror.

She stood face to face with herself, not as a young child nor as a beautiful woman, but just as she was: dressed in blue jeans and a cheesecloth smock with embroidery on the yoke. Her face was white with exhaustion and her eyes bright with unshed tears.

"There will be no need of writing," said the other Felicity, and even her voice was perfect. "They will not know that you are gone."

Felicity stared. After what seemed like a long time, she said, "I don't understand."

Her other self smiled. "It is simple," she said. "An exchange, just as Alys took your cousin and left her poppet behind instead. Except that we both choose freely. You shall go Onward with the others, and I shall live your life." She stopped, as though there was no more to say.

Felicity, too, was silent, but not because there was nothing more to be said. Thoughts tumbled over each other, none of them coherent enough to follow to the end. And when, finally, she did speak, it was not the first or the most important thing. She could not even begin to go there, yet.

"What about Hob?" she said.

Her other self lifted her shoulders in a gesture that was pure Elfrida. "What of him?"

"He never tries to blend in. How would he manage?"

"He goes with you." She said that as though it was obvious, a foregone conclusion.

"But you promised him he could always stay with you. He loves you. Surely he won't agree to this?" Hob's own words came back to her: *Promises are piecrusts.*

"It is one life for another. He cannot stay. He will go with you and the others."

Do you care for him at all?

For now, she let that go. She wanted to sink down, to curl up among the wood anemones that grew thickly here in the dappled shade, and lose herself in the life of the forest the way she had as a child. But she was not a child, and the choice now before her was the biggest of her entire life. *Although if I go Onward, my life will go on a long, long time.*

"Elfrida," she said at last. "Could you show me your own face, please? It's hard to talk to you like that."

"My own face?" Elfrida/Felicity smiled. "That's a thing no being alive has seen."

Too tired to fence with words, Felicity said, “You know what I mean. Please.” And again the wind blew across the water, destroying her reflection. When she could see again, Elfrida stood before her.

“Thank you,” she said. Then, “And ‘Thank you’ doesn’t begin to say what I need to say. Would you really do that, for me? Stay here all alone while I go Onward with the others? What would they think about it? And—and I don’t know how I feel about going without you. Is there no other way?”

“So many questions!” Elfrida brought her hands together, and then spread them apart as though to take in everything around them: the quiet trees and their long shadows across the houses that were yet to be; the birds settling to their roosts; this place on the edge of two worlds, that was soon to be just another patch of neglected woodland.

Felicity waited. At long last Elfrida said,

“They will take you with them, and Hob will make his peace with it. And yes, I would do this thing. You shall go, my Felicity. There will be no need of goodbyes or explanations, for I shall be here in your stead. So there’s an end to questions. Let us go to the others. You leave at dawn.” She reached out to touch Felicity’s hair. “Your fire burns low tonight. I shall give you sweet sleep with no dreams before you start your journey.”

That small touch, that gentle acknowledgment of her pain, almost undid Felicity. Tears began to flow, and she let them fall unchecked, too numb to brush them away. Elfrida said “Come,” and she took one step after her, into the shade under the first trees. Then she stopped.

“I’ll follow you,” she said. “I just want to look at the farm first. They may not know I’ve gone, but I need to say goodbye. I won’t be long.”

Over her shoulder, Elfrida gave her a long look. “Do not tarry,” she said. “And speak to no one.” Then she was lost in the darkness.

Chapter 68

Felicity was alone, for what felt like the first time in a long, long while. For a moment more she stood looking after Elfrida, and then she raised one arm to wipe across her face, and turned towards the farm. She went by the fields, not out of the gate and along the track, so as to come down to the farmyard behind the barns. There were no cows standing by the hedge where they liked to gather after milking, no full churns ready to go down to the lane for collection in the morning.

She felt numb. She kept going, one step after another, but not ready to arrive. *I am going,* she thought, but without any particular emotion, as though all feelings were used up and this was the only thing left to do now. *There's no coming back.* Walking out of the wreckage of her life; going Onward into who knew what, leaving a changeling behind. *What kind of life will she lead?* Elfrida would not care about Cambridge, or Sebastian, or friends and family. She, too, would leave it all behind without a second thought, and the paths she chose would be utterly different from the ways Felicity would have travelled. It could not be helped. In some part of her mind, she wondered where that brief flare of hope and elation had gone, but she was too tired to think about that now.

Suddenly, she could not bear to look at the house itself, and she slipped into the hay barn. It was full of fresh bales; they had been haymaking, at least, though there might be no cattle left to eat it. Perhaps the sheep were not yet gone. And here came the cats, hoping for their share of milk. They milled around her, questing, and she crouched down among them and sought solace there.

"Look after my parents for me," she murmured, and then, *But they won't be here. Will anyone think to care for you?* Somehow, out of all the sorrows of the last few days, this one seemed the most unbearable. Sitting there with nothing to give them in return for their gentle companionship, she wept. After a time, she lay down in the sweet-scented hay, breathing in the living smells of the summer meadows. The cats curled against her, sharing warmth and fellowship. She closed her swollen eyes, and immediately dream images swirled about her. How long was it since she had last slept? Lulled by the purring of the cats, she let herself drift away.

"Who's there?" Torchlight swept the barn, making fantastic shadows, blinding her. The cats fled this way and that as she sat up, blinking, shielding her eyes from the glare.

"Fliss, is that you? What are you doing here?" Her father stood over her. After a few moments he angled the torchlight away, then switched it off altogether. It was dark now, but moonlight slanted in through the high windows under the eaves. He hesitated, then sat down beside her on the hay bales.

"Something wrong, is there? Don't you have exams just now?"

Speak to no one. But she had already disobeyed that by talking to the cats. This would be her only chance to say goodbye, even if her father did not understand.

"Dad," she said. "Sorry to frighten you."

"Barn door was open," he said. "I was just doing my rounds. Well, old habits die hard."

Earlier, she had been full of rage, ready to confront him, somehow force him to change his mind. Now, she could find nothing but a quiet grief. Had he been a friend rather than her father, she would have reached out and held his hand.

"Is it all gone?"

In the dark, she sensed his smile. "Not by a long chalk, not yet. But there's been an auction. The cows went a couple of days ago. Planning permission came through for those two fields the developers were after. We would have told you, but we knew you had exams on. All finished, are they?"

"All finished," she said.

"How did you find out, then?"

She thought fast. "Christine writes to me. I thought I'd come home for a bit, surprise you."

He glanced down at her. "Things not going so well, eh?"

"Sort of." The old defensiveness—but what was the point now? "Dad, I might go travelling for a bit. See the world, you know? Before I decide what to do next."

He nodded slowly, considering this. "Well now, you know, the sale changes things for all of us. Your mother and I, we're thinking to move to a little house nearer town. Something with a bit of garden. And of course there'll always be a room for you. But see," and his voice took on a new strength, "we'll be able to pay off the debts, and when the rest is sold we'll give Bob his share, and there'll still be enough for all of us while we 'decide what to do next.'" There was a hint of laughter; and something else, something she could not remember ever hearing before. *He's excited.*

"What will you do?" She could not imagine her father without the farm. They were part of each other, just as Elfrida and the others were part of the woodland. But by tomorrow night they would be gone, and she with them. *Just because I can't imagine something doesn't mean it can't happen.*

He was speaking again. "Oh, I'll help out here and there, I daresay." Echoing her thought, he said, "I never saw myself as a townie. But it's time your mother got her say. She hasn't had it easy over the years."

All those lost children. "I'm sorry I was such a disappointment to you, not being a boy to carry on the farm. Maybe this wouldn't be happening if you'd had a son."

He looked sharply at her, startled. "Never think that! I've hung on too long, truth be told. Should have let it go years back. Small farms have had their day, Fliss. You've got more choices than we ever had. You'll go far. You've got nothing to be sorry about."

If only you knew. A part of her longed to tell him everything, to be heard and understood and forgiven. To go up to the house and be made a fuss of by her mother, and to lie in her own bed tonight, free of responsibilities. But that was a fantasy. It had never been like that, and it never could be, not now.

Her father was still speaking. "It's not been easy for you either. I know that. But when the money comes through, you'll be able to buy a house of your own, if that's what you want. Give you your independence, and a bit of security. It doesn't make up for how things were, but it's something."

"Dad?" He had never talked like this, not in all the years of her childhood. She had thought he did not care, that they would barely notice if she disappeared into the woods and never came back. "What do you mean, 'How things were?'"

He shifted away a little, and she thought he might simply get up and leave; but after a moment, she realised he was feeling in his pockets for tobacco and papers. That had always been his way, to do his thinking while he rolled a cigarette. She could smell the tobacco, hear the crinkle of the paper, and then came the sudden flare of light in the darkness as he lit a match. He waited to be sure it was burned out before stowing it back in the box with the others.

"You won't remember," he said at last, drawing on the cigarette so that the end glowed bright. "But when you were younger, before you went off to the grammar school, you used to go off by yourself all the time, into the woods. We thought—*I* thought—it was only a matter of time before we lost you."

She sat up straight, suddenly wide awake. "Of course I remember! What do you mean, 'lost me?'"

"You know what I mean," he said steadily. "Lost you to Her. I tried to stop you going, tried all sorts. Barbed wire, punishments, getting you away from the farm with your cousins whenever they'd have you. But it was no good. I knew you'd go one day, break your mother's heart, and it would all be my fault.

"We talked about selling up, but we wouldn't have got enough for the land to pay back what we owed. Small farmers were going out of business right and left, and there were no planning permissions back then. And I thought none of it would do any good. If She wanted you, She'd have you, for sure.

"But once you'd started at the grammar school, things changed. Maybe you just got more interested in other things, or maybe She thought better of it. And now, with university and that boyfriend of yours and going travelling, well, seems like you're making your way in the world. I'll never know the ins and outs of it, but I do know this. When we move away from here, we'll be free of that she-devil and her band, and it can't come a day too soon." He took a deep drag on the cigarette and then ground it under his heel.

Felicity stared at him. She was trembling, a fine tremor that ran through her whole body. He had known. All that time, when she had thought herself uncared for and unobserved, he had known exactly where she was, and with whom. Yes, he had tried to stop her, but never once had he talked openly about Them, as he was doing now. Now, when he thought she had forgotten, and it was safe at last.

"You're cold," he said. "Where are your things?" And then, not seeing her rucksack anywhere close by, he said "Here, have my jacket." He put it around her shoulders, still warm from his body, smelling of lanolin and tobacco, dogs and wet earth; all the layers of his life there to read in the thick tweed. On the inside, she knew you could see the colours it had once held, moss and heather and bark, but the outside was no-colour, the way everything ended up on the farm. She longed to snuggle into it, looking for a safety that had never been there. But the shaking did not stop.

"Dad?" she said. "You said it was all your fault. What did you mean by that? You couldn't have stopped me. No one could, unless we really had moved away, I suppose. It was my choice. You did your best." She wasn't sure that was true, but it felt important to give him—what? Some kind of absolution, before she disappeared from his life forever? But he was shaking his head.

"You don't know," he said, looking down at the wisps of hay under his feet. He reached for his tobacco pouch to roll another cigarette, and she saw with wonder that he was trembling, too. She felt in the jacket pocket for the matches and held them out to him, but he put up a hand as if to ward her off.

"I thought She must have told you," he said. "If you remember Her and the rest of them, then you must have known. I thought that was why you were so shut away, off in your own world, even when you were there with us. Your mother knew there was something wrong, but she never knew the truth of it. Fliss, I'm more sorry than I know how to say. But it's over and done now, long ago, and we've got the chance to start fresh." At last he looked at her, and his eyes were wet, pleading. "You can see that, can't you?"

"Dad," she said again. "What must I have known?"

Chapter 69

He got up abruptly, paced the length of the barn, stopped, and turned at last to face her. "All right, then," he said. "Seems I've got to say it out loud. I've kept quiet all these years. Kept my part of the bargain, even when it tore the heart out of me. Maybe it's time, now, when it's all over and you're safe home. Maybe it don't matter no more."

She waited. He took a deep breath, then came back to sit on the hay bale, near but not touching.

"There's no knowing," he said, "how long She and her kind have been there, plaguing this family. Generations, maybe. I know my father tried to fence off those woods, but back then there was all kinds of coming and going, people cutting osiers and burning charcoal and coppicing the trees, all that. He couldn't keep them out, and he couldn't keep us lads from larking about in the woods, no matter how many beatings he gave out." He smiled at the memory. "I don't reckon a beating ever stopped any child, come to think of it, and I'm sorry for that too, Fliss." He glanced sideways at her. "I just didn't know what else to do."

She said nothing, sensing that he needed to tell his story in his own time—though she thought she could guess what came next.

"So, well, I was a good bit older than you were before She come to me. Thirteen, maybe fourteen, and full of myself like any young lad that age. And she was a wonder, no doubt about that. Not a bit like the village girls, all giggling and telling tales to each other. She was . . ." he paused as though searching for the right words, "Unearthly. So beautiful. I'd never seen the like, and I don't reckon I ever will again." He gave a short laugh. "Spoiled me for regular girls, which was probably her aim all along."

He looked at Felicity then, and said hastily, "Now I'm not saying I didn't love your mother, don't think that for a moment. But she knew there'd been someone else before her, and I know she never felt she measured up. She deserved better, and I hope it's not too late now to make it up to her. Money won't make it right, but we're not too old to start fresh, once we're away from here.

"Anyhow, I don't take pride in how things were, believe me. But She—She had me in the palm of her hand." He stopped, looking into the past, and as though it conjured her up before them, began, "El—"

"Don't!" said Felicity urgently. "Dad, don't say her name!"

He stopped, shocked into silence. After a long moment, he nodded.

"Well. She made me see myself differently, too. When I was with Her, I felt like a prince in a fairytale. I daresay you'd understand that."

"You loved her," Felicity said simply. "Everyone does. You couldn't help it." And she thought of Sebastian, having the gift thrust upon him with no understanding of how to use it. *Or how not to.* "It wasn't your fault."

He was shaking his head; the story wasn't done yet. "She wanted me to go with her. Said we could be together like man and wife, we could live forever and have all the adventures we wanted, and we'd never grow old. Maybe you know that part, too. All I had to do was step out of my everyday life, and I'd be one of them, happy ever after as they say in the stories."

Felicity was watching his face, as much as she could see in the moonlight. "But you didn't go," she said softly.

"Oh, I wanted to! No two ways, I'd have upped and gone and never looked back. Didn't seem there was much to stay for."

Again, he fell silent. But before she could ask the question, he gave her the answer.

"Your grandfather, he got sick, and he wasn't going to get better. You never knew him; he died before you were born. But that changed things. I had responsibilities. Someone had to look after our mother and young Bob, the farm, keep up the ploughing and sowing, milk the cows and keep a roof over our heads. I gave up school, of course, and the neighbours helped out when they could, but I had to choose. If I'm honest, I did wonder whether all those promises weren't just moonshine, head over heels though I was." He laughed. "Suppose I was more of a farmer than I thought, back then. Gimme them matches, would you, Fliss?"

While he made the new cigarette, Felicity drew the jacket closer around her. The trembling had subsided, as though his words had steadied her. Softly, she said, "That must have been hard. But you did the right thing, didn't you?"

In the act of taking his first draw, he stopped. "Don't say that!" He got up, took a few paces, turned back, like a beast in a cage. "When you know—when I tell you—you won't say that. Fliss, I wouldn't blame you if you went off travelling and never came back. There was no right thing, do you hear me? Maybe there never is. It was all wrong and no way out, and I couldn't see the wood for the trees. I'm hoping your mother might forgive me in time, but I don't see how you ever could. I don't deserve it." He looked down at the cigarette, crushed between his fingers.

"So, better get it over and done with." He did not come to sit down again, but stood facing her, so that the moonlight fell on his back and his face was in shadow. "When I went to Her, to tell her I couldn't go with her after all, I don't know what I was hoping for. That we could just go on like before, maybe. But she wasn't having that. Said I'd made a solemn promise, and such things are binding. Hard as granite, she was. I'd never seen her that way. I offered all sorts, anything she wanted that I could give, but she said there was only one thing that could free me from my promise, and that was to find someone else to go in my place."

"A life for a life." Although she did not know what came next, Felicity felt that she had heard this story before. There were so many echoes, from the old tales and from her own experience. "But that didn't happen, did it?"

"It didn't happen. Not then. She made me a bargain. I could go back to the farm, do my duty, and she'd never trouble me again. And if by some long chance I should meet a girl who'd have me, I could marry and settle to the path I'd chosen. And it might never happen, but in time we might have children. If they were boys, they'd grow up to work the farm in their turn. All she wanted, if it should fall out that way, was my first-born daughter."

He stopped, and then spoke all in a rush, as though to make her understand before it was too late, "It just seemed like her way of saying, 'All right then, off you go, farmer boy, and no more magic for you.' I thought I'd got off lightly. Truth to tell, I buried it away and almost forgot about it. It was years before I even met your mother, hard years when I had to be the man of the family. I never realised all the ways She and her band had helped out here and there, until it all stopped. Mending fences, saving the hay from the rain, untangling sheep from the brambles. Well. At least they didn't do any actual mischief after that, or not that I could tell. But I knew what they could do if they took a mind.

"Still, there'd been no sight nor sound for many years, and the day I brought your mother home, I really thought it was a fresh start. We were young and hopeful. Oh, we knew things weren't looking good for farms like ours, but we thought surely things would turn in our favour if we just kept going. Mixed farming, sheep and cattle, milk and poultry; if you keep your options open something's bound to pay off." He laughed, and it was not a happy sound. "Good job we can't see what's coming, I suppose."

Felicity was barely hearing him. The words drifted past her and disappeared like the smoke from his cigarette. *My first-born daughter.* That was the price of his freedom. That was what Elfrida had asked for. Her mind was racing, trying to make sense of it all. *She wanted me, before I was even conceived.*

Hardly aware of what she was doing, she held up her hand. "Wait, wait a minute," she said. He stopped at once, as though he'd been expecting it.

"I know," he said. "Whatever you've got to say to me, it can't be worse than what I've said to myself. She swore me to silence, of course. It's a relief, after all this time, to say it right out loud. But she didn't get you, did she? I don't know what I did to deserve that, either. But here we both are, and we'll walk away from this place free of her and all her tricks. So give it to me straight, Fliss. It's the least I deserve."

She was shaking her head. There were no words, just a mass of conflicting emotions all fighting for expression. Rage, of course, warring with pity for the boy he had been, trapped into a terrible bargain that had bound him all his life. Pity for herself, yearning for magic and, like her father, sworn to silence and a lifetime of secrets. Wonder at the choices she had made, which were no choices at all. *Was everything I did mapped out for me? Even saving Christine? Surely not that.* And what about Elfrida? She could not even begin to look at her feelings there.

But she was a child of silence and secrets, after all. In the end, all she said was,

"Just tell me the rest."

Chapter 70

In the darkness, she could feel the intensity of his gaze, trying to read her thoughts. For a long time, he said nothing. At last, he took up the tale again.

"Well. June and I settled into working the farm, and soon enough there was a baby on the way. Of course, I prayed for it to be a boy. But it made no odds; we lost him at six months, and the next one even earlier, at around four. After the third, we pretty much gave up hope. Your mother, she kind of faded. She was there, and yet she wasn't. And I thought, well, that's my come-uppance. I did wonder whether maybe She had some hand in it, but then, these things happen."

He was looking down at his hands, helpless. Again, a long silence. "And then you came along." He raised his head. "We never thought you'd go to term, never dared to put faith in it. When you arrived, I had to go finding a pram, a cot, all the things you need, all in a hurry. Lucky Angie was about a year old by then, and Bob and Marjorie were very good to us. Your mother hardly dared to pick you up; seemed like she couldn't believe you were real. And I couldn't let myself be glad either, knowing what I knew."

He stopped. Felicity looked up at him, her eyes full of tears. His pain was so real, so immense, that her own feelings were entirely eclipsed. Lost in the past, he did not move, did not react at all.

"It was a week before She came," he said at length. "A week when I started to hope maybe she'd forgotten, and maybe it would all be all right. You were in the pram under the apple tree in the yard. Your mother had gone up for a rest, and I was digging in the vegetable garden, keeping an eye. Everything went still, and I looked up, and She was there.

"She picked you up out of the pram and stood there looking down at you. She hadn't changed a bit, though of course I was a man grown by that time. She looked up at me as I came near, and I waited for that old enchantment to take me over. But it didn't come. And I thought, *I'm a married man now. It's not perfect, but it's real. It's right and proper, and I'll stand by that come what may.*

"I don't like to think about the next part," he said. "It's like it's dark in my mind, though the sun was shining through the new leaves and there was blossom on the tree. I begged and pleaded, and she just stood there with you in her arms, stiller than the apple tree behind her. A bit of blossom fell into her hair, and she never moved. And when I finally ran out of words, when I thought she'd just turn and walk away and leave an empty pram behind, then at last she looked up at me.

"It was as though I'd said nothing at all, like my words were just noise to her. She said,

"'She is my hope of felicity. For this I have waited a long, long time. That is her name: Felicity. And when the time is right, she will come to me.'

"Then she touched your eyelids with one finger and laid you back in the pram. The next minute she was gone.

"Well, I grabbed you, held you so tight you started to cry, and then June came out and told me off for getting mud on your clothes, and she took you indoors. I stood there looking down at the empty pram, and I knew she'd won and there wasn't a thing I could do about it. You were hers as sure as if she'd taken you then and there, though there might be years yet. It *was* my fault, no two ways."

Abruptly, he turned away, walking fast towards the barn

wall, head down, fists clenched. And Felicity doubled over as though she had been punched in the stomach, mouth open, gasping for air that would not come. *Laughing faces among the leaves.* There were no thoughts, not yet; just images falling like a house of cards, the story of her life retelling itself in a new and terrible way. Herself at eight, trying to tempt the fairies with little gifts. Defying her parents, struggling through bog and briar to come to Them. Longing to be one of them, and always denied that final step. Until now.

What's in it for Them? The Professor's words—was it only this afternoon?—just before she had left him. But it was the wrong question. What They wanted was simply to add to their dwindling band. Left to themselves, Hob and Adder and Lovet and the rest would have welcomed her and never looked back; she knew that now with utter certainty. The true question should have been: *What's in it for Her?*

And there it was, the whole story. *My Felicity.* Sebastian had called her that too. She'd always wondered about her name, so out of character for a farmer's daughter. *I was her hope of happiness. She didn't want a baby to look after, the way Alys wanted little Annie. She didn't want a playmate, the way the others did. She wanted me as I am now, old enough to make my way in the world. Offering my life freely to her. A life for a life.*

Dimly, she was aware that her father had come back, was standing over her and then, awkward and hesitant, putting a hand on her shoulder. He had never hugged her, not once that she could remember. That hand carried all the weight of his remorse, his need for forgiveness, and she could not bear it. It was too much.

She sprang up, shook him off and walked, as he had done, the length of the barn until the hay bales blocked her path. As a child, she would have made a den up near the roof, would have found where the cats hid their kittens and smuggled out food for them. But there was no refuge there now.

What am I going to do?

In a few short hours, it would be getting light. If she broke her promise, if she didn't go to meet Elfrida before dawn, what would happen? Would Elfrida just give up, go Onward with the others?

Of course not. Her plans had been laid long years ago, when her father was still a child and probably long before that. She couldn't give up. Even if all the others were gone, she'd come after Felicity—*and she can come to me wherever I am*—and make sure that nothing in her life worked out as it should. What harm might she do to her parents, her friends, to Christine?

No. That way lay only ruin and misery; a long slow revenge. There was no choice, and there never had been. Just a short time ago, she had stood in the shadow of the woodland and declared that she would go Onward; that that was what she wanted with all her heart.

What now?

"Fliss?" Her father stood a few paces away. She did not turn to look at him, could not bring herself to speak.

"Your mother'll be in bed by now. Come up to the house and we'll find you a bite to eat. She'll be pleased to see you in the morning. We can talk through what comes next." He paused, and she could feel the tension in him, the words pushing for expression. Words had never come easy to him, and that was probably Elfrida's fault too.

Then, all in a rush, "It's good to have you home, Fliss."

Now she did turn, grateful for the sheltering darkness, sparing them both the embarrassment of intimacy. She looked at him standing there, slightly bent, hands hanging empty that were usually busy about some task or other. His face was in shadow.

"Dad," she said. "It's all right. You did your best. You couldn't know how things would turn out. Nobody can." Her throat tightened and she stopped, fighting back tears. There were no words weighty enough. *I'll never see you again.*

"Well," he said, and his voice was hoarse, too. "That's by the by. But we'll see you right, don't you worry. It's a lot to take in. Let's get up to the house now, and we'll talk in the morning."

He turned to go. Felicity stood there a moment or two, and then she took off his jacket and walked after him.

"Dad," she said again. He stopped at once, lit by a bar of moonlight falling from the high window.

"There's something I've got to do first. You'd better take this."

He looked at the jacket in her outstretched hand, frowning. "You keep it on. It's cold out."

"I don't need it," she said. "And Dad?"

He waited.

"I hope you and Mum have a better time from now on. Tell her I said so." That was too much. He could tell there was something wrong; she saw it in his sudden stillness, like one of the dogs sighting a rabbit. *Where are the dogs now? Surely they can't be gone too?*

The silence stretched, became almost unbearable. Everything in her yearned to go with him, to make it all right in his eyes, to have just one night in her own bed in the house where she had been born. But it wouldn't be all right. It would be all wrong, and there was no help for it.

At last, he moved. "Don't be long," he said. He held the jacket loosely in one hand, as if he did not know what to do with it. He paused a moment at the barn door. *If he turns back now, if he says one more thing, I'll tell him everything.*

He did not turn. He went out, leaving the door half open, and she heard his footsteps going away across the yard.

She drew a long, deep breath, looked once more around the barn, and whispered, "Goodbye."

Time to go.

Chapter 71

One step, and then one more step. Feeling her way around the edge of the field. It must be well after midnight by now, but the moon was high and almost full, so her side of the hedge was in black shadow. It was alive with movement, sudden rustlings and scurryings as she passed by. She found herself naming the creatures she heard, woodmouse and field vole and shrew, the poppies and cornflowers along the field margin, the bushes and trees at the core of the hedgerow, blackthorn and elder, spindle and may. Great drifts of mayflowers spilled their scent over her, and that brought her back to the mayflower crown.

She stopped dead, breathing in the fragrance of Elfrida's first gift to her. It was no good hiding among the names of things, pretending that somehow that gave her a way to be with the reality of what came next. But there were simply too many thoughts, too many feelings. She stood for a long moment, and then she broke off a spray of flowers, tucked it into her hair, and went on.

Here was the stump of the oak tree with the hollow where once, long ago, she had hidden her birthday watch. The barbed wire was broken and coiled back, and the way lay open, waiting for her.

Would They be there, just beyond the boundary? Maybe they were already watching her, waiting for her to take the next step. But there must be an hour or two yet before sunrise; there was still time. She sat down with her back to the tree, facing out onto the moonlit field and away from the woodland. There were goosebumps on her arms, and she hugged herself, shivering. Her father had been right about the cold; but then, she wouldn't be cold for much longer.

Thoughts tumbled over each other, incoherent, too fast, none reaching any conclusion. *What if?—No, that's no good. Talking never made any difference, anyhow. Maybe Hob and the others?—No, they've followed her this far, they won't back down now. Am I really doing this? I've got no choice. This is what I was born for.*

Think! The memory of Professor Edgerley in his study came back to her, analysing the evidence and weighing up conclusions, clear and precise even when those conclusions were breathtaking in their implications. Felicity had never been like that, she thought now. *I've muddled through my life, reaching out for magic, captivated by the shine, never stopping to wonder about the consequences.*

But that's the way She shaped me, right from the start.

I was just a child! But They were children too. Children driven to extremity, hurt far worse than she had ever been, turning their backs on a world that offered only cruelty. Or sometimes seduced into crossing the border, stolen from their homes and swept away on the tide of magic. Could that be what had happened to Elfrida?

"Remember the stories." The Professor's words as they parted for the last time. Was it only a day or so ago? Somewhere among all those tales there must be clues; but she was so tired, and so full of anger and terror and remorse that there was no room for sorting through stories. Anger and terror, and yes—pity. Whatever had happened to Elfrida all those centuries ago? What must she have gone through, yearning to go back into the everyday world, watching from the borderland as it slipped away from her? For no matter how cold and calculating her actions had been, she was still a child, desperate and terrified.

Children can't really put themselves in other people's shoes. That made Them thoughtless, sometimes cruel, as well as captivating and wonderful. And they changed and grew, but they did not grow up. *I'm a grown up now, or at least I'm supposed to be. I can see things in a way that they never can. But how does that help?*

"I don't know!" she said aloud into the waiting darkness. What else had the Professor said? There must be something!

"What do They want from us?" That was the question that had first caught her eye, that had brought her to his lecture. What Elfrida wanted seemed clear: to be a changeling in the everyday world, while Felicity travelled Onward in her place. But what did she really hope for from that exchange? *If I've learned anything, it's that magical gifts don't turn out the way you expect. What you really wanted slips from your grasp, and you're left poorer than before.*

And then: *Will that be true for me too, if I go Onward?*

The moon was riding lower now. To the east, although she could not see it from here, there would be the beginning of light in the sky. *Will those mountains be there today?* She shivered again, and then abruptly got to her feet, brushed off twigs and insects, put one hand on the bark of the boundary oak, and passed under the trees. She did not look back.

At once, the light became dappled, shifting and dancing with the movement of branches overhead. From old habit, she stopped trying to see her way and let other senses guide her: the sounds of the woodland, the feel of dead leaves or fresh grass underfoot. *This is my place; neither here nor there. The in-between place where anything is possible.*

Following no direction, she walked. *They won't make me struggle through brambles and bogs tonight. They'll show me the way.* The ground was beginning to slope upward now, the trees thinning out, and shapes emerged from between the trunks, keeping pace with her, drawing nearer. To her right a tall wolfhound, stopping as it sensed her gaze, turning its head, waiting. To her left, slinking low to the ground, a creature she had seen only in books; slender and sinuous like a stoat but red-furred with a cream underbelly. She stopped.

I know you.

How long had it been since she had last seen them? Seven years or more! She cried out in sudden joy, dropped to her knees, and spread her arms wide.

They came running, threw themselves at her, became a tangle of limbs, the hound licking her face ecstatically, the marten curling in her arms. And here came Hob, changing as he ran into a crow, circling overhead shouting raucous delight at the dawn-streaked sky. *He doesn't know. She hasn't told him.* Like the child she had been when last they were all together, she gave herself up to the simple physical pleasure of sharing human contact. *I have missed this so much!* For a time, that was all there was.

At last, when the excitement had subsided a little, she was able to sit up again. The beautiful brindled hound laid his head in her lap, became Lovet, and she stroked his curly hair. Adder held her hard around the waist with both arms, butting his head against her shoulder like the marten he had just been, and Hob flew down to lean against her back. In her ear he whispered,

"We thought you might not come."

She turned her head a little, said, "I promised, didn't I?" and drew them all a little closer. *Children. They really are just children, though their faces are lined and their backs are bent. It's in their eyes. I can see it.*

And what do children really want?

Lovet got up and began to tug at her hand. Adder took the other hand, and together they pulled her to her feet as Hob pushed from behind. Together, hand in hand, they walked on, and Hob turned cartwheels around them. Felicity looked down at them all, held those small, gnarled hands in hers, and felt so weak with love that she almost stumbled.

I don't miss the lordly ones, as I used to call them. Here we are, without shine, just our bruised and battered selves. I wouldn't have it any other way.

Chapter 72

"It is near time." Elfrida was waiting for them where the path crested the hill. Felicity looked up to see her, and behind her the long slopes of moorland stretching away Onward, fading into mist. The mountains were not yet visible, but she knew they would be there. To the east, where the shadowy woods fell away to the dark lake and the creature that lived in it, the sky was growing lighter, and the undersides of the clouds shone like gold. *A good day to start a journey.*

"I fell asleep. But I'm here now."

Elfrida swept that aside with one hand; no matter. "You are here now. Are you ready?"

Felicity began to tremble. She took a deep breath. "I'm ready," she said. "There's just one last thing I'd like to ask you before we part."

Adder's hand tightened in hers; around them, Hob stopped his capering. Lovet had put the pipe to his lips, about to play; but no music broke the silence. Felicity was sure now. *She hasn't told them.*

"Name it." Elfrida was utterly still. Waiting.

Another deep breath; she did not seem to be able to get enough air into her lungs.

"You've given me so much. All of you, but especially you, dear Elfrida." She spoke the name slowly, deliberately, hoping the ancient magic might aid her a little. "Please, may I hold you, just this one time?"

And Elfrida laughed. "Hold me?" She came a few paces

nearer. "What singular creatures you humans are. But yes, I have seen that it is customary when bidding farewell. Just this one time, then." She opened her arms, and smiled.

Adder let go of her hand. Felicity took three steps, to stand facing Elfrida, who met her gaze without hesitation, apparently without guile. And so she took one last step and did what she had always longed to do and never dared. She put her arms around Elfrida's shoulders and held her to her heart.

Elfrida's body was cool, unyielding. Her head rested against Felicity's collarbone, and she did not lift her arms to hug her in return. *I think she must hate me, to have wronged me so.* After a long, still moment, she stiffened and made to move away.

Felicity held on.

In her ear, Elfrida hissed, "Enough. Release me now!"

Felicity tightened her hold. In a voice that was far from steady, but loud enough to be heard by the others waiting around them, she said, "I claim you back from the borderland. When dawn breaks you will be free."

Elfrida screamed. With a sudden convulsive movement she seemed to leap upward, and her body changed, becoming one lithe rope of muscle that writhed in Felicity's grasp, serpent-headed, its fangs poised inches from her face. She almost let go, although she knew it was illusion; and the next instant there was nothing to hold on to at all, and swarms of bees flew at her eyes, her unprotected arms and legs. She felt them crawling inside her loose smock, felt their stings driving into her, and it took every ounce of determination she had not to try to brush them off, to hold her arms steady, her hands one over the other, holding the space where Elfrida had been. *She's still there.* She had screwed her eyes shut under the stinging hail of bees, and she kept them shut, knowing this was just the beginning. How long until the sun rose?

The buzzing stopped. It grew cold, and Felicity felt goosebumps rising again on her arms, moisture beading in her hair, and the dank smell of decay in her nostrils. Somewhere close by, there was the sound of lapping water. Her eyes came open, but she could see nothing. She was enveloped in fog, wrapped in it, smothering; and the lapping sound was getting louder, nearer. *Oh, Elfrida. You never forget anything.* She summoned her anger, hard and hot, let it rise inside her like a bonfire on a winter's day. *You used me. You fed my fear and made yourself my protector, made me dance to your tune. I'm not letting go.*

Something cold and slimy touched her foot, began to slide upward, winding around her calves and binding her legs together. She fought to keep from screaming, fought against the surge of panic, and almost lost her balance as the tentacles pulled tighter. *There is earth under my feet. It is not long until dawn. That is all there is.*

She pushed her awareness down into the soles of her feet, imagined them sending out roots deep into the soil, anchoring her unshakeably to this small place. And the next moment, as though Elfrida could read her thoughts, a gust of wind hit her like a solid wall. The fog vanished and she found herself in the path of a whirlwind. Flying leaves and twigs battered her arms, and now she could not help herself; she put her hands over her head and crouched down, making herself small.

You can't hold a hurricane. But over the shriek of the wind she shouted, "Elfrida! I've got you and I won't let go!" And knew, because the onslaught only intensified, that she had not lost yet. So long as her intention held firm, Elfrida could not break free.

The screaming grew louder, more intense. It seemed to come from every direction at once, and the thought came to her with utter conviction: *She's terrified. I don't know how this will end, but she does, and she can't bear it.* Despite everything, despite the way Elfrida had shaped her since before she was born, used and manipulated her, brought about the ruin of everything she held dear, in that moment her anger died and she felt nothing but pity.

It was hopeless to try to shout over the screeching that now seemed to be inside her head, driving out everything else. Felicity, with her hands over her ears and her face buried between her knees, whispered, "Elfrida. It's all right. I've got you. I won't let go."

Had the noise died down, just a little? She gathered herself, spoke again.

"Elfrida, I know you're scared. I'm scared too. But I want you to know that I'm trying to understand. Whatever else you've done, you've given me so much. You gave me magic when everything was dreary. You gave me amazing playmates, and you taught me not to mind when other people didn't like me. You're the most wonderful person I've ever met, or probably ever will meet."

She paused. The wind had definitely died down now. *What's coming next?* Before a new onslaught could begin, she spoke, still quietly, filling the void.

"I know who you are, Elfrida. I mean, I don't know what you look like or whether that's even your real name, but I know you. I know you're young, and hurt, and angry, and frightened. You must have been so lonely, all those years in the borderland, when you couldn't get back to the world you'd known and your companions kept leaving you, kept going Onward where you dreaded to go.

"Were you seduced into crossing the border, and then found yourself trapped there? Or did you take refuge like Hob and Lovet, from a place where people were cruel to you? It doesn't matter in the end. Because I've read the old stories. I went through them again and again, looking for clues. But until now, I didn't know what I was supposed to be looking for."

There was no sound at all. The whole world seemed now to be holding its breath, listening. She took her hands away from her ears, lifted her head and looked around. Not far off there were Hob, Lovet and Adder, clinging together, hiding their faces. The morning mist was still thick in the valley, but on the branches above her the first rays of sunlight were shining.

Felicity held out her arms again. “I’ve got you, my dear. I won’t let go.” Then she recoiled as a foul stench tainted the air. The thing in her arms was rotting, long dead but somehow still living, still moving. Her fingers sank into its flesh, and she almost snatched them away in horror. Her stomach heaved and bile flooded her mouth, but she had not eaten since—she could not remember when. The thing was making faint sounds, a sort of mewing or moaning, and that somehow was far worse than the screaming had been. It clutched at her with sticky fingers, and it took all her conviction to keep from fighting it off. She closed her eyes again, but she could not shut out the feel of it, the reek of it.

Through clenched teeth she said, “This isn’t you either. Is this what you fear you’ll become? Elfrida, look at Hob. Look at any of the others. They’re not repulsive, are they? I used to be a bit afraid of them, but not any more. I love them; they’re wonderful.

“And so are you. I love you, Elfrida, no matter what you look like. With my love I hold you. With my love I set you free.”

Felicity raised her head, and the sun was warm on her hair, on her face, on her closed eyelids. In her arms she held something small, and warm, and trembling.

She opened her eyes.

Chapter 73

The creature she cradled did not, at first, look human. It clung to her, hiding its face against her chest. It was almost bald, with just a few wisps of hair, and its spine curved out at an impossible angle. Under her hands she could feel the hard knobs of vertebrae just beneath the skin, and its own hands, clutching at her, were black-nailed, swollen-jointed, the skin so thin she could see all the blood vessels beneath, and so mottled and marked by age that she could not begin to guess how they had once looked. Its legs were curled underneath it. Felicity was reminded not so much of any animal, but of a walnut newly broken from its protective shell, gnarled and brown and hopelessly exposed.

She found herself rocking, to and fro, murmuring words of comfort and reassurance. After a while she became aware of the others around them. They came closer, looking to her for guidance, and then at her nod they crowded in, pressing their own bodies against hers and Elfrida's, surrounding them as best they could. The words became a sort of song, just four or five notes repeated over and over again, a soothing lullaby; though whether it was to comfort herself or Elfrida, she could not have said. The others joined in, going off on strange harmonies of their own, weaving a net of sound that held them all. Where the growing sunlight struck it, rainbows formed, dancing and shifting around them.

Felicity looked up. She caught Hob's eye and he grinned at her, and then the net was full of glimmering lights, sparkling and vanishing wherever she looked. Lovet unwound his arms from around her neck, took out his pipe and began to play, and the notes became spirals and streamers of colour in the air. And Adder, tapping the rhythm of the music along her arm, made the sound swell and vibrate in the air around them, in the ground under them, so that they were all enclosed in a bright cocoon of light and sound that pulsed to a mighty heartbeat holding them all, children forever, safe in the bosom of the Earth.

At last, Elfrida lifted her head. She looked at Adder, at Lovet, and then at Hob, who touched her face with one finger and put the finger in his mouth. And finally, she looked at Felicity, and their eyes met.

Old beyond old, that face. Long past human, lined and wizened and dark as oak bark, but the eyes; the eyes were still Elfrida's. Almost lost in those webs of fallen flesh, neither green nor brown but a mixture of both, barred like a hawk's wing and alight with—what?

Felicity had braced herself for malice, for hatred. What she saw was shame. Shame that flinched away, that tried to hide but could not. Through her own tears, she held Elfrida's gaze, held her with heart and soul, and they both wept.

How long they sat there she could not have said; only that the sun was fully up when, at last, that gentle cocooning faded away, and they came back to themselves, to the bright promise of a May morning and the joyous chorus of birdsong.

Adder tugged at Felicity's arm, pulling her to her feet, and gently she let Elfrida go. Hob seized her other arm, and together they towed her to the top of the hill. It was a clear day, almost cloudless. The morning mist still lingered in the valley, but there, right at the edge of vision, their snow-capped peaks dazzling in the early sunlight, were the mountains. And there was the path, leaving the woods and snaking out across the moorland until it disappeared over the next hill.

"We go! We go!" Hob chanted, and from somewhere

behind them came the sound of the pipe playing a marching tune. Felicity gazed at those mountains, filling her heart with the sight of them.

For the last time, she turned.

Elfrida stood behind them, once more the dark-haired maiden. Felicity went to her, untangled the spray of mayflowers from her own hair, and offered it to her. She accepted it, with a sidelong look that was a little shy, a little rueful, and tucked it behind her ear. And then, abandoning all caution, Felicity took her hands.

"What will you do?"

Elfrida lifted her shoulders. "I will do what I must do, now."

"But I've freed you, haven't I? That's how the stories go. I brought you back."

Those slender hands tightened their hold, gripping so that Felicity almost cried out with the sudden pain of it. "You humans! You never tell the whole story. You see your own small part, and you think that is all there is."

Felicity looked up, bewildered, frightened. "So tell me! Tell me what I've done!"

Elfrida sighed, and her anger died away like falling leaves. "You bound me to my true shape. Yes, I may cross the border now and live there without finding someone willing to take my place. But only in that shape. No glamour, no other guise. It would be a short life, and a wretched one."

Felicity tried to pull her hands away, but now it was Elfrida's turn to hold fast. After a long moment, looking down at their joined hands, she said, "You named me your felicity. That's always been the part I was to play for you. So maybe your felicity isn't to be found where you thought. It seems to me that magical gifts and wishes never turn out the way we think they will. You taught me that."

Before Elfrida could reply, Hob broke in. "The sun is up, the way is clear!" he sang, dancing around them to the rhythm of the pipe. Speaking low so that he would not hear, Felicity said, "I'm glad he never knew what you intended. He loves you. They all do. They stayed for you when all the others went Onward. They are your family now."

Elfrida smiled, but it was a bitter thing. "He knows; never doubt it. What you said, what you did, made that plain. And if they are my family, then that knowledge is one more thing I must learn to bear.

"But he is right. It is time to be away." At last, she let go. She brushed past Felicity, moving towards the top of the hill. And then, as though it had only just occurred to her, she stopped.

"And what will you do, my Felicity?"

Felicity looked up, startled. "Do I have a choice?"

Elfrida raised her eyebrows. "Not half a day ago, you wished to travel Onward with all your heart and soul. But since I can no longer remain in your stead, you are free to do as you will. Go or stay, as you please."

Felicity stood very still. Hob was running circles around them all, like one of her father's sheepdogs trying to keep the flock together. From very far away, the sound of Lovet's pipe came to her, interwoven with the singing of birds and the everlasting movement of the trees.

All those choices I made, that were no choices at all.

Can I really choose freely now?

In her mind's eye, she saw again the distant promise of those gold-capped mountains. She felt the deep humming of the earth beneath her feet, in this place that was as familiar to her as her own heartbeat. She looked around her at the friends of her childhood: at Hob, always in motion; at Adder waiting on the hilltop; at Lovet making music to speed a journey. Finally, she looked at Elfrida.

She took a deep, deep breath. Then, in a voice that was only a little shaky, she said, "I'll stay."

Elfrida did not move, but her body seemed to change shape

a little, to grow smaller. *Is she disappointed? Is she relieved?* Felicity was not sure what kind of reaction she was hoping for. *I may have seen your true physical shape, Elfrida, but I will never know who you really are.*

"What of your broken heart, your lost home, your life of learning?"

Felicity took another deep breath, and her voice came out stronger this time. "Things never turn out as you expect, do they? Maybe it's not all lost. I'll go back to Cambridge and see what I can salvage. And maybe new and better things are on their way." And she thought, with a sudden lift of the heart, of talking to Professor Edgerley freely and without fear; of sharing good company with Steph; of watching her parents change and grow happier; of helping Christine into a bigger and brighter life than her family could imagine for her. Of Sebastian she did not want to speak yet. *I'll find him and try to help him use his gift. I owe him that.* That hope was too important, too fragile; but it was there.

"So, my brave Felicity," said Elfrida. "We are both free. And we are both bound."

Hob and the others came running then, and for the last time she knelt down to greet them, open-armed. They surrounded her, and she gave herself up to them as though she was still a child, as though the way was still open. She closed her eyes, the better to feel their hands stroking, their heads butting against her, the solid warmth of them leaning into her, and was almost sure that there were not three but four small bodies in the tangle. Someone nibbled at her ear; someone kissed her lightly on the forehead, on the eyelids.

Slowly, slowly, the touching and patting grew lighter, gentler, like the brush of leaves against her skin, like the breath of wind in her hair . . .

She stayed there for a long time, until the warm sun dried the tears on her cheeks and the ordinary life of the woods recalled her; the tickle of an ant crawling over her ankle, a butterfly landing on her arm. Her parents would be awake by now, wondering about her.

It was time to go home.